LILLITH OF ENDINGS

LILLITH OF ENDINGS

OTHERWORDLY ANARCHIST

BOOK ONE

Dreamer's Riot

Podium

Cover design by Kongsi

ISBN: 978-1-0394-8579-2

Published in 2025 by Podium Publishing
www.podiumentertainment.com

LILLITH OF ENDINGS

CHAPTER ONE

New Life

I feel a sudden, sharp, and all-consuming cold like I have been thrown into a bath of ice water. My eyes shoot open, and I gasp as I abruptly sit up in bed, only to be greeted by my mother's screaming.

Wait, my mother? Something about that thought feels wrong, like sitting in a familiar chair but discovering a leg has been shortened, making it wobble underneath me.

"You're okay . . . She's okay!"

My mind is brought back to the present as a familiar . . . well, a voice breaks the moment of silence following my mother's scream. I am in bed, my nightgown and sheets drenched through with sweat. Surrounding me is a group of startled, red-eyed faces. My mom, dad, and three older brothers crowd around my bed before Mom bursts forward to wrap her arms around me and sob into my neck.

"By the Collector, Lily, we thought we had lost you!" she moans out through sobs.

Lily? Oh, that's right, for Lillith. Did I just forget my own name? How could I forget that my name is Annie—wait, no, Lillith. What is going on?

"What is going on?" I ask, only to be met by more confused faces.

"What did you say, Lil?" my oldest brother, Gilbert, asks, concern returning to his face.

"I said, what's—" Oh, I realize I am speaking English. My family doesn't speak English; I need to . . .

At that realization, something clicks in my brain. There is something like surface tension in my mind, a thin barrier dividing memories of my two lives from each other, and suddenly it breaks—and I am completely submerged in the memories of Annie Beckett. A grad student in Chicago with a master's in biology and minors in math and applied physics. Annie—that is, I—had been both a PhD student and a teacher at my university.

Then when I had gone to confront... That's right, I had died. At twenty-seven.

At the same time, my recent memories as Lillith are becoming clearer. I have been sick with what I now realize is most likely pneumonia. My family has gathered in my room to say goodbye; at only seven years old, I had died as Lillith as well, but . . . here I am. Both Annie and Lillith's memories are intact, though Lillith's remain hazier, with that blurry filter of childhood memories. Annie's now seem to dominate my personality, with years of adult experiences and worries overpowering childish ones. I don't even feel sick anymore, other than being exhausted.

"LILLITH!" Dad shouts, and I realize my family has been talking to me as I sort through my two lives.

"S-sorry, Dad, Mom. I'm just feeling a bit disoriented. I'm okay," I say, making sure to use the correct language this time.

Yet again, I watch panicked faces fade to relief, except for my father's; he looks slightly confused for a moment. I realize at some point my mom has stopped hugging me.

"Don't scare us like that, sweetheart!" my mom scolds me, while my brothers compete to talk over each other.

"Lily, I am so glad you're okay." This from Henry, while Edward calls me a little brat, and Gilbert tries to ask if I need anything.

"Let's give her some space with Mom," Dad tells my brothers. "We are only confusing her more, and she needs to clean up. Let's go fetch the doctor, see if we can't make sense of all this."

"You know how she is, Dad, she wants us here!" Ed tries to argue, but Dad grabs him by the ear and pulls him out as Henry and Gil follow. I feel a pang of regret as my brothers leave. My entire life, this life, I have looked up to my brothers. I love and trust each of them deeply, and all three take pride in me as well. I can see that they are just as upset about leaving as I am.

"We'll be back soon!" Gilbert calls into the room as my father pushes him out the door. I feel a sadness that had taken root deep inside me begin to melt away. This was the sorrow and resignation of a child facing their mortality. But I am safe. I am safe and I am surrounded by people I love, who love me just as much.

At the same time a new sadness, Annie's grief, settles into my heart. The sterile coldness with which my parents regarded me. The friends I lost. The lifetime of injustice that weighed down on my shoulders and tried to crush me into the pavement beneath it. This sorrow envelopes me like a familiar friend, a companion I know like my own soul. Unlike the fear I had in the face of death as a young child, this feels as important to me as the woman in front of me, the woman I love as my mother.

After a beat of silence, my mom and I try to speak at the same time. "I'm sorry, Mom, I didn't mean to scare you!" clashes with her "Lily, I can't believe you are still with us!" Then another moment of awkward silence. More like sisters than mother and daughter, we both burst into tears at the same time and embrace each other.

"I'm okay, Mom! I'm really okay, I promise." I sob into her shoulder, and she sobs into mine. We hold each other for an eternity and a single breath, letting all the emotions we had been holding back for weeks pour out of us.

"Uh, Dad's right, Mom. I could really use a hot bath," I say, finally pulling free from my mother's tender embrace.

"R-right, yes, of course, dear, you must be desperate to wash that sweat off. I suppose we can spare the wood to heat a kettle of water," she replies, wiping her eyes with her sleeve. Before she goes to boil the water, I'm suddenly pulled into another hug. "I love you so much, Lily. I'm so glad we still have you," she whispers in my ear before pulling herself away.

I look around the room for a mirror but find nothing. My mom is quite pretty, but I realize I'm not really sure what I look like, aside from knowing my hair is long and black like hers. It's quite greasy too; hopefully, the bath will remedy that. She also has interesting red eyes unlike any I have ever seen. In fact I remember, as Lillith, being told that mine are similar. It doesn't seem like this is a particularly strange attribute to have either, or my family has never treated it as one anyway.

I begin trying to sort through my emotions. Turns out having the lives of two women in your head can be confusing. I feel overcome with a need to act that I have never known as Lillith. A few minutes later, while I work through this, I hear raised voices outside my room. I slip from between the sweaty sheets to press my ear to the door.

"She's ALIVE, Richard! Just take that as the blessing it is!" I hear my mom scolding my dad.

"I am, Joan, I'm so relieved it feels hard to breathe!" he responds quickly. "I'm just remarking that something was a little off . . ."

She snaps back, "What's off? What is off about our little girl coming back to us after she had already stopped breathing? All I see is a miracle."

"I know, Joan. I know, and I agree, but weren't you listening to her? I don't know what she was trying to say when she first woke up, and then once she started talking . . . Have you ever heard her speak so clearly? 'I'm just feeling a bit disoriented'? Where did she even learn that word? She sounds like a noble!" says my father. "I just want to make sure everything is okay with her. Just let the doctor look at her again."

"Richard, for the last few weeks you have been completely absent. Our daughter was dying, and you left me alone."

"I have been right here; I didn't leave you alone!"

"You were here physically, fine, but make no mistake, I was alone. You gave up on her so fast I didn't even notice I was leaving you behind."

"That's not fair, you know that's not fair!" I cringe away from his outrage. "I'm responsible for this family! I have other things to worry about, I can't just stay here with her all day!"

Mom's voice is low. "What's not fair, Richard, is you being absent for our dying daughter, then coming to me with this shit when we are gifted a miracle. You couldn't be bothered to worry about her until she started using big words? Please."

"I just don't want it to be a false hope. I just want to make sure. Joan, can't you understand that?"

"Fine," comes my mother's brusque reply. "But you will have to work extra just to have the doctor tell you what I already have. The Collector had mercy on our little Lily, and she is going to be okay."

I pull away from the door feeling a cocktail of emotions. In retrospect, my dad *hadn't* come to comfort me once while I was sick. Not one story for a dying child, not one word of comfort. Only my mom and brothers visited me. My heart sinks realizing my relationship with my father is going to be burdened in this life as well. At least my mom hasn't rejected me in this life . . . yet.

I also feel like an idiot. I am seven years old. I need to act like it. I'm not sure how I'll handle my memories of being Annie, but I'm not going to tell anyone about them. I don't know much about this place I am in, what religions are practiced here, or what level science is at.

I don't want to tell my parents I'm a twenty-seven-year-old grad student and get sent to some priest to be exorcised or any other dumb shit like that. Or am I thirty-four? If I am Lillith as well, do I add on her seven years? Well, whatever—I need to be seven for now.

I sigh as my mother returns with a bucket of steaming water and a sponge. I should have known there wasn't going to be a real bath.

"Let's get you out of that nightgown, sweetheart," Mom says as she starts pulling it up over my head. I don't resist, and she starts gently cleaning the sick and sweat off with the warm sponge. She turns me away from her and I can tell she is trying to hide her flushed face and chest. My heart breaks as I recognize a woman hiding her unhappiness from her children. The least I can do is pretend I didn't notice.

"I don't sup—" I start before remembering my earlier mistake. "Um, Mommy, can I use soap?" It's not the best impression of a seven-year-old ever, but it's not exactly something I've practiced. It seems when it comes to mentality,

Annie is winning out. I'm not able to slip back into the mind of a child like I was never an adult.

She laughs. "Soap? Hot water is luxury enough, Lily. If you want more than that, marry a nobleman!" This confuses me a bit, as I don't think soap should be that hard to make, although I never learned how myself. How could I have known I'd find myself in a time and place that had never heard of Dove soap or two-day Amazon delivery? Still, I would have sworn common soap was available even in medieval times, if I remember correctly. At some point I'll have to investigate why it's treated as a luxury.

As she's chuckling, I am distracted by a more concerning thought. The divide between me and my original mother—that's how Annie's mother feels to me now—started with a similar harmless joke. My parents and I didn't speak in my past life. For years leading up to my death, I wasn't welcome at holidays, and we didn't so much as call one another. Here, with a new opportunity at life and a second chance to do things right, I have been given another set of parents I love. My skin burns under my mother's soothing touch, and the small part of me that's excited to be a proper member of a family again sags under the weight of Annie's memories. It's not my first concern, however, and I decide to worry about that later. At least Mom is feeling better again.

I pout to myself, yearning for the fresh feeling of scrubbed and conditioned hair, but I let my mom finish bathing me and put me in a clean nightgown. The doctor does come to examine me, and she is just as astounded by my recovery as my family was. She gives me a clean bill of health, which seems to ease my father's concerns to an extent, if not the tension between him and my mother.

I sigh as I lie down for bed that night. Partially because my mind is moving a mile a minute; my stomach feels like I'm on the rise of a roller coaster, just before the fall. Living as a woman in twenty-first-century America had more than a few challenges. Here? I have a lot to worry about and a lot to prepare for. Also because I miss my expensive mattress; truly a tragic loss.

I wonder exactly where, and when, I am. I wonder how advanced math and science are here. God, I hope I'll be able to pursue a similar career in this life, though it feels distant from Lillith's current reality. I just want to learn. Maybe there will be some interesting flora and fauna around I haven't gotten to study before. With these thoughts chasing each other around my head, it's several hours before I fall asleep.

CHAPTER TWO

Learn

I settle in with greater ease than I expected. Part of me, the Annie part, feels like I'm intruding on a family as a stranger. But it isn't like that at all. I, Lillith, have grown up in this family. These are my parents, my brothers, and this is my life.

In other words, I don't have to settle in at all. There are adjustments I have to make; Annie has experienced many things Lillith has not. My father is a city guard. This occupation is bound to cause no small amount of friction in our relationship moving forward, considering how I died in my previous life.

I also lack some of the puppy dog admiration I previously held for my brothers. Where a seven-year-old might want to be just like her brothers growing up, a grown woman isn't nearly as impressed with the antics of children. This seems to hit Edward particularly hard as I fail to pretend I am impressed with his jokes and education. I still feel warm and excited whenever I see them, however. It feels really good to have a family again.

This isn't the only change in my mentality. The last seven years of both lives feel like they have happened simultaneously, and I find myself no more attached to one than the other. My life experience has advanced by twenty-seven years in a single night; my outlook on life and ultimate goals face an abrupt shift with the recovery of my memories.

A fire danced beneath my skin when I was Annie, guiding my hands with the wild and urgent intensity of flames. I now have that same fire to contend with but in the body of a seven-year-old child.

I allow the weeks to pass, letting my family drift back to our familiar regimen from before I got sick. I don't play with my brothers as much, but I love spending time with them. Henry seems to understand to an extent that the experience changed me. Edward doesn't, and his attempts to regain the wide-eyed admiration of his little sister escalate over time. Gilbert? Gilbert doesn't notice a change one way or another. There is something loveable about his obliviousness.

At the same time, I learn what I can about this world. As Lillith, I hadn't had any context, but I can now build a clearer picture. I briefly entertained the idea of time travel until I failed to find any familiar constellations or celestial bodies in the night sky. I am not on Earth.

Some things are not so different, however, as the all-too-familiar stains of corruption and power paint every corner of this city. I clearly live under a monarchy now, and nobles enjoy all the pleasures and benefits provided by a boot on the necks of their fellow men. My muscles ache with nervous anxiety the more I learn and the more certain I become that this life is going to be no less violent than my last.

As a little girl, the change I can effect in my current state is . . . negligible, to say the least. With that in mind, the only thing to do is learn. The first step is to learn to read in this language. Unsurprisingly, a seven-year-old in a medieval culture doesn't know her letters yet.

A few weeks after my reincarnation, I approach my father.

"Dad, can you teach me to read?" I ask, putting on my best hopeful-little-girl face.

At first, he seems exasperated that I am bothering him, but my request shifts his demeanor to one of amusement and he answers me through laughter. "Now, what in the world does a kid your age need to read for?"

"What makes you think he even knows how?" Gilbert helpfully interjects, causing a flash of anger to race across my father's face. Gilbert doesn't notice this, but I hold off a scowl and decide it would be best to move the conversation past this.

"He guards the city; he probably has to read important messages and stuff before letting people inside, right, Dad?" I respond.

"That's right, sweetheart, you are a smart one, aren't you!" Dad replies while pinching my cheek. "But you are much too young for something so complicated. Why don't you work on sewing with your mom?"

At this, the scowl escapes, not to be restrained in the face of so many indignities.

"You look confused; he means you are too dumb to read!" Edward chimes in to my annoyance. Recently his attempts to recapture my childish hero worship have devolved into teasing and occasional bullying.

"Am I too dumb to read, or are you just mad that you couldn't learn?"

"Hmm, nope, definitely too dumb. Which is a shame since you are so ugly too!"

I am preparing to find a place for my knee just south of his belt when Henry interrupts the argument. "Come on, Dad, it won't hurt anything. I'll teach her the letters in the evenings after my chores."

"I suppose you are right. Just don't be too disappointed if you don't get it, okay, sweetie?" Dad condescends, rolling his eyes.

"I won't! Thank you, Henry, I'm so glad I have one single good brother!" I exclaim before sticking my tongue out at Ed and Gil.

"W-what the . . . Lily?" Henry splutters, astonished at my work. "How are you picking this up so fast?"

"Oh, I don't know, letters are fun!" I giggle back while writing *Edward is a dummy* in the dirt. I feel amused and a little proud, which is a bit childish since I have an obvious advantage.

He has been teaching me the alphabet for about a week, and I already have a pretty good idea of how to use it. Now that I have memorized each symbol and its sound, I can sound out most words pretty much immediately.

As in any language, there are a myriad of exceptions and modifying rules I have yet to master, but these are edge cases I don't need to worry about immediately. Even being taught with sticks in the dirt, I am able to read and write extremely quickly, which explains Henry's shock.

"I didn't even teach you how this works, but you can already write full sentences?"

"I'm not dumb like Ed! This is easy!"

"Well, don't get ahead of yourself. You still have to learn punctuation and grammar, as well as a bunch of other rules. It'll take at least a year for that!"

It turns out if you already speak a language with native fluency and have spent over twenty years reading and writing in another one, learning a new writing system is not a herculean task. A month later, I have surpassed Henry, and likely my father, in reading ability. It is time for step two and another request for my dad.

"Dad, is there a place I can read books?" I ask, this time making sure Gil and Ed aren't around to derail the conversation.

"Sweetheart, I know Henry is teaching you your letters, but—"

Henry cuts him off. "I was, but the little genius already reads better than I do!"

"What? Really? It took me over a year to learn . . ." Dad starts before beginning to blush and clearing his throat. "Er—I mean, that's really impressive, Lily, but books are expensive. I don't know if we can afford that . . ."

"Is there a store that sells them? I just want to look around! Please please please please!" I begin begging him the same way I always did before I got sick. I push down the embarrassment that accompanies speaking like this. I don't know how long I can keep up the little kid persona.

"Well, there is a bookstore run by that old mage, but really only nobles—"

"Can we go there? Please, Dad? I just—wait, mage?" I stop as my brain catches up to what he said.

He gets a sharp look of irritation on his face at the interruption before answering me. "Yes, Lily, a mage is a noble who casts magic spells for the king."

"Magic spells?" I feel frozen, like in the moments between sleep and wakefulness before you have control of your body. How had I missed something like this? Magic exists in this world? I race through my memories but find no magic being used. I have to investigate.

"Well, now you HAVE to take me, Dad! Books and magic? Pleeeeaase?" I beg.

"I know, honey, but like I was saying, nobles are the only ones who can afford to shop there. I'm sorry."

"We don't have to buy anything, I just want to see, and I want to meet the magic man!"

My father looks at me for a long moment before finally replying. "Tell you what, Lily, I'll make you a deal. I will take you there, but you have to stop avoiding sewing with your mom. AND you have to put effort into learning it!"

I groan inwardly. Sewing is not my favorite pastime, but it isn't a useless skill either, so I suppose I can learn it. "Okay, Dad, I promise."

He smiles brightly at my concession and agrees to take me the next time he visits the shopping district.

I cough as I enter Godfrey's Bookstore with my father. A thick layer of dust smothers the disorganized piles of books and scrolls, and we leave footprints in it as we walk in. It seems this store doesn't experience abundant traffic.

"Lord Godfrey?" my dad calls into the quiet of the store. "I'm sorry to bother you—do you have a free moment?"

At that, the back of the store echoes with the sound of shattering glass, followed by what is clearly a stack of books collapsing. An old man emerges with a surprisingly mild look on his face and a book in his arm.

"Oh, what a pleasant surprise! Who might you be, child?" he exclaims, either addressing me first or addressing my father like a little girl. Either option endears him to me a little.

"My name is Rich—" my father starts before I cut him off, drawing an irritated glare.

"I am Lillith; pleased to meet you, Mr. Godfrey."

"You should refer to him as Lord Godfrey, not mister," my father reprimands. "Mages are nobles, Lily, and they must be addressed as such."

"It's quite all right, sir," Godfrey responds as I smile innocently. "You can call me Uncle Godfrey if you like. Now, what can I help you with?"

"Lily recently learned to read. I told her we couldn't afford any books, but she was insistent on seeing where they were sold. She also wanted to meet a mage," Dad says.

"Is that right, Miss Lillith? You are awfully young to be reading. Can you tell me what this says?" Godfrey asks, gesturing at the spine of the book he is carrying. My father smirks at this and I realize he doesn't quite believe Henry about my abilities.

I glance at it and reply through chuckles, "*A Magician's Melancholy: A Fantastical Story of Love, Lust, and Betrayal.*"

Godfrey blushes a little as he realizes I can, in fact, read. "Right, well, I was just preparing to put this away; it was a special order for a customer, you see," he explains before pushing his bookmark into the book and tucking it away in his cloak.

"Of course, how kind of you to show such personal care for their order!" I say, grinning. This causes confusion to mask my father's face as I drop the seven-year-old act for a moment. I curse inwardly, but the persona isn't going to help me much in my current goal.

"Right, right, of course. In any case, I'm afraid your father is correct, little miss, I don't believe you'll be able to afford any of my wares."

I stand as tall as I can and announce, "I would like a job!"

"What?" Dad and Godfrey chorus, their voices reflecting shock and amusement respectively.

"I would like to work here. I can clean, organize, and handle customers. In return, I would simply like permission to read some of the books."

"Lillith, dear, you are a bit young to be selling books to noblemen," Dad says, clearly a bit embarrassed and very exasperated, but Godfrey's mirth is peppered with contemplation.

"Tell you what: tell me how you would organize this mess, and maybe I'll give you a shot," he says, to my father's astonishment.

It is a universal constant that small business owners will exploit free labor any time it is offered, regardless of the source. I know I have him on the hook.

"Well, I would begin by separating every work into one of ten categories and give each a range of one hundred . . ." I begin to explain the Dewey Decimal System to him. I replace mentions of technology with magic, but it is clear he is interested. I can even see his calculations begin as he realizes I have something real to offer. Equally clear is that my father is flabbergasted.

At the end of the day, I have a job lined up and knowledge within my grasp. In one stack of books near the back of the store, I spot a spine that reads *Introduction to the Magical Arts.* Initially, I was going to focus on history and government, but if magic is real, learning about it is priority number one.

CHAPTER THREE

Mana, Math, and Mistakes

Have you ever heard of a broom, old man?" I shout into the back of the shop while sweeping up another shattered glass he has left on the floor.

"I am far too busy with more important work to worry about trivial things like that!" Godfrey retorts, injecting all the haughtiness he can manage in a shouted reply.

I smirk to myself. "Reading smut is not 'important work' and I know you are not doing it for a customer, so don't try it!"

"Lillith, child, you are too young to know what 'smut' even is. I am researching the latest literature by the finest artists on the continent!"

"I'm old enough to know fine art doesn't make your face so red nor your pants so often in need of adjustment!"

With my final jab, Godfrey storms into the front of the shop, an indignant look decorating his face, and I do a victory lap in my head while bracing myself for retribution. His demeanor quickly reverts to the wizened old wizard's facade he likes to present to the public as the bell at the front door jingles, and my victory is complete.

I have been working for Godfrey for six months now, and we have built a familiar rapport. I have abandoned all attempts to sound like a seven-year-old around him, and he doesn't seem to notice. I deliberated whether to keep it up, but ultimately decided it would hurt my goals more than help. We get along as well as can be expected, and can exchange good-natured banter to a point, but his temper will boil over at certain things like it very nearly did a moment ago.

It's far from perfect, as he remains a noble. He has me working for free despite his wealth, and he can't help but condescend to me. These friendly exchanges keep work amiable but are always punctuated by a reminder that I am at best an amusement and at worst a tool to him.

His shop is clean and organized—one could even call it presentable—and customers are beginning to be a somewhat regular sight, thanks to me. Those thanks are entirely metaphorical, however, as he has not actually expressed any gratitude.

I turn my attention to the customers who have just entered the shop. "Welcome to Godfrey's, how can we help you today?" I ask politely as a well-dressed man and his son walk in.

The man just scoffs and addresses Godfrey directly. "I am looking for a journal for my wife, a gift. Do you have anything like that, Godfrey?"

"Certainly, Walter, let me show you my reserved collection in the back . . ." Godfrey responds while leading the man, Walter, apparently, into the back of the shop. He leaves his son behind without a word, so I suppose this is a familiar routine for them.

"What are you doing here?" The boy sneers at me.

I pause to look down at the broom in my hands, then respond, "Making a tapestry."

"My father says Godfrey shouldn't have hired a dirty commoner to work here."

"Is that so?" I respond wearily.

"He says we only came here because we were in a rush, but no one will want to buy books from a dirty little girl!"

"Your father sounds like a real noble man, kid."

"Of course he's a nobleman, can't you tell? And I'm not a kid, you're a kid! He's right, you are an idiot girl."

"Yes, well, we all have our weaknesses."

"So?" he asks, looking at me like I've forgotten something.

"So, what?"

"So, what are you doing here, stupid? You are a burden on your betters!"

"Burdening, I guess." I shrug as I go back to sweeping. We might look the same age, but letting a kid get under my skin is . . . beneath me.

"What's that supposed to mean?" he asks, but his father returns before I can respond.

"Come along, Hugh, don't talk to the, uh . . . help," he says, wrinkling his nose at me. "Godfrey, you really must get rid of the little urchin. If you hadn't reorganized this shop, no one would bother coming in at all."

"Oh, take your little snot and go meet your wife, Walter. I have important work to do," Godfrey scoffs while waving him off.

"Well, it's not my business, I suppose. Feel free to ruin your reputation." With that, Walter and his son storm out of the shop, and I let out my barely contained laughter.

"Real gems those two," I say. "Really a shining example of nobility."

Godfrey smirks at me and says dismissively, "Pay them no mind, Lillith. Now, if you'll excuse me . . ." He waves me off as he returns to the back. I realize he probably views those nobles and me as roughly the same, which makes me wonder what his noble rank actually is.

I return home and do my chores for the evening. Tonight is the night. I have everything prepared.

I have been studying magic for the past six months, and I have a good grasp of the concept now. It is well-known that only nobles are mages, but it turns out the reason for this is twofold. Firstly, the few commoners who awaken magic are granted nobles' titles. Secondly, magic can be earned one of two ways, through education or genetics.

Magic is introduced to the body through the use of magic circles. A prospective mage draws a large and intricate circle on the ground and needs to wait at the center while magical energy, or mana, of different essences is gathered from the environment.

The process usually takes several weeks, and the mage can't leave the circle before the energy takes root in their bodies or it will dissipate. After this, the mage has a moderate amount of mana, but can't repeat the process. Magic is passed down, however, and their children can draw their own magic circles. In this way, magical ability grows in families over generations, and even if a commoner does learn the method to gain power, they will be extremely weak in comparison to established nobles.

In other words, for a commoner to become a mage, they need weeks of free time as well as resources to keep themselves fed and cared for while they gather mana. This is for the few commoners with the level of education necessary to understand the workings of magic circles well enough to design one.

No preexisting designs are published, with every family guarding their designs jealously. With all these factors together, it is essentially out of reach for a commoner to become a mage. In some rare cases, however, someone from a mundane family is born with a high level of mana already. These are the commoners elevated to nobility.

I am not one of these lucky souls, but I do have an advantage. Over the months of studying the workings of magic, I began to recognize patterns. Magic works through the precise combination of aspected mana. Mana in its base state is featureless, but through will, it can be infused with an aspect. These aspects include the obvious like heat, cold, light, and other things I've always associated with magic. It can also be infused with less obvious concepts, however, like force, friction, tension, or any other of thousands of different mana aspects.

A magic spell is essentially a recipe of aspected magic. For example, basic fire magic can be created purely with fire-aspected mana but will only create a flash and go out. For a long-lasting spell, a mage needs mana with aspects of wood, air, and heat. To throw a fireball, a force aspect has to be added.

The power, distance, direction, and temperature all depend on how much of each aspect is included in the spell. Most mages treat this like a recipe, experimenting with quantities and ingredients until they find a result they like. This is likely because math in this world has advanced only as far as basic algebra, with some trigonometry that seems to be relevant mostly to architects.

With my knowledge in math, physics, and science, however, I have a feeling I could start with the result I want and write an equation to find the values I need. I just need mana.

This brings me to the magic circles. I only know the basic template, but I understand how they work. Magic circles designate a point as a center and use runes associated with different aspects to draw in mana. The mana then meet runes of force that direct them to that center and gather them around elements that match their aspect.

Eventually, this energy stabilizes, and whatever mana gathered around will permanently carry that magic, even regenerating it when it is used. Interestingly, this method is used to enchant magic items as well as grant humans mana. For a knife, the circle would primarily gather metal-aspected mana and add in a little of whatever aspects were desirable, like sharpness or durability.

For a person, the primary aspects would likely be blood, skin, muscle, and bone, mixed with minor elements for mages who want to specialize in different types of spells. I have a different plan.

The first problem is the weeks needed to gather mana, but I am pretty sure I can get around this. The way the center is specified in magic circles is relational. Generally, the point of reference is the room the circle is drawn in. Other times it's an entire estate or even the country itself, in the royal family's case. The larger the area used, the more mana can be drawn into the circle. The one rule is the point of reference has to be established, and the magic circle has to be drawn in the exact center of that point of reference.

The size of the magic circle is actually about comfort as well. In other words, they are large so the person inside them can move around comfortably for the weeks they spend there.

Finally, the weekslong time frame is just the minimum. This is how long it takes, on average, for enough mana to gather to stabilize in the body. Once enough mana gathers in one place, it will take root in whatever object shares its aspect. In a single moment, the ambient mana in the circle will snap into place. Supposedly, this feels something like waking up or taking an ice-cold drink of water. Once this happens, the mage can leave their circle. But they don't have to. If they don't, mana will continue to gather. In particularly rich and powerful families, teenagers spend months there. One renowned mage even claims to have lived in the circle for years to maximize the amount of power they could accumulate. The only reason anyone leaves is because, well, they want to live their life.

This is where my idea comes in. Hypothetically, as long as the circle is at the center of whatever space I use as a reference, it can be any size. If I choose a space for which the center is trivially large, I can move the circle around inside it. So, by designating the reference space as an ever-expanding universe where either every point is the center or no point is . . . Well, I can carry the center around with me. I can tattoo a magic circle on my body and accumulate mana from everywhere, forever.

There are two problems, however. Most mages accumulate magic inside their entire body, and this would only accumulate magic in one spot. I added outwardly pushing force runes to my circle design, which should push accumulated mana into the object it is attached to—that is, me—as a way to solve this problem.

The second problem is the endless size of the universe. This would attract too much mana; it would overwhelm me and I wouldn't be able to control it. My magic circle is designed in an intricate spiral with dispersal runes that only allow a small trickle of the mana to accumulate. This was a reluctant change, but after thinking it through, I realized a "small trickle" should still be a respectable amount, especially considering I never have to stop accumulating it.

I also made a few other changes, since I have a much more detailed understanding of the makeup of the human body, down to exact percentages, than the mages who came before me. I am not limited to blood and bone, but can instead target the elements of my body much more specifically and accurately, from neurons to keratin. Lastly, I don't want to specialize, so I can focus entirely on accumulating a large amount of adaptable mana.

Now I just have to take a few risks. Seeing as each mage can only use a magic circle once, if my design sucks, I am screwed. It could even be dangerous; a lot of these ideas have never been tried or even considered before. My encounter with the nobles today solidified my resolve, however.

I loathe power dynamics. Nobility, wealth, and every other boot that ever pressed down on my throat in both my lives are going to face a reckoning, and this is what I need to make it happen.

"Nothing ventured, nothing gained," I mutter to myself.

Using ink stolen from Godfrey's shop and a needle from my mother's sewing, I begin the long, arduous task of a highly detailed stick-and-poke tattoo on my stomach. Having never tattooed anything before, never mind myself, this process takes me another two months. I can only stand short sessions, and my skin feels raw and angry. But at the end of it, I am finally ready to ink in the activation rune to begin gathering magic. I steady my hand and breathe in deeply. There is no going back after this, and I have to fight off second thoughts.

"Please let this work. Pleeease let this fucking work," I beg no one in particular as I grit my teeth and finish the last bit of the rune.

Pain.

Pain is the only word I can think of as I am bombarded with mana. The sensation of the tattoo is like a mosquito bite in comparison. This process is supposed to hurt a little, but something I have changed has dialed that up to eleven.

I have been pepper sprayed, I have been beaten with batons, and I have been tased, but this is true agony. Just when I think I have truly made a mistake and am about to cut a line across the circle to make it stop, my vision fades, and I black out.

CHAPTER FOUR

Successes and Failures

Bang bang bang.

"Honey, are you okay in there?"

I hear my mother's concerned voice and an offensive pounding on the door as I crawl my way back to consciousness.

How long was I out? I think as I struggle to get my bearings. The pain subsided at some point, but I can't tell if the circle is working. My room is flooded with light despite the closed panels, so it's late into the morning at least.

"I'm coming in, Lily!" Mom shouts through the door.

"Shit," I mutter, looking down at the tattoo on my stomach. "I'm okay, Mom! One second!" I shout back, scrambling for my nightgown. Too late—she's walking through the door.

"Lily, I have been knocking at your door for five minutes, it's almost noon, what's going on?"

I bundle the nightgown up against my torso, desperately covering the tattoo.

"Um . . . I'm sorry, Mom, I was up late because, uh . . ." I start as she eyes me quizzically.

"Because?"

"Uh, nightmare. I had a nightmare."

"Oh, sweetheart, that's okay. Why don't you tell me about it?" she asks, sitting down next to me.

Fuck, uh, scary, what is something scary . . . ?

"Well, um, I was in space and, uh . . ."

"What space were you in, honey?"

"Oh, the sky, where the stars are. I was on a ship in the stars and there were . . . dead people with extra arms and tentacles and they were trying to kill me!"

Her face contorts a bit at this description. "Oh, that must have been so scary, Lily!" she sympathizes while rubbing my back, before muttering, "I need to talk to the boys about the stories they tell you . . ."

"It was! And so I woke up and couldn't sleep, and then I fell asleep when the sun was coming up so I accidentally slept too long! I'm sorry, Mom!"

"Oh, it's all right, my little love. Everyone has nightmares. Even Daddy and Mommy. Why did you take your nightgown off though?"

"Oh, when I woke up, I was all sweaty and gross and I couldn't sleep with it on."

"Oh, I understand. Why don't I clean that for you? Here, let me—"

"NO!" I shout, startling her. "I mean, it's okay, Mom. I'll take care of it. I'll be down in a little bit," I quickly correct myself.

She looks at me like I've just bitten her, but apparently she decides to let it go since she responds with, "Well, all right, sweetheart. But come down quickly. Lord Godfrey was expecting you half an hour ago."

As she reluctantly leaves me on my own, I groan with relief and let the nightgown fall to the floor. That was too close. I'm not prepared to explain why or how I tattooed myself.

With that, I decide to examine it a bit more closely. I don't have much time, but I need to ensure I'm not in any danger. The design is perfect; I haven't made any mistakes in drawing it. It's just the same as it's looked as I built it up over two months. An elaborate circle with spiraling runes stretches from just above my belly button to just below my sternum.

Focusing, I try to feel if it's drawing in mana. After a moment, I feel an energy radiating through my body, starting at the circle. It's strange, but I have an instinctive understanding of it. I can't manipulate it yet, but I can feel its edges, sense its size. It's . . . much slower than it should be, based on what I read.

I'll have to figure that out later; I'm late for work. I quickly put on my dress and tie my hair into a ponytail, then head out of my room.

"There's our little scaredy cat!" Gilbert's voice greets me as I emerge.

Great, of course she told them. Having been raised by two mothers now, I'm beginning to suspect they're all clueless creatures. Oh well—as long as the tattoo is still a secret.

"Glad to see you return to the land of the living! Oh, sorry, too soon?" Ed chimes in before Mom smacks him across the back of the head. I giggle to myself a little. Ed has been growing increasingly mean lately, but this feels more like standard big brother teasing. He must have also been concerned about the nightmare and is finding his way of showing it.

"Leave your sister alone, you two!" she reprimands.

"We're just poking fun, Mom, she knows we don't mean it, right, Lil?" Gil responds.

I smirk before addressing Mom. "That's right, it's fun! Why don't you tell me about the nightmares they had growing up when I get home?"

Gilbert and Edward pale at the thought and my mom smiles at them. "Why, yes, honey, why don't we 'poke fun' about that old dream you told me about . . . the one with the scary old lady?"

This saps all the humor out of Edward's face as it turns a crimson red. "You know what, I think I needed to check on the neighbors. Bye!" He shoots me a familiar glare as he leaves. Right, his concern was never going to win out against embarrassment. I hope he can snap out of this as he ages; he is so easily upset with me these days.

I laugh until my father comes in and calls to me, an irritated tone in his voice. "Come on, Lillith, we are burning daylight here! Lord Godfrey is probably wondering where you are!"

"Right, sorry, Dad, be right there!" I respond, following him out the door.

Godfrey is not wondering where I am and doesn't even look up from his romance novel when I enter the back room of the shop.

"Lillith, get me a Danish," he grunts when the door closes.

"Get your own Danish, old man," I snort, echoing our daily greeting.

I collect the cleaning supplies and go back to the front, then find a quiet place to sit down and examine the mana flowing into me. I've had some time to consider on the walk over, and I'm pretty sure I know what happened.

First, the pain. I have a few theories here. The final rune opens my body up to mana and turns it into a nexus point. This is what all magic circles do, but no one has successfully imprinted one on a living being before. This is because once something moves, the circle stops working. Mine was successful, however, which gives me a clue.

Magic circles aren't drawn with a person inside but are drawn before the person they're for enters them. I think I'm the first person to experience a space abruptly shifting from mundane to a mana nexus. The space inside the circle is, on a conceptual level, being dismantled and rebuilt as an entirely different type of space. In my case, that space is my body.

I've also targeted the components of my body at a much deeper level than most. My blood, bone, and flesh are targeted, but so are my marrow, the calcium in my bones, the bacteria in my gut, and everything else I could think of. Mana permeates my body further than any known mage in history.

Combining those two factors, I realize I've essentially put myself through a metaphysical wood chipper and forced the fine human mist back together on the other end. No wonder it made me black out. I shudder, remembering the agony that assaulted me last night. I need to be more careful.

The other problem is that the mana I'm collecting is less than I expected or planned for. I have a theory here as well. I'm able to move around and continue drawing mana because I used the infinite universe as my reference space. My theory is that all points are at the center of an infinitely expanding space.

That's just the problem. Yes, I'm always at the center of the expansion, but so is everywhere else. The mana isn't collecting anywhere other than where the circle is, but it's targeting every point in existence simultaneously. This means I only receive an infinitely small fraction of the possible mana.

I groan inwardly, beginning to regret how many dissipating runes I've used. It's entirely possible using none at all would still have resulted in enough mana to kill me. I just wish I had used a lot fewer. This isn't terrible though. As things stand, I estimate the efficiency of this circle is about sixty percent of a standard mana circle, all things being equal.

It's going to take me nearly twice as long to gather enough mana for it to stabilize. It's also going to take longer to match a noble in total mana available. To match a mage who'd spent six weeks in their circle, I'll need around nine. Compared to the more patient and dedicated mages who weren't driven from their circles for months or the one who supposedly spent years in his, I am years behind. This doesn't even account for generational mages who started with a large amount of mana.

I'm not terribly upset, however, as that still gives me the overwhelming advantage. I'm seven—or maybe eight now. I'm never going to stop accumulating mana. Unless I get a deep enough cut on the tattoo to interrupt the ink, I guess.

Note to self. Do not run with scissors. Or at all if I can avoid it.

At the end of the day, I will far surpass all but the most stubborn of mages by the time I'm an adult. I haven't cast a spell yet, but I have a feeling my approach to designing them is going to give me a leg up as well.

Pleased with my overall appraisal, I stand up and brush off my dress. I am about to begin organizing the nearest bookshelf when I see Godfrey. He's standing in the middle of the shop, staring at me, slack-jawed.

Fuck.

"By the Collector, girl, what is happening to you!?" he bursts out as I make eye contact with him.

I have a feeling I know exactly what he means, but I have to make sure. The magical theory I read never mentioned mages being able to see mana in other people, and I can't see anything weird about him. Better safe than sorry.

"Um, do you think you could be more specific?" I ask.

He gives me a dangerous look and I realize I'm speaking to Godfrey the noble, not Godfrey the amiable bookseller. He will make me speak if he needs to. Yet another reminder that even when kind on the surface, he is still a noble and, at least on some level, cruel. I don't know to what extent yet, but I know it's there. It doesn't matter that he doesn't usually make me treat him as a lord; he can insist on it whenever he wants. "You know damn well what I mean, child, don't play me for an idiot! You are gathering mana! Your body somehow looks exactly like the space above a magic circle. What in the three planes did you do to yourself?"

Again, fuck. Godfrey is looking at me with a mixture of anger and greed. A pang of anxiety seizes me as I realize how much more valuable I just became to him.

I have lived long enough to know that there are plenty of flavors of the rich and powerful. There are the rude, openly entitled, and arrogant. There are the polite, charitable, and humble. Under the surface though? Under the human skin and the mask of wealth, there are a few things you will never find: true kindness, trustworthiness, and empathy. There isn't a way to amass or maintain power and wealth while also having empathy.

So I like Godfrey in the way you like any boss while knowing they can and very well might put you out on the streets for their own gain. I joke with him, I banter with him, and I fear what he will do if he thinks he stands to gain from it. I certainly don't trust him, and I'm not going to let him get in the way of what I have planned for this world. Although I could, perhaps, use him.

"Well, let me explain," I start as he guides me into the back of the shop.

CHAPTER FIVE

Power and Pride

Let me get this straight," Godfrey starts, his fingertips pressed together and resting under his nose as he tries to come to terms with what I have done. "You, in the last eight months and using only the books in my shop, learned how to create magic circles, designed your own, and circumvented the necessity to stay inside it. Is that right?"

"Sort of?" I reply, a sheepish look dancing across my face.

"And you only have to spend a couple of hours in this circle each day?"

"That's right," I lie. "As long as I return for enough time every day, the mana will continue to focus on me as if I hadn't left."

He allows silence to fall as he studies me for a moment. "Lillith, that is simply not how it works. That's not possible."

"And yet," I retort, gesturing to myself.

"Can I see this circle?"

"Well, I don't think that's a good idea," I respond, smiling sweetly.

This earns a sharp look, followed by a quiet pause as his calculating eyes try to read my expression. Just as I prepare to break the awkward silence, Godfrey beats me to it. "Lillith, become my apprentice."

I pause as if shocked but smile internally. I can tell he is upset I didn't immediately teach him how I did this, but he is smart. He knows if he really wants to understand it, he needs me on his side. "R-really, Mister Godfrey? You'll teach me magic?"

"Yes, Lillith. I will teach you what I know. But you have to promise me something, and it's Master Godfrey now, if you are going to be my apprentice."

"That's what I said, Mister Godfrey, right?"

"I know better than to fall for the little-girl gimmick, child. You can't invent a new magic circle but not know the difference between *mister* and *master*." He glowers at me.

"I've no idea what you mean, mister." I smile back.

"Whatever. I need you to make me a promise." He sighs, appearing irritated at the perceived disrespect but, I suspect, too focused on the potential gains of my discovery to pursue it further.

"I can probably do that, what do I need to promise?" I reply.

"Don't share this new magic circle or any spells you design with anyone else. It's fine if you don't share them with me, but you mustn't share them with anyone else either."

There it is. I can see right through this request. He isn't the first "mentor" I ever had who wanted to profit off my ideas. He expects to be able to discern any spells I invent from the mana flow, and will most likely follow me to find the magic circle. I'm not worried about that, however; lies can be met with lies. There is no honor among nobility, not really.

"Okay, I can promise that."

"Let me know the moment your mana stabilizes. I'll show you some basic light and sound magic."

"Thank you, Mister Godfrey!"

"Why don't you go home for now? I wouldn't want you to lose the chance for your mana to stabilize because of meaningless work here. In fact, you should stay home until your mana is ready to be used, just to be safe."

In other words, he doesn't want another mage seeing my mana and getting the same greedy look that keeps slipping through his mask of curiosity.

"Okay! I'll be back soon, Mister Godfrey," I say, happy for the excuse to continue my own research.

"A-apprentice!? Lord Godfrey wants to teach you magic?" My father gapes at me, hardly able to grasp what I have just announced to my family.

Edward glares at me before accusing, "You're a liar! Commoners can't learn magic! Pretending you can read is one thing, but there are limits to boasting!"

Ed has been struggling with this for a while now. He had given up on learning to read before I started and didn't take it well when I progressed so easily. It seems to be getting worse every day that I go to work while he isn't allowed a job yet. Not only has he failed to regain my childish admiration, he is starting to worry I have surpassed him. His inferiority complex seems to boil over with the announcement I'm going to learn magic.

"Mom, make her find a switch, no one is going to want to marry a liar like her," he begs our mother.

I'm a bit hurt when my mom replies, "That's a bit much, Eddy, dear, but he is right, Lily—are you sure you are being honest with us?"

What would be the point in lying about this? It would be too easy to check. I guess an eight-year-old might not consider that, so I can't entirely blame them for their skepticism, but it's not like I've ever been a terribly dishonest or boastful kid before. It still twists my stomach in knots that she thinks I'm a liar.

"I'm sure, Mom. He even gave me the next couple of months off from work to make my mana nice and strong," I reply patiently, trying to refer to mana stabilization like a little kid would.

This earns a smirk from Edward, who exclaims, "Aha! I bet you got fired and just don't want to admit it! I knew you couldn't actually read. I'm surprised Lord Godfrey let you get away with it this long!"

"Is that true, sweetheart?" my father asks, looking suspiciously self-satisfied as well and crouching to address me. "Did you lose your job with Lord Godfrey?"

"No, Dad. Eddy is just being a cock," I reply, enacting my plan for minor revenge for his attitude.

"Lillith! Where did you hear that word!?" my mom gasps.

"What do you mean, Momma? Eddy taught it to me! Is it bad?" I ask. Okay, maybe I *was* dishonest, but I was much smarter about it than they were implying, and I would prove it, dammit!

With this, my mother's fury is redirected at Edward. "Edward! What kind of words are you teaching your little sister? I should boil your tongue!"

Edward gapes. "I—I didn't, I don't even know that word! She's lying about this too!"

"I don't think she is lying . . ." Henry interjects, to Edward's horror. "I know she can read, and she can do it well. I don't see why she would be fired."

"Henry is right," Gilbert adds. "I've been to Lord Godfrey's shop and she really turned it around. She is so smart, maybe he does want to teach her magic . . ."

I grin triumphantly, before adding the final nail in the coffin: "You can always go and ask Mister Godfrey, he'll tell you I'm being honest!"

If I had been lying, I would have wanted to avoid verification at all costs, so this suggestion seems to convince my parents. My father's face falls for a moment before suddenly brightening. My work with Godfrey has always bothered him for some reason, and he has a similar reaction to Edward when I learn something new. It hurts having my own father seemingly hoping for my failure, but I am not unfamiliar with it. My original dad felt challenged by my education as well, and I suspect both imagined me growing up to be a housewife.

It's not long before I discover what changed my father's mind this time.

"Our daughter, a mage," Dad reflects, stunned by the implications. "That means . . . that means we are going to be a noble family!"

I hold back a grimace. I can already tell this is going to be another point of contention between us. "Well, I don't think so, Daddy, we're just gonna be normal people still," I reply.

"You don't understand, sweetheart, mages are all made nobles. You will elevate all our statuses!" he reprimands, a little put out at being contradicted.

I understand this perfectly, but I'm not planning on "nobility" being around for very long. Once magic is available to everyone and the monarchy has been . . . But those plans are for the future. I can't very well explain that to him now.

As my mother processes this information her demeanor changes. "Oh my goodness, you really are a little angel, aren't you, Lily? Apologize to your sister, Edward!"

Edward glares at me and is about to begrudgingly obey when I cut in, "It's okay, Momma! None of you believed me, so I'm not mad at him!"

It's better not to foster any further hostility in Edward, and I don't much like the idea of a forced apology. You can't force remorse, you can only explain why it should be felt. He's also just a kid and a little jealousy is to be expected. I also already got my revenge for his rudeness.

This only seems to further wound his pride, and the glare he shoots my way tells me his childlike rage has only been stoked. Oh well, I can handle any petty bullying this inspires.

A couple of months have passed while mana continues to gather around my body when my peaceful day is interrupted by a familiar little pest. Hugh and his father visited Godfrey's Bookstore a few more times in the months I was tattooing my circle, and I have grown familiar with his snide antics. I'm not sure why they suddenly started visiting so often, and I have no idea why he's visiting my home.

I'm outside my house, reading a book borrowed from Godfrey, when Hugh's taunting whines demand my attention.

"Father says Lord Godfrey finally fired you, commoner," he says.

I blink at him.

"Too embarrassed to admit it, huh? Well, that's okay. I felt bad for you, so I have come to rescue you from your misery," he announces, looming over me with his fists on his hips.

I just stare blankly back at him, completely unimpressed.

Confused at my lack of response, he forges on, "I have come to offer you a position as a kitchen maid in my father's estate!"

What the fuck is this kid on about? Why does he keep . . . oh. A fountain of amusement wells up as the pieces fall into place for me. He has a crush on me, doesn't he? That's kind of cute, poor kid. Sorry, but I'm a bit too old for you.

"Um, no thank you," I reply as politely as I can. "I am happy with my current position."

"You really are an idiot urchin, aren't you? I am offering you, a commoner, a job in a noble house!"

"I understand. Thank you. However, I am happy with my job at Godfrey's."

He sniffs at this. "You haven't shown up to your supposed job there in months! Commoners shouldn't have too much pride to accept the scraps that are thrown to them!"

This isn't that cute, actually, but I can't lose my temper with a child. "Hugh, I am sorry if I hurt your feelings. I am simply not interested, but I appreciate the sentiment."

"Stop trying to talk like a grown-up, and it's *Master* Hugh. I am a baron's son! Show some respect!"

I just look at him with as sweet an expression as I can until he realizes I don't have a response for him, and he adds, "Whatever, stupid commoner. I'll come by again in a week, once you have gotten over your silly pride and admit you lost your job."

As he storms off, I roll my eyes and close my book. That's enough outside time for today. I am greeted with another ray of sunshine as I enter the house and Edward harasses me.

"Begging the noble kids for a job now that Godfrey fired you, huh?" he chides.

"Edward. All this pride is only going to make you miserable if you hang on to it so tightly. Just let it go. We don't need to compete all the time."

"Stop trying to sound like a grown-up!" Edward echoes Hugh's observation from a moment ago. "And if we are letting things go, maybe you should stop lying before you get caught! Mom and Dad are gonna notice when you never do magic. You are getting their hopes up for nothing!"

I just sigh and head to my room to finish my book. It breaks my heart what is happening with Edward. I still remember how happy I was to see him every day growing up. How much I admired him, how much I wanted to be like him. He thrived off my older-brother hero worship, and now he seems to be starving. I love him, and he seems to resent me more with every passing day. I'm worried this is going to escalate past sibling rivalry, but I don't know how to fix it! I can't return to being the kid I was before, and I won't hold myself back for him! I just have to hope he can work through this and learn to value a new dynamic.

That night, Edward is proven wrong definitively. I feel the mana take root and stabilize in my body. I had estimated this would take at least a few more days, but it is impossible to predict with a newly designed circle like mine. As such, I am taken off guard when it hits me. The textbooks didn't do the feeling justice. I stumble as it happens, needing to brace myself against the wall and take a sharp breath. I feel as if I just walked from a warm house into a freezing blizzard, but it feels refreshing. Like finally putting on a pair of glasses, the world takes on a new clarity in an instant. I am officially a mage.

CHAPTER SIX

Magic, but No Chemistry

Learning magic is hard, actually. After my mana stabilized, I immediately realized how Godfrey had spotted me. Mana is quite visible to anyone who has it permeating their body. It looks like waves of heat in the desert but flows like a river. Different aspects of mana have different tints of color, making every spell look like an ever-shifting mosaic of liquid glass. When a mage uses magic, mana clings to them like mist, rising up, trailing behind them, and shifting in color as it interacts with its environment.

I was speechless the first time I saw Godfrey cast a spell. It looks like an artist gathering colors from the air and sculpting it into what they desire. The sight made my heart sing! They don't typically need to use physical movements for this, but the effect is dynamic and visual. It's almost like they are dancing with their minds. I see now why spells are treated more like recipes than equations; it is natural to treat them as an art form.

It's been almost four years since I started studying magic, and I am only now starting to get the hang of it. I figure I've turned twelve by now. My plan to create spells like equations does work, but it is harder than I expected to aspect mana in specific quantities. I learn the standard way with Godfrey and practice my method in my own time.

To my immense disappointment, I didn't get to cast a spell for a full two years. I spent all that time focusing on hiding mana around me. It was not the grand discovery I had been looking forward to, but it is essential no one spots me gathering mana after I leave home. It all paid off, however. I can now completely suppress the mana radiating from my body, containing it inside myself when I'm not casting. What takes even more control is manipulating the energy swirling around me. Using the same method of suppression, I also learned to condense it as it gathers, hiding it not in my body but in the air, the light, or the shadows around me. I realize that any concept that can have a mana aspect can itself contain mana the same way I do. Since I don't use this to cast, I never have to reveal it.

Godfrey was beyond frustrated as well; I had taken far longer than he expected to find an effective method of doing this, and I don't look quite so brilliant to him anymore. It wasn't until a little over a year ago that we finally began working on sound and light magic like he initially wanted. I only know two of Godfrey's spells, but now that I have a decent understanding of light and sound mana, my experiments should go much more quickly. Initially learning an aspect is what really takes a long time, and I don't want to do too much in front of Godfrey anyway.

I felt such a thrill when I first mastered a simple lighting spell that illuminates a room. I expected it to look like an orb of light, an assumption based mostly on books and games, but it doesn't. I can discern the origin of the light, but it's just an empty space sending light in all directions. And the first sound spell Godfrey taught me creates sound at a designated location. It's useful for throwing my voice or speaking without moving my lips, which means I've had plenty of fun tricking Henry, even if it can't do much else, for now.

Tonight, while the rest of my family is asleep and unlikely to notice the flashes of light through the cracks of my doorframe, I am doing experiments on my own. One of the reasons I took so long learning what I have is that a huge amount of my focus has been on learning other aspects behind Godfrey's back. He thinks I can only aspect my mana with light and sound, but I've managed with speed and force as well. I figure no matter what magic I learn, vectors are going to be useful. With the spells I can do now, however, speed is going to make the most difference.

The darkness of my room vanishes in an instant as I weave my light spell. From the center of the ceiling, a bright glow illuminates my bed, my small table, and the little chest that holds my small collection of clothes, sending sharp shadows in every direction. I feel a familiar flexing of a nonexistent muscle as I add in speed mana. It's like descriptions of phantom limbs or a sixth sense; a part of myself that feels natural to access yet it never existed before. As natural as this has become, my attempt to try to change the color fails, and the room just goes dark again. Huh, that should have worked. The spell is still in the air, but now the only light comes from the moon outside my window. So adding speed to an established light spell won't work. Right, the spell creates white light in its default form, which already includes every frequency of visible light. In that case . . . I dispel the current instance of light, then gather speed mana first. Once I have the correct amount of speed forming the basis of the spell, I add in the light and cast it just as before.

The room immediately illuminates with a soft green light, giving my room the appearance of an indoor aquarium. Ha! I'll have to keep this in mind for future spells. With that, I begin writing equations for different colors. If I practice each, I should be able to build any colored light in an instant. I also create equations outside the visible spectrum. Although some of these won't be safe to practice, I do think they will come in handy someday, especially since I don't know any offensive or defensive magic yet.

With that in mind, I have two other experiments I want to try. I need to figure out how to target a frequency of light and change it just as it hits my eyes. This way I will be able to discern infrared, ultraviolet, and even X-rays while a spell is active. I also want to be able to cast light directionally instead of filling a room. I will spend the next few months figuring this out, but for now, I think I've done pretty well. I settle down and roll over on my old, lumpy bed. I close my eyes but it's some time before my mind stops chasing new ideas and planning different spells.

A few weeks later, Hugh visits to harass me *again* as I sweep my family's porch. His crush is growing less and less harmless as time goes on, and the kid does *not* like being turned down. Things have gotten even worse since he reached puberty—he doesn't even look at my face anymore, instead condescending entirely to my chest. What's there to even look at, kid? I've barely started to develop; I hardly boast an hourglass figure. I suppose kids look different to kids, but damn, it does not make sense to me. In any case, the open lust causes bile to rise in my throat.

"I have decided," Hugh announces to me, "you and I are to start courting immediately."

I guess he got bored with his . . . *subtle* approach. I give him my usual unimpressed stare.

"I have been giving you opportunities to get closer to me for some time now, but it has recently been pointed out to me that uneducated commoners like yourself can easily miss such cues. As such, I have decided to make things clear to you. We are now courting." He ends his ridiculous monologue with a curt, matter-of-fact nod.

"No, we aren't, Hugh."

"Don't be a simpleton, commoner, I have declared it so, and as your better, I am to be obeyed. My father is a baron, after all."

"Congratulations on your daddy failing to pull out a decade ago. You must be very proud of your achievement. I'm not courting you."

This comment hits Hugh like a smack in the face and he splutters. "H-How dare you insult me! I am going to be a baron! Don't you understand that? I could have you whipped!"

"I doubt it," I reply, unintimidated. I am the apprentice of a powerful mage, or at least Godfrey considers me his apprentice; I think of him as more of a Wikipedia page. Either way, my hypothetical prospects far surpass a local baron's. "As charming as threats of violence usually are to women, I can confidently say you have zero chance of ever wooing me. Give up."

Hugh's face hardens and I can see him steeling his resolve. "I have told you the way things are, and I highly suggest you accept them. Now, come with me so we can tell my father," he demands through gritted teeth, before grabbing my wrist and trying to pull me away.

I twist my wrist toward his thumb, opening up his hand so I can pull my arm free. I then shove him away from me. My face is stone and my voice is cold as I respond. "Do NOT fucking touch me."

"Did you just strike a noble? I really will have you whipped!"

"Go ahead. Call your daddy for help. Try to punish me. But if you touch me again, I'm breaking something."

He looks like he actually might try again, but as the broomstick in my other hand splinters in my grip, he reconsiders. "Y-you'll pay for this, bitch!" he yells over his shoulder as he runs, no doubt to request his father's help.

I have a lot of patience for children, but this is a lesson he needs to learn now. If he tries that on me in a few years, he is losing a few pieces. I head back inside, no longer interested in my chores. Did I really splinter the broomstick? I couldn't have done that as Annie, especially at twelve. I'll have to figure that out later, however, as my examination of the broomstick is interrupted by Henry.

"You okay, Lily? You look ready to tear someone's spine out," he says. I guess I still wear my heart on my sleeve sometimes.

"I'm okay, just Hugh visiting again."

"That kid's still after you, huh? I'm sorry, Lily. You want me to sneak some itching powder down the back of his shirt?"

This makes me chuckle but I turn him down. "It's fine, I can handle that little creep. Thanks though."

Henry is my favorite brother. He is training to be an alchemist, so he probably could make itching powder. It isn't a real solution to the problem, but I do need to shake it off somehow. I'm glad he was the one here. Gilbert would have ignored me and tried to fight Hugh, and Edward probably would have told me to court him. Henry is the only one who actually respects how I feel about it.

That gives me a thought. "Where are Ed and Gil, by the way? Neither of them came home last night," I say, only to see Henry's face fall.

"Well, Gil probably spent the night at Hannah's house. Or Ella's. Or Abbie's.

You get the idea. And Ed . . ." he responds, putting as much meaning as he can into the pause after Ed's name.

"Edward's out gambling again?" I guess, my stomach churning. My relationship with Edward has not improved over the years, just grown increasingly hostile. He seems to have lost all self-confidence and spends all his time gambling. Henry and I have both proven time and again that, despite being younger, we understand things quicker. We're both more mature and use our time to improve ourselves. The more either of us learn, the more Edward's inferiority complex grows.

"Yeah," he sighs. "Took my research stipend again."

I curse to myself and pull out part of the allowance I have received from Godfrey since becoming his apprentice. "Here, take mine," I offer.

"It's fine, Lil, you earned yours too." He waves off, biting back tears. I suspect he is crying more for Ed than for his wallet.

"You know he'll just take mine as well anyway. This way he won't know where to look first. Besides, even if he didn't, Dad would," I grumble. My dad doesn't go to gambling dens, but when he does take my money "for the family," I never see any returns on that.

"But now Dad will accuse you of hiding it or wasting it on sweets before you get home!" Henry protests.

"And he does the same when Ed gambles my money away. Besides, if my theory on what Dad does with my money is correct, I think I'd rather just get yelled at. He's also a *little* right—I don't let them take all of it," I respond. My parents' relationship has not been improving over the years either. They share about as much of their intimate life with me as any parents would with a twelve-year-old, but I can see the signs clearly enough. Mom pulls away when Dad touches her. He switched to later patrols and doesn't spend nearly as much time at home. The glassy look behind my mom's eyes and her "allergies" she complains of whenever I find her alone . . . There are only so many things a man like my dad would use that money for when his wife is rejecting him.

Henry flinches at the implication. "Okay, you're right. But you still deserve it just as much as I do."

"And I don't need to buy materials for my magic. You need it, Henry," I insist, pushing the tin coins into his hand and closing his fingers around them.

"All right," he reluctantly accepts. "Thanks, Lily."

"Have you spoken to Gilbert yet?" I inquire. Gilbert has been womanizing for a long time, and as soon as he was of age, he stopped caring about risk at all. He has never been as bad as Edward, just oblivious, but he is hurting people. Ella came to me weeping and heartbroken when she realized she wasn't going to marry a nice guy but was just one of many hookups.

"I . . . I tried," Henry says, sitting down. "He just . . . doesn't understand. It's like a game to him. He just . . . blows me off."

Henry and I had talked about confronting Gilbert. Edward wouldn't listen, he practically hated us. This fact still hurts my heart. Gilbert is just genuinely oblivious, possibly willfully ignorant, to the pain he causes. So Henry has been trying to get him to sit still long enough to allow him to explain it to him.

"I . . . see. Okay. Thanks, Henry," I respond, smiling sadly. "I'm going to go practice my spells."

"Yeah. Good luck, Lil."

Aha! My mood is much brighter now, as I've finally figured out how to direct light. Trying to create a cone, or any other shape of light has failed, and I've decided it's because I was trying to make it act in a way light just doesn't. It's always going to go in all unobstructed directions. I feel a little silly I even tried it, truth be told. My current method creates a sort of container for the light to emit from, made of a barrier that stops light from bouncing against it. I create this with a circular opening on one side, then I initiate the light spell inside it and voilà! I now have something of an uncanny flashlight that guides the light in a certain direction. From the back, it looks like something of an eerie black orb. Not quite a black hole, but you just don't really see anything.

This will be useful for many things, particularly experimenting with light waves outside the visible spectrum, which might have cooked me before. Not a weapon I would prefer to use, and one that rapidly drains me of mana, but it'll do in a pinch.

My celebration over the perfect circle of white light on my wall is cut short, however, as I hear my father's clearly angry voice calling me to the living area. When I come out, I am greeted by Hugh's smug face as he stands in the middle of my home next to his father.

Here we go.

CHAPTER SEVEN

Confrontation, Violence, and Kidnappings

When Godfrey doesn't suppress his mana, I feel like I am wandering through the desert. When I walk past a strong mage in the market, it feels like opening an oven. The multicolored heatwaves of mana don't literally feel hot, but the intensity of another mage's mana is extremely similar.

As I walk in to see Walter, Hugh's father, for the first time since becoming a mage, I am astounded. This man, whose power and influence Hugh has been propping himself up on, the man who has been brought here specifically to put me in my place . . . is really weak. He doesn't have even a fraction of my mana. I am keeping mine suppressed at the moment, but I have nothing to worry about.

I figured a baron wouldn't be incredibly powerful, but nobles do usually have some generational power. But, I realize, Hugh doesn't have any mana at all. In other words, Walter gained mana *after* Hugh was born. He must have earned his barony through service and been gifted mana afterward. It explains the family's lack of surname. This man is the middle manager of nobles. Such meager power and so much pride in it.

"DID YOU STRIKE LORD WALTER'S SON?" my father shouts at me. Clearly, he does not realize how small this man is.

"I pushed him away when he tried to assault me, yes," I reply, smiling.

"YOU CAN'T PUSH A NOBLE CHILD, LILLITH!" he berates, before turning to Walter. "I am so sorry about my daughter's behavior, Lord Walter. I promise I will punish her appropriately, I swear—"

"That won't be necessary," Walter's almost whiny voice interjects. "She simply needs to apologize to my son and comply with the previous instructions she was given, and all will be forgiven."

Hugh jumps in to add, "Make it a sincere apology, bitch. I want you on your hands and knees. You can come with us when I am satisfied!"

I stick my pinky in my ear to clear out wax as I reply. "I'm not sorry, so that wouldn't make much sense. You are lucky it was only a shove. And no, I will still not comply with 'the instructions I was given.' I am not courting this little creep."

"You stupid little cunt," Walter snarls. "When you are given an order by your betters, you fucking comply!"

He rushes toward me with an open palm, ready to slap me, as I'm sure he has done to many women before. I examine the wax on the end of my pinky, and just as he enters my personal space, I stop suppressing my mana.

Walter staggers, his mana dwarfed by mine. There aren't many mages I can do this to so thoroughly yet, but Walter is definitely one of them. No one else in the room notices, but Walter falls backward, catching himself as my mana overwhelms his senses for a moment.

"Do not. Fucking. Touch me," I growl, watching a bead of sweat run down the side of his face.

Only Walter and I know what this means. I may not technically have a noble title yet, but in this fucked-up society, power is everything, and I have magnitudes more of it than Walter does. For all intents and purposes, I outrank him. If he had slapped me, he could be executed. I wouldn't wield the power of the state against someone, but he doesn't know that, and he just lost the power to wield it against me. He is terrified.

My father picks up on this, but Hugh, who is standing behind Walter's back, is oblivious.

"How dare you insult my father! We'll have you in the stocks for days. I'll—" Hugh is ranting at me when he is cut off by his stuttering father.

"Shut up, Hugh! M-my apologies, L-lady Lillith. I didn't know what your status was. Lord Godfrey didn't tell me he had taken on an apprentice!" He leans forward and literally starts to grovel in front of me. It's disgusting.

"Don't fucking do that, stand up. Just get out and tell that little pervert you raised to leave me alone," I command. I'm not done with this family, but I certainly don't plan to leverage any authority my mana gives me. Fuck that. No, I'll deal with these creeps my way.

"Father, I don't understand, why are you—" Hugh inquires, still confused, before he is yet again cut off by Walter.

"I SAID SHUT UP, CHILD!" he yells, grabbing his son by the wrist, the same way Hugh grabbed me earlier today. "I-I'll be taking my leave now," he says curtly, and pulls his son out of my home.

I glare at my stunned father. "Way to look out for me, *Dad*."

"W-what just happened?"

"I showed him my mana. I have too much of it for him to challenge. A better question is what the hell just happened with you?"

"Do not talk to me like that, young lady!"

"I'll talk to you however I like. That man was trying to punish me for defending myself, to force me into a relationship with his son, and you what? Rolled over?"

"I—I didn't know you could send him away like that! If I had stood up to him—"

"If you had stood up to him what? He would have sent the guards after us?"

"YES! He would have, at the very least, had both of us arrested!"

"So, to be clear, you were going to let your daughter be abused because if you hadn't . . . people like *you* would have been sent to punish us?"

"Lily, you have to understand, this is how the world works—"

"The world works with fathers screaming at daughters for not getting dragged away? Your excuse for that can't be that people like you enforce it, then it's still your responsibility."

"Lily, I was just trying—"

"I don't want to hear it," I cut him off a final time before storming into my room and slamming the door shut.

Walter

That is the most humiliated I have ever been in my life. I fought my way to my position, sacrificed my time, my wife, and my health, all to have the power that I have today. All that for a fucking child to shame me in front of my son?

No. This will not stand. I don't care how much mana the little bitch has; if she is still living in that pathetic hovel, the lord doesn't know about her yet. Let's see her humiliate me while she is in chains. I can't send the guard after her, but she was too cocky. There is more than one way to put an arrogant little brat in her place. The little idiot hasn't seen how cruel this world can be yet, but I'll teach her.

A little money in the right hands and I will own her all the same.

Lillith

Dad disappointed me, but he didn't surprise me. He was always going to have to choose between his work and his family. The guards are not my friends. Maybe today gave him something to think about. If he wants to work with pigs, he can learn to farm.

Right now, I have more magic to study. Earlier I gripped the broom so hard it splintered. That takes a great deal more strength than a twelve-year-old girl has. Strengthening spells exist, but I don't know any, and I certainly wasn't casting at the time. It must have something to do with how thoroughly mana permeates my body. I don't get tired like I did in my past life, but I've been attributing that to youth.

In retrospect, I practice magic every single night and usually only get about four hours of sleep. I should be far more exhausted than I am; I was when I was staying up to do my tattoo . . . Could my body be drawing from the mana I am constantly pulling in? I need to do some experiments. How strong am I? How long can I stay up? Can I survive for longer than usual without food and water?

Nothing I've read about magic implied any of this, except that mages live longer than other people. Longer is relative, however, as commoners in this world tend to die around fifty or sixty . . . I thought it was just wealth and healing magic, but maybe having mana in your body does more than that.

I'm going to have to get to the bottom of this. I'll experiment with sleep first. I wonder if I can stay awake for days at a time . . .

It's been a week since I last slept. I am exhausted, but I am considerably better than I should be. If I, as Annie Beckett, had stayed up this long, I would be hallucinating. My life would probably be in danger. Instead, I feel like I just did a day or two of intensive exercise or labor. Ready to pass out when I make it to my bed, but not in any danger.

As I leave Godfrey's shop for the day, ready to head home, I spot a cloaked man across the road. He is eating an apple and staring at our storefront. Well, that's a bit creepy, but Godfrey can take care of himself. He can afford it if he gets robbed, in any case.

Unfortunately, it seems I've misjudged the man's motives. As I head home, he departs as well. Every woman knows the feeling of a man paying too much attention to them, and this man's eyes drip down my back like sweat. I speed up and take a few unusual turns, hoping I am mistaken, or just too tired to think straight.

He matches me turn for turn. After a few minutes, I spot another man ahead of me, dressed the same way and locking his gaze on me. I break into a run, turning so I am fleeing from both men. They match my pace and soon I see a third man waiting for me. I turn again but find myself facing a dead end with two more men waiting for me.

Fuck.

Fuck fuck fuck FUCK!

This is bad.

"Lord Walter sends his greetings, little lady," the first man says behind me, and I spin around. "Seems you've caught his eye."

"She's a bit young, don't you think?" another man asks.

"Not for a noble; they've bought 'em much younger than this," a third replies.

Shit. That fucking family. I haven't tested this spell yet, but no time like the present, right? I cover my ears and close my eyes while I conjure the brightest flash of light I can, alongside the loudest and sharpest bang possible. I hear it through my hands, but it's okay for me. My makeshift flash-bang seems to have worked on the men, however, as all of them are covering their ears, a couple with blood leaking between their fingers.

The first man seems to be recovering fastest, and I run for him. I pull a dagger from his belt and bury it in his side. As he screams and tries to grab at me, I slip away and sprint past him, running toward freedom. But I hear rapid footsteps behind me; it seems they are beginning to recover. One of the men catches up to me and scoops me up like a . . . well, little girl.

"Fucking got you now, you little bitch—" he starts, when I cast the first part of my flashlight spell in front of his eyes. He reaches up when his vision goes dark, allowing me to slip out of his other arm. I kick up between his legs as hard as I can and he screams, doubling over. As I turn to run again, I notice blood on my foot.

Oh yeah. I'm fucking strong. Only one man pursues me now. I guess two of the others stopped to help their injured friends. I turn down an alley that splits a second time. I turn right and hide behind an old, ruined wall. I use my sound spell to throw my voice down the other path, screaming for help. When the final man takes the bait, I emerge behind him, an old brick in my hand. Before he gets too far for aim to matter, I throw it as hard as I can at the man's head.

It caves in the back of his head. The man collapses, convulsing on the ground. I see pink foam escaping his lips as his body shudders. Looking around briefly, I realize no one else is chasing me. I am a violent woman but not a cruel one. I pick up the brick and slam it into his head twice more. His body stops shuddering as I put him out of his misery.

Finally free from pursuit, I drop the brick and run home.

As I arrive home, my mother runs out and wraps me in her arms, ignoring the blood and gray matter splattered on my dress and face.

"Oh, thank the Collector you are okay, Lillith!" she sobs into my shoulder.

"I'm fine, Mom, I just—" I start, but she cuts me off.

"Someone has taken Henry, Lillith."

CHAPTER EIGHT

Rescue

Henry

Gilbert and Edward are both older than me. My big brothers, men I am supposed to look up to, are complete idiots. Yet again, it has fallen on me to retrieve the useless jerks from wherever they spent the night. Edward is easy enough; there are only a couple of gambling dens close enough for him to sneak off to. When he isn't passed out at the bar, I realize it must have been a particularly rough night. I order a glass of water and head around to the nearest back road, passing a hooded man, and find him passed out in nothing but his underclothes.

I dump the water on his head and toss him the tunic and trousers I, unfortunately, know to bring with me.

"Wake up, moron," I chide as he jerks awake, looking around rapidly to get his bearings.

"Collector below, Henry! Are you trying to kill me? A gentle nudge would have worked!"

"Not pissing away all my money would prevent this too, but here we are."

"Fuck, it's not like you deserve that money any more than I do. Just because I won't unbuckle my belt for some old creep like you and Lillith doesn't mean—"

"Shut the fuck up, Ed. I don't know when you started believing your fucking excuses, but Lily and I earn what we make honestly."

"Yeah, like a weak kid like you could do anything worth paying for. Lily at least figured out what women are good at while she was young, but you could at least do a man's work."

"Does telling yourself this bullshit actually make you feel better about being a fucking failure?"

"I may be a failure, but at least I'm an honest one."

"You can't even be honest with yourself. This isn't worth my time. Where is Gil?"

"What am I, his keeper? I don't know where he went. He could—"

I stop listening as the hairs on the back of my neck rise. Something is wrong. That man I passed earlier has been joined by two others, and as I look to the other end of the road, three more men are approaching us. They are rapidly closing the distance and cutting off escape routes.

"Shut up, Ed, something is happening," I interject. He looks up and realizes the same thing I do. We are surrounded.

"Did fucking Bart send you guys? I told him I would have the money in a couple of days, he said he would give me time, I'm good for it!" he tries to reason with the men. I roll my eyes internally, realizing he already has plans for my weekly stipend.

"We don't care about your debts, kids. We are here for you. Both of you," the first man replies.

What does he want with both of us? Ed I get, but I have no enemies . . . My thoughts are interrupted as a few of the men get out rope and a couple of bags. Shit. I reach into my pocket and pull out a small bag of powder I keep for emergencies.

"Ed," I whisper, "I'm going to distract the two on the right, I should be able to blind them long enough we can team up on the guy on the right and push our way through to escape before the other three get to us . . . Can you do that?"

"Fine," he responds. "Do whatever you are going to do now though. I don't know what these guys want, but few people dragged away like this are ever seen again."

I don't hesitate once I get his assent, and I throw the now untied bag of powder in the nearest two men's faces. This formula is highly acidic and will make their eyes burn for hours, as well as leave them with a nasty rash for weeks. As they clutch at their faces, no longer able to see us, I begin to turn to help Ed with the third man. I don't get the chance, however, as I feel myself being shoved into him.

Dazed, I struggle with the man but am quickly overpowered. As he ties my hands behind my back and another from the group lowers a bag over my head, I catch a glimpse of Edward running to freedom. To the third plane with that asshole.

I'm going to fucking kill him if I get out of this.

Walter

"You mean to tell me," I begin, completely dumbfounded by these thugs' incompetence, "you only caught one out of the three?"

"They are tricky little fuckers, Lord Walter. We will get them!" Nigel, the thick-headed third-in-command of the Manticorps, explains. I knew they were just a third-rate street gang when I hired them, but it wasn't exactly a complicated job. I didn't even send them after the oldest kid, the only one who should be able to fight.

"I sent you after three children, barely off their mommy's tit, and you barely managed one? And why are you the one talking to me anyway, where are the two who can actually read?" I ask, exasperated.

"Um, well, sir, the kid we got had some sort of weird powder, he got Theo in the eyes and he's not doing so well . . ."

Theo . . . I think he was the second-in-command? What an incompetent idiot. "Okay, so the stupid shit got himself blinded. What about your boss?"

"Uh . . . dead, sir."

"Dead. How the fuck did he die?"

"Well, Piers went after the girl, seeing as how you said she was the most important and all, and well, you didn't tell us she was a mage, sir . . ."

That's odd. Even with her level of magic, she shouldn't be able to cast any spells yet. What in the third plane could she have done to kill a grown man? "You are telling me a child, a little girl, cast a combat spell that was able to kill him?"

"Um . . . it was some kinda explosion, I think. It made our ears bleed, and by the time we figured out we were okay and all, she had stabbed him in the side. We couldn't afford a fancy healer or nothin', so, uh . . . you know . . ."

I rub my temples, a headache growing with each word this useless fool says. "So, your leader, the best among your entire gang, was killed. By a little girl. With a knife. Where did she even get it?"

"It was . . . well, it was his, sir. She stole it from his belt."

"You are all idiots. Thank the fucking Collector I had a backup plan. Send a letter to the family. We'll have that little bitch meet you tonight to get her brother. Grab her there."

"Um, none of us can write a letter, sir."

I grit my teeth. Absolutely fucking useless. "Fine. I will write the letter. Deliver it to the family."

"Yes, sir."

"And Baldwin?"

"Sir?"

"Try not to let the little girl kill any more of you."

Lillith

I read the letter that was left on our doorstep before my father or mother gets the chance. My father is off alerting his captain and trying to enlist aid from the guards. Apparently, Edward had arrived home about twenty minutes before me and told my parents about Henry's kidnapping. He claimed it was probably "our pimp" responsible for it. The little shit seems to have actually convinced himself that Henry and I get money from sex work and not apprenticeships. That only makes me more angry—why would you steal money from . . . But never mind, that's not what matters right now.

I know who is behind this. Lord Walter, another small man with inflated pride. This note is instructing me to come to an alley in the beggar's quarter after nightfall. I am clearly the real target here. The creep must be trying to take care of me before I can be officially anointed as a mage and noble by the church. Well, fuck him. I still don't have any safe combat magic, but it doesn't matter. I am going to find Henry before the meetup tonight.

I put a cloak on over my dress and raise the hood to cover my face. I need to sneak out while Mom is heating water to bathe me. She will probably not be on board with my plan to hunt the street thugs who abducted her other child. Moms, am I right?

I try using sound magic the same way I use light magic, creating a barrier where sound waves can't pass through. This doesn't work like I hope, however. My flashlight spell uses light mana to stop light waves from bouncing off the barrier, and I can only cause this effect in a small area, a sphere with a radius of about a foot. It works more or less the same way with sound mana, but the sound I create just sort of . . . bounces around inside it. That's pretty obvious in retrospect, but I don't have time to experiment. I will just have to sneak out the old-fashioned way.

I manage to steal out my bedroom window and head to the gambling den Edward mentioned in his story. Well, he mentioned a tailor, but I knew where he would actually have been. Asking around gets me exactly nowhere; everyone is too afraid of the local gangs to answer questions about them. Even the ones who aren't are, for some reason, reluctant to send a small child after them. Hours pass, and I have no luck, especially since the city guard is most likely on the lookout for me by now.

Just when I am about to give in and head to the meeting point, a tactic I am loath to use, a man shoves his way out of the building. He is clearly in a bad mood and likely just had a run-in with one of the bouncers. What is important, however, is the angry rash decorating his face. His eyes in particular look like someone smashed a ghost pepper in his face. If that isn't Henry's work, I don't know what is.

My suspicions are confirmed as I follow him and he meets up with another man.

"You look like the third plane, Theo, that rash is somehow even worse now!" the man bellows as the first man, Theo, I guess, approaches.

"Shut yer fuckin' mouth!" Theo snaps. "This job has been more trouble than it's worth. I'm gonna make the kid pay in flesh for this little trick. And show me some goddamn respect, I'm the boss now that little bitch killed Piers."

"Uh . . . sorry, boss. Aren't we suppose' to be using the kid to get to the girl?"

"We don't really need him, you idjit! The stupid kid will show up and we'll grab her. She won't know whether her brother is there or not!"

"Won't her parents—"

"Leave the thinkin' to yer betters. We made sure she was the one who got the note!"

Well, that confirms just about everything I need. I follow the two of them for the next half hour, an easy enough task as neither seems to care about their surroundings. They eventually enter a large shack in the slums. I wait outside until I see another man go in, one I recognize, one who tried to abduct me earlier today. I sneak around back.

"Get the fuck out of here, kid, if you know what's good for—" a man, mid-piss, yells as I appear around the corner. I cut him off, creating a bubble of sound mana around his head. As he starts looking around, startled, I try aspecting as much speed mana as I can to my own body and charge him. I punch him in the groin with all the force I can muster, and he doubles over. Don't judge me, I'd aim for the solar plexus if I was taller! Probably.

Knowing I have very little time, I grab his head between both hands and begin slamming his head against the ground. The sound bubble seems to work as I feel the pressure of each impact but never hear a sound. As he begins reaching up to wrestle with me, I apply pure force mana to his head with my next push. It cracks open, his arms wildly flailing at me for a few more moments before falling limp.

Bad start, Annie.

I creep up to the back door of the shack to peek in. There are eight men inside, including the two with rashes I noticed earlier, and three of the men who had attacked me earlier. The man I stabbed is probably dead, and the guy I kicked . . . well, he probably just didn't have the balls to show up. More importantly, a teenage boy is tied up with a sack over his head in the corner. It's Henry. I recognize his clothes, handmade by our mother, and the chemical burns on his hands from his work.

I need to get him out of there. I can't fight eight grown men. I don't have any spells intended to kill and I only know basic self-defense. Even as Annie, most of my combat experience involved covering tear gas canisters with traffic cones. I'm also exhausted. I haven't slept in days.

No more sleep deprivation experiments, Annie.

I need a plan. Interestingly, the speed mana earlier didn't actually speed me up at all, or rather, not in the way I expected. I think it sped up my metabolism rather than my movements. So that's out. With little else to try, I grab a knife off the dead man's belt and cast a loud noise down the road a little and . . . nothing happens. The thugs in the shack look over, but apparently don't care enough to investigate.

Well, shit. I try again, this time creating a voice calling for help.

"Shut the fuck up, help yourself!" one of them calls out in response.

I roll my eyes, my exasperation growing by the moment. I try one last time, and the voice I create yells, "Help! It's the little bitch who killed Piers!"

This, finally, gets their attention. "Shit," the man I recognize as Theo exclaims. "Ray, Os, you stay here with the kid; everyone else with me."

With that, they finally rush out the door. I have no time to spare, and I can't use my flash-bang spell or the six who just left will come back. I burst in through the back door and try casting my light shield in front of both remaining men's eyes. This is a mistake, however, as I seemingly don't have the skill to cast it in two places at once.

"You little shit." The closer man scowls and rushes me, picking me up by the waist. I wrap my legs around his back, locking my feet together, and cup my hands around his ears. With my hands in place, casting is much easier as I don't have to specify a location. I create the loudest sound I can directly in his eardrums, bursting them instantly.

The man lets me go at the pain, but I tighten my legs and hold on to his left ear with my right hand. With my left, I begin stabbing him with the knife, over and over as fast as I can. I stab him in the back where I can get as much force as possible, but before the man falls, I feel myself being pulled off by my hair and thrown to the ground.

"Get off him, you little cunt!" I hear a man yell as my skull bounces against the wood floor. Dazed, I try to discern where both my enemies are. Fuck, I'm so tired. I lost the knife when I was pulled off. Shit. I feel a foot make contact with my rib cage and follow through, with enough force to crack a rib and throw me into the wall, which my head hits again.

Beginning to panic, I shoot off a wave of light in the direction I think the kick came from. I climb to my feet to see my spell worked; both men have stopped for long enough to clear my head a bit. I see a club in the corner of the room previously hidden from me and I run for it, fighting through the pain in my side and head. The uninjured man recovers too quickly, however, and tries to race me to it. I apply an upward force to my body and feel myself grow lighter, giving me the burst of speed I need to beat him to the club.

I grab it and turn around, swinging it full force into his leg just as he catches up to me. His leg bends at an entirely unnatural angle and he crumples in an instant. Without a breath of hesitation, I raise the club over my head and collapse it into the man's skull, killing him on impact. I turn to face the injured man, but he's gone. Shit. I turn again to catch him behind me, but I'm too late.

He grabs me by the throat and throws me against the wall.

"I don't fuckin' care about keeping you alive anymore, you little shit. Walter can fuck himself. You die. Here," he declares through gritted teeth. His ears are bleeding and so is his back, but his eyes reveal he is beyond madness at this point. I doubt he can even feel the pain as he starts choking the life out of me. I drop the club and grasp at his hands, but the adrenaline running through him plus his superior leverage make him impossible to overpower.

Feeling around for anything I can use, I search every part of him I can reach. Just as my vision starts to fade I find it. The knife is still in his back. I grip it in my left hand and pull it down, shredding his back more but he just grips tighter. With the last strength I can muster, I pull it free and shove it into his temple. He collapses immediately and I feel delicious air fill my lungs, my vision returning. I collapse myself, the pain catching up to me and the sharp breath reminding me of my broken rib.

As I cough blood onto the wood floor of the shack, I hear Henry's voice. "Who is there? I need your help, I think they are after my sister!"

Once I catch my breath, I start to reply. "It's okay, Henry. It's me, I'm—" But that's all I get out before I feel a sharp pain in the back of my head and everything goes black.

CHAPTER NINE

Every Petty Tyrant

The throbbing in my head, the aching in my throat, and the stabbing pain in my side compete to torture me as consciousness returns. My rib cage wins my attention as I try to hold my hand to my side, only to discover my hands are cuffed behind my back. I groan, trying to focus my vision and take stock of my surroundings.

I am in some kind of stone basement. There are only tiny, barred windows near the ceiling, about fifteen feet up. In the middle of the ceiling is a wood panel that looks like a hatch, and a rope ladder hangs from it. I can see all this due to lights mounted on the walls, not torches but not electric either. They must be magically enchanted. In other words, I am in some rich asshole's basement.

The cuffs behind my back are chained to the wall, but I can't move much in any case. I am on my knees and have a cloth gag in my mouth, apparently placed here with some intent. The skin of my wrists and knees feels raw. I finally focus on the far side of the room, where a rug and comfortable chair have been left, likely out of reach of my chain. Walter sits there, smug satisfaction owning his face.

"So you are awake, child, good," he says through a grin. "You did well, you know. I'm told you killed five men. What a ferocious little girl you are!"

He pauses to take a drink, just to show me how relaxed he is. I roll my eyes.

"And there she is!" he laughs. "Fierce little Lillith, the girl who can put noblemen in their place! The powerful child with so much mana I can't challenge her!"

He cuts off his chuckle and draws his face into a scowl. "But that's not the case anymore, is it, Lillith?"

I furrow my brows in confusion as he continues, his smile returning to his face. "You used up all your precious mana trying to save poor little Henry, only to fail. And yes, that's right, what you should be realizing right about now is completely accurate. The chains you are wearing prevent your body from accumulating mana. You are trapped here, powerless. Stupid bitch." He smirks as he holds up a key to taunt me before putting it in his breast pocket and patting it.

I tug at the chains a bit, even more confused. I can feel some kind of enchantment on them, although I can't interpret the mana without seeing it. The confusing part is . . . he's wrong. I am suppressing my mana like always, but it is accumulating just fine. I don't know how long I have been unconscious, but I already have twice his mana. Is he some kind of idiot?

I raise an eyebrow at him and his smile vanishes again. "You don't seem to understand the situation you are in," he growls. "I own you now. Body and soul."

I start laughing through my gag and he snarls, launching from his chair and closing in on me. I don't flinch and he backhands me, knocking me to the stone floor. With my hands behind my back and my broken ribs, I have pretty much no chance of sitting up on my own. Instead, I just cough a few times and begin laughing at him again.

This elicits even more rage and he yanks me back up by my hair, then punches me in the face and knocks me back down again. With this punch, the rag tied around my head comes loose and the gag falls out.

When he pulls me back up to look at him, I spit out blood and a tooth before finally speaking. "Is this helping, Walter? Do you feel better?"

"You are bloody and beaten, chained and helpless in my estate, and you want to know if I feel better? You are more full of yourself than I thought, child. I'm fine. I am in control. You, however? Your life is over."

I smile, showcasing the gap he just created in my teeth, before responding, "In control, are you?"

"Yes. I am in control. And you will learn what kind of man you insulted."

"Oh, I know what kind of man you are. You think I haven't seen this shit before?"

"Oh, have you? You, a little fucking child, have seen this kind of power before? The kind of power that holds your sad little life in the palm of my hand? Enlighten me. Where have you seen 'this shit' before?"

"Every goddamn day, Walter. Do you think you are unique? I can't spit into a crowded market and miss a sad little man like you. You are—" I am interrupted as he punches me again. I sputter and spit more blood onto the cold stone before I continue, "You are fucking commonplace. Run-of-the-mill. You are just vanilla cruelty with a little bit more money."

"I think," he says, slowly and deliberately, "you will find I am anything but commonplace."

"I think not, Walter."

"It's Lord Walter, you cunt! And you have never met a man like me, I assure you."

"Half the men I meet are like you, Walter. Half the people I meet are like you. You are every sad little bully of schoolchildren. You are every landlord, every employer, every tiny little king of their tiny little kingdom." I scoff, genuinely amused that he thinks he is special. "Every petty tyrant who revels in denying a tip to a barmaid, every rapist, every child with a spear and shield and oath to protect their pathetic little lord. You are all the same, just with varying levels of wealth."

"Am I? I'm so ordinary, huh? Except none of them own powerful little stuck-up mages, do they? None of them can kill you if they want, can they?"

"Some of them can. But that's not what makes you the same. You are the same because you are so. Fucking. Sad. You are so insecure. Your pride is so fragile. How much money did you spend, and how much are you going to spend, because a little girl told you no?"

"A trivial amount, that's how much. You really think you are that special? I just want you as a pet for my son. You aren't special."

I laugh again at that, still collapsed on the floor. "You don't give a fuck about your son. You care that I challenged you. You care that I hurt your sad little pride. That's what I mean when I say you are ordinary. You are all the same. Give someone like you any amount of power, and you cherish it. You hold it close to your heart and treasure it. And you snarl like a rabid dog over rancid meat when you think someone doesn't respect it enough."

He just stares at me with cold eyes as I continue, "A waitress doesn't laugh at your shitty joke? You withhold her livelihood. A maid gets angry when you assault her? You get her fired, even beaten. A twelve-year-old girl tells you no? You get five men killed and risk everything you have to put her in her place. And why? Because of your pride. Because you are afraid of us. Because you are desperate to believe you deserve the little power you have."

"I'm afraid? Of you? The child chained and bloodied in my basement? Don't make me laugh!" he snarls.

"Fuck yeah, you are afraid. You are terrified. You are shitting your noble little pants. Because if we don't treat you like you are in control, you aren't. You are afraid of feeling small. You are afraid of realizing you are nothing. You are afraid women you don't own won't tell you how handsome you are and men who don't fear you won't praise your wit. You are afraid that if the little girl who didn't want to date your son can kick you out of her house, then maybe you really are nothing but a little prick in a pretty suit."

"Is that so?"

"It really, obviously is."

He pulls me up so I am facing him again and crouches in front of me. "Well, you know what, child? Maybe I am ordinary. Maybe you are right about everything you just said"—he gets right in my face so I can smell his stale breath—"but I still own you. I still control your life. And in a few months, you will be telling me how handsome I am. You will be laughing at my jokes. You will be doing whatever I ask and thanking me for the privilege."

"Is that so?"

"It really, really is. See, us petty tyrants? We have a saying," he says, and moves his mouth to my ear so he can whisper, "every bitch can be trained, and every mare can be mounted."

"Where I'm from, we have our own saying."

"Really, and what is that?"

"Eat the rich," I whisper back, then flare my mana at full force, completely blindsiding and disorienting him. Just as he starts to pull away, I move, sinking my teeth into his neck and using my mana-enhanced strength to grip his flesh like a vice. He frantically tries to push me off him, but I use force mana to increase my weight, using my body like a steel ball.

As he feels his flesh begin to tear, he stops pulling away, terrified I will pull his throat out. In the brief moment he relaxes, I release the extra weight and use all my strength to push off the ground, shoving him onto his back. I now bombard him with force mana, pummeling him into the ground so hard he can't even lift his arms to fight back. I feel him pushing back with his mana, but I pour everything I have into him, crushing his mana like a cockroach beneath my heel.

I tear a piece of his neck off, spit it out, and go back in, biting directly into his throat. I tear it open and hear a gasping sound directly from it. I spit again, and as his blood runs down my chin, I glare.

"Because you couldn't handle a little girl hurting your pride. Let me ask again. Do. You. Feel. Better?"

He stares into my eyes, convulsing and shaking, fear and desperation painting his face alongside the blood and foam escaping his mouth. I keep eye contact for what feels like an eternity but is probably only a few minutes, until I see the life leave his eyes. With that, I release the mana and collapse on top of the ruined corpse. I rest for a few minutes before I know I have to move.

I scream in pain as I roll over and try to move up on his body. Finally, I manage to get my hands to his breast pocket and fish the key out. It takes several desperate, frustrating minutes to get the key into the lock of my manacles. I feel like I am going to pass out by the time I unlock the chains. I still have to find Henry. Not even bothering to hold back my tears, I cry out in pain and frustration as I climb the rope ladder with my broken body.

The first time I get to the hatch at the top, my strength gives out as one hand tries to open it. I slip and fall the fifteen feet to the stone, feeling something in my leg fracture and wailing in agony. After a few minutes, I take a series of rapid breaths to calm myself down and work through the pain.

I begin actively circulating mana through my body, feeling the flow of energy like water through pipes, and drawing strength from the external mana I am still collecting. This gives me the energy I need to slowly climb the ladder again, this time successfully throwing the hatch open. I emerge into a well-decorated study, with a rumpled red rug that must have been pushed off the hatch. I try not to think about why Walter already had this fucking dungeon in his home, or how standard the practice likely is.

I unlock the door to the study into a hallway where I come face-to-face with a maid. Well, waist to face. After a moment of silence, she starts screaming.

Oh good, she didn't know I was here. That's a good sign.

These are my final thoughts as I fail to bully myself into consciousness any longer and pass out on the most comfortable surface my face has fallen onto all day.

CHAPTER TEN

Cover-Ups and Curiosities

I gasp for breath as I suddenly wake up, and immediately regret both actions. Pain courses through every inch of my body. The sharp breath passing through my bruised throat and expanding my broken rib works in concert with my broken leg, swollen face, and raw gums to punish me for every choice I've ever made. I feel like hell.

"You look like you walked to the third plane and back," a vaguely familiar voice greets me.

I start to turn to the voice but quickly decide I don't need to see them as my broken body protests. Instead, I just lie down and face an unfamiliar ceiling. "Does a baron's basement count?"

"In this case? I think it just might. Hopefully this clinic is a little more comfortable. In any case, you certainly got close to passing into at least one of the planes. Again," the feminine voice responds.

The mention of my previous brush with the afterlife jogs my memory and I understand who I'm talking to. "Oh, I made it to the clinic, huh? That's nice," I respond, relaxing a bit more.

"'That's nice,' she says," scoffs the woman who treated me for pneumonia five years ago. "I don't know if you are incredibly lucky or cursed by the Collector."

"I don't understand the difference," I quip through a groan. This elicits a confused look as she enters my field of view. That's right: people here don't usually make sarcastic jokes about being cursed by God. "The Collector" and I were never going to be on good terms anyway, so I don't even think about it.

She's pretty, I think to myself as she wipes sweat off my forehead.

This transforms her confusion into a gentle smile before she responds, "Thanks, you are too. Uh, probably. Under all the swelling."

Oh. I didn't think that. I said that. Well, she is, so whatever. I guess my inability to filter things through a fever followed me across planes of existence. How lovely.

"Your mother is here. Are you feeling up to seeing her?" she asks, breaking my train of thought.

Honestly, no. I feel like someone ran me through the drier with a bunch of socks full of loose quarters. I'm also having some trouble thinking straight. All I want to do is go to sleep again, but I need to find out how Henry is doing.

"Let her in," I sigh, ready to be bombarded. She nods and leaves for a moment, and I am left in silence for two breaths before my mother charges into the room and pulls my torso from the bed, embracing me with far more vigor than I am prepared to respond to.

"Lily, by the Collector, what have you done to yourself!?" She weeps into my hair.

"P-pain . . ." I wheeze as her aggressive hug creates all sorts of fresh agonies in my body.

"What, dear? Tell me what's wrong, sweetheart!" she frantically inquires, squeezing me tighter.

"I said *pain*. My rib is broken, Mom," I manage to get out between squeezes, and she panics, pushing me back down into my bed and holding her hands up in front of her.

My head hits the bed frame and I wince. "Thanks, Mom," I intone, just glad she's not crushing me anymore.

She runs her hand along the less swollen side of my face before asking again, "What happened to you, Lillith? They won't tell us anything!"

"It was Walter. Didn't care for my plucky young attitude, it would seem."

"This isn't funny, Lillith, you almost died! You were abducted by a noble? How did he get in the house without me noticing?"

"Oh, uh . . . he didn't. I went to find Henry on my own . . ."

"After you had already been attacked? Lillith, what were you thinking? Your father has the other guards on it, why would you go out alone?"

"Because. I'm the one who found Henry. Dad's the only guard who cares. If they had been looking, I wouldn't have found him first!"

My outburst is met with a palpable silence and my mother's eyes widen. "Y-you . . . you found him?"

Wait, why is that surprising to her? I found him, he should be . . . Oh shit.

My memories catch up to me and I realize someone knocked me out before I untied him. I have no idea what happened to him after that. *Walter is dead though—surely those thugs have no use for him now?*

"He's not . . . home yet?" I ask, little hope behind my weak voice.

"No, Lily, Henry is still missing! Where did you find him?"

I give her directions to the shack, and forgetting my injuries again, she pulls my head to her and kisses me on the forehead. "Oh, you sweet, stupid, angelic, moron of a daughter. Thank you so much. I'm so glad you are alive . . ."

"Go ahead, Mom," I allow, seeing her eager to relay my directions to the guards.

With my permission she dashes to the door before briefly pausing. "I love you, sweetheart," she pushes past tears.

"I love you too, Mom," I respond as she departs.

Oh fuck, I hope they find Henry.

My worries are interrupted by the doctor. "Now, you are pretty beat up. You'll be spending the night here, and you'll be confined to your bed for at least six months."

"I understand," I respond blankly, before she follows that information up with a question that returns all the adrenaline of the past day to my veins.

"Now that your mother is gone, how about we discuss that tattoo . . ."

Shit.

Baldwin Tudor

I approach my father's study, irritated to be called away from the new maid I was entertaining. *That old man has always had the worst timing,* I think before rapping at the door. The maid hasn't been properly broken yet and I have to leave her in the care of one of my aides so she doesn't make the mistake of running off. It would be a shame to have to kill her so early.

"Enter," he drawls, ordering more than granting permission. I comply and enter the ornate room. My father, Viscount Reynold Tudor, the City Lord of Satusmor, sits behind his desk.

"How may I attend to you, Father?" I ask politely.

"It seems one of my aides has caused a problem. I'd like you to look into it," he instructs, not bothering to look up at me.

My father is weak. Considerably weaker than me, as a mage, so he leans into his authority at every opportunity. Nothing is surprising about that; it's the nature of magic that every noble is surpassed by their children. The iron grip on our children's lives is the only reason most of us survive to my father's age. That and intentionally cutting their magic circle training short.

Father failed to pull me out of my circle prematurely, however, so my strength threatens him more than any of my siblings. The pathetic old man has no idea how to handle me, but tries his best to be intimidating anyway.

I smirk and retort, "So you couldn't keep one of your dogs leashed and you want me to put it down for you, is that it?"

He lets out an amused grunt before he responds, "No need for that, seems the fool got himself killed."

"Oh? So what's the problem? It sounds like an issue that worked itself out."

He finally looks up from his desk. "The fool man abducted a commoner child from the lower city and tried to train her, either for himself or for his son who is the same age."

"I'm failing to see the issue. Did an idiot upstart guard try to arrest him or something?"

"No, no, you know our guards are thoroughly vetted. Any of them who would have bothered investigating a baron are assigned busywork, fired, or killed. No, the problem is the girl managed to kill him and escape on her own."

This sends my eyebrows up my forehead. "Really? How on earth did she manage that? Exactly how weak of a mage was he?"

"That's where the tricky part comes in. It was Baron Walter. He was fairly weak, a former merchant who bought a magic circle design off the black market to earn nobility. So yes, he was weak, but not weak enough to be killed by a twelve-year-old girl. Even a mundane man should have been able to handle her easily."

"How did she manage it, then?"

"Bit his throat out, it seems. The commoners are growing even more savage. But that isn't the truly interesting bit. He had her chained in mana-suppression chains. The child is a mage, possibly a powerful one. She apparently killed five mundane street thugs before killing Walter."

"Really? Naturally occurring or a bastard someone failed to kill?"

"That's one of the things I intend for you to find out," he says, pensively folding his hands together. "Her mother was a tavern wench before getting married and a fairly pretty one. A few nobles have probably sampled her. It's also possible it's neither. The girl is seemingly a secret apprentice of Godfrey's; he may have provided her a magic circle for one reason or another."

"That old man isn't dead yet?" I huff. "So essentially you need me to cover up your aide abducting an unofficial noble of higher technical standing than him, find out where the girl got her mana, kill her, and teach Godfrey another lesson. Is that right?"

"Yes. And," he adds, "find out what kind of circle Godfrey used, if any. If she is that capable at twelve, the circle may be more dangerous, and valuable, than she is."

"As you wish, Father," I agree, bowing. "I will take my leave, then."

"Very good. Keep me updated." He dismisses me, returning to the paper-work on his desk.

This should be interesting.

I'll head to Godfrey's shop first. If he didn't draw the girl's magic circle, he'll know where she got mana by now. I also don't want him getting in my way when it's time to dispose of the girl.

Lillith

"So you expect me to believe," Dr. Clarice begins, an unamused look of disbelief coloring her face, "that you gave yourself this giant tattoo, with a sewing needle and a bottle of *expensive* ink . . . for fun."

I shrug. I can see why she doesn't believe me, but it's the truth, except that last bit. "Yes?" I respond.

"Is that a question?"

"No?"

"Okay, Lillith. I suppose if you won't tell me, I'll have to ask your parents about it," she says, giving a shrug herself and beginning to stand from the chair at my bedside.

Shit. I need to stop this here if I can. I can't have this design getting out yet; it would just end up in the nobles' hands.

"Okay! I'll tell the truth!" I desperately exclaim. She simply raises an eyebrow and sinks back down, inviting me to continue. "Mister Godfrey gave it to me. He said not to tell anyone though! Promise you won't tell!"

At this, a look of pure disgust transforms her usually elegant features as my lie inspires more than a few incorrect assumptions. "Fucking disgusting noblemen," she growls under her breath.

Damn, Clarice knows what's up. That's not an assumption I'd like to spread around either, however, so I quickly correct her. "He didn't do anything like what you are thinking. It's a, uh, he said it was a medical charm. It makes me heal quicker and stuff. It's, like, a noble secret or something."

Her face relaxes at this. I figure this will be believable since a few of my cuts and bruises are already scabbing over or healing. It's even kind of true, apparently. Most commoners know as much about magic as most kids back on Earth knew about how their computers worked, so she doesn't know mages can't enchant a moving or living object.

"I see," she responds, still looking irritated. "How lovely to hear there is yet another kind of medical magic being denied to us common folk."

"There is medical magic?" I ask, interest piqued.

"Oh yes, I could have you up and about in a week with that. But as things stand, you will need to heal on your own. Hopefully, your, uh, charm helps."

She then begins examining me more thoroughly. She looks confused as she holds her fingers to my wrist, before moving to my neck. Confusion turns to concern and she gets up.

"One moment, Lillith, I'll be right back," she excuses herself as she briskly marches from the room.

What's that about?

Curious, I hold my fingers to my neck, then my wrist.

What the fuck!?

I don't have a pulse.

CHAPTER ELEVEN

Missing

Godfrey

Shit.

This is pretty much all I can think as Lord Baldwin Tudor walks into the back of my shop like he owns the place. He might as well. His father is City Lord of Satusmor, and Baldwin is the most likely successor. This man and his father are the people most responsible for my fall in status and, indeed, the only reason I am forced to attend to a small bookshop in a backwater city instead of advising the king.

What does he want this time? He's already taken everything from me.

I remain seated and we both refuse to speak first for an awkward, prolonged moment. I sigh, giving in first as usual. "What do you want, Baldwin?"

He smirks before responding, "I heard an interesting rumor, Godfrey . . ."

"Can we skip the foreplay and get to how you plan to fuck me?"

"You've always been so boring, Godfrey. But if that's what you wish . . . Tell me about the girl—Lillith."

As his face travels from smirking to cold, my heart sinks into my stomach. Of course he found out about Lillith. "Lillith? She's just some common brat I have clean my shop. What about her?"

At this, he raises an eyebrow. "Oh, is that so? So you don't mind if I employ her as a maid at my estate?"

I scowl, as frustrated as ever with this infuriating child. "She would be wasted as your plaything."

"Oh? Some 'common brat' would be wasted as a maid? Is there something you aren't telling me, *Count* Godfrey?" He sneers my title at me in a mocking tone. Nothing pleases him more than having a noble of higher standing than him completely in his power.

"Fine," I snort. "Lillith is my apprentice. She can't be your maid because she is a mage."

A cruel smile conquers his face as he responds. "Oh, I know, Count. She killed six men, including a baron, yesterday."

That stops me in my tracks. "She what?"

"Oh, you didn't know? How interesting. Quite the spirited apprentice you've found, Godfrey. Tore Baron Walter's throat out with her teeth, it seems."

How in the three planes did that happen? She's barely managed basic sound and light creation, not nearly enough to overpower an experienced mage, even a weaker one . . .

"Well, that's to be expected," I retort aloud. "She is a very capable mage, might even give you a run for your money."

"Oh really? And how, pray tell, did she earn her mana? Is she a bastard? Or did you draw her circle for her?"

I pause for a moment, considering the best response here. Lillith's magic circle is a big deal, and Baldwin won't be subtle. If he gets the design from her . . . "All right, you have me. I drew her circle."

He cocks his head and scans my face with calculation. "Is that so?" he finally says. "So are you willing to take responsibility for Walter's death?"

"Yes. She is my apprentice, she gained mana from my circle, and she is my responsibility," I lie. I smile internally as Baldwin assaults me with his greedy grin.

That's okay. Gloat over your small victory. What I've got is worth so much more than this pettiness.

"Well, then," Baldwin announces, "that's all I need from you. If you'll excuse me, I'd love to meet our little killer myself. Don't worry—she has been found innocent, so you will suffer no consequences for this."

Wait, what? That's not right. If he didn't want to pull me into some petty trial . . . Shit.

Lillith

"What do you mean he wasn't there?" I ask, panic chasing bile up my throat.

"No one was, sweetheart. There were signs of a struggle, some bloodstains and splintered wood, but the shack was empty. Are you . . . are you sure that's all you know?"

Oh shit oh shit oh shit! Those fucking thugs still have Henry. I have to get him back!

My desperate internal cries don't change anything, however, as I am still unable to walk, much less search for my brother. I'm home now, stuck in bed for months while Henry is who knows where. The only decent lead we have is that the gang was hired by Walter, but the city guard simply doesn't investigate the criminal connections of nobles.

My mother interrupts my internal turmoil as she curls up in the corner and wails, feeling every bit of agony and even more helplessness than I do.

"I'll find him, Joan, I swear, I will find our son . . ." my father struggles to say as he wraps his arms around her. I can see the look of resignation on his face, however. Like me, he knows the city guard is done looking. He doesn't expect to ever see Henry again. I don't think my mom does either.

Fuck. That.

I am going to find Henry. I am going to bring him home. I won't be here for six months. Next time I run into that fucking gang, I'll be ready for them. I'll kill every last one of them and I'll bring Henry home. I just need to be patient. I need to learn more magic and more aspects of mana.

I would stay up all night every night learning magic until I passed out, but . . . I feel my gums with my tongue and feel a new tooth growing in where Walter knocked one out. That shouldn't be happening. Something is weird with my body. My blood flows through my veins without pumping, I need a fraction of the sleep I should, and I can crack a grown man's skull with my hands . . . None of these things were predicted side effects of my magic circle.

This may sound like nothing but upsides, but . . . human bodies aren't supposed to work like that. My optimism was torn from me piece by piece over twenty-seven years as Annie, and I can't just enjoy these benefits. If my blood isn't using my heart to flow, that means it is mana running my body. So . . . what happens if I use up all the mana I have? Maybe my organs will kick in and do their job, maybe my body will use the mana I am still drawing in, and maybe . . . Well, I can't risk it.

But I can push. I can push myself to the limit and I can grow stronger. I begin cycling my mana, pushing it through every cell of my body while I try to grasp another aspect.

"I won't let this stand, Mom. Henry will come home," I say into the mostly silent room. My mom looks sadly up at me, her wails having died down to a whimper.

She gives me a shipwrecked smile that fails to reach her eyes. She doesn't respond to me with more than that. Just agony, terror, and resignation chained behind her tight, upturned lips and glassy eyes.

Henry

This bag is still over my head. It's been over a day since I've eaten, I think. They moved me after they took Lily. I don't know how far, or why, or anything really.

I called out for Lily a few times, but if she's here, she's unconscious or tightly gagged. We have to get out of this. We have to get home.

My wrists are raw, bleeding from all my attempts to free myself from the rope. I am still struggling, however, when the sack is finally, *finally* pulled off my head. The room I'm in is dark and damp, and I barely see better than with the sack on. I look around frantically until my eyes adjust and I see a woman crouching in front of me.

"Your little sister killed five of my men, Henry."

She what?

"I—I don't understand."

"She killed five of my men and, apparently, my employer. Do you know what that means, Henry?"

It means you're out of the job.

Part of me wants to respond with snark. To make fun of her, take a shot at her like I would with Ed, Gil, or any other bully. But I'm scared. I'm so fucking scared and they have Lily. They have my little sister.

"N-no, ma'am . . ." I respond instead, sounding even more meek than I feel.

"It means I don't get paid. Which means my men don't get to eat. Which means we have to get that money somewhere else."

"I—I'm sorry, ma'am, I don't—"

"DON'T FUCKING CALL ME MA'AM," she screams in my face, and I fall over on my back, trying to scramble away before she composes herself just as suddenly as she lost her temper. "Sorry, Henry. See, I don't much like being treated like an old maid. You can call me Rosalind. *Lady* Rosalind."

"You're a lad—"

"You can call me. Lady. Rosalind."

"Yes, my lady . . ."

"As I was saying. I lost workers and I lost money. That means I need to replace both. What do you think I should do about that, Henry?"

"I'm sorry, ma—Lady Rosalind. I'm not really sure . . ."

"The boys want to take what we are owed from your sister, you know. Pay for blood with blood, flesh with flesh, if you catch my drift."

I pale at the thought of that. I can't let them—not to Lily—I—

My terror-driven panic is interrupted as Rosalind continues, "Yeah, I don't care much for the idea myself. I'm a lady, see, and we ladies have to stick together, right? But I just couldn't think of another way to get what we lost."

I just stare with wide eyes, waiting for her to continue, and she doesn't leave me waiting long.

"I was downright stumped, you know. But then I remembered something. I remembered a couple of my boys got something real nasty in their eyes. Imagine my surprise when I learned you had caused it. You are an alchemist, aren't you?"

"Um, I'm just an apprentice, ma—Lady Rosalind," I reply.

Rosalind gets a dangerous look in her eyes. "That's twice you've slipped, Henry. There won't be a third."

"I won't, Lady Rosalind."

"An apprentice is just fine. See, we don't get many alchemists around here, and we could really use one. So what do you say, Henry? We spare your sister, I keep my men out of her sweet little dress, and you do some work for me? Sound like a deal?"

"I want to see her!"

She waggles her finger at me. "Nu-uh-uh, Henry. That's not how things work. You don't get to see her. You don't get to demand anything. You will work for me, or you will die and your sister will work for me. What's it gonna be?"

I gulp. I know they have her. I know I heard her voice and I heard those men carry her off. I have no choice.

"Okay, Lady Rosalind. I'll work for you."

CHAPTER TWELVE

Questions and Preparations

"Will you please talk to me, Mom?" I ask as my mother drops off a bowl of soup on my nightstand. I am met once again with tightened lips and weary eyes. She hasn't spoken much, at least around me, since the shack Henry was in was found empty. She had been holding it together before, she was even energetic when I was found, but . . . I got her hopes up when I said I had found him. Realizing he wasn't coming home twice in the same day pushed her too far. I had hoped when I was allowed to come home from the clinic her spirits would improve. It was a hollow hope.

"I love you, Mom," I follow up as she heads out of my room. She pauses for a moment and I can see her tense up, a slight tremor affecting her body language. She doesn't respond, however, and leaves the room. All I can do is give her time. That and figure out how to get my brother back.

Thinking about Henry breaks my heart. Seeing what it's done to my mother shatters me. Intellectually, I know it's not my fault Henry is gone. The blame for every act of cruelty belongs to its perpetrator alone. It's not my fault a rich asshole wanted to ruin my life. It's not my fault I couldn't save Henry from a dozen grown men. I know this, but part of me still blames myself for failing to save him.

My mom isn't processing things very well right now, and I think she blames me for what happened. It would be easy to blame my failure to submit to abuse for what happened. That much I know I carry no blame for. I can't really explain that to my family though. All I can do is grow strong enough to resist. To save Henry and to pull down every fragile monster like Walter. So I need to work on myself.

Even though I have a decent reserve of mana that is growing all the time, I still need to ration. Part of each day I try to master new aspects, another part I try to design new spells with my current aspects, and part I try to focus my mana on accelerated healing. This last one is actually the most interesting. As I cycle my mana, I realize I have an instinctual understanding and control over everything in my body. It's sort of like proprioception, but I can sense more detail than ever before. I have a sense of where my heart is even though it isn't beating. I can feel not only where my hands are but the individual tendons running into my fingers. I can feel the healing as it happens, and I can even adjust it.

I feel my broken leg hasn't set correctly, and I am able to adjust it over time and hold it in place as it heals. I find this fascinating; if I can do this to other creatures, I can gain an almost immediate understanding of their biology. I'll need to test this on a flower or something.

I wonder if—

My musings are cut short as I feel an immense magical pressure. I've been focusing on my leg healing since Mom left the room. Beads of sweat form all over my body and my limbs grow heavier as what feels like all-encompassing, oppressive heat consumes my thoughts. My father steps through the door. "There is someone here to see you, Lily, are you awake?"

I look around panicked and he notices my distress. "Lily? What's wrong? Are you okay?"

I don't get to respond, however, as the source of my anxiety enters the room. A large man in his thirties and far too finely dressed for my comfort responds for me. "She senses my mana. She is fine."

"Oh, of course, Lord Tudor," my father responds quickly. "Lily, this is—" he starts but is cut off.

"You may leave us now." Tudor dismisses him. "I'd like to speak to Lillith alone."

Fucking great, another noble, and a much stronger one at that. What is he, a count? A marquess? I've never felt a mage this strong before. As my father leaves, Tudor speaks up again. "I am Lord Baldwin Tudor. Son of Viscount Reynold Tudor, City Lord of Satusmor. I have a couple of questions for you about your . . . encounter . . . with Lord Walter."

The son of a viscount? Shit. How much mana does the damn king have? I have a long way to go. I should have known who the Tudor family was. Hell, I barely even use the name "Satusmor" to describe this city. I admittedly slacked on history and geography when I discovered magic.

"Ask away, Mr. Tudor," I respond, eliciting a raised eyebrow at either the lack of title or the flat tone. He doesn't say anything about either, however; he's more interested in the events with Walter, I suppose.

"Start from the beginning. How did you learn magic?" he asks.

"I started working at Godfrey's Bookshop when I was seven. I learned magic while I was there."

"And did you always have magic, or did Godfrey draw you a magic circle?"

"I used a magic circle."

"I see . . . And how much mana did you accumulate? I don't sense any from you."

"Oh, Godfrey wouldn't share an advanced magic circle with me, and I didn't have the freedom to sit inside one for very long."

"That's not an answer."

"Is it not? My mistake."

He rolls his eyes at my consistent question-dodging before I feel all his mana converge on me at once. I don't stand a chance of defending myself, although I do reflexively throw my hands up, as if they could block anything. My defenses shatter and I fail to continue suppressing my mana, which draws an interested appraisal from Baldwin. I didn't know mages could just *force* my mana out like this, fuck!

"That is quite a bit more mana than you should have been able to accumulate in your position, isn't it, Lillith?" he asks.

"I don't know how much is normal! Godfrey has always suppressed his around me and I rarely meet other mages," I answer honestly, relieved that he hasn't noticed mana continuing to accumulate around me. It would be easy to miss, with the rest of my mana surrounding me, especially for anyone who wasn't looking for it.

"Are you certain you didn't inherit some mana from your parents?" he inquires, studying me.

"I don't know, let me examine my genealogy real quick," I quip, annoyed by the questions. I wasn't prepared for someone this powerful to ask these questions so early.

He smirks. "You may want to watch your tongue, girl; I am patient but not infinitely so."

I really am helpless at the moment, and I know from two lives how dangerous men with injured pride can be, but I can't bring myself to pretend I respect this one. I should probably dial the sarcasm back for now, however. I don't respond and wait for him to continue the interrogation.

"Well, no matter. I have more questions," he continues. "Walter had a mana-suppression chain in his basement. I don't imagine he failed to use it on you. How did you overpower him?"

"He thought I was out of mana already. He likely thought I'd be of more 'use' to him a bit more mobile," I respond. I'm careful not to lie directly, as I have no idea what kind of magic he knows and I've read priests have spells that can discern lies, although I haven't the faintest idea how they would work.

He studies me for another moment before his body language relaxes and he says, "Well, that's all I have for you. I may be back later if I have more questions."

I raise my eyebrow at him. None of his questions were about me killing Walter; the only thing he cares about is my mana. This guy is going to be a hassle, I can tell already.

"Farewell, Lady Lillith," he says, adding the noble honorific to my name. Gross. He departs, and after a while I feel his mana begin to fade. Shit, that was unpleasant. He definitely wants to use me for something. As the pressure from his mana finally eases off me, my father enters the room again. I sure wish he would knock.

"Lily, are you okay? What did Lord Tudor want?" he asks.

"Nothing much, Dad. He just wanted to hear the story of what happened."

"And everything is okay? He's not going to—"

"I don't think I am being charged with anything. It's okay, Dad."

I see his shoulders relax like I just lifted a six-ton weight off his shoulders. "Thank the Collector for that."

Baldwin

This is going to be a very lucrative investigation. Godfrey was clearly lying through his teeth, and I never once got a straight answer from the girl. One thing is clear to me, however: Godfrey didn't draw her circle, and I don't think she is a bastard either.

It was subtle, hard to see through her mana, but it was still accumulating. How in the third plane did she manage that? If I'd had a method of accumulating mana that didn't keep me tied down . . . I could be king. I need to find out the secret to this. Everything else can wait. My father would be a fool to kill this girl. We need to bring her into the family. Under our control.

If I own Lillith, I own her mana and the method she uses to accumulate it.

A wide grin decorates my face as I leave her shitty little family home. I haven't been this excited about a new toy in years . . .

Lillith

Now that Baldwin is gone I can get back to work. I need to come up with a way to fight back against overwhelming power like that. This thought brings me back to my musings about biology.

I can use my mana to control how I heal . . . why stop there? There are hundreds of ways animals in the wild defend themselves from stronger predators, and I know how some of them work. If I'm careful, I can find ways to defend myself by mutating my own body. I'll have to add these experiments to my preparations.

Curious, I pull a flower from the vase on my nightstand and try filling it with my mana. Most living things have no resistance to external mana sources, and it enters easily. While it's in my hand it works as intended; I can sense the inner workings of the flower. When I put it down, however, I sense nothing. Picking it up reveals the mana is still there, but I can't sense it unless I am making contact.

I probe gently, then start trying to modify it. The flower rapidly wilts in my hand as I essentially direct it to die one change at a time. This will work. I snatch up bloom after vibrant bloom. I modify one to need less sunlight, another to change color, and a third to need less water, placing the first two back in the vase and leaving the third on the nightstand. Over the next week, I'll observe them.

I adjust a few more flowers in minor ways before putting them back. I then pull out a journal, stolen from Godfrey's shop, and begin flipping past pages of calculations for new spells. I have a dozen modifications I want to try on myself, and since I'm not confident it's safe yet, math calculations are all I can do right now.

One thing is for certain though: just because I can't be safe around mages like Baldwin doesn't mean they will be safe around me. I get to an empty page in my journal and write *Golden Poison Frog* and *Slow Loris* at the top.

These two animals secrete different types of poison. The frog is far deadlier, but the loris, a type of primate, has a unique poison that is only dangerous once it comes into contact with the animal's own saliva. If I design something with both traits in my sweat, preferably something I can control, I can excrete the poison first and the activating protein only when I touch a target I want to kill.

Ideally, I can figure this out in time for the thugs holding on to Henry to regret it.

CHAPTER THIRTEEN

What Just Happened?

Henry

I've been here a week now, and I don't see any way out of this. Rosalind has me creating medicines with half my time and illicit drugs with the rest. Her and these other morons sell both to different clientele. She has already forced me to dilute the formula three times so she can sell more with fewer ingredients. I've never seen someone so unwilling to spend money on anything, nor someone so easily provoked to rage.

She feeds me something resembling food once a day and leaves me a bowl of water to drink from. I'm kept in a makeshift cell and expected to create reliable potions with no tools and cheap ingredients. If she would just let me see Lily, I could handle all this, but she won't even entertain the idea. How am I supposed to be certain they aren't using Lily like she threatened if I can't even see her?

That's the thing that makes all of this unbearable. I don't know what they are doing to Lily, I don't even know if they still have Lily! I can't gamble though; if Rosalind is protecting her as long as I cooperate and I stop . . . I could never forgive myself. Especially since this is all my fault.

I don't know if these guys were after Edward for his gambling debts or me for my alchemy. Rosalind implied they found out about me when I tried to escape, but I don't know whether that's true. Alchemists are valuable, even just apprentices like me. It's possible whoever hired them knew about my apprenticeship and wanted me before Lily ever, apparently, killed any of them. That's the part I find hardest to believe—I've never seen Lily hurt so much as a spider. Although it certainly sounded like she was fighting hard when she came for me . . .

Whether I was caught up in Ed's problems or targeted for my alchemy doesn't matter, however. What matters is Lily came for me after I was taken. She exposed her magic, a secret she was keeping closely guarded, and came to save me. If Rosalind is to be believed, she even fought either Rosalind's boss or whoever hired her to get to me. In either case, it was someone wealthy or intimidating.

In other words, I got us into this and anything that happens to her happens because of me. That being said, I can't trust Rosalind either. So I have to comply to keep Lily safe, and I can't comply in case she isn't safe. I need a plan to escape, but I have to find out where they are keeping Lily first. At the very least I need to find and talk to her.

"You seem awfully relaxed, Henry." Rosalind's voice pulls me from my inner turmoil. "You sure you don't have better things to be doing? Like, I don't know, working?"

"S-sorry Lady Rosalind," I stutter, and quickly scramble up from the corner of my cell. As I bend over the meager supply of bottles I say, "I . . . I could get this done faster if —"

"Oh, can you? That leaves me fairly curious as to why you haven't been. Maybe I should go ask your sister?"

"N-no, my lady! I meant, if I had a proper place to work, a room with tools and a table to sit at, I could create more potions, if I had that, is all . . ."

"Oh? And where do you suppose I am going to find you fancy tools? Who goes without a room for you?"

I can see her irritation building, but I push forward. It's a comparatively small risk. *Lady* Rosalind has some kind of hang-up about nobility, although she clearly lacks the education such a background would have provided her. I have to try.

I brace myself before responding. "I—I don't know, my lady, I just thought . . ."

"You thought what?"

"It's just, the other noble ladies I have worked with, uh . . ."

I see a dangerous glint in her eye. "What about the 'other' noble ladies?"

Gulping, I carry on, "The other noble ladies had all prepared tools for me when they hired me, so I just thought—"

"I know that! You think I don't know that? Of course I have them! You think I'm not as good as them just because I'm not an official noble? I just meant why should I let *you* use them?"

"Of course, my lady. I—I just wanted to offer, for your sake! I know you, of course, match up to them—no, surpass them in every way! I just wanted to be of more help!"

She settles down at that. I guess my lying worked. I have never been hired by a noble, and I only use my master's tools. Even if I had been, I doubt a noble lady would have alchemical tools for me. When someone wants you to think they know about something they don't, however, it is very easy to manipulate them.

As she puts on her noble facade again, she says, "Well, I'll think about letting you use them. Just think about it, mind you, if you behave."

"Of course, Lady Rosalind."

"Just to be sure, I know some lesser ladies may not bother to provide the proper equipment, but you are working with me now. What tools are you used to working with?"

I smile internally and begin listing standard tools I think she might be able to steal. Some I need for what she asks me to do, and others I need for my own plans.

Lillith

It's been a week since I killed Walter and met Baldwin. My flower experiments didn't all work exactly as intended at first—extending their lives without water took a few attempts—but now I can manipulate them freely. Today, I plan to start human trials, so to speak. I am going to start with poison. I should be able to create two unique types of sweat: the first will be the poison, and the second will contain the protein that activates it.

I've done my best to mimic the golden poison frog, whose poison kills in under ten minutes when ingested and can even cause paralysis on physical contact. But, like the slow loris's toxin, it will be neutral unless activated with the correct protein. This should give me a few options and protections, provided I can get it working.

I've also gotten started on a new light spell, an attempt to create a personal radar. I don't plan on anyone sneaking up on me again. Both projects are slow going, however. It will be months of trial and error for the poison, and I'll have to be extremely careful with it. My radar spell should be a bit faster, but I am having trouble designing a way to receive and interpret signals.

I don't have time to keep experimenting this morning, however, as Gilbert enters my room.

"You okay, Lil?" he inquires, failing to knock like his father before him.

"I'm fine, Gilbert, what do you need?" I respond brusquely. I haven't gotten along with Gilbert for the last couple of years. I don't care how many partners someone has or whether they have them at the same time, as long as everyone is aware. That's not the case with Gilbert, however. He's just a typical jerk who lies and manipulates and leaves when he gets what he wants. Basically? He's a creep.

Taken aback by my tone, he responds, "I'm just checking on my little sister, Lily. Why are you always so hostile to me?"

"It's Lillith. And I think you can figure that out on your own," I retort.

"Fuck, 'Lillith,' I don't understand what happened to you. You are kind of a bitch these days."

I roll my eyes. "Yeah, well, I understand exactly what happened to you and I'm just not interested in chatting. So what do you really want?"

"Shit, you are always like this with me and Ed, I don't get it. Well, your boss is here. Lord Godfrey wants to talk to you. I can tell I'm not welcome, so I'll just send him in."

Figured Godfrey would be around at some point. It's honestly weird it took him this long. Gilbert storms out, and a few minutes later, Godfrey enters, also failing to knock. What is with that? I know knocking is a convention in this world—is it just me who doesn't deserve the courtesy?

"I brought a Danish," he starts, offering me the expensive pastry he is constantly demanding from me at work. "Heard you got into a bit of a scrap with Walter?"

I accept the Danish; I haven't turned down a dessert since I came to this world. "Just a bit. I'm fine though."

"What happened exactly? How did you get away from him?" he asks, that familiar greedy stare hiding behind his eyes. As usual, he is mostly here to see if I've discovered any more world-shattering magical abilities.

"Just took a bite out of crime," I quip, eliciting a confused look.

"What?"

"Nothing, sorry. I just took him by surprise."

"I . . . see. And did you use any magic?"

"No, he had me in some kind of chains that prevented it," I lie between bites of the Danish, causing his shoulders to slump.

"Did anyone . . . else come to ask you questions about it? Any other mages?" he asks. He's not dancing around the point much today. Something about this feels wrong. He should have been here the day it happened, and he should have tried to disguise his real purpose for visiting. I have no reason to lie though; it would be too easy to check.

"Yeah, a guy named Baldwin came by," I respond. I can see the anxiety seize him at Baldwin's name.

"Did you . . . tell him about your magic circle?"

"No . . . I told him you drew it for me."

Relaxing again, he asks, "Did anything else happen?"

"He forced his way through my suppression, so he knows how much mana I have," I say. His face pales.

"Lillith, listen to me, you have to be careful of him. If he—" He is cut short when we both feel it. The same shimmering mana as before is nearby. Godfrey seems unbothered by the pressure itself, but he is clearly afraid. Magical ability isn't the same thing as power. Baldwin scares him.

I'm not terribly pleased to talk to the noble again either, truth be told. He's the type of man whose very presence slithers across your skin. It's a few moments before Baldwin has spoken to my father and comes back to my room.

"Well, what a surprise!" he exclaims to Godfrey's chagrin. "I didn't expect to find you both here!" I'm skeptical of that, but I don't bother challenging him as he continues, "Fortuitous though, as I would just love to speak to both of you!"

"What about?" I ask unceremoniously.

He smiles. "Why, your magic circle of course. It seems both of you made a mistake!"

"I don't believe I did," Godfrey responds, sounding afraid but also angry. These two seem to have a history.

Baldwin laughs and says, "Is that so? So you both expect me to believe that you, Godfrey, designed a circle that allows travel?"

Shit, he must have seen the accumulating magic when my defenses were down. I look at Godfrey but am just greeted with panic. Whatever. I shrug and reply, "Who else would have?"

"That's exactly what I intend to find out, Lillith dear," he tells me, a broadening grin almost contorting his face.

I blink and everything feels wrong. I can't quite put my finger on what. Everything feels wrong. Like the world stuttered while I was blinking. What the hell was that?

"Well, that'll be all," Baldwin announces. "I have other duties to attend to." *What? That can't be all, he barely asked me anything.*

He leaves, apparently satisfied with that short conversation.

"I'd better get going as well, Lillith," Godfrey follows up.

I sit, dazed, as he departs. I can't figure out what the fuck happened. No matter how I look at it, that conversation was too short. Why would he come all the way out here just to say that? It doesn't make any sense. I can't examine it any further as another intruder enters my room.

"Those guys must have stamina if you entertained them that long," Edward quips.

I ignore his crass delusion about what I do with my time and hone in on the other part of what he said. "What? What do you mean 'that long'?" I ask, confused.

"You were with those guys for over an hour. Honestly, I'm impressed, Lily, still working in the state you're in."

Over an hour? It felt like maybe ten minutes to me. Something is very, very wrong.

CHAPTER FOURTEEN

Father-Daughter Dance

I t's been two months since Walter abducted me and died for it. Two months since my mother spoke to anyone in the house. Two months since we've seen Henry. Every week for the past two months Baldwin has stopped by, held maybe five minutes of pointless conversation, and spent over an hour with me that I never recall. I never see him weave a spell; I just feel a sense of wrongness and the time has passed.

I don't believe he has been assaulting me, if only because he wouldn't need to hide or heal the evidence or use magic at all, for that matter. If that was his purpose, there would be nothing I, currently, could do to stop him. Which means he has some other purpose. I need to know what that is. This is one of the reasons I, now able to move around with a crutch, am visiting Godfrey's Bookstore.

I am not allowed to walk here alone anymore, which is a fairly normal response for parents but is still annoying. I put up with it, however, because I really need more information. I need to find out what Baldwin is doing, and I need to learn about this world. I admittedly put history on the back burner while I learned about magic, but I can't put it off anymore. Growing my magical ability is great, but it's only a solution to immediate problems.

It's a bit like a woman carrying a gun. Yes, I'm technically allowed to defend myself, but if I do so, I'll still be punished for it, even if not by the law. I suspect the only reason I faced no consequence for killing Walter is because Baldwin seems to have some other use for me. Magical ability only grants power because it grants nobility. I'm not a change-the-system-from-within type of girl, so that's not really on the table. I need to show people a better world is possible and give them the means to burn the current one to the ground.

It is the pursuit of these two goals I am researching today. This is a bookshop rather than a library, so my options are limited, but there are a couple small sections of history and policy. I take my first stack to a chair near the back room and start with a dusty, thick political tome. I stop as my eyes scan various laws, the twisting of my stomach reaching a critical point.

"What the fuck is this, Godfrey?" I ask incredulously.

He looks up from his smut to respond, "What's the problem this time, child?"

"Women always have a male guardian? What's that about?"

"It's really nothing, child, no need to panic. Your father is your guardian until your husband takes over. It's perfectly reasonable, really. You would starve otherwise, or just make exclusively emotional choices."

This causes the hardest eye roll of this life so far. "And if I don't ever get a husband? What about orphans or sex workers?"

Putting his book down, he sighs before explaining my foolishness to me. "Women who choose not to get married are the property of their employers. They can be a seamstress, a maid, a waitress, a whore, or any other job suited to women's talents. They will be paid with food and shelter until they do get married, if they haven't chosen whoring. This is common for women who wait until they are exceptionally old to get married and can't live with their parents. But none of those are an option for you anyway. As for orphans, they are the wards of the church."

"Putting aside the many, many asinine assertations you just made about women and what we are capable of, why is that not an option for me, exactly? I'm a mage. I'm already more qualified for most jobs than almost any man."

"Exactly, you are a mage, Lillith. A brilliant one too, and you will learn a great deal of magic, but after training, you are only to use it under your husband's supervision. And make no mistake, you will have a husband; it is the moral and legal duty of noblewomen to pass on their mana to keep the nobility strong."

There are quite a few things in that statement I am uninterested in, but I choke on all my competing retorts. I pause a moment, then say, "No wonder everyone still camps out in giant circles for weeks. You have been locking magic under the supervision of the stupidest people on the planet."

"Don't be ridiculous, child. You may have made a profound discovery, but you are the exception to the rule."

"Yes, I'm sure no man has ever taken credit for a woman's spell or circle design before," I quip, eliciting a quickly covered look of guilt in Godfrey's eyes. *Yeah, I know what you're planning, asshole.*

This apparently strikes a chord with him because he lashes out. "No need to throw a fit—this is why all of you need a guardian, you are too easily upset!"

"Yes, of course," I begin in an unimpressed monotone voice, "I can't believe *I* got so emotional. Whatever would I do without your wisdom guiding me."

Godfrey just grunts, and I take it as a sign he is no longer interested in the conversation. I return to reading but I regret it. This law is just the tip of the iceberg. Women and children are legally considered property for all intents and purposes. Crimes against either are identical to property damage. If someone is caught raping a commoner woman, the punishment is a fine paid to her husband. If it's a noblewoman and mage, the punishment is death, unless the culprit was a noble of higher standing than her husband. Turns out my mana is the only reason Walter even bothered hiding his plans.

I suppose it's no surprise. Women are treated like children and children are treated as subhuman. Just power on top of power on top of power and greasy assholes shitting downhill wherever they land in the hierarchy. It's no matter. I am not going to have a husband. I'm not going to be some kind of magic baby farm. I will tear every pretty noble little thing down long before that happens, and anyone who tries to force it, well . . . I'm an anarchist. Walter wasn't the first and he won't be the last.

I've had about as much of this as I can stomach. Time to figure out what Baldwin has been doing and how. I can't find any reference to anything like what he is doing in magical texts. I start collecting different legends and fairy tales, even grabbing a couple of religious texts. If it's not something that is openly talked about, perhaps it is something that stories are told about.

I'm interrupted by my father entering the shop. "It's time to head home. Lily," he calls as I gather up the books I've been reading.

"All right, can you help me carry these?" I ask.

"Are you sure you can take those out of the shop?" he inquires, looking in Godfrey's direction.

Godfrey just waves him off and says, "Whatever, just bring them back," without even looking up from his book.

"Well, all right, then," my dad says, and picks up a couple of my books, grinning when he sees a fairy tale on top. "Finally reading something more age appropriate, are you? It's good to see you drop the 'grown-up' act sometimes."

"Grown-up act?" I raise an eyebrow at the phrase as we depart the shop.

"You know, you always imitate the writing in the books you read, trying to sound like you aren't a little girl. It's not quite convincing with your voice, you know."

I glare at him. I guess I have been a bit lax about acting my age, so to speak, for the last couple of years. It's just exhausting being an adult woman pretending to be a clueless child just for my parents' sake. It feels pretty similar to teaching math to rich frat boys or responding to work emails, actually. I always have to play dumb or risk hurting my parents' pride and drawing their ire. I have completely failed that with Edward already.

I don't have the energy to argue, however, so I just let him believe what he wants. This is clearly not an impression that will end when I get older anyway. I change the subject instead. "How is Mom doing? Is she eating more?"

My father's face falls at my question. "She's having a hard time, Lily. She lives for you kids. Losing Henry was . . . not easy on her."

"I'm sorry, Dad. She'll be okay when we find Henry. I'm sure of it."

He gives me a half smile in response, but his eyes betray his true hopelessness.

My heart aches whenever we talk about this. I miss Henry. I miss my mom, even if she never really related to me. I want to help her. I am going to help her; I'm going to bring Henry home. I am healing fast—another week and I can probably go looking for him. I have mastered a few more aspects. I can now create a small, dense pebble with earth mana and propel it with force mana.

My poison skin experiment is going . . . poorly, especially with no ethical way to test it on humans. But that doesn't matter; in its current state it couldn't even kill a fly. I am missing something I can't put my finger on. I can, however, copy the light in an area and create an illusory barrier I can hide behind. I am confident I can handle a group of thugs the size I ran off last time. I just have to find him, a task I am working on two spells to help with. I haven't given up on my radar idea, even though I still haven't cracked how to receive the signal. And I'm trying to enhance my hearing, magically and physically.

"There's something I want to talk to you about," my father says as we walk in silence, interrupting my planning.

"What's up, Dad?" I inquire.

"It's about your position as a mage . . ."

Shit. I hate it when he brings this up. The man is so damn eager to be part of a noble house, he doesn't understand why I haven't gone to the church to be officially christened as a noble yet. I don't intend to ever do such a thing, but it's getting harder to get him to drop the subject.

"Yes?" I cautiously ask.

"I've arranged for you to meet with an etiquette tutor. You are going to be a noblewoman, and to be honest, Lily, you are a bit crass, even for us commoners. We need to start preparing you for marriage in a noble society."

Ah, of course—ready to marry me off already. Not a chance.

"I'm not going."

"Lily, this is important. I—"

"I said no. I don't have time for something useless like that."

"Now listen, young lady, I am very patient with you, but I am your father. This I'm-so-grown-up-I-don't-have-to-listen-to-you act can only go so far. When I tell you that you are going to do something, you are going to do it."

"The answer is no, Father. I am not going to waste my time on that garbage."

"Lillith! You cannot behave like this. You have to prepare to be a nobleman's wife someday! Wives are submissive, Lily; you'll never be married if you keep making a fool of yourself like this!"

"Oh no! You're saying I won't get to tie my life to some arrogant pig who locks little girls in his cellar and uses me like the dirty socks you hide under your bed when Mom is sick? Whatever will I do?"

"LILLITH! SHUT YOUR MOUTH NOW," he shouts, before calming himself. "I am going to be the head of a new noble house, and I will not have you embarrassing us."

"Embarrassing you?" I balk. "You're just a petty bully who gets paid to round up 'criminals' for richer men to use as slaves! The only chance you have at nobility you have because of me! If my presence makes the comfort you bought with me less stable, then try to get that comfort without me. How about that?"

His rage races mine to boiling as I snap back at him. The knowledge that his daughter is the reason the nobility values him pricks at him, but throwing it in his face turns it into a gaping wound. As we approach the house, he points at a tree. "Fetch me a switch. If words won't get through to you, maybe this will."

"No. If you want to try to beat me while I'm still injured, you can get your own. I don't recommend it, though, *Father*," I growl at him, ready to defend myself if he tries anything.

Beet red, he stomps to the tree, snaps a branch off, and strips it efficiently into a switch. As he marches back to me he pulls his arm back, ready to hit me across the face rather than spanking me. But I don't flinch. "Try it," I taunt. "See what happens."

He swings full force, trying to punish my independence. The switch flies from his hand, snapping as it comes in contact with my force mana. I stand still, unfazed by his attempt to hit me. We stand in silence for a moment before I speak.

"You do not own me, Dad. I don't care what my age is. I don't care what my gender is. I am not a tool to elevate your status. I am not clay to be molded into whatever image you desire. You will not try that again."

Realizing he can't touch me, he spits at my feet. "You ungrateful brat! I can have you arrested for assaulting and defying your guardian. I can have you made a slave. You really think you can insult me like this!?"

"Go ahead and try. See what happens to your dreams of nobility. You have me or you have nothing. So go ahead," I snarl, thrusting out the hand that isn't holding my crutch, "arrest me."

He glares down at me, his pride irreparably damaged. He doesn't try to arrest me and I withdraw my hands.

"The way I behave isn't an act," I say. "I'm not emulating a book. This is me. It's not the image you had for your little girl, and I understand that it doesn't make sense to you. But this is who I am. You can't change it, and you can't force me to fill that role. I don't fit. If you get over your pride and accept that fact, maybe we can move past it. But I'll be honest—I don't think you will. I've known for a while your pride is more important than your family."

I begin walking the rest of the way home, but he calls after me. "It's your fault Henry is gone, you know. It's your stubbornness, your bitterness that brought this on our family. If it weren't for you, I'd still have my son. Your mom would be okay. If you just knew your place and did as you were told, this family would be whole!"

I turn around to face him. "Have you even been looking for him? You say he's gone because I don't do what I'm told, but you are a city guard. You could have found him by now. But you've been ordered to stop investigating, haven't you?" I glare up at him. "Henry isn't still gone because I didn't do as I was told. He's gone because you did."

I leave him with that, retiring to my room with my stack of books like a shield.

CHAPTER FIFTEEN

Saving My Siblings

I snap shut yet another fairy tale. I haven't found anything promising in the books I brought home. I lay my head back against my headboard and rub at my eyes. Baldwin is using some kind of magic I can't understand or see. My best guess is that he's somehow removing my memories after whatever happens. That way I would see the mana in the spell, but not remember it. I just can't figure out how he is doing that.

A mage can actualize almost any aspect they can think of. With willpower, they grasp a concept they understand and imprint it on mana, which then behaves according to the properties of that concept. For example, where I use force mana to propel things, another mage may use power mana. I use force because I understand physics and so I have a great deal of control over whatever I apply it to.

This should not work with mental manipulation, however. First of all, everyone's body has a natural resistance to outside mana. It's one reason I can modify my own body, but I would have a great deal of difficulty modifying someone else's. Even the flowers were a bit of a challenge. It would take immense amounts of mana. The mind is even more protected, and a mage's mind even more so. Even the king likely wouldn't have enough mana to do so.

Finally, it takes understanding. My projectiles fly farther and straighter because I apply both forward and upward force, whereas power mana works more like throwing a punch: holding an object with power and moving it at great speed. In other words, my projectile spells are better than most because I understand how to manipulate them. The same applies to body and mind manipulation.

The only way mana can be used to alter a person's mind, even if enough mana is expended, is to fully understand how the human brain works; that would require knowledge far beyond even old Earth. If a mage without that tried, they would simply kill their target. What Baldwin does every week is impossible. I love a good fairy tale, but these aren't getting me anywhere. I need to find a library.

I drop the book onto the pile beside my bed with a *whumph* that flickers the candle flame and stand up, stretching my body. It's been a few days since my confrontation with my father, and my accelerated healing has finally done the job. Well, enough of the job. I no longer need a crutch and I can move about on my own. All I need is a pair of pants and I can start looking for Henry in earnest. I mean, I don't need them, I guess, but these dresses and skirts are not easy to move around in and certainly don't do me favors in a fight. Alas, my parents seem to believe pants are immodest on women.

As I lament my lack of wardrobe options, I pick up the faint click of my parents' door closing. Finally, everyone is in bed. This is my first opportunity to find Henry! I pick my least restrictive skirt, blow out the candle, and gently open my door, closing it behind me with a soft *snick*. As I suspect, the common rooms are empty. I creep heel to toe to the door, minimizing the sound of my footprints. I don't need to, as I also use magic to block the sounds around my feet, but old sneaking habits die hard.

I successfully escape the house and relax my posture as I head in the direction of the seedier part of the city. I jump as a voice calls out to me.

"Going looking for Henry?" Gilbert asks, leaning against the house and taking a bite out of an apple. Shit, he was not there a second ago! I really need to figure out my radar spell.

"That depends; are you planning to stop me?" I respond.

"No. I know you don't trust me, Lillith. You don't even like me. But I love him too. I have been looking every night for months."

This gives me pause and I raise an eyebrow. Can I trust him? He's a creep. But he always did care for Henry. Maybe I can get a head start. "Well. Come along then," I reply, deciding I need all the help I can get, for Henry's sake. At least it's not Edward. He tosses the apple aside and jogs to catch up with me. "So what do you know so far?" I ask.

"I've checked every tavern on the south side of town. Every gambling den, even every brothel. No one has seen him," he explains as he walks alongside me.

"What kind of questions did you ask?"

"What do you mean?"

"What did you ask people when you were looking for him?"

"I just described him, I guess? Asked if anyone had seen him. That sort of thing?"

"All right, there's your first problem."

"What do you mean?"

"You aren't asking the right questions. Think about it, Gil. Walter is gone, so assuming Henry is still alive, why would the men who attacked us still want him?"

"Well, that's why I asked around the brothels, and anywhere else he might be forced to work."

"Sure, that's why they might want to keep any random kid like Henry, but he is special. He knows alchemy. If they were planning to kill him, telling them about that would be more than enough to keep him alive."

As we walk, the residential buildings give way to inns, taverns, and gambling dens.

"So . . . you think he works for an apothecary? I doubt a street gang can afford a shop, Lillith."

"No, but that doesn't mean they can't sell potions. He would be valuable for healing potions, sleeping potions, even green mist or—"

"Collector's grace, Lillith, he can make green mist!?" Gilbert interrupts, startled that his little brother might know how to make the drug.

I just roll my eyes. "Of course he can, alchemists make all of the potions that nobles use to minimize its risk, and that is certainly one. Henry and his master probably sell their own stable version for richer clients. They would obviously know how it's made."

"Nobles don't breathe mist, Lillith, it's a crime. They are the ones who made it a crime."

"Nothing is a crime for nobles except insulting higher nobles. But you're getting sidetracked."

"Right, sorry."

I make sure my voice is low enough not to echo down the empty street. "We need to ask if a new source of drugs and potions has shown up in the last couple of months. We find that, we find Henry."

"Holy shit. I belong in the third plane, Lillith. How could I have missed that?"

"I suppose it's not entirely your fault. I've known this the whole time. I just . . . didn't think you were out looking for him."

"You really think I'm that shitty of a person, Lillith? That I just sit on my ass while my little brother is missing?"

"Dad does exactly that, and he literally gets paid to handle these kinds of things. Supposedly."

"Yeah well, I'm not Dad," he says, passing a hand through his hair. "Look, Lillith, I just fool around a little bit. Can you at least tell me why that makes you hate me so much? I'm not even hurting anyone!"

I look at him appraisingly. He really believes he isn't hurting anyone. "All right. I can explain it to you. Will you listen? I mean really listen and think about what I'm saying."

He stops walking for a moment and I can see him processing the question. That's actually a good sign; if he just wanted to bully me into agreeing with him, he would've answered offhandedly. "Yeah, I can listen, Lillith."

"How often do you check in with the women you 'fool around' with, after the fact?" I ask, and his face takes on an embarrassed shade as I tug him down a side road to our left.

"I don't, really. I mean I do, but I just let them down easy and move on, I guess . . ."

"Right. You get what you are looking for and then you dump them. It doesn't even seem that bad to you, that casual cruelty. But that's not the worst part," I say. He gets a flash of indignation when I mention casual cruelty, but he polices his face as I continue, "Do you know what marriage is like in this country, from a woman's point of view?"

"I guess not, but it's not like I ever promised to marry any of them."

"Gilbert, we are traded like horses. Our fathers sell us off to the highest bidder. We have to live our lives in fear of who we will be sold off to. I just found out our husbands literally become our new guardians when we are married. Imagine for a moment that you could be sold like that. Any woman, even a man, could buy you, whether you liked them or not, whether you found them attractive or not, and they would just have authority over your life forever!"

"Okay, I understand that," he says a little petulantly, "but what does that have to do with this? I didn't buy any of these girls—they all agreed to everything we did!"

"Imagine it was you, Gilbert, with no control over how your life ends up. Then you meet a charming, beautiful woman who seems to really like you. You can trust her. You are safe. And she says she loves you. You think maybe, just maybe, you can actually choose who you'll spend your life with. Then she uses you and dumps you like trash."

Gilbert sucks his teeth. "Okay, I guess that bit would suck . . . but I would still have fun, and I would move on!"

"You aren't getting it." I shake my head. "Okay, imagine it was me. Imagine a man did that to me."

I see a flash of understanding on his face and he doesn't respond, so I continue, "And here's the thing, Gilbert. You boast about it. You tell all your friends. You spread rumors about your conquests. Do you know how a woman is treated when that happens?"

"I mean, she's considered a bit loose, I guess?"

"You guess? You know. You would never marry a woman who wasn't still 'pure.' A woman who had slept with someone other than you. It's considered shameful to take someone like that as your wife. As if it even means anything."

As I lecture, I see a couple walk by and give us a strange look. I pull him into a quiet corner, and when I look back I can actually see him processing what I'm saying and I don't let up. "Now these women, whose entire lives hinge on being valuable as a wife, are suddenly untouchable. How do you think their lives end up, Gil? They risked everything for a man who said he loved her because they were that desperate to choose their own life, their own husband. And you didn't even have the decency to do it to one woman at a time. Half an hour of gratification for you and their lives are over. You didn't even think about it enough to know what you were doing."

"No, Lillith, now you are pushing it too far. Their entire lives? It's just a little fun!" he pleads at me, badly wanting to believe his own words.

"You don't even know what happened to Hannah, do you?" I retort, and he looks at me, startled.

"What happened to Hannah? She was upset last time I saw her, sure, but she was fine!"

"Her father heard one of the rumors about you two. By the time you had moved on to another woman, he had beaten her even more badly than those thugs beat me. He didn't even face any consequences for it—he's her guardian. And you were too busy doing the same thing to another woman to even hear about it."

This revelation stops him cold and he stares at me, wide-eyed. "Collector, Lillith! I—I didn't know, I—"

"You didn't care to know, Gilbert. That's why you and I don't get along. You let your dick lead you around, lying to women, ruining their lives for a quick dopamine fix."

"What's dope—never mind, Lillith. I—I need to think. Collector, Hannah is hurt that badly? I really do belong in the third plane . . ."

After venting my frustration to Gilbert, I allow silence to prevail as we walk through the filthy southern district. I'm assaulted by the familiar itch of eyes slithering across me and I wrinkle my nose at the uncaring stench of what is clearly the criminal quarter. As I scan the various people, loitering or peddling illicit goods from different corners, I consider my brother. . . I'm honestly impressed by how receptive he is to what I said. It doesn't change how he behaved, but it might change him.

Just a few minutes later, I notice careful footsteps following behind us, and start directing Gilbert to a more isolated area. This is exactly what I was looking for. Gilbert doesn't notice, too lost in thought to pay attention. As I reach a dead end in an alley, three men with knives corner us in.

"Leave the girl and any money you have, and we'll let you go," the man in front says, a sickly grin skewing his face sideways. Gilbert looks up and horror takes over his previously conflicted expression.

"I—" I start as Gilbert speaks at the same time.

"I won't. Leave now, while I'm being nice!" he blusters. He is scrappy, but hardly at an advantage here, and the men know it. They laugh together and the man on the left just taunts him in response.

"Oh relax, we are just gonna take her for a test ride for you! We'll return her to you, mostly intact!"

"We might even teach her a few new tricks for you!" the last man chimes in.

"You won't touch her, I'm warning you! Leave. Now!" Gilbert responds, his voice steady despite his clear anxiety.

"Or what?" the first man asks. "You're unarmed, you're alone, and no one around here will care if you scream. So what'll you do if, say, I don't leave?"

The man is still grinning, his eyes on me in obvious anticipation.

"I'll—" Gilbert starts, but I put my hand on his shoulder. I have been conjuring three small, round stones since I noticed the men, and finally, they are ready.

"I've got this, Gil, watch and learn," I say reassuringly as he looks back at me, confused.

All three men burst into laughter and the third man shouts, "Look, boy, your girl is sacrificing herself for you! You're a lucky man, you are! Maybe I'll—"

We never find out what he is considering as a stone flies through his throat and he falls to the ground, spluttering and trying to hold the blood in.

I stand next to Gilbert, pointing finger guns only I understand in that man's and the second man's directions. I don't actually need the gesture—I fired the stone with my mana mentally—but I can't help myself.

"W-what just fucking happened?" the second man yells, looking at his fallen comrade.

"M-mage. The bitch is a mage, shit!" the first man, wide-eyed, gasps, and the second man turns to flee. He makes it two steps before a stone enters his skull through the soft spot at the back of his neck and he falls dead instantly.

"Run if you want the same," I calmly explain, tossing my last pebble in the air and catching it. The remaining man falls to his knees.

"M-my lady, I'm sorry, I didn't know, had I known you were a mage, I never would have—"

"Tried to rape me?" I interrupt. "I know. That's why I didn't tell you when you started following me."

His and Gilbert's eyes widen at the same time.

"Yes, I knew they were there. Who do you think will be most likely to answer our questions?" I ask.

"Questions?" the man asks, no longer looking at me with lust. "Isn't this a bit extreme?"

"Yes, questions. I need you to tell me about the potions on the market," I respond.

"Potions, my lady?" he asks.

"Yes, potions. Has there been a sudden influx of potions on the black market? Healing potions. Green mist. Has anyone started selling more of those recently, in the last couple of months or so?"

I see recognition in the man's eyes, and he replies immediately, "Yes, my lady, both of those and more, a lot more than usual!"

"Good. And do you know who is selling them?"

"I'm—I'm not too sure, my lady. They have been at quite a few stalls lately. I"—I raise a finger at him so he hurries on—"I think the Manticorps were the first to sell them, ma'am!"

"The Manticorps? And who are they?"

"A local gang, my lady. They are local mercenaries for hire, but they have been selling products lately too!"

"And where can I find them?"

"I—I don't know, ma'am! I'm not part of their gang, I just hear about them, that's all!"

I look at his desperate eyes and decide he is telling the truth.

"All right, that's all I need, then," I say, and as his face relaxes in relief, my last stone flies through his eye socket, lodging in his brain. Gilbert blanches at the brutality.

"Why did you kill him? He surrendered! He gave us what we wanted!" he sputters.

I look over at my brother. "I did it for the next girl who needs to walk by this alley. I did it for all the girls who have walked by before and didn't have mana to protect them. I did it because I grieve for them, and I won't have another woman to grieve for because I didn't."

Gilbert falls to his knees, retching. I let him empty his stomach. I am closer to Henry now, that's what matters. The Manticorps, huh?

Time to put an end to a street gang.

CHAPTER SIXTEEN

No Woman Is an Island

It seems the Manticorps don't exist. Or, to be more accurate, they have bullied and threatened everyone around town into pretending they don't exist. This makes the night unfruitful and frustrating. If I approach someone to ask about them, I am, admittedly reasonably, chastised for wanting to know. If Gilbert approaches anyone, they vehemently deny knowing of any such gang. People don't aggressively deny the existence of something they are hearing about for the first time, however, so we are on the right track.

Gilbert and I reconvene in the dark of a cramped alley, and I come to a decision. "We have a name now," I say. "We may have better luck during the day."

Gilbert, deep in thought about something, startles as I break the silence, but he responds, "Won't people be even more afraid with more people around?"

"I find it unlikely," I explain. "Being approached by strangers at night always puts people on guard. If we bring it up when we have a natural reason to be there, in the light of day, we'll run into fewer people in fight-or-flight right when we approach them."

"What do you mean 'in fight-or-flight'?" he inquires. Oops. Though it sounds intuitive to me, maybe the way I phrased it confused him.

"It's what I call the physical response to perceived danger. Our bodies sort of . . . energize and prepare us to either fight or flee."

He nods, recognizing the feeling and looking contemplative. As we walk back toward our home, he speaks up after a moment. "Lillith, I think there is something . . . wrong with you."

Lovely. I'm sure a conversation that starts like that will be a pleasant one. He heard me out, however, so I can return the favor. "Care to elaborate?"

"You . . . you are cold, Lillith. Calculating. You are what, twelve? Thirteen? You speak like a mortician examining a corpse. People don't analyze what their body is doing when they are afraid!"

"Well, that's not—I mean, it's not an original concept, it's just the name that's new."

"That's beside the point! Our brother is missing, Lillith. And he is missing because of people who were after *you*. For months! And your only response? Saying you'll get him back then going right back to reading and practicing your magic like nothing ever happened! He could be dead, Lillith."

"Gilbert, that's—" I start before pausing. I wanted to respond with my reasoning for all that, but maybe that's his point? What he's saying doesn't exactly ring true all the way through, but the sentiment . . . well, it might be fair. I need to examine that. I have seen a lot of death and lost a lot of people to the pride of those in power. I still grieve for all of them. I still worry about the ones I never found.

In this life, however, Henry is the first. Yes, I knew Henry was too valuable to kill. Yes, I needed the magic and knowledge I was practicing to save him. Gilbert is right though; that's exactly what it means to be calculating. I must look like I have no empathy at all. I do, but I am jaded. A lifetime of loss and abuse, my relationship with my original parents, and two lifetimes of watching the same happen to the people around me.

I have to be careful. I can't let myself lose sight of why I'm so angry. Why I am learning what I am. I can try to explain some of this to Gilbert, but he at least partially has a point. Something I need to reflect on.

"I understand what you mean, and to an extent, you are right. I have been calculating. But I want you to know I'm not being cavalier about this," I say. "I am cold. But not in the way you mean. I am cold not because of a lack of emotion but because of its abundance. It's a frigid anger, an icy grief. And I am calculating, you are right about that. I'll examine that, but I don't know how else to be right now."

I see Gilbert take in what I am saying, and I continue, "I think it's unlikely Henry is dead. I've always thought so because I knew he was valuable to anyone who had him. And you're right that is a calculating response. On the flip side of that, however, is that I can't entertain the idea that he is! It's a more real possibility than I have been willing to admit to myself! But I don't know what else to do! I can't act on his death, I can only act on his life, and that's what I'm doing!"

I realize I've begun raising my voice, and I wipe one eye as I feel water running down it. When did that happen? Saying this all out loud is breaking some kind of barrier. I hadn't realized the lack of a confidant was affecting me this much. Annie had a group of like-minded friends and allies, and I to an extent had Henry, but for the last couple of months, I haven't had anyone I trust.

Gilbert starts raising his voice as well. "Lillith, you didn't change when Henry was taken! You didn't change when you killed Lord Walter! You have been like this, your behavior is exactly the same! What are you, always angry? Always grieving?"

"YES! I AM ALWAYS GRIEVING!" I shout back. My voice echoes through the empty streets, dancing across the cold cobblestone and knocking on the doors of curious families. I have to take a deep breath and center myself before I draw more attention. "The way I live my life and the beliefs that drive my goals are all an expression of grief! I came into this world in mourning! Yes, for Henry, but also for every other Henry out there! I am grieving for every little girl in every secret cellar, for every barmaid followed home by an angry customer, for every slave in the fields, and every slave in the marriage bed. I'm grieving for every Hannah," I finish, starting fast and slowing down as I fight through my growing tears.

That final word hits Gilbert like a slap across the face. "Okay, Lillith. I understand. But you killed three men in cold blood tonight. You didn't even flinch, much less hesitate. One of them was fleeing! The other had surrendered! That wasn't justice, that was just revenge!"

My eyes harden at that. "No, Gilbert, it wasn't. You have made some good points tonight, things I will think about. You've made me realize I am isolating myself too much. But you are wrong about this. That wasn't revenge, that was responsibility."

"Responsibility? That was murder! There was no honor in that!"

"Honor is just a word nobility came up with so we would think fighting back against unbalanced scales was immoral. Empathy is what matters. And I am never going to meet someone who was hurt or abused by someone I could have stopped."

"And if they could have changed?" he asks, a look of desperation in his eyes.

I have composed myself by this time, so I reply, "Look, Gilbert, I understand why that's important to you. And we can talk about the complexities of your guilt in another conversation. But the victims of those men don't deserve to continue being exposed to and fearing them based on a what-if. And I certainly won't be gambling any future victims on one."

"So what about me? Are you going to kill me someday too?"

I look over at his vulnerable face and steel myself. "Not as of now, but if you do what they did? Absolutely. You were casually cruel, and you knew that, but you didn't understand the extent of it. There is a longer conversation to be had about your choices, but I can't kill every ignorant creep. The line between educating and ending has to be somewhere between you and men who follow women into alleys."

His expression is stricken. "By the Collector, Lillith, 'maybe' was not the answer I was expecting!"

"Look," I say, turning back to the dark road ahead of us, "you have done a lot of harm. Part of coming to terms with that, part of changing, is accepting that you shouldn't be trusted. If those men I killed did truly change at some point, if they really understood what they had done? Felt the weight of it? Well, they would have accepted what I did. Accepting that I won't trust you is the least you can do."

Gilbert quiets at this, and I give him time to process. I have some things to think about as well. I have isolated myself. If I had shared my insights with Gilbert months ago . . . shit. I killed the man responsible for taking Henry, and that man owns the blame for that, whatever others might think. But not sharing my plans was a mistake. That was arrogance, and Henry has suffered for it. It took me a single night to find information, and I could have helped sooner.

We arrive home and, both of us contemplating our mistakes, head to bed.

The following day Gilbert and I head out. My father watches us step out the door with a smug look on his face that worries me. It's the first expression other than anger I have received from him since our confrontation. I don't have time to worry about it, however; now that I can move freely, I want to find Henry as soon as I can. I push worries about my father to the back of my mind.

Today we visit the seediest shopping district where people seemed the most afraid of the Manticorps's name. I figure this is likely the closest to their territory. A few vendors and bartenders might be able to help us, and if not, I have another idea. We aren't having a lot of luck so far, but as Gilbert warily exchanges questions with an uncooperative baker, I spot a kid pulling a loaf of bread off the stall while its owner is distracted.

The baker, apparently more vigilant than the kid expected, immediately turns his attention to where the bread had been.

"Collector-damned urchins! Girl, did you see where he went?" he asks.

"Nope, sorry," I respond flippantly. "I'll be right back, Gil," I say before following the boy to the alley I saw him turn into. It takes me a minute to catch up with him, and he has apparently noticed me as he suddenly jumps out from behind a corner and tries to swing at me. I dodge easily enough and use his momentum to push him past me.

"Whadda ya want?" he scowls, after recovering. He is a couple of years younger than me, but only a little shorter. He obviously lives on the streets and he looks at me with a familiar distrust.

"Just to ask a couple questions," I assure him, flicking a tin coin over to him, which he catches easily. "I'm looking for someone."

He looks down at the coin with a mixture of gratitude and anxiety as he clutches his bread to his chest with his other hand. "Wot kinda questions?"

"I'm looking for a group called the Manticorps. I hear they've been selling interesting potions lately."

He tenses up and, interestingly, his anxiety is joined by concern. "You don' wanna poke yer nose aroun' there, lady," he says. "It ain't safe." He begins to hand me my coin back, but I wave him off.

"Don't worry about me," I say reassuringly as I form a rock above my hand to demonstrate my mana. "I can protect myself. I plan to put an end to them tonight." I fire the rock into the wall with force to demonstrate my point.

Eyes widening, the boy closes his fist around the coin. "Truly, yer gonna stop 'em?" he asks.

"Truly. But I need to find them first."

The boy has an internal debate for a few moments before his resolve steels. "I'll show ya," he announces, his anxiety replaced with anger and determination.

I retrieve my brother and we follow the boy, who tells me his name is Tommy. It's a fairly complex route to the Manticorps's hideout; unsurprisingly, this city isn't built on a grid. But we arrive and duck behind a nearby building so Tommy can point it out to me. It's a large building; it looks like it would be used for storage. Gilbert stands at the other end of the building, keeping watch.

"They come 'n' go from there. Got a dozen rooms 'n' a big one under a hatch. They make me and my family bring money 'n' food," he explains.

I tap my lips as I think. "Anything else I need to know?" I ask.

"The new boss, she's a crazy lady that gets all bent up about bein' treated like she's rich or somethin'. She's weird, got some sorta power," he says, causing my eyebrow to raise.

"What kind of power?"

"She's fast. Like, she'll hit you from behind when you was just talkin' to her face-to-face fast. And quiet. We're all afraid to talk bad 'cause she can show up outta nowhere when you say somethin' bad about her," he says, clearly worried about just that happening.

"Here," I say, having mercy on him, and hand him my entire coin pouch. "Try to warn all the kids you can to stay away from here tonight."

His eyes widen as he sees the pouch. He takes it, clear happiness and hope decorating his face, then he grows concerned again and pleads, "Summa my family work there, miss. They won't fight you, but they hafta be there! Can you keep 'em safe?"

"I won't hurt your family, Tommy, I promise. I will only fight people who fight me, okay?" It's inconvenient, but I knew coming into this that not everyone stuck with the Manticorps would be guilty. Legal slavery isn't the only kind in this world.

"Miss?" Tommy says, a questioning tone in his voice. I raise an eyebrow, indicating he should continue. "Can I . . . Can I help? I wanna come with you."

I'm really starting to like this kid. "Sure," I say, "but I can't guarantee I can protect you. You'll have to be careful. But if you want to fight, you have the right to fight. No one can tell you no."

With that, he leaves in a hurry, and Gilbert and I head home.

"You really think we can do this, Lillith?" he asks, worried.

"I think we have to. I'm a lot stronger than last time though. If we prepare and are careful, we can do this."

"Okay. I'm with you."

Problems with Gilbert aside, it feels good to have someone who can help me again. Tonight is round two.

CHAPTER SEVENTEEN

Assault

On a torn-out sheet of my journal, I draw a magic circle to attract light mana. I also include absorption and emission runes, so any substance imbued by sitting in the circle should absorb and immediately emit light. More specifically, it's targeting ultraviolet light. In other words: I've drawn a fluorescent magic circle. For a brief moment, I think of using a circle like this for a person and chuckle.

I weigh the paper down in the center of my room, the space I am using as an anchor, and place a sack of flour on top of it. Typically, enchanting an object with a circle takes a few days to a few weeks, depending on the substance and mass of what is being targeted, but I can get around that. Since I am using mana aspects I have grasped and control directly, I can channel and stabilize it much more quickly.

After about six long, boring hours, I have a sack of fluorescent flour. Flourescent, if you will. Okay, that was pretty bad; I should sleep more. I cast a flashlight using a black light–wavelength and confirm the flour does, in fact, glow. Perfect: step one complete.

I spend some time forming several stones as lethal projectiles. I can technically use any stone for this, but since my spells are more equation than recipe, I am far more accurate when I know the mass exactly. Finally, I sneak a few dozen eggs I'd liberated from Walter's old estate into my room and hollow them out. Thoughts of childhood Easters perk me up a little as I poke a small hole in the top of each, and a bigger hole at the bottom. Fortunately, I don't need these as pretty as Easter eggs, so the process is quick.

Using the paper with the magic circle as a makeshift funnel, I pour the flour into the eggshells, applying a gently rotating force mana to expedite the process. As I wrap a few dozen glowing, flour-filled eggshells in my socks and put them in my bag, I can't help but laugh to myself. Prepping to rescue my brother from a dangerous street gang is feeling a lot less "action movie" and a lot more "arts and crafts" than I would have expected.

This is the best I can come up with to deal with such a large group safely, however. Especially if I want to hold back on lethality. I push down a spike of anxiety as I remember what Tommy said about the gang's current leader.

She is inhumanly fast. She is uncannily quiet. She is hung up about nobility. She is a fucking mage, I think again, trying to account for these factors in my plan.

Going up against another mage is always a gamble until you can feel their mana. Is she more powerful than me? Does she have more aspects? What else can she do? There are too many variables to plan for all of them, but I refuse to leave Henry with the gang any longer. I have to rely on what I do know.

She is a mage, but she probably isn't a noble. Tommy said she wants to be treated like she's rich. It's unlikely she is actively avoiding noble recognition like I am. In fact, she has probably tried to be christened as one before. Or she is a noble and runs a street gang as a hobby, I guess. *Fuck, I guess that's not impossible either*, I realize, my anxiety spiking again. Meeting Baldwin was a reality check. A magical reality check, which I find surreal. I do find that unlikely, however, based on Tommy's description.

This leaves one option I consider most likely. She is probably an illegitimate child of a local lord. Either that or an ostracized one. In either case, noble recognition is most likely being actively withheld from her. Hopefully, this means she never got her own magic circle and is relying entirely on inherited magic. This is a lot of *ifs* and *probablys*, but they'll have to do. Henry deserves immediate action.

I compartmentalize my anxiety as I gather my supplies and head down to meet Gilbert. The time for worrying has passed.

Gilbert and I meet up with Tommy behind the same industrial building and I immediately fail to suppress my panic. He has been beaten, badly. His lip is split open, his face is bruised all over, and his left eye is swollen shut. He limps to get to me.

"Tommy, what the hell happened? Are you okay?" I ask, running up to him and catching him as he begins to stumble. Gilbert runs to his other side and wraps his arm around his back to help support him.

He groans out his response. "M'okay, ma'am. Just some scrapes 'n' bruises," he assures me shortly before taking a sharp breath through his teeth as I examine a welt on his arm.

"I repeat, what the hell happened? Do we need to get you to safety?" I ask, panic ballooning.

"R-rosalind," he begins, clearly biting back pain. "I wus warnin' 'em all like ya said to, and alluva sudden Rosalind came outta nowhere an' hit me, knocked me flat."

At this, my hackles rise and I quickly scan our surroundings. This was not the plan. "I'm so sorry, Tommy. Is she here now? I understand if she is, but I need to know, now!" I interrogate desperately. Gilbert begins flicking his eyes back and forth across the alleys and rooftops near us.

"No, ma'am," he says, "but she knows yer comin'. I told 'er about you an' yer brother. She got all my friends locked up 'n the cellar 'n' she says she's gonna kill 'em if you don't come in unarmed. Says she got yer brother too."

"All of them? Are you sure?"

"'M sorry, ma'am, I don' unerstand . . ."

"Your friends, they are all locked up? Was there anyone innocent left free in the main building?"

"I—I don' think so, ma'am, but I dunno fer sure."

"Did you see the cellar? Could you tell if anyone you didn't know was there?" Gilbert interjects, inquiring about Henry.

Tommy shakes his head as he responds. "No, sir, sorry. She sent me 'ere right off."

"That's okay," I say. "Do you know how to get there? Is there a way to sneak into the building?"

"Yes'm." Tommy nods. "I can get in, but I dunno if I can get back out all quiet 'n' all."

"That's okay. Can you get Gilbert in?"

"Yes'm, I can 'elp with that."

I turn to Gilbert for my next question. "Gil, how are you in a fight? Can you take a couple of thugs?"

Gilbert taps the club he brought at his waist. "I can take a couple of these creeps. Do you have a plan?"

"I do, but it'll be hard to pull off with hostages. I need someone to get into that cellar and handle any guards posted on the prisoners. Tommy, are you in good enough shape to get Gilbert there?"

"I dunno, ma'am, but I can try . . ."

"That's fine. I'll provide the distraction. Give me a signal when it's safe in the cellar, then tell everyone to get down until the light comes back."

"The light?" Gilbert asks, before realizing it's not the important question. "What kind of signal?"

I put my fingers in my mouth and let out three shrill whistles in short bursts. "Can you do that?"

Gilbert imitates me, then nods. "Easy enough."

"Perfect. Neither of you has to do this if you don't want to, or don't think you can. But if you'll trust me, I think we can do this."

Gilbert

When we get closer to the Manticorps hideout, Lillith separates from us and I help Tommy in the direction he indicates.

"There's a panel o'er there, 'n the side a the wall." He points, directing me to our way in. I help him over and find the panel in question. I try to pull it from the wall and my heart practically beats its way out of my chest as it creaks.

"No!" he whispers frantically. "Push o'er, don' pull it!"

I do as he instructs and lead him inside. We enter a cramped storage room, where I hear voices.

"Your plan was to attack us with pebbles and eggs?" I hear a woman laughing from somewhere nearby. We are close, shit. I feel sweat drip down my forehead as I try to creep out of the room. The hallway outside is empty, and I begin slowly, carefully following Tommy's pointing finger as I help him through the old building. The conversation continues somewhere nearby.

"Well, that remains to be seen, doesn't it?" I hear Lillith's voice at one point.

Wait, did the other woman say she brought eggs? Eggs? What in the third plane is she planning? I think. I am jolted back to reality where Tommy is waving, frantically trying to stop me from doing something. I look around for whatever he is panicking about before I take another step and realize what it was.

A loud creak echoes through the hallway as I step on an aged floorboard. Ah. *Fuck, I can't believe we didn't discuss signals for this kind of thing ahead of time! When will I stop being so fucking oblivious!?*

I realize the conversation outside has stopped and footsteps are coming in our direction, followed by a loud *THUNK*. That's when I hear pure chaos.

Footsteps are suddenly roaring in the other room, the first woman screaming commands and men yelling. I stop sneaking and pick up Tommy in a bridal carry, something he groans through, but he keeps directing me. A moment later a man bursts through a door in the hall in front of us. His eyes widen as he sees us and he opens his mouth to yell when I see Lillith appear, kick him in the back of his knee so he falls, grab him by the throat, and throw him back into the other room.

I gape. *How the fuck did she do that!?*

No time to consider, however, as I have to get to the hostages. They could be in trouble with all this commotion. I run in the directions Tommy gives me and finally come to a room with an open hatch in the ground. "Sorry about this," I say, before jumping in with Tommy in my arms.

I land and collapse to the ground, rolling onto my back to protect Tommy. In the middle of a torch-lit cellar are a couple of ramshackle cells thrown together with old wood absolutely full of terrified street urchins, mostly younger than Lillith. A panicked thug stares at me from in front of one of the cells as I recover, and there is a moment of silence as we stare at each other before he charges at me.

I leave Tommy on the ground and scramble to my feet, narrowly avoiding the thug's club. He is clearly no match for me, and I push him into the wall as he misses. Pulling out my own club, I hit him in the back and he falls to the ground. I pin him with one knee and hold his hands behind his back, satisfied he is subdued. Thank the Collector there was only one, or I would have had to kill him.

My relief fades quickly as I scan the faces in the cells, however.

Where is Henry? Henry isn't here! Oh shit, what if—

I don't get to finish my thought as Tommy lets out three shrill whistles.

"W-wait, not yet, my brother isn't—" I stutter as the world is swallowed by darkness.

CHAPTER EIGHTEEN

Colors in the Dark

Parting ways with Gilbert and Tommy, I march right in through the front doors to confront the people who took my brother from me. I am greeted by a large, gruff man and his scrawny partner, both armed with clubs. The skinnier man grabs my arm and tries to pull me along without saying a word.

"Where are you taking me?" I ask, refusing to move. The only response this receives is an angry blush from the skinny man while the bigger man grabs my arm and tries the same. Still unmoving, I repeat the question. "Where are we going?"

It is the skinny man's turn to laugh as the larger man struggles. Coming to a decision, the larger man goes to pick me up, only to fail as force mana increases my weight.

"Tell me where we are headed, and I'll go with you," I explain through a sweet, girlish smile. I should have a few minutes before I need to cause a commotion, and I want to know if they plan to just lock me up or confront me now.

The two men glance at each other before the skinny man speaks up. "We ain't supposed to speak with you, kid," he explains, and the big man face-palms.

"Well, you have officially failed that order, so you might as well tell me so you can get one thing done," I quip.

"Fine," the big man says. "We are taking you to the main audience chamber to meet Rosalind. Now come."

"Audience chamber?" I laugh. "Real fancy abandoned warehouse you have here, huh?"

"Just shut up and follow us," the big man grumbles and I comply. The "audience chamber" turns out, predictably, to be what was probably the main storage area. Somewhere around thirty men are in the room armed with clubs or daggers. Hopefully, this is everyone not directly guarding the prisoners. If it's not, the rest will likely come when I start causing real trouble, and if any decide to join the guards instead . . . well, they won't be able to find their way to the cellar in total darkness.

In the center of them is a woman with crossed arms. Rosalind, then. I steel my resolve as we approach her. This is where things get dangerous. Henry needs this, and Tommy is taking a huge risk for this. I can't mess it up, and I've never properly fought another mage before. I can confirm she is, in fact, a mage as I get closer. I can feel her mana radiating off her as she flips a small knife in one hand. It's not as strong as mine, but it's not as much weaker as I'd like. I don't have thirty grown men fighting on my side.

"You're that little bitch who killed Piers!" a man near the front shouts at me just as Rosalind is about to speak, drawing a hateful look from her. She stares at him for a moment. "S-sorry, boss."

As he is sufficiently cowed, she turns back to look at me and finally addresses me. "I should thank you for that, Lillith. You did me a huge favor!"

"I aim to please," I respond dryly.

"The boys here were awfully loyal to him. I can kill any man here, but they wouldn't have followed me if I took leadership by force. But when an unarmed little girl overpowers and kills him, well. That's hardly my fault."

"You're very welcome—Rosalind, was it?" I smile. "I look forward to doing this gang the same favor again."

Her mouth draws to a line as she responds. "It's *Lady* Rosalind. It would serve you well to show me proper respect," she growls at me. Hang-up indeed.

"Refusing to refer to you as a noble is the most respect I will ever show you, Rosalind. Or did you forget what happened to the last noble who insisted on my respect? I believe he hired you, no?"

"Walter was an idiot, I'll give you that. But I am not. You will respect me."

"Demanding a title and expecting respect is exclusive to idiots."

"Is it as idiotic as marching into a hostile environment unarmed?"

I smile brightly at this. "I'm not unarmed at all!" I see her tense up briefly and zero in on the two bags I have strapped to my sides. Then I pull out an egg and a pebble and present them. "See?"

She stares at me, dumbfounded. After a moment she starts laughing and exclaims, "Your plan was to attack us with pebbles and eggs?"

"Defend myself, actually. Which brings me to the rest of you. If you want to survive, leave now. I don't know why you are with this gang, but if any of you are unaware, they abduct children and sell them," I announce. I receive the expected chuckles in response and continue. "Anyone who stays here dies."

"Threats from a little girl aren't going to sway them, kid," Rosalind laughs, "especially a little kid with rocks and eggs. Trust me, I am much scarier than you are."

"Well, that remains to be seen, doesn't it?" I say, my smile remaining on my face. "I haven't thrown any eggs yet."

"You have a lot more spirit than your brother, don't you?" she chuckles, and my hackles rise. I have been avoiding talking about Henry, drawing out this pointless conversation as long as I can. She is trying to bait me, make me angry so she can control me.

I glare at her for a moment and prepare to respond as the chuckling fades, but I'm interrupted by a loud creak somewhere nearby, and Rosalind's head snaps in its direction. Fucking shit.

"Go investigate—she brought someone else with her!" Rosalind orders. Men all around the room tense up and grip their weapons. I see one man run toward the door nearest to the sound, and Rosalind begins casting with an unfamiliar hue to her mana. No more stalling; the hard part starts now. I retrieve two pebbles from my pouch by controlling the mana I built them with and fire them one after the other.

Before he reaches the door, the man falls to the ground dead, but the pebble I fired at Rosalind just stops in place and falls to the ground. Figures it wouldn't be so easy. All hell breaks loose and I am under attack from all sides. I am prepared this time, however. I throw up a shield spell of force mana that bounces back attacks on me with equal force.

I do this just in time as a throwing knife bounces harmlessly off me like my pebble did to Rosalind. I have little time to think of anything as men descend on me. I dodge past the first man to reach me and use one foot to trip him as I push him over. I then retrieve an egg and fire it in his direction without aiming carefully.

I don't have time for precision strikes, so I am marking anyone who attacks me. A club descends on my head and I dodge out of the way, swinging a force-enhanced fist into the man's rib cage before ducking backward away from another man's knife. Him I hit with a pebble, catching him in the solar plexus and removing him from the fight. I run through the crowd, dodging and tanking blows while returning my own. Whenever I get a half-decent shot on someone but can't kill them, I fire an egg as well.

I am hit from behind and fly forward, barreling into two men. I scramble up and realize it was Rosalind; she'd gotten through my shield with that kick somehow. As I regain my footing, I see a man has made it through the door. He's after Gilbert. Shit! I put up a wide wall of force mana to delay Rosalind and launch myself in the man's direction at the same time.

As I get there I see he is in a hallway preparing to call for help. Before he gets the chance, I kick out as hard as I can at the back of his leg and he crumbles to his knees. Now that he is closer to my level I reach around and grab his throat, using all my strength to launch him back into the room. Rosalind is already on me again and dodges out of the way, then course-corrects straight for me.

I put up another force wall in front of me, and one on the door. I can't keep too many up at once, but I can leave that one up for now. Now that Rosalind is fighting, I am struggling to keep up. I am fairly certain I can beat her. She is fast but so am I, and I hit a lot harder based on that kick, but the numbers are holding me back. Rosalind is sticking to hit-and-run tactics, appearing from seemingly random directions and charging me like a bullet.

I keep her off me by moving my force walls as needed, but that's practically all I can do. I manage to throw an egg between attacks, but I don't have the time to fire off a lethal attack against any of her men. They are all covered in flour, but something needs to change soon. My force walls take more mana than her acceleration, and I will lose this fight after long enough.

Not to mention I am still rebuffing mundane clubs, daggers, and fists from all directions. I don't even have time to throw a punch in retaliation or Rosalind will reach me. Fortunately, I don't have to. Three shrill whistles ring out from somewhere nearby, and I grin. I already have everyone but Rosalind painted, and I push out the spell I have had prepared since I walked into the building. A dark box envelops the entire building. Rather than a wall, I have created an entire space of light mana that will allow exactly two frequencies to pass through it.

Brilliant colors soar toward me in the absolute darkness, and I put up a force wall to stop it. While mana can be perceived by a mage's eye, it doesn't emit real light, so our spells are still perfectly visible, even if we aren't. The only other thing anyone can see is thirty or so glowing splatters of flour as I fill the room with my black-flashlight spell. You may expect this to emit a purplish light, but that's just a result of Earth technology. My black light is truly invisible. Ultraviolet waves fill the entire space and all Rosalind's men glow.

I shove my way through the barrier of bodies surrounding me and bowl my way to freedom, then stop gathering mana around my body. Rosalind is finally stationary, unsure how to find me. She is thankfully either unable to suppress her mana or hasn't considered the need, and I can pinpoint her easily. I quickly fire off three pebbles at a few of her glowing subordinates and all three fall to the ground.

She spots the mana from these spells and charges me, but I manage to move and she hits the wall behind me. I swing out a kick and make contact, but my foot meets the same mana barrier I hit earlier. She seems unhurt from either impact as she screams, "Got you now, you little bitch!" and tries to stab at me.

I don't know how she kicked through my force barrier earlier, but I don't want to risk this, so I use force mana to propel myself toward the center of the room. I think it's the center anyway, as I can see several men still scrambling about. To my delight, in their panic, there have been a few friendly-fire incidents, a few more seem to have fallen on the ground, and a couple are still grappling.

I decide to handle a few the mundane way so Rosalind can't spot me. I grab a man's ankle and pull him to the ground, then scramble up, grab him by the hair, and force his head into the pavement with all my strength. My strength has grown and I hear it crack immediately. A couple more glowing lights charge me and I throw my force shield back up. Within moments, Rosalind has spotted me and charges in a second time, but I anticipate it, using force mana to pull from all directions before she launches herself.

The two lights running toward me and four other men get pulled in as I duck. I feel blood splatter across me as Rosalind and her mana shield collide with them like a cannonball. I hear screaming from two sources. One of her victims is alive and crying in pain, and Rosalind is screaming in fury. I try to back away but trip over something and fall to my back. I accidentally touch it and my hand comes back wet. Picking it up, it becomes clear I just picked up a man's arm.

How fucking fast is she flying? This is like fighting an unstoppable force. The battle continues in this vein for a few minutes: I pick off her men, narrowly avoid her attack, or force her to change course with a force shield, lather, rinse, repeat, until I am fairly certain we are the last two standing. We both stand still, and I try to catch my breath. There are a few groaning or weeping men on the ground, but she still locks in on my location just from my breath.

As I narrowly avoid her charge, I notice sound mana around her head. That's right, Tommy said she was quiet, of course she has sound mana! This gives me an idea and I shout at her, "You'll never be a noble, you know!"

She screams and charges me again. Dodging without mana is hard, but my physical strength and speed help. I carefully make it to another part of the room, running into a wall once, and avoid another attack, then I shout again, using mana to amplify my voice. "Although the way you killed your own men with incompetence, maybe you will after all!"

I avoid her again as she yells, "Shut up, bitch! I'll tear you apart!"

Now is the time for the final step. I begin casting sound magic and run toward the glowing bodies in the center of the room. I stop but keep sending my spell forward to the center of the room. The sound spell shouts in my voice, "And just like every other noble, you are sad, pathetic, and dead!"

The vibrant colors of her mana paint the darkness as it collides with my own and I enact my final plan. I throw up four thick force walls around her, trapping her in a box. As she begins bouncing from wall to wall at breakneck speeds, I see actual dents in the thick yellow mana of the force walls around her. That explains how she got through my shield—she must have hit me with more force than I could generate.

"You can't keep me in here forever!" she screams, pausing her attempts at escape. "Eventually, you'll run out of mana, and I'll still have plenty. And I'll be able to see you then. And I am going to make your death as painful as possible."

Apparently, this fight hadn't gone as she expected. I sigh wearily before replying, "No, you won't." At that, I collapse all four walls into her. They stop at her shield, whatever kind of mana it is, and she panics, realizing what is about to happen.

"W-wait, I can help you, I can get you your br—" she starts, but my mana overpowers her and she is crushed into a paste in an instant. I collapse and release all my spells at once, the bright light shocking me. I recover my breath and look around at the carnage surrounding me. I, on the other hand, am in much better shape than the last time I fought this gang.

Now it's time to save Henry.

CHAPTER NINETEEN

Familiar Failure

I let out three whistles to signal to Gil and hear three in return. I run in the direction of the sound, signaling a couple more times before finding the room with a hatch in it. I climb down the ladder to be met with Tommy and Gilbert arguing.

"I jus' did what the lady told me to!" Tommy protests as Gilbert, who appears to be sitting on a prone man, glowers.

"We hadn't found my brother yet! It was too early to signal!" he shouts back.

"But the plan was—" I cut myself off and ignore the two of them as I scan the room. Cells are filled with mostly young children and a few older ones. Very few approach Henry's age, however, and I can tell at a glance he's not here. My stomach twists in familiar knots as the reality of this hits me. I failed to save him, *again.*

They fucking took him to get to me and I failed to save him, twice.

"Fuck!" I scream, falling to my knees, startling the frightened inmates and drawing my companions' attention. "Fuck fuck fuck fuck!"

"Lillith, are you okay!?" Gilbert exclaims, looking at my bloodied dress with wide eyes. I can tell he wants to run to me but stays with his apparent captive.

"I'm fine; it's not my blood," I respond half-heartedly. "He's not here, Gil. I still haven't saved him." Tommy sees Gilbert's dilemma and relieves him. I see they tied the guard's hands up and gagged him with cloth at some point and are just holding him now. With Tommy weighing their prisoner down, Gilbert rushes over and pulls me into a tight hug.

"We'll find him, Lillith. If anyone can find him, it's you, and he knows that," he reassures me. He's right, we will find him. As much as I want to break down right now, I don't have time. I still did something that matters tonight. These kids can eat their own food now. They don't have to live in fear of this gang ever again. It's not a permanent solution, but it'll help.

"We have to let these kids out, help me, Gil," I say, gently pushing him off me. He nods and we both head to a cell. They are each locked with a padlock, but I just yank one off while Gilbert is searching the man on the ground for a key. I get more than a few wide-eyed looks at this, but I ignore them and swing the door open.

I address the group. "We have to finish searching the building for any remnants, so I recommend staying here for a while. But you are all free now. You don't have to work for or be used by the Manticorps ever again."

"And what about the next gang that pops up?" an older kid near the front exclaims. "There will always be someone doing this!"

I nod. "Yes, you are right. Someone will try to fill the power vacuum. If not a new gang, then the city guard, and I understand there isn't really a difference to any of you. But they all know they have something to fear now. For now, I won't let them forget it. And eventually, you won't either."

"Easy for you to say, you can rip a lock off with your bare hands. But if any of us try to fight back, we'll just be arrested and enslaved!" the same boy responds, and I nod again.

Slavery is technically illegal in this kingdom, but it is legal as a punishment for a crime. The natural result of this policy is that the definition of "crime" expands. Some things only commoners bother with become illegal, or only commoners are arrested for other things. Any act of violence on the streets results in an arrest, including self-defense. Just stealing from the stalls results in slavery if you are caught.

Even worse is that the local gangs, collections of most of the actually dangerous people, all have a deal with the guards. They are essentially an extension of the city guard since they are a source of income and control. Assaults on gang members are treated as assaults on the guard, and violence by a gang member is treated as law enforcement. As a mage, if I allowed the church to christen me as a noble, I would never be investigated. Any of these kids, however? If they got caught fighting back, they'd be marched off in chains within hours.

"I know," I respond, "and right now I'm not expecting you to. Like I said, I will keep them afraid. I'll even give you the tools you need to be able to fight back. All I ask is that you remember that I did and, when the time comes, remember that it's an option."

"W-what about R-Rosalind?" asks a little girl from Gilbert's cell, which he and Tommy have finally opened.

"Dead. As are most of her men." This announcement causes a murmur through the kids. "She won't come after you again, and it's unlikely you'll have to confront another like her for some time." I can feel they don't trust me, but I don't mind. I answer a few more questions before they are satisfied that it's safe to leave.

They decide to wait for the rest of the building to be cleared before leaving, however, and Gil and Tommy stay to watch their captive while I do so. I find one room full of what looks like shoddy alchemical tools and am reminded of my failure again. I was so damn close. Where is Henry now; why wasn't he here?

I sit down on a stool in the room and hold my face in my hands. I need to hold this back; I'm not done yet. I need to finish tonight, and I can process it all later. As I sit there, I see a glint through my fingers and reach down to the dirty ground. I pick up a steel button with some kind of bird engraved into it. It looks too nice to be owned by anyone here, unless Rosalind managed to pilfer it.

I pull myself together and tuck the button away. Then I systematically search every room in the building, which doesn't take too long. Finally, I interrogate the injured in the main room. After finding out all I think I can get out of them, I finish them off. They were warned and given the opportunity to flee. Finally, I return to the cellar.

"Everyone is clear, it's safe to leave," I announce. "Get far away from here. I don't know what the guards will do if they find you near here, and I don't want to find out." At this, most of the former prisoners depart, several of them greeting and hugging Tommy when they do. Tommy, Gilbert, their prisoner, and one young girl remain after a few moments. I see her, huddling in the back of her cell, too afraid to move.

I am about to approach her when Gilbert asks, "What do we do with this guy, should we let him go?" and my answer is provided for me as the girl panics and retreats farther into her cell. She is staring wide-eyed at her former guard. Terror dances across her face when Gilbert suggests we let the man go, and I see tears forming in her eyes.

That's all I need, and I walk up to the prone man and stomp my foot on his head full force. His skull crumples under my foot and Gilbert scrambles away. "What the fuck, Lillith, he was helpless!" he exclaims. Tommy seems unfazed and the little girl bursts into tears. I just point at her.

"As long as he was alive, his victims would never feel safe. I don't know exactly what happened, but look at her! Look at how afraid that child was, how much tension she just let leave her body!" I lecture to Gilbert's grimace.

"Still, Lillith, he was helpless! We can't just kill helpless people!"

"He was helpless until we let him go. Then he would have gone back to being the monster under that little girl's bed," I say as Tommy enters the cell and hugs the girl, who begins sobbing into his shoulder. "No one who inspires that much fear, that kind of fear in children, will be allowed to live after meeting me. Not one."

Gilbert nods slowly. He doesn't seem to have the stomach for killing, but he is at least beginning to understand why I do. Tommy emerges from the cell holding the girl's hand. "Thanks, lady. I don' know how tuh thank you . . ." he says to me, clearly getting emotional himself.

"Like I said to the others, Tommy. Just remember, and be ready to fight someday." He nods and begins to head for the ladder with the girl before I follow up, "Tomorrow afternoon, meet me where we met the first time. I'll help you."

"Yes'm," he agrees. "Jus' say the word." With that, they depart and I am left alone with Gilbert. I am going to design a magic circle for these kids, step one in arming the world against the nobility. I can worry about that later, however; Gilbert and I need to get home.

I try to stop Gilbert from seeing the room where I fought, but he glances in and immediately evacuates his stomach again. At least they can't test DNA here. That's something I had to think about the first time I had to kill someone, and a single hair almost caused a serious issue in that life.

We stop at a local well and draw water to clean the blood and dirt off my skin. Gilbert doesn't speak much, and a melancholy pall accompanies us as we make our way through the city. Neither of us has much to say. Gilbert also continually gives me an uncomfortable look, like he's not sure what to make of me.

We do eventually make it home, and Gil helps me sneak into the house. I make it to my room and hide my bloody dress. Then, alone in the quiet, I finally, blessedly, allow myself to weep. I curl up in a ball on my bed and cry into a pillow I clutch close to my chest. I can't keep failing Henry. I have to find him.

I continue to cry until I eventually fall asleep.

I'm rudely awoken by the overwhelming presence of Baldwin's mana enveloping the house. This is the absolute last thing I need today. I can't stand the thought of dealing with him. The thought of having my memories stolen from me or being helpless to whatever he has been doing again. I just want to run away.

I actually consider it when my father bursts into the room. "Get dressed and come out, Lily, we have news for you," he announces, smirking at me. This isn't how Baldwin's visits usually work, and I feel a burst of panicked adrenaline. I don't like how this feels; something is wrong and I am definitely not in the mood for variables.

I get a dress on, lamenting, as I do every day, my parents' strict antipants policy for girls. That fight last night would have been much easier in some damn pants. I stop distracting myself, however, and head out to meet my father and Baldwin. The two men's self-satisfied grins do nothing to improve my mood as I emerge from my room.

"Congratulations, Lillith," my father announces as I meet his eyes, "We have arranged for your marriage to Lord Baldwin!"

Plans

Henry

I've been with the Manticorps for a month and a half now. I've made a great deal of progress on multiple fronts. Rosalind did at least try to put a lab together for me, so I don't have to work in that cramped cell anymore. There are still too many guards to run but it's a step in the right direction. An old table lies before me, full of dirty or broken alchemical tools. The few working ones do speed me up enough that Rosalind stays off my back, although the quality of my potions has fallen so much I don't know why she needs me. Any of her men could make these insults to alchemy.

That doesn't matter anymore, however. I am convinced she is lying about Lily. Lily either already escaped or has already been handed off. The gang seems to employ the labor of local street kids, forcing them to steal food and coin. Now that I have the freedom to move around a little bit, I have tried asking them about her a few times. Many times they seemed either confused or afraid.

But the most telling was when a young, scared girl was trying to answer me and Rosalind appeared out of nowhere and smacked her across the face. After that, none of the children would let me approach them, but it was answer enough. That little girl had no idea who I was talking about. So why would Rosalind want to hide what she had to say? My best guess is the lack of information is the information. No one who comes here has ever seen Lily.

In either case, the risk of her being hurt due to my escape is lower than the risk of her being hurt because I didn't. This makes my course of action clear. I am getting out of here. I don't have Lillith's abilities, but I have my own plans. For the past couple of weeks, I have been asking for minor additions to the ingredients I need. Originally, I wanted to lace the thugs' food, but apparently, street gangs don't sit around a dining room table for scheduled meals.

My backup plan is to put a sleeping concoction in a few vials of green mist. Green mist is a potion that evaporates on contact with air, and the drug fills the space it is in. By slightly modifying it, I should be able to knock my captors out with it. In a few more days, I'll have enough vials to escape. The primary problem with this is avoiding exposure myself. I can pull my shirt over my nose, but that won't do enough. I need to release the vials in strategic locations and leave myself a path to freedom.

As I cork my latest trap potion, my blood runs cold. One second I am gently reaching the vial toward the small box I am keeping them in, and the next I am putting it in Rosalind's hand.

"L-lady Rosalind!" I stutter, stumbling back as she begins tossing the vial up and down in her hand. "I wasn't expecting you!"

She begins circling me. "Really? I would have expected me if I were you."

"W-why is that, m-my lady?" I ask, sweat dripping down the side of my head as I eye the vial.

"If I, an alchemist for a generous lady who kindly put together such a nice lab for me, were producing product so slowly, so poorly? If I were so ungrateful, I would certainly expect a visit from my benevolent employer," she elaborates, clenching her fist around the vial and sending a spike of anxiety through my body.

"I'm sorry, my lady, I will work harder!" I promise, desperate for her to stop mishandling the vial.

"No, you won't," she replies, a dark mood casting itself across her face.

"L-lady Rosalind?" I inquire, my panic increasing, until her face suddenly snaps into a smile.

"You, my little alchemist, have been sold," she announces.

What? How could I have been sold if I'm not even legally a slave?

"But what about my sister?" I ask, confused and desperate to find out more. This could ruin my plan completely.

"Oh, I wouldn't worry, little Henry," she responds cheerily. "The same man has expressed interest in purchasing her too!"

I have trouble processing this. Is she just lying again so I'll go with this new buyer? Was I wrong—is she here after all? Has she been charged with killing one of those men? Is she a legal slave now? I mentally move up my timetable. I need to get out of here as soon as possible. If I work through the night, I'll have enough sleeping potion to escape tomorrow morning.

"When am I being sold, Lady Rosalind?" I dig, trying to plan my escape around this new information.

"Why, he is on his way right now! You may want to make yourself present-able!" she laughs at me, clearly enjoying my discomfort. Shit. Shit shit shit. I have no time at all! In a snap decision, I pick up the box of trap potions and throw them all at Rosalind's feet, running without looking to see if it worked. As I exit the room, I see a couple of thugs in the hallway looking confused.

"Boy! Did you hear glass shatte—" one man says, but I barrel into him, shoving my head into his stomach and knocking him over. I pull his knife from his belt and scramble to my feet to run away from the second man, heading for the exit. I keep having to turn and change routes as I run into more men, all aware I am not allowed to leave. They close in on me, blocking off my avenues of escape.

I am smaller and weaker than all these men, and I have no potions. Even if I had saved one, it wouldn't help against this many people. I have been backed into a corner and I hold my stolen knife out, pointing it at any man who approaches me. Then suddenly, my body seizes up and I lose all control over my limbs. I feel myself being caught by the back of my shirt and a voice grumbles, "At least it works on you. I was worried your entire family was resistant."

I am then dragged back to my makeshift lab. The sleeping mist still fills the air alongside the intoxicating effect of the green mist. I feel myself losing consciousness as my body is dropped to the ground next to Rosalind—who is completely awake. The man, also mysteriously unaffected by my potions, leans over me and slaps me across the face to bring me to my senses.

"Foolish boy," his gruff voice complains. Then, over his shoulder, "How did he get away from you, you idiot?"

The last thing I hear before losing consciousness is Rosalind explaining herself. "My apologies, Lord Baldwin. His little plan was just so cute . . ."

CHAPTER TWENTY

An Interesting Theory

That's certainly an interesting theory." I address Baldwin directly, completely stone-faced. I am livid, but there isn't much I can do at this moment beyond clenching my fists. I struggled against Rosalind, a weaker mage than me, and Baldwin is stronger by orders of magnitude. More importantly, he has the authority of the country behind him. I can buy time but not much else. "I'm twelve; you and I both know you can't marry a noblewoman any younger than fourteen."

He grins as he responds, "You aren't a noblewoman, are you?"

"No. But I'm a mage, and the church will never approve the match if I'm not christened as a noble first," I retort, crossing my arms.

"Lily, it's harvesttime," my father interjects, looking self-satisfied. "That makes you thirteen now."

Baldwin leans against our table and begins peeling an apple in the air, using some kind of mana I haven't grasped yet. He doesn't bother looking at me as his bored voice explains, "I am the son of the city lord. Our wedding will take a year to plan anyway; arrangements will need to be made and guests will need time to travel. You'll be old enough when the time comes."

If I had a heart rate, it would be leveling out at this. I have time. A year at least. I can work with a year. One year to find Henry, learn what Baldwin is doing to my memory, and plan to deal with the wedding. I've dealt with more in less time.

I'm drawn from my racing thoughts as Baldwin continues, "Of course, you do make an excellent point. The church has demanded you be christened as a noble. They have already approved the engagement, but you will need to establish your house. Pick a house name. I won't be marrying an unnamed noble. You will be Lillith of Tudor before long, so anything will do, but pick something suitable for your family."

My father and I make opposing expressions at that. I have zero interest in a noble title, and he has been trying to make an appointment with the church for years. He would have succeeded if either Godfrey or I had been open about my mana. He is beaming as I reply through gritted teeth, "And when, exactly, am I to be christened?"

"In one month. I look forward to welcoming you to the nobility, my dear fiancée," he answers through a slimy grin, then gives me a sarcastic bow.

I can worry about that later, I suppose. It's not like the church can make me act like a noble just by putting my name on a piece of paper. Probably, women aren't allowed in the church without an escort and rarely before they are "adults." I have read some accounts that priests use unique magic, so I shouldn't write off the possibility of manipulation magic. Though that shouldn't be possible, thoughts of Baldwin's unique trick flash through my mind.

"Very well. Will that be all, Baldwin?" I ask, policing my expression and tone for the rage I feel at having to pretend I might comply.

"Nothing of import, although I would like to discuss something in private if you don't mind. Your father can work with you on the rest of the details afterward." He requests this in a tone indicating it isn't an actual request.

"Of course, Lord Baldwin!" my father eagerly agrees. "I'll be waiting just outside!"

I stare Baldwin down as my father exits the room. I am absolutely determined to respond to whatever he is doing, or at least figure it out. I let my mana boil out around me. I am ready to respond at a moment's notice. I will react the second I see Baldwin crafting any new spells.

A breath later Baldwin says, "That will be all today. I will be back next week to speak again."

I stand completely still. I hadn't even moved; my individual fingers are still in the same position. The only change is that I'm sweating and my stance is tense. I feel like I just flexed every muscle in my body for as long as I could stand. Adrenaline courses through my veins and I begin pacing, desperate to use the energy on something.

"That took quite a while, didn't it, Lily?" my father asks as he reenters.

"What do you want, Richard?" I snap back, furious with him. Furious with Baldwin. Furious with myself. In this moment, however, he can have all of it.

"Richard?" he echoes, completely aghast. "Lillith, I am your father. You will refer to me as *Father* or *sir*. Is that understood?"

"Father? I don't have one of those. If I did, he wouldn't sell me."

"Sell you? SELL you? Lillith, I am doing this FOR you! He is the next Lord of Satusmor! You are going to be his wife, you'll never have to worry again, none of us will!"

"You are doing this for you, Richard. Do you think I can't see the greed behind your eyes when you talk about nobility? Do you think I can't see the disdain behind them when you look at me? I'm just your only child who failed to be a son."

He takes a menacing step toward me. "You are my daughter! And this is the best life you can hope for! The only life where you don't have to struggle every day to survive! We'll have power, authority, wealth, everything we ever wanted or needed!"

"I never wanted any of those things!" I say, hearing the thirteen-year-old in my voice. "That's everything *you* ever wanted!"

"THAT'S THE SAME THING!" he screams in my face, before taking a few deep breaths. "I am the head of this family. What I want for us is what we want, and soon what Baldwin wants will be what you want. I have fed and taken care of this family for years with my money. You would be starving on the streets or selling yourself without me. So would your mother. You can finally do something to return the favor, and this is how you behave? You should be ashamed of yourself!"

"Favor?" I retort, practically spitting the word in his face. "You can't take all the options from us and call it a favor to let us survive in the one option left! You're a jailor, not a father."

"Well, that's just the way the world works. You'll have to deal with it, or did you expect me to ignore thousands of years of culture so my daughter would be happy?"

"YES! I don't care how the world works; I don't care if that's how the world always worked!" I say, and wish I didn't have to look up at him. "You could have done better; you could have been better than the man you are."

"Well. I'm sorry to disappoint you, Lillith, but I just don't see why I would do that. Now I have Lord Baldwin's backing. You will be seeing an etiquette tutor before you get married, and you will not give me lip about it."

"Fine, Richard. I'll see the tutor. But I won't be getting married. I'll warn you now, do not pin your hopes on this engagement."

"Do not call me Richard," he snaps, and then his lips twist into a smirk. "And yes, you will. There is nothing you can do about it. Just trust me: this is what's best for you."

"I'll decide what's best for me, Dick," I respond, technically complying with his demand. "Now if you don't mind, I need to bring Mom her dinner."

Later in the day, I work in my room. I still can't modify my body like I want to. I've figured it out with plants just fine, but the changes won't stick on my own body. I've tried adjusting the size of my pores and glands, adding toxins and activation proteins to my sweat, and further enhancing my strength. Not a single change lasts a day, and each is reverted before I even finish them. Poisonous skin would be extremely helpful with a man trying to force me into a marriage.

I finish internally scanning my body for the poison I had tried to create yesterday, but was once again met with an unchanged physiology. I don't understand this; it can clearly be done. Mana controls my blood flow and enhances my strength and body. Mana can modify my body, I'm sure of it; I'm just missing something. I feel like I am trying to make a handprint in water. Frustrated, I throw my journal on the ground and scream into my pillow.

I am not in the mood to fail at something else. I decide to move on from this experiment and meet up with Gilbert. I want to meet Tommy and set up a magic circle for his group, as well as look for new leads. I still don't like Gilbert exactly, but he seems to have my back when it comes to finding Henry.

I approach his room, knock on the door, and immediately hear two heavy thuds, scrambling, and a yell through the door: "One moment!" I chuckle, wondering what he had been doing that I startled him so badly.

Finally, he arrives and swings his door open. He looks a bit embarrassed as he greets me. "Sorry! I was just, uh, doing some studying. What do you need, Lillith?" I lean over and look behind him, where I see his chair on the floor and laundry thrown on top of his desk. His quick disguise of the drawing on his desk fails as a draped tunic slips to the floor and reveals it: an awkwardly rendered deer in charcoal. It looks like he was trying to learn to draw.

". . . Right," I say, chuckling. "We need to meet up with Tommy. We have more to do. And I need you to buy me some pants."

"Pants? Lillith, you're a girl," he laughs.

I roll my eyes. "Gilbert, my dress could've gotten me killed last night, and we haven't found Henry yet."

"Yeah, but it just wouldn't be prop—"

"Do you want to fight the next mob?"

". . . No, not really."

"Then I need pants. A few shirts too, and some better boots."

Gilbert looks at me skeptically but nods. "Okay, Lillith, I'll do what I can, but nothing is going to fit you that well."

"Oh no, are you saying my girlish figure won't stand out while I'm searching the slums for our kidnapped brother?" I gasp, feigning horror with my hand to my mouth.

"No, that's not—I mean—oh, never mind," he sighs. "Let's go."

"Speaking of pants," I add before we leave, "yours are unbuttoned. Looks like you were studying too hard."

His face flushes and he scrambles to button himself up before we depart.

* * *

The tailor gave us a little trouble; he didn't quite buy our story. Gilbert claimed he was buying clothes for his brother who was about the same size as me, but he didn't understand why Gilbert would take me instead. He wouldn't allow me to try the clothing on and insisted on eyeballing the sizes.

Nevertheless, I have some actual clothes for the first time in this life. A new pair of pants, boots, and three shirts. They're fairly baggy but not too bad; I can move much more freely now. After a stop at home to change, I tied up my hair in a messy topknot and felt much more prepared for the night's activities. The next stop was Tommy. We stopped and bought a boatload of the cheapest food we could find from a shadier stall in the area.

In late afternoon light, we made our way to the alley I met him in and found him waiting for us. "Miss Lillith! I didn' know if you was gonna show up!" he exclaims as soon as we are in full view of each other.

"Of course we came, Tommy, I promised, didn't I?" I respond with a smile. I am so glad he's okay. "How are the rest? Anyone hurt? Arrested?"

"Not a soul, miss, guards 'n' folks came tuh look at the ol' hideout, but none did nothin'. I don' think none of 'em even thought tuh ask us!" he informs me, clear relief in his voice.

Tension leaves my shoulders as well and Gilbert grabs Tommy and pulls him into a hug. "I'm so glad to hear that. Can you take us to the rest of your friends? Your family? This food is for them," I ask.

Tommy's face lights up like the sun and he gives me a bigger grin than I knew he could. "Yes'm, I'll lead the way!"

Gilbert and I follow him down the winding roads until we reach an encampment. There is no cover, just a large number of makeshift tents and shelters surrounding various communal firepits and resource piles. It reminds me of unhoused camps back in my old world, except it is occupied almost entirely by children.

My heart breaks for them, but I steel my resolve. Gilbert sets up near the middle of the camp and announces, "I've got food! Anyone hungry come this way!" I probably could have told him how to handle this more smoothly, but Gilbert remains as oblivious as ever. As it stands, half the children swarm him and the other half seem too scared to approach.

"We'd better go help him," I say, and Tommy nods, laughing. As we walk over, I say, "This won't do at all. We need somewhere sheltered, more private . . ."

"For wut, miss?" Tommy inquires, and I look over at him.

"Well, to teach you all magic, of course," I explain as if it is the most obvious thing in the world.

CHAPTER TWENTY-ONE

Leads

Are you really gonna help us do magic, miss?" a wide-eyed girl asks me, hope and disbelief warring on her face. Tommy, once I convinced him I was serious, announced this news to all the kids collecting food from Gilbert. I've been met with all sorts of reactions. Some are distrustful, others are excited, and plenty have a familiar look of greed in their eyes. I'll have to disillusion them of the notion this will be an opportunity for them to gain power, but I have to deal with one thing at a time.

They aren't going to be unique in this. I'm out here to level the playing field, not build tiny kingdoms on the streets. There are any number of problems I'll have to try to head off and respond to. That can't be helped; I have to give people a fighting chance. I deliberated for a long time about whether I would try to spread magic equally or not. Ultimately, I realized I had no choice.

Magic exists here. The planet lives and breathes mana, and there isn't anything I can do about that. The only thing someone needs to acquire magic is a surface and something to draw on. It's not like guns, which can't be manufactured without great knowledge and resources. I learned to give myself magic with a few books. In other words, my options are to leave magic in the hands of just a few who are already part of a culture that abuses it, eliminate it entirely, or share it.

To eliminate it I would have to burn books and control knowledge for all time, which isn't exactly in line with my ideals. I would also have to genocide the people who already have it, which isn't an option either. Yes, almost everyone with magic is a noble, but most of them are born with it. "Noble blood" doesn't make someone evil any more than it makes them deserving of worship. It's few choice to continue living a noble's life that condemns them.

On the flip side, it's a spectacularly bad idea to leave that kind of tool exclusively in the hands of people who grew up in luxury earned through the oppression of others.

So that leaves me with equal distribution. I want to make education in general more widely available in any case, which would eventually lead to the same thing. This way people will be able to fight back while they learn.

"Yes, I'm going to teach you magic. I'm going to teach everyone I can," I respond, hopefully reassuringly. The little brown-haired girl smiles delightedly and turns to whisper with a girl next to her.

"Was da catch?" a burly kid asks, skepticism clear.

"Well, there is certainly more than one catch," I start, to groans of disappointment, "but not imposed by me."

"Waddas dat mean?" the boy asks, irritated.

"It means magic is the domain of the nobility, and they want to keep it that way. It means—" An older kid interrupts me.

"It means we'll be nobles!" he shouts, causing gasps and cheers in the group, much to my chagrin.

"No, I'm sorry, but no," I contradict him. "One commoner with mana is one thing. They can explain that away, they can elevate their status, or in cases like Rosalind's, I suspect, suppress them individually. An entire group, however, is a different story. A group of kids from the street with the knowledge to earn and harness mana is nothing more to them than a threat."

This sobers the group a bit and a couple of faces pale, while some younger ones simply look confused. I continue my explanation, "The nobility will want you dead. Not with the casually cruel indifference they already have; they will actively hunt you."

I see rising panic and try to head it off. "But you won't be alone. You'll have each other, and I am going to offer the same thing to a lot more people. You'll have me, and you'll have each other. I'll teach you to hide it. I'll teach you to use it. And you can teach others the same way. Yes, it'll be dangerous, I won't lie. None of you has to do this if you don't want to. But it'll give you a fighting chance."

"Yer oudda yer mind," the burly kid says, giving up and turning away to focus on his food.

"I'm in," Tommy announces loud enough for the whole group to hear.

"Me too," the quiet voice of the timid girl chimes in. After that, I get a few rejections, but overwhelmingly the kids want to learn. I smile warmly at them.

"Okay, I'll teach you all. First, however, we need to find a place to do it.

Somewhere covered, private. A large house or a cave, something like that," I say to the annoyance of my audience.

"If we 'ad some'ere like that, why would we be 'ere?" Tommy scoffs.

I nod in concession. "I'm aware of that, but you are forgetting something."

"Oh ya? What'd that be?" he asks.

"Now you have support. Everyone look for a place that fits the description. I don't care where—if it fits, tell me about it. I'll look too. If it's a viable option, I'll figure something out," I explain. "Just keep an eye out, and soon, you will all be mages."

An excited chatter breaks out as they realize I am done. I hear some of them already discussing different possibilities. Many of them are silly or immoral, but I am hopeful. I spend a while mingling with the group, trying to extract information about Henry. Unfortunately, I don't get much. A few of the kids recognize his description and can confirm he was with the Manticorps for a while, but they can't say much more. Apparently, each kid didn't encounter him often enough to pinpoint when he disappeared. I ask if anything strange has happened recently, but the situation with the Manticorps was too unstable for anything to stand out. And if anything out of the ordinary did happen, the kids would hide and keep their heads down to avoid becoming a casualty. The sun has gone down, and sighing, I give up and join Gilbert, who has been in quiet contemplation ever since I spoke to the kids about magic.

He talks quietly to me as we depart, headed toward the large market together in search of new clues about Henry. "You sure about this, Lillith?" he inquires with a raised eyebrow. "You want to do something that'll have the nobles hunting you?"

"More than one something," I retort. "Besides, it looks like I don't have much choice."

"What do you mean?"

"Dad has arranged a marriage for me. To Baldwin Tudor."

Gilbert stops walking, his mouth agape as he processes this revelation. "Lord Baldwin Tudor, as in the future Lord of Satusmor, is your *fiancé*? Shit, Lillith, I wondered why someone so important visited so often. Congratulations!"

I glare at him. There is a moment of silence before his exuberant face shifts to confusion and he follows up with, "Or . . . I'm sorry?"

"Gilbert. I am not marrying that finely dressed sack of leeches!"

"B-but you would be Lillith of Tudor—any woman in town would kill for that!"

"Yes, you have displayed a thorough understanding of what women want, you're probably right."

"Okay, I deserved that, but, Lillith, our entire family would never have to worry again! We'd become a noble family like Dad has wanted for years, we'd even get our own name! We could be something cool like *Flames* or *Blades* or something. Gilbert Blades would be an awesome name! Or we can do something more feminine, *Flower* maybe; Mom can be Joan of Flower. We'd be wealthy and never have to worry ag—" He stops as he sees my face contorting in disgust.

"Gilbert, I have no interest in being a noble."

"B-but we would never have to struggle to survive again, we—"

"We would survive on wealth earned by other people struggling to survive. Do I seem like the kind of person who would be happy doing that? Think about it for a moment, Gil; with all you've seen me do, with what you just saw me do. Does it seem like wealth is my aim?"

"I guess not . . . but Mom has been so miserable lately. You could make her happy again!"

"Mom is miserable because her son is missing. She thinks he's dead, and her husband, a man supposedly responsible for helping people like his missing son, barely bothered to look!"

"I know that, Lillith, I'm not an idiot. But maybe a little luxury will at least cheer her up? Some fine food never made someone's life worse."

The run-down homes and businesses we pass as we walk, with patchwork roofing and cracked windows contradict him. I skirt around a pothole that was never fixed because the nobles needed their luxuries, and I have to resist spitting at the thought.

"It would taste like ash in her mouth. Besides, you are missing the point. I am not interested in getting married, Gilbert."

"All women get married. What, are you going to live with Dad forever?"

"No, but that's a discussion for another time. I don't want to be a noble and I don't want to get married. Dad didn't arrange for our future—he sold me to a cruel man for his own comfort."

I see Gilbert's face darken as this comment reminds him of our previous conversations. "Look, Lillith, I know you don't like how a lot of things work, but you need to be realistic. I listened to you before, so listen to me. If Dad arranged a marriage for you, it's because it's the best thing for you."

"It's really not. And even if it was, that's my choice to make. I know you are trying to change, Gil, but the way you view the world is still backward."

Gilbert sighs, realizing he's not going to convince me, but I continue, "I'm going to stop this marriage, Gilbert. It's going to be ugly, and you may not understand it. But I'm going to do it. I need you to support me in this."

"I . . . I'll think about it, Lillith. I really don't think you are making the right choice here. But I'll think about it," he reluctantly concedes.

A moment of silence passes, and something occurs to me that I glossed over earlier. "Wait, why would I be Lillith of Tudor and Mom be Joan of Flower, but

Baldwin is just Baldwin Tudor and you would just be Gilbert Blades?" I ask, suppressing an eye roll at the silly surnames he chose.

"Huh," he responds, startled by the shift in subject, "well, women aren't main household members in noble families. Men have a family name and women have an affiliation. So Baldwin Tudor and Lillith of Tudor," he explains, and I groan. Of course that's how it works.

"So I, with my mana, would be earning a family name . . . for you guys? But I am just affiliated with the family? The family that is noble . . . because of me. Is that right?" I gape.

Gilbert has the decency to look a little sheepish at this. "I suppose so; that's just how it works . . ."

I don't bother suppressing the eye roll this time. "Jesus Christ, that's absolutely asinine."

"Jesus who?" he asks, confused.

"Never mind that, let's just . . . not talk for a while," I respond, my irritation reaching a boiling point. I swear I'm going to find whoever's idea that was and boil them alive. Well, they are probably dead, but I'll still boil them. Fucking affiliated with my own family name.

"Oh, we're here, that was fast," Gilbert exclaims as we arrive at the market. It's thinner than it is during the day, but some vendors still stand by their emptying stalls and wagons. Gilbert is right; we did arrive quickly. He adds, "I thought we just left. It feels like I went through confession."

"Yeah, well, time flies when you're having fun," I sardonically dismiss him. "What's important now is finding Henry. I have a button I think we can use—it was in what I think was his lab." I pull it from my pants pocket to drop in his hand.

"That's an interesting emblem," he responds, examining it. "Someone will recognize this for sure."

"That's the hope," I reply.

We begin the tedious work of extracting information from the grumpy, tired vendors. As usual, we don't make much progress this way, but I think vendors are a better source than street kids in this case. After a while, I trail behind Gilbert, barely listening. Something is nagging at the back of my mind, like an itch you can't scratch or a word that's on the tip of your tongue.

"Gilbert, what did you mean?" I ask, the issue dawning on me.

"What? The fruit looks good . . . What else could I mean by—"

"You said it felt like you went through confession; what did you mean?" I say seriously.

"Oh, sorry, I forgot girls don't do that until they are fourteen. Confession is a ritual at the church. It's pretty normal, everyone does it. Help clear our minds and cleanse us of flaws, that sort of thing," he explains.

"And why did it feel like that, exactly?" I say, flexing my fingers as adrenaline begins flowing through my veins.

He picks up on my serious tone before he answers, "Well . . . because it goes by in a blink. You meet a priest, and the next thing you know, you're done. You don't even remember it. It's a pretty odd experience."

CHAPTER TWENTY-TWO

No More Charging In

I have to go to the temple," I immediately announce, walking off before Gilbert can finish questioning the fruit vendor.

"Wait, Lillith, hold up!" he shouts after me, jogging to catch up with my brisk pace. "What about Henry, what about the button?"

"We'll ask around there. I need to check something, now," I respond matter-of-factly. Finally, FINALLY, I have a lead on what Baldwin has been doing. I should have figured it out months ago, but I am apparently an idiot. The very first thought I had when Baldwin first came to question me was basically *I should avoid lying; I have heard people like priests have unique magic that can detect that.*

I only treated that as a mild risk I didn't really believe in, however. I've never been religious and I instinctively brushed off rumors of priests' special divine powers. While I know mana can affect a mage's own internal mind and body, I am equally certain it is next to impossible to use it to affect someone else's. At least, not without their explicit cooperation.

What I didn't consider—what I moronically ignored—is that magic exists in this world. If magic exists, why would I assume it was the only thing this world has that my old one lacked? It's the academic's arrogance that has always plagued me. You learn all about biology and you assume you are an expert in chemistry as well. You learn astrophysics and you consider yourself an expert in linguistics. "I'm smart," I would always tell myself. "I'm educated." Every single time, I would find myself humbled and embarrassed when an actual expert came in.

A dozen times I've reprimanded myself for this exact mistake, and here I am again. Twice dead, in another world, probably another reality, still letting myself believe I have understood all disciplines as soon as I learned one. My heart is . . . well, as still as ever, but adrenaline rushes through my veins as I hurry to the temple district. I don't know what power this is, and I don't know how Baldwin has been using it. I don't know what he has managed to do to my mind or get out of me while I was stupidly narrowing my search. I do know where I can find out now, and I am going to. No more delays.

Gilbert puts his hand on my shoulder and shouts, "Lillith! Stop for a moment and tell me what's going on!" He fails to hold me back, which clearly startles him as he stumbles and I keep walking. He circles in front of me and yells again, "Lillith! Stop, you're scaring me! What in the third plane is going on?"

I finally stop, scowling as he stands in my way. "Fine," I respond through gritted teeth. "I don't know how confession works, but Baldwin has been doing the same thing to me. Every single week, he comes into our home, into my room, and does something to my mind. I never remember his visits, if I perceive them at all."

Gilbert just looks confused at this. "Lord Baldwin isn't a priest—he can't conduct a confession, Lillith. And like I said, you aren't due for one for another year at least."

"And yet," I tersely reply, "here we are. What he does is exactly the same as you've described. I am going to find out what it is."

"I understand, and that makes sense, but what if you're wrong? What if it's not the same? What if it's just a spell you don't know?" he asks.

"That's not how mana works, Gil! I'm not wrong, I'm—" I cut myself off. I'm making the same mistake again. It sounds like the same thing, but that doesn't mean it is. "Okay, sure. It's possible it's not the same thing. But this is my only lead. I'm going to follow it. Now can we go?"

I see fear dance across his face that I don't quite understand as he says, "I don't think that's a good idea, Lillith . . . It's not like those thugs—you can't just . . . you know . . ."

"What are you talking about? What do they have to do with anything?" I ask, completely thrown off by the non sequitur.

"This is the temple, Lillith. They have as much power as the Tudor house, maybe more! You can't kill your way to answers here!"

This comment takes me completely off guard and I rub my forehead with my index finger in exasperation.

"Gilbert. What exactly do you think I'm planning to do? Why would I kill someone?" I say, growing irritated. "Who exactly do you think I am?"

"Well, I mean—Lillith, that is how you've solved all your problems since I started working with you! And now you are marching to the temple with a storm cloud over you, looking like you are ready to—to burn the place down!" he stutters, seemingly unable to believe I'm not planning a murder spree in the temple district.

"Those were rapists and human traffickers," I explain, gesturing vaguely behind us. "I kill as a matter of necessity, Gilbert. I do it because there is no version of the world where people like that can exist safely, and the world is genuinely better without them. I don't just kill everyone who is in my way!"

"You didn't even hesitate for a second! With any of them! You didn't even blink!"

"No, because I am prepared to kill if necessary. I am willing to if I need to. That doesn't mean I am eager! I don't fucking enjoy it; it's not my first resort!"

"Well, how was I supposed to know that!? Last time I saw you looking this angry and serious, you crushed a man's skull under your foot!"

"He was keeping children starving in a cage, Gilbert! I had to—" I start raising my voice but stop myself. Gilbert has stopped walking and my tone is starting to draw looks from the people around us. "Okay, look, fine. Whatever. I can see how you came to that conclusion. I'm annoyed, but I understand. I am not planning to kill anyone, okay?"

Gilbert doesn't seem convinced, but I try to have grace. The first time you see something like that, it leaves an impression. "Okay," he responds, "so what exactly are you planning to do?"

"I was just going to—" I stop myself short yet again. Shit, he's right. What am I going to do? March into the temple and demand they tell me their secrets? That wouldn't work if I were a Gilbert, and I'm a twelve—err—thirteen-year-old girl. I have a tendency to forget what I look like to other people. I do need a plan, and I'm reluctantly grateful that Gilbert stopped me. "Yeah, fine, I got caught up in the realization about the priests. I may not exactly have a plan," I admit to Gilbert's apparent relief.

"Yeah, I know you don't," he says. "The temple isn't accepting guests this time of night. If you want to investigate confession, you'll have to go back tomorrow."

I didn't realize that, actually. The relief at maybe understanding what was happening followed by the anger associated with it carried me away. I didn't stop to think things through. Yet more evidence that I can't do this alone. I've always needed someone to talk some sense into me before I jump headfirst into things. Maybe if I had spoken to someone before, I wouldn't have gone after Henry alone and after days without sleep. Maybe I could have saved him.

At the same time, I know I can't trust Gilbert to always be that person. He is trying to take a look at himself, he is trying to be better, but he's still . . . Gilbert. Obliviousness and ignorance can only explain away so much. He came through this time, however, and I'm not doing something stupid tonight.

"Okay, yeah," I respond, "that makes a significant difference. I can't just . . . sit still though! I'm no good at that. Having someone affecting, or trying to affect, my mind makes me sick to my stomach. It's violating. I want to be able to do something now."

"I get that, Lillith. I'll help you, tomorrow. We'll come up with a plan together," he reassures me. It's hard trusting him with this. Trusting anyone is hard for me, and he doesn't have a history of reliability. I have to, however; he's willing to help and he's all I really have. Him and Tommy, I guess, but I doubt Tommy will be allowed within a mile of the temple.

"You're right. We'll go tomorrow," I agree. My adrenaline draining, I start to feel how tired my body is, the effect of the mana I expended in the fight last night, the lack of sleep.

We leave this market behind, having exhausted the vendors, and walk vaguely in the direction of a smaller night market. We are quiet for a while before Gilbert works up the courage to ask me something. "What about Dad?"

I furrow my brow, not pleased to be talking about my father and confused by the question. "What about him?"

"To you, is there a world where he can be safe? You described what he was doing as 'selling' you. Are you going to kill him?" he asks, and I see tears building up in the corners of his eyes. I realize in this moment that Gilbert is afraid of me, and my stomach twists in knots. I can understand it; he doesn't come from the past I do. The last couple of days must have been an emotional trainwreck for him.

"I'm not planning to kill Dad, no," I reassure him. "I'm sorry, Gilbert. I know I have done a lot of things that look unstable recently. But I am not looking for people to kill."

"Lillith, you were so angry when you were talking about the engagement. At Lord Baldwin, and at Dad. Someone with that much pain and anger behind their eyes, someone who can kill as readily as you do . . . Is he really safe?"

"I am angry. I am livid at Dad. If I never spoke to him again, it would be too soon," I say, causing a pang of sadness to flash across Gilbert's face. "But I don't kill out of anger, but necessity. The unfortunate, sick truth is there is hardly a marriage in this country that isn't arranged. There is hardly a man who doesn't believe he can arrange his daughter's life for her, and hardly a father who doesn't believe he deserves absolute authority over his kids."

I idly rub the back of my head while I try to explain my philosophy to him. "It's sick and it's wrong," I start, then head off the response he is clearly forming. "I know you don't believe that, but it is. And that's the thing. I can't change it by killing every man who believes that and tries to do it. It won't change anything. I would just be creating pits of bodies in every city."

I do believe every woman, every child, really, has the right to fight back in this way when this type of authority is exercised over them, but saying that won't help right now. That also doesn't really apply to my situation. My father doesn't have power anymore and he knows it. His hopes for a wealthy future are all on me, so he can't arrest me for disobedience. I displayed that he couldn't beat me into submission either, which left him with no power over me.

It's Baldwin's power that he is leaning on, and I can take that away too, given enough time. "My goal," I continue, "is to deprive these people of that power. I want a better world, Gilbert. I will kill when I have to, but I believe people can be convinced to give up that power. Dad . . . Dad is just a man consumed by pride. I don't kill people for being ruled by their pride if they don't have the power to hurt someone with it. In this case, he doesn't."

"Okay, Lillith," Gilbert says, "thanks." I can tell he is still worried but there isn't much more I can do about that.

Instead, I decide to change the subject. "While we are out, let's get some flowers for Mom." This elicits another pang of sadness in his eyes, one I understand well. The thought of my mother is hard for both of us. She doesn't speak at all anymore; she hardly even eats. Our efforts to save Henry are equally about saving her. The house feels hollow while she stays locked up in her room, never interacting with us.

"Yeah, she'd like that," he says, not believing it any more than I do.

He's coming home, Mom, I promise her inside my head. *I'll stop Baldwin, I'll find Henry, and I'll keep you safe. I swear.*

CHAPTER TWENTY-THREE

Finding Allies

"Mom, you need to eat," I urge, holding a bowl of grits I brought her for breakfast. I'm met with the same weary smile and nod of assent as always, and my heart breaks a little more. *He's alive,* I want to announce. *I found evidence; I know he's alive!* I know by now this won't work. Small hopes and forward progress are meaningless to her. She will not allow herself to hope; she is too afraid of breaking all over again.

Instead, I sit next to her with the bowl in hand and give her one bite at a time. When her mood falls this low, feeding her is all I can do to keep her alive. My heart cries out for her, but right now I can't do much else. Dad refuses to talk about the problem, Edward seems annoyed by it, and Gilbert . . . well, Gilbert tries but he is his own special brand of unhelpful.

"I love you, Mom," I say, giving her a soft hug before I depart. I've gotten her to eat enough for now; I can come back tonight. Leaving the room, I am greeted by the sight of my father choking down the rubbery grits he made for his own breakfast. It has been a point of contention between us for a while that I didn't pick up my mother's cooking duties for the family, only preparing food for the two of us. He has given up on pushing this chore on me for now and has to suffer through his own failures every morning now.

"Lillith, good. I need to speak with you!" he grunts as I come into view. I sigh as I wash the bowl from Mom's breakfast.

"What is it?" I grumble. "Will it be quick?"

"It will be as quick as I want it to be, Lillith. Don't forget I am still your father," he chastises me, and I raise one eyebrow.

"I suppose that's true," I intone, "but I'm on my way out the door, so if you want an audience, I'd recommend spitting it out while I'm still in the room." I see him tighten his grip around his spoon and his jaw quiver at the quip, but he holds himself back.

"Your etiquette tutor will be here tomorrow afternoon. I expect you to be present and to be respectful and attentive. She is a very respected tutor employed by Lord Baldwin's estate."

"Oh, a very fancy Tudor tutor is she?" I quip. "Don't worry, I will be as respectful to her as she is to me, and as attentive as you are to your wife."

He chokes on his breakfast as I add that last bit, but I'm out the door before I can find out what furious profanities I just incited. I have no interest in etiquette lessons, but I can't turn away Baldwin's tutor without causing further problems. She would likely be the one punished if I did. I can work on my magic while she chitters about inane noble customs. Today I have bigger concerns.

This morning I am meeting Gilbert at Godfrey's shop. I've decided I don't want to knock on his bedroom door ever again, so meeting up is preferable. It's time to get to the bottom of the priests' abilities. I arrive at the shop and Gilbert waves me over. "You look much nicer this way," he praises, gesturing at my nicer dress and the French braids in my hair. "This is far more decent than men's clothes. I'm glad you changed your mind."

I don't know why baggy pants and a shirt would be "indecent," but I don't bother quizzing him right now. "I didn't change my mind; these clothes make more sense for what we are doing today. Those clothes made more sense yesterday. Now, we have work to do." I lead him around the back of the shop and create an audio barrier around us. In this case, I make a one-directional sound barrier that prevents noises moving out, but not in.

"All right, Gil," I start once I'm sure we have privacy, "we need to find a way to witness a confession."

Gilbert looks at me completely aghast. "Lillith, that's blasphemy! Confessions are a sacred rite protected by the Collector! We can't sneak into one!"

"If it's protected by the Collector, why is some noble prick practicing it outside the temple?" I challenge.

"W-well," he stutters, "I'm not convinced it is the same thing . . . It could be completely different!"

"And I'm not convinced the Collector is real," I retort to Gilbert's horror. Although I do have to further consider the possibility of some kind of powerful being. The presence of magic, the special abilities given to priests, and my reincarnation all indicate a powerful supernatural entity could exist. That sounds like a possible enemy to consider at a later date, however. "You are half right," I concede. "We can't just sneak into some random person's confession, especially since we don't know what goes on during it. It would be violating to whomever we picked."

He seems a bit relieved at this and raises his hand. "Well, if you insist on doing it at all, I suppose I can volunteer." I just look at him with my brow furrowed.

"Gil, that is a phenomenally terrible idea," I intone, and he seems to wither before me.

"Why is that? I really don't mind; better me than anyone else, right?" he asks.

My fingers go to my right temple as they so often do when talking to Gilbert. "It's called a confession," I explain. "If I had to guess, and I'm going out on a limb here, at least one purpose of it is confessing things. I can't send someone who knows I massacred three dozen men. Yeah, the temple might not care as much as the guard and I might get let off since I'm engaged to a Tudor, but it's a hell of a risk."

He looks a bit sheepish as he replies, "Right, that makes sense, sorry. Who, then?"

"That depends. Do confessions take place in a private room, or is it more like a two-sided booth?" I inquire, and Gilbert looks at me like I'm an idiot.

"Why in the third plane would we have confession in a booth? What kind of sacred ritual takes place in a booth? Of course it's in a private room," he scoffs. Yeah, that's fair. I figured as much but I couldn't shake the image of a Catholic confession from my head.

"That's good, then I can sneak in—there will be room. So we're looking for someone who has a reason to help us, doesn't know I am *technically* a mass murderer, and can camouflage any magic I need to cast," I respond, ignoring his snickering.

"Oh, is that all?" Gilbert quips. "Well, someone like that will be easy to find!"

I just roll my eyes and gesture in the direction of the bookshop. "Yeah, I think we might be able to find someone," I retort.

He looks confused for a moment, not picking up on my hint. I gesture my head in the direction of the shop again, and he just holds his hands up and to the sides in a sort of *what? what are you talking about?* motion. I sigh again and just explain it. "Godfrey. He has enough mana that no one would spot me if I cast a spell, even another mage. He only knows one of my secrets and only half of it. He doesn't seem too fond of Baldwin, or at the very least he definitely doesn't want Baldwin to have access to my magical knowledge. Finally, he was there the first time Baldwin did it; it's likely he is a victim of it as well."

Things seem to fall into place and Gilbert snaps his fingers. "Oh! Of course, I don't know why I didn't think of it! Godfrey has always helped you, we can trust him! Good thinking, Lillith!"

"Well," I hedge, "not trust, exactly. It's more like we share common interests for the time being. It's also a bit of a gamble, truth be told. The one secret he half knows could definitely cause trouble if the church knew it, but just more of the same trouble I already have. The real question is how willing he will be. It requires trusting me more than I trust him."

"You don't trust Godfrey? He's your master, Lillith, of course you can trust him! I don't know why you have to be so cynical about everything," he says, looking almost disappointed in me.

"I'm no one's apprentice. Besides, if you see a noble, powerful mage who owns a luxury shop for the rich and assume he is trustworthy just because he is friendly . . . well, I don't know what to tell you. You just haven't been paying attention," I reply.

Gilbert wilts at this, then tentatively replies, "So if we don't trust him, then why are we asking him?"

"Because," I announce, "I don't have any better ideas. Let's go!" At this, I dispel the sound magic and enter the shop with Gilbert. "Godfrey, are you in here?" I call into the back.

"Depends, do you have a Danish?" I receive in return. With this confirmation, I head into the back of the shop where Godfrey is covering a book with a stack of papers. "What do you want, child?" he asks, turning away from me in his seat to hide the effects of the hidden book, I suspect.

"I need to ask for your help with something. Something . . . fairly big," I begin. He gives me a dismissive nod to indicate I should keep going. I explain the situation to him the best I can. I see a look of recognition and anger paint his face when I discuss our last meeting with Baldwin together, and he confirms he lost time as well. I see his calculating eyes stare back into mine for several moments as I finish my explanation.

"I can't do what you are asking," he responds. I expected this was a possibility; Godfrey has his own secrets and, if I'm right, a few things he doesn't want me specifically to hear. I tsk, annoyed but already moving on to my next plan, when he holds up his hands in a placating gesture. "I'm not saying I can't help, just that I can't help in the way you are asking. Mages of my power and standing aren't expected to participate in the rite of confession. It would draw a lot of attention if I did."

I raise an eyebrow at him. "Okay, care to explain how you can help?" I invite.

"I know a young priest at the temple. He's a good lad and he owes me a favor. I can arrange a meeting for you, perhaps he can help you out," he offers. I bristle at the thought; I don't have the fondest memories of priests in my past life. Religious people are a tricky demographic for me. Many in high positions in any church will just use it as a tool for control, wielding their own sacred texts like a knife or as a pedestal to amplify their own voice.

On the other hand, many true believers with compassion genuinely believe they can help you. The problem is they are all mixed together and it's a bit like a bag of mystery jelly beans. The other problem is that genuine, well-meaning belief doesn't mean you are right, but joining the priesthood often means you are dogmatic. In other words, even the well-meaning ones will try to save my soul for the Collector.

That would be more of an annoyance than anything, however. I can brush that off, and if I can get someone to actually help me, it'll be worth it. If this guy turns out to be the rotten sort, I'll just burn that bridge when I come to it. "All right, we'll do it your way," I concede.

"Very well, I will contact him now; I'm a bit curious myself. I've never been to a confession before, and I'm embarrassed to admit I didn't consider that's what had happened. I knew Baldwin shouldn't have the power to alter my memories, but I lost time. Let's talk to him together. I'll ask him to join us here." I nod in assent, and Godfrey pulls a metal sphere out of his desk. He casts a spell I don't recognize, and I'm startled as an exuberant voice comes out of it.

"Lord Godfrey! A pleasure to hear from you!"

Apparently, the nobility has long-distance communication. My mind starts spinning—this will accelerate some of my plans a great deal. I only need to learn how it works.

CHAPTER TWENTY-FOUR

Faith of a Mustard Seed

After some time, a tall blond man in a robe finally enters the bookshop, and Godfrey flips the sign to Closed.

"Hello! You must be the plucky apprentice Lord Godfrey told me about!" He beams. "I hear you have need of a priest!"

Gilbert and I are a little taken aback by the energy he's brought with him, and Godfrey titters in the background.

"She does! Lord B—" Gilbert begins before I cut him off by clearing my throat loudly. Is this idiot really going to start by declaring that I'm an enemy of one of the most powerful men in the country? We literally just met this guy.

The priest chuckles gently and lightly reprimands Gilbert, "Woah there, lad! I think the young lady would like to speak for herself!" This ingratiates him to me a small amount; so often it feels I'm fighting to be heard. It's not enough to trust him, but it does help set me at ease. This, of course, immediately puts me on guard. Okay, I'll admit to a few trust issues—but a lot of untrustworthy people make an art of setting people at ease! I can't help that.

"I would," I confirm. "My name is Lillith, by the way. I prefer that to 'young lady,' if you don't mind. And you are?"

He throws his hand to his mouth, an exaggerated shock at his own rudeness. "My apologies, how impolite of me! I am Acolyte Emeric of the Temple of the Collector. A pleasure to meet you, Lady Lillith!" He bows and holds his hand out palm up as if to accept mine. I grab his hand and turn it into a shake, which he laughs off. Gilbert gives me a quizzical look while Godfrey pretends to be distracted by a book.

"It's just Lillith, thank you. One moment," I say before casting my sound barrier around all of us. Emeric raises his eyebrow, recognizing the spell for what it is, but politely waiting for me to speak. *Two for two so far, Emeric, well done.* Once I am sure we have privacy and have found various chairs to pull up, I say, "I need to speak to you about the rite of confession."

He rubs his chin in one hand and looks at me for a moment before responding. "Surely you aren't quite fourteen? Have you done something so grave you feel a need for the Collector's grace early? And in a remote location? Whatever you have done, Lillith, I'm certain it couldn't be so serious as that!"

"It's not that I want to experience the rite, at least not as a participant; I need to understand it. How it works and what it does," I explain.

"May I ask why?" he inquires, smiling but losing some enthusiasm.

I decide to take the risk and be upfront about the issue. I don't know if this man means well or if he is a zealot; I don't know that he won't attack me just for suggesting the Collector's power is being used incorrectly. I don't have a lot of other options, however, so I lay my cards on the table. "I believe a man is using the rite on me, regularly and in my own home."

He loses all his cheerfulness at this and draws his mouth to a line. "Lillith, that is very serious. If that's true, we need to apprehend him immediately. Is this man a priest?"

"I don't believe so, although it's not impossible he has some training with the church. You won't be able to apprehend him though," I respond.

"And why is that?"

"For one, I am not going to tell you who it is. For two, it just isn't possible."

"Lillith, this isn't something to play games with. If you know who this man is, action must be taken."

"I'm not playing games; I mean it. The church handling it won't lead anywhere."

He opens his mouth to either argue or try to explain that I am wrong, but Godfrey chimes in, "She's right, kid, telling you won't do anything. That's not the kind of help we need."

Emeric's face pales, then hardens in response to this.

"I see. In that case, this is even worse." After a moment, he says, "Tell me what kind of help you require."

"I need to understand the rite. And . . ." I say, bracing myself for backlash at my next request, "I need to know how to fight it."

Emeric looks aghast for a moment, then composes himself. He glances at Godfrey, who gives him a gentle nod.

"All right, Lillith. I can't tell you how it works; I'm sorry, I just can't. But I can tell you how to defend yourself against it when it's wielded by the wrong hands. It may take some time to master, however," he says.

"That's fine by me. I just need to defend myself, for now. What do I need to do?" I ask. It's not everything I need, but there is no point arguing over it right now. If I can learn how to stop it, I can work from there.

"How much do you understand about directional aspects?" he asks.

"Like mana aspects? I know how to aspect mana; what do you mean by directional?" I respond.

Godfrey chimes in at this, assuming his "master" role. "He means the direction of effect an aspect has. Mana aspects are either exoaspected or endoaspected. All the mana you use is exoaspected mana. This is mana that creates an external effect, like firing a projectile, creating light, or shooting fire." This makes sense. I do have mana that creates internal and external effects.

"And endoaspected mana has an internal effect, like altering my body?" I venture. For some reason, Emeric's face contorts at the guess.

"No! You must never use mana to alter your body," he berates. "Altering the body from its natural course is the domain of the Collector and is both deeply wrong and immensely dangerous!"

I'm a bit taken aback. That's an interesting reaction I file away for later. I have seen women with earrings here. I've even seen tattoos on religious men. He must mean alter in the same way I have been attempting . . .

My pondering is interrupted as Godfrey continues his explanation. "Emeric is right, Lillith; alterations to the body are dangerous and often necessitate banishment of the afflicted. It was a good guess though. No, endoaspected mana is mana that observes an external concept and causes an internal effect. It's sometimes called emotional mana because it is a result of abstract concepts. Joy mana, for instance, is endoaspected."

I nod, the concept clearing up some past reading for me. I have read about strange aspects of mana like hunger or sadness. I never understood what they would be used for. Gilbert looks back and forth like we are speaking a different language, but Godfrey carries on, "Magical bards are masters of endoaspected mana. They create emotions in their audience that reflect mana of an aspect they have internalized. This increases their exoaspected mana in various ways. Anger can increase the power and efficiency of fire spells, for example."

This is extremely useful information, and it clicks into place for me. "So there is an aspect of mana that can increase my defense against religious rites?" I hypothesize.

"Sort of," Emeric chimes in. "It won't change the effects of official rituals under the supervision of the church, but it will protect you from bad agents who are using the temple's knowledge to steal from the Great Collection."

"The Great Collection?" I ask before thinking better of it and moving on, "Never mind. So you are saying with a certain endoaspected mana, I can defend myself from the man doing this, but not from actual priests? What kind of mana can do that?"

"Well, it *will* defend you from priests actually, just not if it's used for its intended purpose. You need to aspect and internalize faith mana," he explains, and I wilt. "If you aspect faith mana, then the divine magic of a priest will only be effective when directly enacting the Collector's will."

This doesn't sound all that promising, truth be told. It is a lead though, so I may as well investigate. "And how do I do that, exactly?" I ask.

"To internalize endoaspected mana, you need to embody the aspect in question," Emeric says. "You need to truly understand and represent that aspect, or you won't be able to assign it to mana. To defend yourself, you essentially need to hand yourself over to the Collector completely."

"I . . . see. Thank you, Emeric, that is very helpful," I say, only half lying.

"I can teach you more about the Collector, enough to help you grasp faith mana, if you like?" he inquires hopefully.

"Another time perhaps," I answer. "I have a lot to consider."

His shoulders slump a bit, but he doesn't push any further. "I understand, Lillith. Let me know if you change your mind," he says. "In that case, I'd better get back to the temple." He stands up and exchanges a look I can't interpret with Godfrey, then leans down to me and whispers in my ear, "You deserve to feel safe, Lillith. If you ever need me, I'll help you." He then departs, waving goodbye to us.

"Well, that's not gonna work," Godfrey and I lilt at the same time. Gilbert looks back and forth between us, confused.

"Why not? I don't understand mana, but if all you have to do is have faith, maybe you should try?" he says.

I give him a long-suffering look before responding, "It just won't, Gilbert. Even if I wanted to, you can't force yourself to have faith in something you don't."

"Indeed," Godfrey agrees, "it's not so simple as that."

"It was helpful though. It gives us a place to start," I say as my mind races. I will likely never manifest faith mana, but I am not a woman who has left her emotions behind. I just need to find a substitute.

"You can't use it, but it was helpful? What do you mean?" a confused Gilbert asks the room.

"It was, indeed," Godfrey confirms. "We know we can fight divine magic with mana. We just need to find the right aspect." Godfrey has come to the same conclusion I have, although he probably should have earlier. I suppose he is just as susceptible to academic arrogance as I am.

Gilbert and I leave the shop. We decide to question a few more people about the button I found before heading home. My mind runs laps around my head as we conduct today's search. I have a few ideas for mana aspects I can probably manifest. Defiance, anger, and independence would all make sense. I just need to pick something before my next meeting with Baldwin.

CHAPTER TWENTY-FIVE

Who Am I?

I prepare my lunch the following day, still unsure what aspect will work best for me. Last night I tried to aspect mana with the concept of *defiance*, but it didn't quite feel right. The mana and the concept slid right off each other. I contemplate the issue as I swallow a spoonful of bland grits. I considered anarchy mana, but it felt a bit trite and didn't quite connect. My other ideas, anger and independence, felt wrong as well.

Emeric said I need to truly embody a concept in order to aspect it for internal use. Each aspect has its own issue that disqualifies it. I am defiant of someone else's will. That's not about me, or rather it's not something I identify with, it's just my reaction to an attempt to exercise power over me. Anarchy, well, I don't embody it like I'd like to. Truth be told, it is impossible to stay alive and truly represent anarchy until the concept has spread beyond myself.

Independence doesn't work at all. Relying solely on myself has only ever been a mistake. Yes, I am independent in the sense I can take care of myself and don't actually need anyone else to survive, but my feelings toward the aspect are far too complex to condense my being into it as a concept. As I finish my meal I give anger another go. This aspect feels the closest to what I need; I can feel myself grasping it, but, while it's solid to the touch, it evaporates when I try and grasp it, melting like ice over hot coals.

My ruminations are interrupted as my father leads in a finely dressed woman with auburn hair in careful curls. "Lillith, I'm pleased to introduce you to Lady Sybillia of Capet, your etiquette tutor," he announces.

I stand, brush the crumbs of bread off my dress, and offer my hand for a shake. "A pleasure to meet you, Ms. Sybillia." I'm not too fond of the idea of etiquette lessons, but this woman isn't the one who ordered it. No need to take it out on her.

"What in the world are you doing?" she scoffs, making a shooing motion at my hand. Well, all right, that one's on me. Handshakes aren't a thing here. It threw off Emeric as well, after all. "You've got a . . . peculiar child here, don't you?" she asks my father. Okay, that was fucking rude. I'm right here, lady!

No, Lillith, she isn't in a much better situation than you, not really. Yeah, she's rude. Looks a bit pompous. Clearly a rich piece of . . . Wait, what was I thinking about? I try to avoid making too harsh a snap judgment.

"You will refer to me as Lady Sybillia in the future, and you will curtsy when greeting someone. Is that understood?" she says, redirecting her attention to me.

"Oh, I understand perfectly," I respond, a hint of irritation in my voice.

Her expression sours further as she picks it up.

"You are going to be more than a handful, aren't you?" She sighs. "Well, there is no accounting for taste, I suppose. Collector knows what Lord Baldwin was thinking with this one. All right. Show me to your room, child, we have more work to do than I feared."

I head to my room without a word. I was going to be there regardless; I have no reason to refuse just for the sake of it.

"Tidy, I see, a mark in your favor," she approves. I just roll my eyes, uninterested in her appraisal. I'm trying not to project my irritation at her presence on her. Her rude comment and her nobility are certainly strikes against her, but she is as much in Baldwin's power as I am. "All right, seems like we need to start with basic greetings," she begins.

I nod along with her instructions, but my mind drifts off. I am aspecting mana internally, so she shouldn't be able to spot it. Where was I before? That's right, anger mana. It was slipping through my grasp. I wonder if fury mana will work, but decide they are essentially the same thing. I keep trying anger, however. It's like standing in front of my childhood home after a new family has moved in. The simmering hot rage is familiar. The mana rushing through me flows over the aspect like water around stones in a river. Still, I think if I work at it long enough I will be able to grasp it. I need something faster though. Time to move on.

I begin trying to aspect mana with *autonomy*, but this feels more slippery than anger, so I dismiss it. I am pondering what other aspects might work when I am snapped back to reality and have to catch Sybillia's wrist as she tries to slap me. "What the hell do you think you are doing?" I snarl before I see her face looks concerned, then frightened, rather than upset. Oh, I focused way too hard on aspecting anger. I let go of her wrist and she pulls her hand back.

"Young lady, what is wrong with you!? You weren't responding to anything I said or did; even shaking you didn't work! I was preparing to call a doctor!" she hisses at me. Okay, so upset, but not the kind of upset I was expecting. I can give her credit for that. Damn, do I really get that out of it when I am doing this? That's a weakness I'll need to account for.

"Sorry," I respond absent-mindedly, "I was just focusing on something." This explanation hardly placates her, and the anger I was expecting floods her face.

"Focusing on something? It wasn't my lesson, I can be sure of that. So what was so important, Lady Lillith? What were you focusing on so hard you couldn't be bothered with the lessons paid for by the Tudor house?" she rants at me. I do actually feel a little bad . . . if only a little. I was never going to pay attention to these lessons, but I could have at least warned her.

"I'm going to be up front here, Ms. Sybillia. I am not going to answer that. And . . . I'm never going to care about these lessons. I'm sorry, but I have more important things to focus on. It's got nothing to do with you, but that's the truth of the matter," I explain.

"That's not acceptable at all! You are to learn etiquette, Lillith. Lord Baldwin commanded it, and there is nothing you can do about it. You are going to have a hard life if you can't accept reality in times like this! Don't be an idiot!"

"Maybe. You are probably right—my life is going to be hard. But this is what I have to do. Now, if you'll excuse me, I was busy."

"And what am I supposed to do? Sit here and watch you? I won't. I'll use mana if I have to!" she threatens, flaring her power at me. I just flare my mana back and give her a disinterested stare. She withers at my greater mana. "Please, Lillith. I have to teach you this." I see her demeanor change and I realize there is actual pleading in her voice.

My heart breaks a little for her as I realize I have been misreading her. She does want to whip me into shape. She wants to mold me into a polite noble girl. She even planned to use her authority and position to do it. All pretty gross things to do, but that concerned look I saw when she tried to slap me to get my attention was probably her most honest moment. The fact that her method of helping was trying to hit me also speaks to her character, but I'll let it go for now.

She's afraid. She was given an order by Baldwin, and she doesn't have any recourse if she fails. She's not a good person. She's not absolved of her complicit role in the state of society. But she is afraid. It's easy to forget in a world like this that power is not a straight line down; it's a pyramid of smaller power dynamics, and abuse drips through it like grease, coating everything on the way down. I can't say I like her, but it's in my nature to grieve for people in situations like hers. If I completely refuse to learn etiquette, I won't be the one paying the price for it.

I decide to meet her halfway. "All right, I'll make you a deal. I'll pay attention to your lessons. I'll learn whatever it is you need to teach me. Every other visit, starting next time," I concede, and relief washes over her. "In exchange, I want to ask you questions about Baldwin. I need to learn about his history, what spells he knows, and his schedule."

She looks startled for a moment but regains her composure. Her back straightens out and her pompous demeanor returns. "A deal like this indicates you have a great deal to learn about etiquette," she sniffs, "but I suppose if it gets you to pay attention, I can play along. What do you wish to know?" It's a bit jarring how quickly she snaps back into her "noble lady" routine and I wonder if I've just been manipulated.

Oh well, my reasoning still stands and she can still be useful. I'll just have to build trust before I ask anything serious. It seems unlikely she would understand me well enough to know how to manipulate me like that . . . unless Baldwin has learned more during his visits than I think. If he has, I suppose it would be easy enough to arm her with just the right buttons to push. That thought sends a chill down my spine and I shudder. I needed an endoaspected mana concept yesterday.

I shrug it off and begin to question Sybillia. "Start with his daily schedule. Do you work with him enough to know how he spends his days?"

It turns out she doesn't; she's been hired for this job specifically. She does, however, interact with him at social gatherings and official events enough to have a little useful information. I grill her on Baldwin's habits for an hour or so and the "lesson" comes to an end.

"Thank you very much, Lillith," she says as I escort her back to the entrance of my home. "I will see you tomorrow."

My stomach twists as I realize this is going to be a daily engagement. Great. I should have negotiated better.

"Right, tomorrow," I respond half-heartedly. "See you then."

Meanwhile, my father looks satisfied with himself. "I'm glad to see you finally accepting reality, Lily. It makes me happy to know you are finally putting effort into securing your future," he says in his best wise-older-man voice. I just scoff and go to boil water. It's time to bathe my mother, and I don't have the energy for a shouting match with him.

As the water boils, I realize that's why anger mana isn't working right.

I have a vast capacity for anger, rage, that whole cocktail of dangerous emotions, really. The depth of my anger is significant and the results of it can be extremely violent. It's not who I am though. I don't want to be angry, and I don't even have the energy for it every time it's justified. I don't embody it.

I bring the sponge and the hot water into my parent's room where my mother is seated, staring out the window. She helps me along as I undress her and begin bathing her. Her grief is so deep I can feel it. I have to wade through it when I move through the room. She can't even take care of herself and it shatters me.

With that sadness comes the familiar rage that has carried me through so many conflicts and driven me to fight back in both lives.

In that moment, it is obvious. I should have known immediately. I'm not defiant because I am naturally defiant or contrary. I'm not angry because it's who I am. I am who I am because of grief. It's the very core of who I am. It's always what inspires my rage and my defiance. Grief is why I fight so hard against control, and it's what has always kept me going, driven me to fight for a better world in the face of everything. It's why I never cared when people called the world I longed for impossible, childish, or stupid.

Telling me only a stupid child would believe in a world without a boot on our throats just makes me mourn for both of us. That makes me fight harder. I grieve for the world I am in and struggle through the blood and the dirt and the bodies to reach a new one.

I begin to aspect the mana coursing through my body with the concept of grief, and it slides into place like an old friend.

CHAPTER TWENTY-SIX

I Am in Charge Here

Endoaspected mana makes a massive difference. I feel like I've just dropped ankle and wrist weights, left mud I was wading through, and taken off my bra after a long shift all at once. My entire body feels lighter, and mana is easier to channel. I need less of it as well, spells forming with a fraction of the power and effort it took before. With this, I could have crushed the Manticorps in the full light of day without having to move a muscle.

Godfrey is useless. He either completely neglected to teach me about this, didn't think I could handle it before it became necessary, or intentionally withheld it. I suppose it's possible not everyone can actually manage to aspect mana this way, but he still should have said *something*. Who knows how much earlier I could have responded to Baldwin? Although, Godfrey was affected as well. I suppose it's possible Godfrey hasn't managed it himself, or whatever endoaspected mana he has doesn't help against divine magic.

That last point has me a little nervous, actually, as I won't know if grief will work until I try it. I suspect it will, at least for me, since grief is what has always led me to shed the collars other people tried to fasten around my neck. I will find out soon enough. It's been a few days since I first aspected grief mana, and I am due for another visit from Baldwin.

For the first time since meeting him, I am glad Baldwin visits me in my own home for this. I had forgotten what Emeric and Godfrey said about bardic mages, but I remembered it quickly the first time I left the house after internalizing my new mana. Bards evoke emotion in those around them, which empowers their endoaspected mana. They could use music or even cutting words, so to speak, and they would become more powerful.

The effects of this are more dramatic than I thought, as the farther I got from my mother, the weaker my mana was. She was literally empowering me with her grief, which felt both appropriate and gross at the same time. I have always been empowered by mourning; it has always spurred me to action, and in a way, this felt like an extension of that. The greater the sorrow of the world around me, the greater my ability to fight for it.

For a while the concept of my mother's grief benefitting my abilities felt supremely uncomfortable; It wasn't dissimilar from how the nobility benefits from our suffering. Now, however, I have more perspective on it. Nobles benefit from causing suffering. I get stronger when I serve the suffering, like an extension of their will or a sword on their behalf. I can't really test this without a reason, but my innate understanding of the aspected mana gives me the feeling it wouldn't work otherwise. I don't think I can intentionally cause grief and then benefit from it, like a bard might. That's just not the kind of grief I identify with.

As I walked in the sunlight that first day, I was hyperaware of the strange new mana in my body. I could feel my abilities waxing and waning on my walk through the city. One large dilapidated building I walked by flooded me with so much power I nearly collapsed, sobbing in the street outside of it. I had to head straight home after that just to recover; apparently, the mana can amplify the emotion in me as well.

I plan to revisit that building another day when I am prepared for the emotional backlash; I am incapable of ignoring that level of sorrow once I become aware of it. It's possible I won't be able to help at all, but I have to check. I have also had a couple of etiquette lessons with Sybillia now, actual lessons where I pay attention and am not entirely surprised that her presence gives my power a small spike. Interestingly, that spike ebbs after the lesson but before she leaves. Something about the lessons themselves is making her grieve, a troubling revelation.

Today is all about Baldwin. I'm still in bed when the immense pressure of his mana sweeps over me and sends me into a cold sweat. Even with my recent increase in ability and my ever-growing mana pool, I don't stand a chance in a fair fight against this man. It's a good thing I don't fight fair, although I suppose it's unlikely he does either. I brace myself as I hear him in my living room exchanging words with my father and clench my fists as the door to my room swings open.

"Well, hello, dear fiancée!" he exclaims as if happy to see me. He has a smile on his face, but it doesn't reach his eyes. "I always look forward to these little meetings of ours. They are so satisfying!" I understand the double meaning he is trying to imply but I also don't believe him. The sick fuck just wants to inspire despair, but it won't work.

"Let's just get this over with," I scoff, my voice laced with venom.

He laughs. "Oh, it'll be over before you know it, I can promise you that!" This prick thinks he's really clever. I just roll my eyes.

That's when I feel it, my entire body freezing in place. I can't so much as wiggle my pinky. Rather than the panic this would usually invoke, elation floods me. The mana coursing through my body is fighting back, protecting me like Emeric said it would. I can instinctually tell that I can break this hold if I need to. It works. It fucking works, and Baldwin is fucked when I get my hands on him.

I am aware and I can break free, but I don't. I need to find out what happens when he believes he is in control. I need to find out, and I need him to believe it's working. If I break out now, worst case is I get myself killed. Best case, he finds a new tactic I can't fight. The feeling of being paralyzed in place, unable to do anything, sends adrenaline and panic through my body. I don't let it control me, however. I stay steady and wait.

Baldwin examines me for a moment, leaning in and looking directly into my eyes. He examines my face in silence for a moment but never touches me. I'm not sure if that's a choice or a condition of whatever divine spell he is using, but either way, I am relieved. Just his proximity makes my gorge rise; if he touched me, I would probably break free from his control without even thinking about it. Finally, after several minutes of examining me, he speaks. "Let's try this again. Speak clearly and plainly. Do not utter gibberish. Speak in the country's common tongue. Tell me where your magic circle is."

I feel my lips moving on their own as I answer his question without hesitation. "My magic circle is tattooed on my abdomen," I obediently explain, following all his instructions to the letter. His brow furrows and he sighs in frustration. Meanwhile, I am practically giddy on the inside. I want to laugh in this creep's face. I did everything he told me to. I never spoke in gibberish, and I exclusively spoke in the common language of "the country." I also interpreted that last bit loosely, however. *Tattoo* and *abdomen* were in English, the most common language of the country I am from.

He gives me slightly altered instructions, telling me to speak in the language of "my country," which results in silence as I don't hold loyalty to nor identify with any country. When he commands I speak in the language of his country, he gets the same, as I don't recognize his ownership of any country.

"Speak in the language most people speak and understand," he snaps, exasperation clear in his voice. "Tell me how you leave your circle and still accumulate mana!"

"Circle," I say in Mandarin, the only word of "I'm always in my circle" that I actually know of the language he, from my perspective, requested. Apparently, however divine magic works, commands are open to interpretation. He scowls and writes something down in a journal. He seems familiar with this song and dance, and I realize I have been fighting him to some extent the entire time. Even while I was unconscious, he was failing to control me.

My glee rises with his anger but dies off as he mutters to himself. "Not much progress today, but no matter, I'm getting closer." At this, I realize I have been particularly successful today, which means I haven't always been. In that journal is information he has gotten from me and I don't know what that is. What else would he have questioned me about? Which of my plans was he aware of, and what countermeasures did he have in place? I got too excited; of course he had been more successful in the past. I have more defenses now than I ever had before; there is no way today was the standard result. I was able to choose what words to translate this time. What if I hadn't always been?

My joy vanishes entirely when he puts his journal away and composes himself, running his hand through his hair. "Particularly troublesome today, are you? Well, no matter. Perhaps I'll have more success with the marital preparations," he says ominously. I was so relieved that he wasn't getting the information he wanted from me that I relaxed too much. Now, hearing that he is doing something else, I almost break free from his control at that moment.

He gestures his hand in a complex motion, holds it out to me, and clenches his fist. Regular magic doesn't require hand movements, so he must be using divine magic. Suddenly, my entire body feels weaker. A pained aching reverberates through my flesh, like the feeling of having too much blood drawn, enveloping every cell. Shit. I'm still certain it's impossible to change someone else's body without either immense mana or that person's help. With regular magic, that is.

As I feared, it seems completely possible with divine magic. I scan through my body with mana and feel a foreign will gripping it. The absolute piece of shit really believes he owns my body. He is wrong. I examine the intent and realize he is using a hammer, whereas I use a scalpel. He has no understanding of biology; he is enveloping me with the image of the finished product he wants to impose with no complex understanding of the exact changes he needs to make.

Frustratingly, it seems to work to an extent. Beads of sweat form on his head as he focuses his twisted will on me. The first thing that changes are my own most recent revisions. My sweat purifies, the poisonous chemicals dissipating as their production halts. Apparently, inhuman poison sweat conflicts with Baldwin's ideal image of me. This takes nearly an hour with the method he is using, but eventually, they are almost completely gone. I feel like a Grade A moron for never checking on them before and after a meeting with Baldwin. It never occurred to me that my failure in these experiments was in any way related.

Through the pain, I read the other changes he intends. He is trying to accelerate my development, shape me into his ideal figure, and even increase my fertility. I have to use mana to literally hold back the vomit and bile rising in my throat at this realization. Thanks to my other changes taking his focus, he has thankfully made no progress at all on this design. Subtly, I begin reintroducing the toxic chemicals and activating proteins while denying his grotesque attempts at molding my figure like clay.

As I suspected, he doesn't notice. My control and understanding of the human body surpass his to a degree he can't even comprehend. I find it easy enough to overcome his will, and his efforts are now just a slight pushback against my own designs, until they pitter out entirely.

I am in charge here, you fucking snake, I think as I thwart all his efforts. He has not gotten a single inch from me, but the violation of the attempt makes me sick. It is rare for me to be tempted to exact an intentionally painful death on someone, but this man is pushing that boundary to its breaking point.

My toxic sweat already matches my previous design when a gasping Baldwin composes himself and mutters, "You can't fight it forever, you stubborn bitch . . ."

Oh yes, I can, and it's about to get even harder for you. You were impotent while I was basically unconscious and defenseless. You'll be less than nothing now that I can fight back, I think defiantly.

He casts some kind of spell that cleans the sweat off his brow and combs his hair. Composing himself completely, he stands where he had been when my body first froze. He shifts his expression back to the fake smile and I feel control returning to my body. "That will be all today. As always I appreciate your cooperation," he says, feigning satisfaction.

I glare at him as he leaves and stay where I am until I feel his mana is gone, then I double over and puke onto the ground. I hate to imagine how violated I would feel if my own changes hadn't been stymieing him, if he'd been able to affect my body, considering how I feel even now.

Baldwin Tudor is not long for this world.

CHAPTER TWENTY-SEVEN

The House of Penance

I wouldn't go in there if I was you, young lady."

The gruff man's voice comes from the shadows beside the tall, narrow brick building I'm peering up at: the one that caused my grief-aspected mana to nearly overwhelm me. Today, I am prepared for the intense mana spike; so far, I haven't collapsed in the road. With yesterday's events, I am freshly fueled with rage at Baldwin, and I use that as an anchor.

"Why not? What's in there?" I inquire of the watching man. I wonder if this is a sick house or something of that nature. It's closer to the walls of the city and a bit more isolated than a lot of buildings of similar size.

"That there's a gatherin' place for undesirables, kid. It ain't safe for a lady like you."

I furrow my brow as I feel the overwhelming grief radiating from the building. I guess it's not impossible it's controlled by another street gang; there are plenty of gangs thrown together more out of necessity than ill intent. Not every gang is like the Manticorps, human traffickers and thugs for hire. Some are just adult versions of Tommy and his friends. People doing what they can to survive, too large and noticeable to swipe a loaf of bread from vendors with any consistency.

"What kind of undesirable? Dangerous? Sick? Something else?" I ask, to the man's consternation.

"What's it matter?" he snaps. "I told you they was undesirables, listen to your elders, girl. Don't go near there if you know what's good for you!" He huffs off, grumbling something about *kids these days*. It seems to be a multiuniversal constant that no matter what days they are, the kids are unacceptable to older generations.

I consider for a moment. If it is a gang, even if it's a dangerous one, I can probably handle them. Rosalind was a rare case, and I am pretty much beyond regular thugs at this point, especially right now. Then again, I don't think I can be empowered by grief mana to fight the people who are grieving, so maybe I can't count on that. In the same vein, this emotion is raw and genuine. Even if it is a dangerous gang, they have a real depth of feeling I have to empathize with. If they turn out to be a problem, I'll deal with them.

It could be a sick house, quarantine for some sort of contagious illness. I think I can handle that as well. I can directly alter my body and, knowing why it was failing before, keep it that way. I should be able to counteract any dangerous side effects. I'm not actually certain I can get sick, come to think of it. I haven't so much as sniffled since drawing my mana circle. My body seems to run on pure mana; I don't know if a virus could even affect me.

I might even be able to help in that case. I can't alter someone's body by force, but I can walk them through helping me. It's not exactly healing magic, but it could work. Actually, shit . . . wait, maybe it is healing magic? Intuitively, healing and the church are associated with each other here. Maybe what Baldwin was trying to do was a perversion of magic meant for healing? Food for thought.

For now, I can feel a heart-wrenching sorrow emanating from the very stones of this building, and if I could ignore that, I would never have been able to aspect this mana in the first place. I have other things to worry about. I have to find Henry, care for my mother, and wring the life out of that slimy creep with my bare fucking hands. I don't have time to be sidetracked, but now that I've found this place, I can't ignore it.

Steeling my resolve, I start up the smooth steps. I feel a growing sense of urgency as the deep well of sadness I am walking into envelops me. I bound up the last steps, desperate to do whatever I can to heal this all-consuming pain.

As I push open the unlocked, rotting door and enter a wide foyer, the sickly smell of neglected people seeps over me. I stop cold, my eyes widening. Undesirables? Did that man fucking say undesirables? I feel an urge to track him down and permanently disable an undesirable part of his body. These are just normal people in pain! People suffering and hurt, or abandoned! This place doesn't seem to be a sick house, not really. As I peer into the large rooms to either side of the entrance, I see plenty of sick people, but they don't all appear to have the same illness, and some have no visible ailment at all.

There is a man sitting against a wall with his head forward, apparently sleeping with no regard for the environment he is in. He is missing his left leg. There is another man with the milky eyes of someone who has been blinded by an infection. There are people with limps, missing digits or hands, and even one woman with a missing nose. These people aren't undesirable; they just make typical people uncomfortable.

"What the fuck is going on here?" I say under my breath, frozen in place. I gape as I try to process the scene in front of me.

A woman's voice breaks me from my stupor. "You must be one of us, then." I feel a small spike in my mana. I turn to face her and immediately recognize the sores around her lips and hands: probably syphilis. "You're so young—talk about shit luck," she continues.

I then realize what she means by "one of us." She isn't crippled or injured in any way. She was sent here just because of a fucking STI. She must think I was as well. She's either a former sex worker, a slave, or she ended up with a man who couldn't keep it in his pants.

"What is this place?" I ask, feeling sick to my stomach. The conditions here seem horrendous. The space practically groans as it struggles to contain all the people; what furniture is here is ripped, broken, and dirty. Is this just some quiet place to tuck away people you don't want around? My mind races through my memories and I realize with horror that I have never met a blind person in this life. Not one deaf or disabled person of any variety. I should have noticed this years ago. People with some of these injuries should be more common with the level of medicine here, not less.

What do they eat? How do they survive? A clinical part of me wonders what the point is. If you are going to lock up and abandon groups like this, why wouldn't you just . . . kill them? It doesn't make sense to store them away as if they're broken tools in a junk drawer.

"We call it Penance," the woman answers me, her voice husky. "This house, that's what it is." Her lip quivers a bit, and I can tell she is biting back tears as she explains it to me. I get the feeling she is always biting back tears.

"Penance? Penance for what?" I ask, dumbfounded.

"Let me guess, sweetheart. You went in for your first confession and you woke up walking through that door?" she ventures, and my heart turns to ice. The implications of what she just said fuel a deep fury that threatens to consume me.

"Is that how you got here? The rite of confession?" I ask.

"It's how all of us got here, sweetheart. Well, most of us. A few, like Ozzy over there, were slaves dropped off by their masters." She gestures at a boy, maybe fifteen or sixteen. His left arm is curled up in an unnatural position, his hand clenched in a hard fist. I notice it is flexed and considerably more muscular than his right. It only takes a moment to realize he likely doesn't have control over it. "It's a shame what happened to him; he says he was working in his master's stables and that side of his body went numb. He tried to ask for help, but his words wouldn't come out right. He fell over and his arm has been like that ever since."

"A stroke," I lament quietly, more to myself than to her.

"A what?" she asks.

"It sounds like a stroke—it has to do with the blood in your brain not flowing correctly," I explain absent-mindedly, focusing on the boy. "You said his master just left him here after that?"

She looks at me with a look of confusion and concern, probably caused by my explanation, but decides to drop it. "That's right. It happens from time to time. Injuries in the fields or other such things, and a slave either loses usefulness or presentability. That's why they have to come here for penance."

"Penance for what, exactly?"

"Well, in his case, he was a slave, so he was likely a criminal. Don't know what he did, but if he can't repay his debt to society through labor, he's gotta come here to do it. Besides, none of us fit the design of the Collector anymore," she says, her voice laced with melancholy. I see, so "not fitting the Collector's design" is the sin of most of these people.

"How does he do it here? Do you do some kind of work or something? And why are the rest of you here?"

"Only the Collector knows that, sweetheart. Some sin found in our hearts, I suppose. In my case, I poisoned my husband, same as you, I suspect. You can see the marks of the curse on me plain as day. He has the same."

"How do you know he didn't poison you?"

"Oh, that's not how it works, sweetheart. This is the curse of a failed wife, you should know that. It's the same curse that visits women who do carnal work instead of getting married . . ." She trails off and I clench my fists harder, anger rising rapidly. Is that what they fucking tell people?

I decide to save that conversation for later. She missed the first part of my question. "And in what way is this penance? How does this misery serve anyone?"

"Like I said," she answers, "only the Collector knows. I just know we do something, this isn't forever. You just have to push through for a couple of years at most."

"You live like this for years? What do you eat and drink? How do you survive?" I probe, getting more and more furious.

"They leave food for us. They drop off a bag once a week, and if you are quick, you can squirrel some away. There is a stream running through the yard for water, so we have plenty of that to spare," she answers in a soft voice, one I realize she is trying to use to comfort me.

"Who leaves food?" I ask.

"The priest. The same one who collects us when it's time."

"Time? Time for what?"

"To serve the Collector, of course. Once we have paid the price for our sins, the priest summons us out, like we are going through confession again, and we are brought to rejoin the Great Collection," she explains patiently.

This is fucking sick. What are they using these people for? Why? Why don't they just help these people? If Baldwin's power is the same as the priests', they should be able to.

The boy from earlier, Ozzy, has noticed me and is approaching. He looks nervous and his left hand is in front of his chest, rapidly strumming up and down. "Hey, I'm Ozzy! I don't get to meet a lot of people my age around here!" he exclaims in a heartbreakingly upbeat tone. He is clearly overjoyed to see me; he is literally rocking back and forth on his feet like an overstimulated child. His red, irritated eyes indicate he was crying before I showed up. I process this like I'm swallowing lead.

It's no wonder I was floored when I first passed this building. The weight of the collective grief in this house threatens to crush me beneath it. "It's a pleasure to meet you, Ozzy," I say, holding out my right hand for a shake before remembering I'm the only one who does that. As I retract it, his left arm shoots out and clinches my wrist in a vice grip.

His face rapidly devolves into the unique panic of someone used to being unfairly punished. "I'm so sorry, I can't control it. I don't want to hurt you, I don't! I don't mean it I don't mean it I don't mean it!" he pleads, his voice rapidly devolving into sobbing as his arm refuses to listen to his commands.

In that moment I mourn for this kid, for the life he has led. I want to pull him into my heart and keep him safe from every cruel thing. I stand up on my toes and pull him into a tight hug, his left hand still gripping my wrist. He sobs into my shoulder and I just hold him like that. Behind his back, my other fist clenches tight enough that my nails draw blood. Gilbert wanted to know why I didn't hesitate to kill? Whoever left this child like this is certainly going to find out; the Collector himself is going to pay for this if I have my way.

As I hug him, the woman I was speaking with rubs Ozzy's back, and after a few moments, I feel his hand release my wrist, but I let him cry into my shoulder a little while longer. I notice a familiar bird symbol branded on his neck. He calms down and I let him go. "It's okay, Ozzy, I know it wasn't your fault. What happened is completely normal. I don't mind at all," I reassure him.

"R-really?" he sniffles. "I didn't ruin everything?"

I smile warmly at him. "You didn't ruin anything, I promise. In fact, I'd like to be friends, if that's okay?" I ask.

He gapes at me for a moment, then gives me a huge grin, which is missing a few teeth. "I'd really like that!"

The woman smiles warmly and Ozzy begins rocking again. I don't want to, but I have to ask: "Ozzy, I'm sorry if this is upsetting, but it is very important to me; can I ask you a question?" I see apprehension seize his face, but he hesitantly nods. I ask, "The brand on your shoulder, what's it for?"

His face sours but he answers me, "It's my slave brand, miss, the seal of my master's house."

I take a big breath. Something deep inside me tells me I already know the answer to my next question, but I ask anyway. "Which house?"

"Tudor, miss. My master is Lord Baldwin Tudor."

CHAPTER TWENTY-EIGHT

The House of Penance 2

My mind reels at Ozzy's words. So many thoughts and emotions grip me that I feel like I am suffocating. Panic, horror, shock, fury, and sorrow all tear at the fibers of my mind, and I unravel like the seam of an overburdened wineskin. I fall to my knees and begin to sob, oblivious to the people packed into the room with me. I am vaguely aware that the woman is now comforting me as she had Ozzy, rubbing my back and whispering that it's okay.

I am certain of it. That emblem, cruelly branded onto this boy's neck, is the same as on the button I found in Henry's makeshift lab. Baldwin has Henry. I mean, I don't know it for sure, but something in the depths of my soul wails that it is true. It makes too much sense. The cruelties and violations Baldwin has been trying have failed. Again and again, they failed. A man so used to owning people, so confident in his own right to govern their very bodies, and a child who won't be controlled.

He needs a backup plan. He needs leverage. He likely considers my entire family his property. No wonder he never lost his confidence. He always had an ace in the hole. A point of leverage he could use.

Shit, what if he takes his anger out on Henry? What if my stupid language tricks send him into a rage and he goes to Henry and beats him? What if Henry is dead? Baldwin has no need of an apprentice alchemist, he could just kill him as an example! Oh fuck oh fuck, did I get him killed, did I—

I stop my spiraling thoughts short. No, I can't think like that. Only Baldwin is responsible for Baldwin's actions. Henry is still valuable to him as a pressure point for me.

I start to calm down. Annie Beckett would be hyperventilating right now, but the mana in my body seems to have blessedly spared me by managing my oxygen flow directly. I need to focus. This is good, I can use this. Two of my problems just became one. I can focus all my efforts on tracking Baldwin's movements and planning to take care of him. Dealing with Baldwin will lead me to Henry.

I take in a few more deep breaths. I realize at some point I wrapped my arms around the woman. I suddenly become aware that my reaction spooked Ozzy; he is huddled up and crouched. On the balls of his feet, he has one arm wrapped around his knees while his other jerks to the side with erratic movements. He is mumbling, "I'm sorry I'm sorry I'm sorry I'm sorry," and rocking back and forth. Oh fuck, the poor kid thinks I am reacting to something he did!

"Ozzy! It's okay, I'm okay, you didn't do anything wrong!" I reassure him, leaving the arms of the woman I've been holding. We both move to him and crouch near him.

"You have to be more calm," the woman whispers to me. "The panic in your voice is only upsetting him more." She's right, of course. I have to be a calming presence, not another frantic one. I nod in acknowledgment and lean down close to him.

"Ozzy," I say gently, placing my hand on his arm, "I'm not upset with you. You have done nothing wrong. It's all right." His rocking begins to slow and the muttering quiets. He looks up from behind his good arm with clear apprehension. "I want to apologize to you, Ozzy. I shouldn't have startled you like that. Will you forgive me?"

"You're not mad?" he sniffles, his voice reflecting the same fear and uncertainty as the rest of his body.

"I'm not mad," I reply, giving him a soft smile and a nod. "Will you forgive me?" He looks at me for a moment, then nods rapidly. I stand up and offer him my hand to help him up after me.

I feel him tense up as another man sitting against a wall nearby complains, "When is someone gonna shut the little shit up for good?" Ozzy looks around like he's scared of being hit, then scurries over and hides behind the woman who introduced us. I glare daggers at the man, but he shows no sign of remorse.

I open my mouth to snap at him, but the woman beats me to it. "Shut it, George, he's a fair bit more pleasant to listen to than your constant bellyaching!"

The man just waves her off and I feel no need to escalate this further. I like this woman more by the moment. She seems fairly deceived about the level of her guilt in her sickness, but that's hardly her fault. It's a rare gem who can find themselves in a situation like this and still make room to feel compassion for others.

"What's your name?" I ask, looking up at her, and she smiles down at me.

Ozzy glances around from behind her and I wave at him before returning my attention to the woman.

"I'm Diana. A pleasure to meet you," she replies warmly, even giving me a curtsy. "And you are?"

"Lillith. My name is Lillith. A pleasure to meet you as well, Diana," I respond, giving a soft bow, as I wore my practical attire today. This seems to amuse her and she rewards me with a laugh.

"So which is it? Did you end up here after confession, or were you dropped off by your master or husband?" she inquires, looking me up and down.

"Neither. I came here on my own," I reply, eliciting a look of confusion. "Do you mind if I ask you a few questions?"

Her face dances with concern at my answer but she nods. "Well, all right, but you really have no business here if you aren't serving penance. You need to get home as soon as you can, young lady!"

I smile at her concern. "I'm all right; don't worry about me. Can I ask, do you ever get any visitors?" This confuses her even more, but I continue, "Priest, nobles, anyone who checks in on you?"

"Before you? Never. No one would come in here willingly. The only person who approaches is the priest. He drops off a few crates of food about ten paces from the door and then leaves. We can't leave to get it until he is far enough away. When he comes to get one of us, they'll just go blank; they walk to him and then they're gone. Those are the only times we see anyone else."

"You can't leave? Who stops you, if the priest is the only one who ever comes near?"

"What do you mean? We can't . . . just . . ."

I furrow my brow at this. Is it more of the priest's mind control? They keep the inconvenient members of society locked away, unable to leave until they fetch them? "Can you . . . ever leave? Besides to bring the food in, I mean," I ask, and she shakes her head, looking at me like I just asked if she ever wears her bloomers on her arms. Well, this could work . . .

As I am contemplating her answers, Ozzy finally emerges from behind Diana. I see his arm twist behind him in a position that looks incredibly uncomfortable, and I decide to try to help. "I might be able to fix that for you," I offer. "I'm a mage; I know a few tricks."

Diana laughs again. She is a very cheerful woman for one who has been banished to live like an animal. "You're a mage, are you? Come on, girl, don't toy with the lad like that!"

I just smile up at her and cast a small flashlight above my hand, drawing the eyes of everyone in the building for the first time. A sense of fear washes over the room and I realize that may have been a mistake. Oops. "By the Collector, my lady . . . why is a noblewoman visiting us?" she exclaims.

I banish the light and put my hands up placatingly. "I'm not a lady! Well, I'm a lady, but not a *lady* lady. I'm a commoner, I'm just also a mage. I really can help!" I explain, reducing the suspicion and fear in the room not a bit.

Diana shakes her head at me, but Ozzy speaks up. "You can help me? How?" I see the hope in his eyes, and to my great relief, I feel the intensity of my mana drop, just a little.

"It's hard to do, and I'd need your permission and help, but I can use mana to alter your body a little. I can try to find where the problem is and show your body how to adjust so you can use your arm again. I can even make other changes if you like, maybe get rid of that brand? I think I can do pretty much any . . . thing . . ." I trail off as I realize the entire room is gaping at me in horror.

"No no no, please don't, I didn't do anything wrong, I'm sorry!" Ozzy begs as if I've just threatened to have his arm severed from his body.

"Are you a fool, girl, or are you just cruel?" Diana reprimands me. I look at her, dumbfounded.

"I—I don't understand, what did I say?" I stutter out, absolutely lost.

"You said you were going seize the Collector's work and alter the poor boy's body! Do you want him to be banished to the woods?" she lectures me, clearly upset, and pulls Ozzy into a hug.

"Banished? For allowing himself to be healed? Weren't you already banished here for being sick and injured?" I ask. I can't understand why they are so afraid.

"To the woods, idiot girl," she snaps, forgetting all her fear of mages from a moment ago. "I'll die here before I let that happen. Any of us would!"

"Why the woods? I don't understand?" I ask.

"Why the woods? Because that's where all the monsters are! That's the only place you'll end up if you go trying to alter the Collector's designs!" she fumes.

So it's more like an execution than a banishment. They refuse to heal them, lock them up here, bringing them just enough food to survive, and send them to be killed by monsters if someone else heals them? There is something sinister going on here, something more complex, and I intend to find out what. First, I think I can help them another way.

"I'm sorry," I say. "I didn't know. I'm a fairly new mage. Can I help you in a different way?"

Diana cocks an eyebrow but softens a bit. "All right, but no more of this talk about messing with anyone's body, okay? What did you have in mind?" she asks.

"Well, I know some kids who could use a sheltered place. They can come here, bring extra food and supplies, and help you contact people outside of here. In exchange you let them use the building and care for them if they fall sick," I explain, hoping I'm not threatening them with some other taboo.

"Kids?" Ozzy asks, clearly getting a little excited.

Diana looks more skeptical. "This is no place for kids who haven't been sent here, Lillith. I don't know if that's such a good idea."

"They're orphaned and alone, Diana," I say. "You would do them as much good as they would do you."

Her expression softens and she nods her head. "I see. You are trying to help both of us, are you?"

"Yep." I beam. "and one more thing."

"What's that?" she asks, folding her arms.

"I want to teach all of you to use magic," I announce to the entire room, and everything goes quiet.

CHAPTER TWENTY-NINE

Sinners and Thieves

I'm feeling encouraged as I walk to Tommy's camp. It took some work and quite a few demonstrations of spells, but the residents of the penance house agreed to my offer. None of them are interested in my attempts at healing, but learning magic and working with the street kids are on the table. Interestingly, many of them are more interested in the kids than in magic. This group included Diana and Ozzy, who both did their best to convince the rest to work with me.

It turns out quite a few of them have people on the outside they are worried about. Family members and friends they never got to say goodbye to. The priest's compulsion prevents them from seeking them out, but with the kids' help, they can contact them again. This possibility alone swayed more than half the residents.

I also made an interesting discovery while displaying my spells for them. When my grief mana is particularly charged, the color of each aspect is far less vibrant and opaque. While its potency is greater, it seems to lose some visibility at the same time. I have a few theories about this, and I'm excited to investigate them.

Finally, I also have a lead on Henry. Next time Baldwin visits me I am going to try to follow him. This is an immense risk but has the potential to change everything. I am also going to ask Godfrey for information. His distaste for Baldwin was enough to get his help before; I can't ignore the resource now. If I find enough threads of Baldwin's corruption, I can unravel him and find Henry in the process.

I arrive at the camp and am pleasantly surprised to find Gilbert already there, playing some kind of game with a few of the younger kids. He is blindfolded, and their call-and-response reminds me of Marco Polo as the giggling children run around his feet and he tries to catch them. While this doesn't restore my trust in him, it does rouse a bit of my childhood affection for him. He must be coming here regularly to visit and bring food. "Got you, Mary!" he cries as he picks up a giggling little girl. My heart is bursting at the seams as I realize she is the same child who had been so frightened of the last Manticorp I killed. I smile and wave as Tommy sees me and walks over.

"Ms. Lillith! What're ya doin' 'ere?" he asks, and my brother stumbles at the sound of my name. I laugh as he is swarmed by kids while trying to peek out of his blindfold.

"You've conquered him!" I call over, the lilt of a laugh carrying my voice. "Do you mind if I borrow him for a moment? I'll return him afterward, I promise!" This causes a cacophony of boos and complaints, so I follow it up with: "Actually, I have something to talk about with all of you!"

This perks them up again and I find myself the new target of their energy. They run over and swarm around me, shouting over each other to get my attention.

"What's up, Lillith?" Gilbert asks as he approaches, completely removing his blindfold.

I hold up my hands to the group, allowing the sound to die down and giving the older kids a chance to join us. "I think," I announce, pausing for dramatic effect, "I have found a suitable place to teach everyone magic." Excited chittering and cheers immediately break out again and even the older kids start whispering under their breath. I catch another glint of greed I don't like in a couple of their faces and make a mental note to keep an eye out for them.

"How'd ya fin' a whole empty 'ouse?" Tommy asks. Gilbert cocks his head and looks at me, indicating he has the same question.

"Well, it's not empty. It belongs to, or rather is occupied by, another group of people," I start. I then begin to describe my experience at the House of Penance. I get quite a few questions from the crowd and do my best to answer everyone.

At one point a girl wrinkles her nose and asks, "So we hafta help a buncha old sick people?" and I give her an admonishing look.

"You don't have to do anything you don't want to, but it will help you. They aren't just a 'bunch of old sick people.' They are a group that's been kicked around and beaten down the same way you have. They need your help and you need theirs," I explain.

"I don't see how we need their help," an older boy says, crossing his arms. "Seems to me we'd just be doing a buncha chores for 'em."

I sigh but remain patient. This response pretty closely reflects the residents' response to the idea of the kids joining them.

"Well, you need a sheltered and hidden location that the city guard will never check. That no one will ever check. You need a safe environment and a support system, and somewhere safe when you get sick yourselves. They need help getting more food and clothing and contacting their loved ones. You will also both need each other while gaining your mana," I explain. I answer several more questions for a while, but it's not so hard to convince the group to agree.

Once I have their consent, I offer to bring them right away, and the excited kids agree eagerly. As I send them off to collect their few belongings, I pull Gilbert aside. "I found out where the button is from," I start, and immediately grab his full attention. "The bird is the seal of the House of Tudor. Baldwin has Henry."

Frustratingly, Gilbert's face lights up at this news.

"That's great news, Lillith! He's safe and we know where to find him. We can finally bring him home! Mom will be so happy!" he exclaims as I begin rubbing my temples again. Gilbert is still convinced my engagement is a good thing. He doesn't understand the extent of the violation of what Baldwin has been trying to do. When I told him about the attempts to change my body, he just shrugged it off because women "usually want to be more fertile and curvy."

I am having a hell of a time shaking him free from a lifetime of accepting the cruelties of the world as normal. Gilbert's sometimes kind, sometimes casually misogynistic view of the world is exhausting. I can see clear as day that he has the capacity for empathy; he can care when he is slapped in the face with reality. He's also thoroughly socialized to believe some of the worst shit I've ever heard.

"No, Gilbert, it's not. Baldwin has had Henry since before we raided the Manticorps. He has had him this entire time, and he let us believe he was missing," I say, and the idiot just looks confused.

"Why would he do that?" he asks. "Aren't we going to be an extension of his house soon?"

"Because—he is not a good man, Gilbert. He could be doing any number of things. It could be to punish me or it could be to control me. The one thing I do know is if we want to see Henry again, we have to get him back ourselves. Baldwin is not going to return him to us, at least not for free," I explain, anger rising in my voice. My clueless brother is completely taken aback by this but bites back his first response.

"You really think he won't let us see him?" he asks softly.

"He hasn't even told us he has him, Gilbert. What do you think?" I ask in response.

He pauses for a moment of contemplation.

"And you are sure he has him?" he checks, clearly hoping I am wrong.

"Intellectually? I can't be completely certain. But I can feel it, Gilbert. I know he does. And soon enough I'll have proof," I assure him. He doesn't respond to this, just withdrawing into contemplation. He'll come around. If there is one thing that always sways Gilbert against his preconceived ideas and biases, it's concern for his little brother.

By the time this conversation closes, the kids have all prepared themselves and are ready to depart. "Ready 'n' waitin'!" Tommy announces to me, and I smile. I begin leading the group through the streets to the House of Penance. We get more than a few looks as we travel en masse. Many steer as clear of us as they can. Some give us nasty looks and a few shout at us. One man actually tries to rescue me from the group.

When he insists after I wave him off, I am forced to display my magic. This succeeds in scaring him off and probably starts some fairly strange rumors. Hopefully it's just dismissed as an oddity and the guards don't investigate. Maybe I should have brought them one at a time, but I'd really like to talk to the entire group before leaving any of them alone.

Finally, we arrive at the worn-down home. None of the kids seem to care about its state, however, as it surpasses their makeshift tents by a mile. I lead them inside and the expectant residents move to one side of the foyer, heads peering out from all the rooms around us. I can see they are chomping at the bit to send messages out to their loved ones.

As the kids finish filing in, I have to lean against the wall and take a few deep breaths. Both of these groups have had harder lives than me. Both of them have experienced loss and heartbreak on a level that can completely break some-one. Both of them cause a significant spike in my abilities, and bringing them together actually makes me a little dizzy.

Once I manage to regain my composure, I begin introductions. Diana and Ozzy take to the kids at once, and Ozzy is excitedly making friends with as many of them as he can. I had the foresight to warn them about his arm, and they all either keep enough distance to not worry about it or react to it only briefly. The kids display a mix of reactions to the residents. About seventy percent openly stare at their various injuries or disabilities, while the other thirty percent try so hard not to look at them it has the same effect.

For the residents' part, they seem to be equal parts eager and annoyed. Not much to be done about that; all I can do is try to help everyone work together and trust they will be able to do so. Finally, I speak up again.

"I have explained to everyone what the general purpose is here. There is one more thing that everyone will need to help one another with, however."

I go into a brief explanation of magic circles and the need to stay inside one. I'd like to give them each a tattoo like mine, but I can't spread that around the city as fast as I need to. It also causes enough pain that it could be dangerous for some, and the risk of the group getting caught increases exponentially. Finally, the need to guard and provide for one another while some are accumulating mana helps further cement the idea of mutual aid in their hearts. If everyone is out for themselves, no one learns magic.

I have also redesigned my original circle for mass use. I'll still use the ever-expanding universe as the space. This way I can encourage people I teach to share with others, and mana can spread much faster, because I don't need to teach how to find the exact mathematical center of a room, nor how to adjust the design to accommodate it. I have removed many of the dissipation runes so their accumulation rate will surpass mine. This should help counteract the inability to accumulate it continuously, at least a little.

I have also had to scale back the extent to which mana permeates the body in their circle's design. I don't target aspects of electricity, carbon, calcium, or other elements most mages wouldn't think of. I am still unsure of all the side effects this has had on me and I still think it's possible expending all my mana could kill me. Instead, I use the typical aspects of bone, skin, and muscle. I use water instead of blood, which is a change I consider safe that still offers a small advantage. Kids will show less restraint, and apparently, the changes it caused to my body are some kind of cardinal sin that people actively avoid. This makes me wonder if the clinic reported my lack of heartbeat to the church at some point. It could spell trouble if they did, but it's too late to worry about that now.

Diana shows me to the largest room in the building, a sort of salon at the back of the house. We clear the furniture away from the worn wooden flooring, and everyone watches as I start to sketch out the circle in white paint with my fingers. I've worked on my design so long I have it memorized, but I've also drawn out a reference sheet with the updated and safer design.

"Now, one thing to remember is that you will all be relying on one another," I say as I draw. "You will be protecting and feeding one another. Another thing to remember is I am not doing this because you are all special. I am going to do this all around the city for all sorts of people like you."

They nod along and I continue my warning. "If you get your magic, then decide not to help the second group get theirs, you will be at a disadvantage. You will have fewer magical allies and friends than everyone else in the city. If you use your mana to control and bully one another, it will have the same effect." I allow my words to sink in before adding my final warning. "If you use your magic to control and hurt people, to gain authority for yourself or force yourself on others," I hiss, pausing to make eye contact with the members of both groups who had been looking at the circle with greed, "you will be my enemy, and you will be the enemy of everyone else in this house. Do you understand?"

I get nods and affirmations of varying levels of sincerity. It'll have to do for now; I have a few weeks to keep teaching them and talking to them before any of them have magic. It takes me hours to draw the circle, especially since I am going slowly and teaching each detail to the small group that remains once the task has become monotonous. As the sun goes down, I finally finish the circle and help the residents and kids decide who will enter it first. It can fit about eight people maximum, and four from each group enter.

Gilbert and I finally depart and begin the walk home. He doesn't talk much, still considering our conversation from earlier. I let him contemplate until we get home and are greeted by my smiling father. Edward is even here, although he refuses to look at me, and that concerns me. Ever since the engagement was announced, he has been avoiding me. First, our father suddenly considers my existence this family's greatest success. And I have consistently failed to be offended at being called a sex worker. These combined factors have left him unable to face me.

"Welcome home, Lillith! Great news!" my father announces, too excited to even smirk at me. Neither Edward nor I like where this is going, and we share a grimace for opposite reasons as my father continues, "Lord Baldwin has secured an earlier appointment with the church. We officially become a noble house tomorrow!"

CHAPTER THIRTY

Lillith of Endings

After my father announced the christening ceremony would be today, I sighed wearily. The last thing I need is to have my family with access to noble authority, especially Edward and my father. It presents no small amount of temptation to Gilbert as well, and while he has stopped carelessly sleeping around, he remains stuck in his old view of the world. No one can reliably be trusted not to abuse their power when they still view other human beings as inherently less than them. I mean, no one can be reliably trusted not to abuse their power, full stop.

It seems Baldwin has spared no expense for my christening ceremony, or to make my family appear as 'noble' as possible. He purchased an entire estate for us, full of luxurious furniture and new clothes for everyone, although this didn't stop me from packing my own dresses. It irritates me how our family was uprooted in a single day and without warning, but I seem to be alone in this. I am sitting in a gorgeous bath attached to my room in our new home, properly cleaning myself for the first time in years. Typically, I would be ecstatic to have a proper bath, but I am too irritated to enjoy it. I eye the bowl of liquid soap that has been provided and realize I can finally analyze it's components. I dip my hand in and flood it with my mana, trying to discern its composition.

This is easier than I expected; it seems to have only two main ingredients, fat and lye. I could make this with wood ash, water, and a piece of meat. Why the fuck is this a luxury item? I mean, I know why. If they keep the recipe secret and limit supply, they have a cheaply made product at luxury prices. I would think selling it en masse might be worth the money, but I discovered over the past few years that most of my peers have little interest in it. I guess a lack of knowledge about bacteria combined with ignorance of the blissful feeling of being freshly clean has robbed them of their senses.

No matter, I know how to make it now. I'll make it popular if I have to scrub everyone clean myself. Actually, I may be able to conjure soap magically. I lose track of my thoughts as I finally scrub the dirt off myself with more than water. My daydreams of magically summoning soap and never feeling so gross again are dashed as I remember how long it takes to aspect mana properly. Conjuring lye and oil would be a massive waste of time I don't have. At least the ingredients are easy to come by.

I also clean my hair with something not quite like shampoo, another mixture of ashes that seems to include an assortment of herbs and egg whites. Done bathing, I examine the dress that has been set aside for me as I dry off. This seems to be a dress Baldwin ordered with measurements he assumed I would have by now—which means it clearly won't fit me at all. I could probably store a couple of cantaloupes in the top with room to breathe.

Next to it, on top of a note, is a gloriously ornate hairpin that is likely worth enough to feed Tommy and the residents of the House of Penance for several months, if not a full year. It's studded with rubies from top to bottom to match the highlights of red in the dress and, as I can clearly see in the expensive mirror for the first time in this life, my crimson red eyes. I've been told they are red before and have seen my reflection in water, but I've never seen them this clearly. I didn't expect them to look so . . . unearthly. They are even sharper and more vivid than my mother's. I quite like them, actually, especially when I compare them to Annie's brown eyes.

All in all the outfit is well chosen to suit me, if my figure were three balloons tied together with string as Baldwin imagined. Or if I'd ever had any interest in dressing like a mannequin in a museum. As I examine the hairpin, no doubt bought through the suffering of so many people, I feel my anger rising. I pick up the note.

> *My dearest fiancée, my darling Lillith,*
>
> *I have prepared for you a gift with all my love. I look forward to seeing you today, adorned as you always should have been, and representing your new noble house. Your introduction to noble society is an important one, and I expect you to represent both our houses with dignity.*
>
> *Baldwin*

The insincere scrap of paper reads like a lecture. I feel bile rising in my throat, and at that moment, standing naked in the washroom of this grand estate, Baldwin's bribe for my father and cage for me, I make a somewhat rash decision. I dig through my discarded dress and find the knife I carry as a last resort. I grab my hair in one hand, hold it above my head, and begin cutting. I hack away at my long hair with little care for the end result.

Finally, I stand in the middle of a pile of black hair on the ground and look in the mirror at one of the messiest pixie cuts I have ever seen. What a shame the beautiful hairpin will go to waste—I'll have to sell it and use the money for something more mundane like, I don't know, feeding and clothing the victims of the Tudor family's governance, maybe. I use the cooling water in the tub to rinse the loose hairs from my body and go to get dressed. I briefly imagine myself actually showing up with cantaloupes in my dress. As amusing as the idea is, I ultimately just put on one of my old dresses, sewn by my mother. This dress has the opposite problem, as I have grown since she last altered it, but it's comfortable enough.

I emerge from my new room to find my family waiting for me. Well, most of my family. My mother is still not very active and is apparently not invited in any case. It seems women are only allowed at this type of ceremony if they are the subject of it. My father, Gilbert, and Edward stand next to one another, dressed to the nines. All three of them widen their eyes as I emerge. Gilbert shifts from shock to an almost amused look, while Edward and my father quickly become angry.

Edward can't stand to see me disregarding the prestige he is so jealous of. He thinks I am genuinely stupid for not accepting a noble position earlier. Personally, I think it would have been idiotic to intentionally give men like him and my father even more power. In exchange for what? Increased scrutiny and less freedom? The only thing he is capable of is thinking about what he would do, and what he would do is live out his fantasies of greater power. Seeing me in a position he desires and rejecting it inspires far more fury than surpassing him in reading ability ever did.

My father, however, recognizes what I have done as the act of defiance that it is. His face is beet red and he begins to lecture me immediately. "LILLITH! Today of all days you have to throw one of your childish tantrums!"

I raise an eyebrow as he throws his own tantrum, but he doesn't notice.

"Do you have any idea what you've done? This is going to humiliate our entire family! This is going to humiliate Lord Baldwin! Some of the most prominent nobles in the city have been invited to witness this, and this is what you wish to present?"

"I mean, yeah, pretty much," I respond, disinterested in his ranting. His fists begin to literally shake as he holds back his rage, and I realize he wants to hit me. He is only stopped by the knowledge of his inevitable failure. The desire to impose his will without the ability to do so only makes him angrier, and he leans down close to my ear.

"You may be able to defy me like this, but Lord Baldwin won't stand for it. This will be your last act of defiance today. You will not humiliate us any further. Now go and put on the dress Baldwin prepared for you," he demands.

I cross my arms in response. "While that dress will certainly leave a lasting impression, I doubt it's the one you and Baldwin want it to be. I suppose I haven't quite filled out like he was hoping I would. If you are so concerned about embarrassing the family, I don't recommend insisting on this, but if it's important, I suppose . . ." I trail off as I let my meaning sink in. The red in his face takes on a new meaning and he stutters for a moment before recovering his anger.

"N-no matter! Lord Baldwin and I have chosen a name for our house. When the priest asks you, you will provide him with the name *Serf.* I will not take any argument about this, and if you defy us, there will be consequences!" he says, choosing a new battle.

I scoff. "Serf"? Baldwin is making fun of us. My father is here worried my hair will embarrass us while he's agreeing to a house name designed to signal our status as lesser than the "true" nobility. Baldwin wants me to go up in front of that crowd and declare we are his servants, and my father is eating out of his hands.

"Richard, do you know what *serf* means?" I ask, and his face wars between angry and perplexed.

"What does it matter what it means? It's the name we have chosen for ourselves and it's the name you will give the priest," he declares.

I roll my eyes, but I don't argue. There's no point explaining to him that he's being made a fool of.

"Whatever you say," I lie.

My brothers have nothing to say, and we prepare to head out. Edward, still refusing to speak directly to me, calls me a stupid bitch under his breath, and I just sigh wearily. It seems to be my fate in both lives that self-impressed men will call me names for not behaving in the way they decide I should. The way they would, with no real consideration for anything but their passing whims. It's hard to really care what Edward thinks at this point. Gilbert hears as well and tries to comfort me by rubbing his hand on my back. I appreciate the sentiment, but it's not really helpful.

When we leave the estate, we are greeted with the sight of an ornate carriage. Something about it irks me, like he is holding my hand to make sure I don't run away from the ceremony, but it's probably just standard practice. I'm just used to walking everywhere I go, and all the extravagance around me has me in a sour mood. I am at least relieved to avoid the morning crowds as we climb inside and let the driver begin the journey.

After a short ride, we arrive at the temple. This doesn't do much to improve my mood, as it is easily the tallest and most richly decorated structure in the city.

The coachman helps me out of the carriage and my family escorts me past the towering, ornately inscribed pillars at the entrance, and I am ushered off to a private room with a group of priests. I am confused at first as they circle me, and I feel the familiar feeling of control being asserted. I can no longer move my body. Without my mother's presence, my grief mana doesn't aid me to the same degree. In a city like this, however, there is always someone nearby in grieving, and I am able to maintain my consciousness. I can tell I do not currently have the power to break free, however, especially with multiple opponents asserting control.

I am not questioned this time, but I feel their will coursing through my mind and body. There are two separate intents behind their actions. They are trying to discern changes in my body, and I panic. After a moment I realize they don't recognize the changes I have made, however. Like with Baldwin, my understanding surpasses theirs. They appear to be mostly looking for STIs or disabling injuries, the kind of thing to send me to the House of Penance for. They find none and focus all their efforts on their second intent, that is, to mold my mind into a more compliant one.

This makes me even more furious, and I fight it with everything in me. I wonder if they do this to everyone or just women. Or perhaps just those they don't already control completely. The worry feeds my own anger and grief. My grief, when felt on behalf of others like this, seems to synergize with my mana, although not as well as when I feel the grief of others directly. I enter into a mental tug-of-war for control of my mind, pushing my entire being into denying the priests' intent. I don't have time to worry if they will be able to feel this and I am forced to bet everything on them being as unaware as Baldwin was.

I now understand why the ceremony was pushed up. Baldwin needs me to be more compliant, and he couldn't force it alone. This part of the ceremony is the only important part. I feel tears welling up in my eyes. In all my encounters in this life, this is the one that has inspired the most fear in me. I cannot allow my mind to be taken from me. I begin to sweat as I defend my mind, my will wrestling with the creeping, unnatural aching of the priests' divine magic. It's like my skin is too tight and I have too little blood, but I can dig my nails into the feeling and pull it out like an infected hangnail. Slowly, incredibly slowly, I push them back.

After what feels like an eternity, I finally regain control of my body. Much like in the moments after finally escaping that nightmare between sleep and wakefulness, that terrifying paralysis that denies you access to your limbs, the returning sense of control feels almost physical. It's over. We can finally move on to the rest of this pointless ceremony, and I am still the master of my own body.

I want to puke, but I hold it back with mana. The priests don't seem to notice they've failed as they withdraw their divine magic and lead me to the next stage of the ceremony, and I can't afford to let them realize.

I am led to the main sanctuary of the temple, an open space not dissimilar to a church or synagogue in my old life, except all of the pews circle a central stage. I'm nudged up onto the circular platform in the middle of a crowd of finely dressed noblemen, each attempting to appear taller, richer, and more dignified than those around them. Gasps and snickers ripple through the crowd at my hair and attire, and when I see Baldwin, I recognize the cold hatred of a man with injured pride, promising retribution with a single look. *Don't get angry yet, Baldwin, I'm far from done.* The priests pour water over my head and place a simple wooden tiara on my shorn hair. One leans in and asks me for my family's chosen name.

This makes it clear this ceremony was designed around men; allowing me to choose a family name that will only belong to my father and brothers is clearly a flaw in their designs, but I'll take it. Baldwin wants me to announce that we are his serfs. His slaves and servants. He wants me to announce we aren't real nobles, just tools he is using.

He wants me to tell the crowd what I represent to the nobility? I can do that. I can tell them exactly what bringing me here means for Baldwin, for every single one of them and their luxurious lives, built on the backs of others. I answer the priest quietly, and he looks at me with skepticism painted across his face but continues the ceremony.

"My lords," he announces, holding one of my hands in his, "it is not every day we get to introduce a new noble family to our beloved city, and it is my pleasure to present a new one to you today. May I present the noble lady, the first mage of her house and the beloved of Lord Baldwin Tudor, Lillith of Endings!"

CHAPTER THIRTY-ONE

Threats

My father glares scorching daggers at me as I stand on the podium, but that doesn't bother me in the slightest. Baldwin's gaze, on the other hand, is pure ice. I've openly defied him twice today, and I did it in front of the most important nobility in the city. I can feel his cold fury radiating off him as he stares at me. A tension in his jaw suggests his teeth are clenched, and the mana seeping out of his body quiets many of the other nobles in the room.

The priest on the platform with me is reciting some kind of prayer, but my eyes are locked on Baldwin. Our cold gazes hold through the rest of the ceremony. In this crowded room, one of us on a platform to be judged and the other surrounded by sycophants, we have a silent conversation and we say the same things. *You will pay. I will not bend, I will not rest, and I will not give an inch. What you have done will not be forgiven and no one can save you from me.* We each read this in the other's eyes and the rest of the world ceases to exist.

An eternity passes; a single moment passes. The priest finishes his ritual, and our quiet dialogue ends as he steps between us and leads me off the stage. I am directed back to my family and my father fumes. "I thought we had an understanding, Lillith! Do you have any idea what Lord Baldwin will do to us? He had a name picked for our house and you openly defied him! He can take the estate back, you idiot girl!"

I stare at my father, completely uninterested in his anger. "A serf is a servant and basically a slave. He wanted us to declare ourselves his property. Instead, I declared us something else entirely," I intonate.

"S-so what? I knew what it meant, and perhaps that's what we are! Unlike you, I can acknowledge my position and that of my betters! He is Lord Baldwin Tudor, you stupid bitch! If he wants us to declare that he owns us, that's what we do!" he splutters. I guess my father is the type with great pride until he meets someone rich enough to idolize.

It's always been strange to me how people will fight for their pride to the ends of the earth, even alienating their family and friends, until someone rich or famous enough comes along. That happens and, even when their idol treats them like a loathsome dog, they will happily bark along, abandoning their pride and defending their chosen master like their lives depend on it.

"It's quite all right, Lord Endings," Baldwin says, approaching us. "There is no need for your anger. If you don't mind, I'd like to take my fiancée on a walk. I'll talk to her about her choices today. Don't worry yourself a single moment more," he commands.

"L-lord Baldwin," my father stutters, "Of course, my lord, whatever you say! Thank you, my lord!"

This sends a pang through me. I haven't had a good relationship with my father in years. He didn't even consider letting me choose my own spouse or future. He didn't consider running with me either time a noble tried to claim me as property. He abandoned me when I was dying. Somehow, even after all that, it still hurts to see him being such a weasel. To yet again abandon me to abuse without so much as a protest but with a thank you.

"You are dismissed," Baldwin orders, sending a clear message to my family.

"Of course, Lord Baldwin, thank you," my father promptly responds, turning to leave. Edward seems to have already gone home, unwilling to spend more time around me than necessary. Gilbert, bless his heart, lingers. I can see the fear seizing his face. His hands are shaking and his knees wobble, but I see him preparing to speak. I just shake my head at him and he pauses. Yet again I have a silent conversation with a stare. *Go home, Gilbert. I'll be okay. I knew this was coming when I did this.*

After a moment of deliberation, Gilbert seems to understand the gist of my message, and he reluctantly follows my father.

"Come," Baldwin barks, and leads me away from the temple. I follow; I know he won't kill me yet, and I want him to take his anger out on me before he next sees Henry. I don't think he would hurt him too badly—he still needs him to control me—but a confrontation now is preferable either way.

We walk for a few minutes, taking different twists and turns down the road until we are in a mostly quiet alley, with only a few people passing by and a couple city guards playing dice. Baldwin spins on me and swings his fist into my stomach, doubling me over. I consider using a force shield but if this becomes a contest of mana, I will lose. He can't hurt my body in its current state, not easily.

Nevertheless, I fall to my knees and gasp for breath for a few moments.

Baldwin paces back and forth, waiting for me to recover. The guards look up briefly, see a young girl in a peasant dress gasping in front of a well-dressed noble, and go back to their game of dice.

"You humiliated me today, Lillith," Baldwin lectures. "You humiliated me twice."

At this, I have finally regained my breath, but he grabs me by my freshly shortened hair with both hands and drives my face into his knee. I splutter, spitting out blood from a cut inside my mouth. "Do you know what the other nobles will be saying? That I picked a whore to marry. An ugly commoner. An idiot girl who can't even pick a proper name." I recover as he says this and begin to stand, but he punches me across the jaw and knocks me to the ground again. I spin this time, falling to my stomach and facing away from him.

His hits aren't hitting as hard as he thinks; my body is stronger and sturdier than even his, I suspect. That's not the point, however. The point is to demonstrate his power over me. It's why he chose an alley with guards to witness what he was doing. "I'm going to have to kill at least one of them, you know. Just to teach them all a lesson. Just so my wife won't be treated as the shame of my house," he chastises, pacing behind me again.

I pick up a rock in one hand, closing my fist around it as I climb to my hands and knees. I'm here to let him take his anger out on me, but I'm still going to get a hit in. I'll probably regret this too, but I have other plans than just letting him vent. He kneels down closer to continue berating me as I begin to recover my footing. "Is this how you intend to behave when we marry? Like a petulant chi—"

I wing my rock-laden fist full force into the side of his head, sending him to the dirt.

I hit considerably harder than he has managed to hit me so far, and it takes him a moment to recover. At this, the two guards are finally roused and begin to gather their spears to confront me, but Baldwin pushes himself away from the ground, holds out a hand to waylay them, and clambers up off his knees. He spits out blood, along with what looks like a couple teeth. His jaw is broken and clearly sitting wrong on his skull for a moment. He stands and uses his hands to force it back into place, where I see it rapidly adjusting under his skin and hear the sickening sound of crunching bone and squelching meat. Even his torn skin begins to knit itself back together, and he completely heals in less than a minute.

Of course, if he can alter my body, he can alter his. Just another thing to plan for.

"I'll handle her," he says, and the guards salute him, offer their apologies, and return to their game. "You're going to regret that, Lillith of Endings," he says, fixing me with a furious glare. With that I see him cast. I don't recognize the mana he uses and try to put up a force shield this time but quickly learn it is useless.

It's wind mana, or something of that nature, and he uses it to hold me captive in the air, tendrils of wind rapidly blowing around each limb and holding them in place. He uses pure mana to shatter my force shield, leaving me defenseless.

"I know a threat when I hear one. Let me educate you on why I am not afraid of the ending you bring," he fumes, hate-filled eyes locked on mine. He runs his hand gently along my face, caressing my cheek with his thumb, then moving it down to my throat and holding it in a vice grip. He pulls his other fist back and swings it into my jaw. My head whips back a little but is held in place by his grip on my neck. He pulls his fist back another time and hammers down on my eye.

He doesn't move quickly. He doesn't hit me with rapid punches or try to beat me so I don't know what's happening. No, each punch is slow and deliberate. His fist is covered in rings that increase its brutality. He pulls back and aims with precision, ensuring each hit lands to maximum effect. Even my body isn't invulnerable, and I am bloodied and bruised long before he finishes his assault. Finally, he feels like his point is made, and he throws me to the ground like garbage. "Do not challenge me again, or it will be much worse than this," he warns, and stalks off.

I wheeze on the ground for a moment, trying to regain my senses after his beating. After a moment I sit up, wiping blood from my left eye. The blood is quickly replaced as I realize I am badly bleeding from a wide gash that vertically bisects my brow and cheek. I channel mana to close it up, but it doesn't work with anywhere near the speed Baldwin's healing had. No matter. I crawl over to where Baldwin fell earlier and begin looking through the dirt. I struggle to focus out of the one eye without blood in it.

After a few moments, I find what I am looking for. A small puddle of blood on the ground with two teeth in it. I smile and pick both teeth up, clenching them in my fist before I force myself to stand and begin my walk home. All things considered, today was a good day. I am one step closer to Henry, and Baldwin is one step closer to death.

CHAPTER THIRTY-TWO

Blood in the Water

Baldwin

That fool child—her stubborn struggling can only amuse me so far. It will bring me no end of joy when she finally realizes her place. For now, she has created a great deal of work for me. Had she done as she was told, her pathetic little noble house could have at least ridden on my coattails or hidden in my shadow. Had she declared her house my property, as I'm certain she was instructed, none would have dared insult them for fear of insulting me.

Instead, she walked into that ceremony, dressed like a beggar, her hair cut like a man's, and declared her house over before it started. Her childish attempt at a threat only served to undermine her. It makes me want to spit just thinking about it! Why can't people understand when you know better than them? I do not have the time to spend validating my choice of wife in the eyes of lesser nobles, dammit!

Of course, if they knew what I know about her magical abilities, I would never have to worry about this. If she wasn't so damn resistant to divine power, this wouldn't be a problem either. I tamed a fucking duke with my divine magic, and a child is shaking it off like it's nothing. I don't know how she convinces herself that the gibberish she spits at me is an answer to my demands, but I do have a theory about her resistance to physical change. A theory that may have been confirmed today.

I have fought with grown men three times her size and I've never been hit so hard. The bitch managed to break my jaw—a thirteen-year-old girl not using mana. I don't know what she was hoping to accomplish, but she revealed her hand today. Either her circle targets some sort of strength-enhancing endo-aspected mana, or she is making her own body modifications somehow.

Both options seem impossible, but clearly one is true. She certainly didn't aspect a strength-focused mana naturally, not at her size. She could never have embodied it. She could have built it into her circle, but the secret to making that work is hidden from all but the highest-ranking nobles. I suppose she may have discovered it herself, as she did with a mana circle that allows you to leave. It's also possible Godfrey taught it to her, but the man's stupidity doesn't reach those depths. He would lose all hope of regaining his former glory if he shared a royal secret like that.

I consider the other option far more likely. I dismissed it almost entirely at first for a few reasons, but considering my divine modifications are failing, it is the most likely cause. I have been assuming a normal base state when modifying her. This means I have been expending my effort returning her to that state before my changes could take effect. I have to figure out what state she is in before I can successfully modify her, which means I'll have to break her. Whether through divine magic or more mundane means, I need her cooperation.

I am yet again impressed with her. Using divine magic is one thing, but if she had access to that, my control never would have worked in the first place. I haven't gotten enough information out of her, but I've gotten enough to know she isn't faking it. It was extremely unlikely in any case; divinely chosen like me only appear once every hundred years at most. I am likely the only natural divine mage in all the kingdom, probably the entire world. It's impossible for a girl her age to have earned divine powers through the temple, and the Collector has never allowed a woman access to his powers.

This means she has been doing it with mana alone. She wouldn't be the first to try it, but she would be the first to succeed without mutilating and maiming themselves. She was able to enhance her muscles and her durability as well, if that beating I gave her is any indication. And to do it at such a level that my changes still haven't reverted them all? She must have some sort of genius insight into the workings of the human body. She is the first to successfully defy the Collector in this way.

This only makes her more desirable. With her genius collared and cataloged among my assets, I'll be the next king. My heirs will be a force to be reckoned with as well. I suppose I'll have to produce them in a dark room at first if she keeps rebuffing my designs. Oh well, it is well known you can't have everything in a wife, and I can always keep a mana light on her expression alone. I do have to keep the temple from investigating her, however; I suppose I'll need to get her exempt from confession. It would be a waste to have such a brilliant asset wasted with . . . such an undignified punishment.

"I hear he fell in love with a local whore; can you believe he invited us to see such a low and stupid girl be inducted as a noble?" I hear a man's voice whispering as I enter one of the finer restaurants in the noble district. I usually have the chefs at the estate cook for me—they are the finest in the city, after all—but I need to make a point today. I have been lenient with the nobility in recent years. Coming home with a member of the royal lineage under my control had successfully cowed them, and few dared openly ridicule me.

This man's remarks confirm my fears, however. I have been complacent. I have allowed them to grow too comfortable, and Lillith openly embarrassing me today pushed a few of them over the edge. Even if I killed her now, aside from losing a valuable asset, it would just be an admission of a mistake. They already see the engagement as a sign of weakness, thanks to her stubborn childishness, and that would just be confirmation I have grown weak.

Thus, I find myself in a restaurant, a place for the poorer nobles to find fine dining. "I hear he chose her because of the short hair," the man's wife replies. "I heard he wanted a boy the same age and only chose her so she could produce an heir!" she chuckles, reveling in the scandal behind the implication.

"Maybe he did," the man smirks. "I could see 'her' being a boy. That was an awfully strong jawline, and did you see how broad her shoulders were? It wouldn't surprise me a bit if this 'Lillith' was just a pretty boy and Lord Baldwin planned to raise a couple of bastards as his heirs!"

I approach slowly to get a better look at them. The couple is dining with two other couples around a round table and have their backs to me.

The woman clearly doesn't notice her friends going quiet and pale, as she continues joking, "Oh, she looks a bit too pretty for that, even if she was dressed in rags and looked like rabid dogs had been at her hair. But who knows, maybe you are right! Maybe that silly name she chose was because *he* has an extra ending?" She and her husband laugh together for a moment, still oblivious to the fear in their friends' eyes.

This couple looks perfect, as I don't recognize them. They are likely the cousins of some viscount or baron, hardly important for the meal they are eating. They weren't even at the ceremony; street nobles of their level weren't invited. The man has apparently never been to a christening if he doesn't even realize his wife would never have been allowed to attend. Just rumors from the fools who did show up. Perhaps I should thank Lillith. I have needed an excuse to remind the nobility in this city to fear me.

"Do you think so?" I ask, pulling a chair from another table and sitting between them. The entire restaurant is silent; I can practically hear the lord's and lady's rapidly beating hearts as they, too late, realize their mistake. "Tell me more," I say, pulling the man's plate in front of me and using his fork and knife to cut through his steak. "Tell me all about what you think of my chosen wife," I command.

"S-she's lovely, my lord," the man splutters. "Truly a prize for us all to envy!" A bead of sweat forms on his head.

"Really?" I ask, raising an eyebrow. "You wouldn't lie to me, would you?" I put a bite of steak in my mouth and stare at the nervous man.

"N-no, my lord, I wouldn't dare to!" he reassures me, and the other nobles at the table fidget nervously, a couple of them with tears forming in their eyes.

"I'm so glad to hear that!" I declare jovially, to his brief relief. "So you were at the ceremony, then?" I add, returning to a cold, expectant stare. The man realizes his mistake.

"I'm sorry, my lord, I—I d-didn't—"

I use half a dozen wind drills to tear holes through his body. His wife wails and people around the table scream as his blood sprays across their faces. After a moment everyone in the restaurant attempts to flee.

"DID I TELL YOU THAT YOU COULD LEAVE?" I shout, magically enhancing my voice, and the room freezes. "Take your seats," I order the now mostly quiet restaurant. They all hurry to comply, and I smell the air sour as at least one person soils themselves. The only sound that remains is the man to my left, kept alive for now with divine magic, attempting to scream without the aid of intact lungs, and his wife sobbing to my right. "Now," I continue, addressing his wife, "if you were not at my fiancée's christening ceremony, do you care to explain what exactly you were talking about?"

She starts sobbing louder, unable to answer. A brave woman at the table tries to answer for her. "My lord, I'm certain she was just repeating baseless rumors, she is only visiting and she didn't know—"

I hold up a finger to silence her. "I didn't ask you, did I?" The gossiper is reaching out to her struggling husband. "Well?" I ask. "Explain yourself."

She starts taking in sharp breaths, trying desperately to regain her ability to speak through her sobbing and answer me. I don't have the patience to wait, and I impale her with a spear of wind. She collapses on the table, joining her husband in his suffering but no longer fighting sharp breath.

I continue to cut the steak and take another bite. "I'll say this once. I will not stand for insults or assumptions about my house. I don't care if it is my servants, my slaves, my dogs, or my chosen fiancée. You will not use any of them as an excuse to disrespect me." The brave woman from earlier reaches out to the bleeding woman next to me and holds her hand in a vain attempt to comfort her. I notice their hair and eyes are similar, and I realize they must be sisters. That explains how she still has the audacity to look at me with hate.

No matter; she can do nothing about it. All these insects should have known better than to disrespect me. I take a drink of water from a glass on my left which has a swirling pattern of blood permeating it. I don't particularly enjoy the taste, but drinking it is effective for inspiring fear and asserting dominance.

I feel the power in my mana spike as my inner aspect is fed by the people around me. This display should do nicely for now.

CHAPTER THIRTY-THREE

The Light in Her Eyes

I make it home, to the new estate my family lives in, only to find a small crowd surrounding the entrance. I recognize a couple of guards who work with my father, or used to work with my father, I guess, but most of them I have never seen before. I rub my temple out of habit but immediately regret it as pain radiates throughout my face. Instead, I just sigh wearily and approach the back of the crowd to attempt to navigate my way to the entrance.

"Now, what exactly do you think you are doing here?" I am almost immediately stopped by an older, sneering woman at the back of the crowd. "This is no place for beggars, girl, away with you!" she shoos. I lazily tilt my head toward her and raise one eyebrow, only to yet again regret expressing my exasperation.

The cut on my eye freshly trickling blood down my face, I respond with clear irritation, "While I'm certain your diligence is well-intentioned, I would greatly appreciate it if you simply fucked off instead of bothering me with it."

The woman's eyes widen in fury and she snaps at me, "Clearly you have already been shown how welcome you are around here, so scurry off while I'm being polite!" I examine the woman for a moment. Her dress is of similar quality to mine and, all things considered, I am actually cleaner than she is. What exactly is this lady's problem?

"Why," I ask through a sigh, "do you give a shit where I am? What does it matter to you?"

I am met by a smug, knowing grin and she puts her hands on her hips, clearly excited to answer the question for some reason. "I'll have you know this is my family's estate. My cousin, Lord Richard, was just raised to baron today!" she announces proudly. "And one thing a new noble house does not need is a beggar looking for pity loitering about. Now, off with you!" I grimace internally as she introduces herself as my father's cousin. I suppose he comes by his glowing personality honestly. I don't have the energy for distant relatives, though.

"Look, lady, between you and me, I don't want to be here much either. Unfortunately, that decision was taken from both of us. We'll have to suffer my presence together, I'm afraid," I dismiss her, and go back to what I was doing. As I see a man next to the woman reach for me, I put up a thin force shield. I use a minor outward force that won't knock anyone over but will make it more difficult to grab me, like reaching through a block of Jell-O. This is enough to give him pause, and he looks at his hand with confusion, then starts bickering about something with the rude woman.

My efforts don't pay off much, and I just receive a lot of attempted shoves and further rude remarks from my "family" but don't progress through the crowd. After my first interaction, I begin to recognize familiar features on the faces in the group. My father's jaw or my mother's eyes. I suppose I should have expected this, vultures descending on my family once they smelled fortune. I don't really blame them, honestly; a lot of these people are so desperate for a better life that they will grasp onto anything they can find. It still feels like a slimy way to do it, however. Especially if that woman before was any indication.

Irritated, I decide to try a spell I have been considering for a while. I'm certain I can do this but haven't had much need for it recently. I know, roughly, the force of gravity. I can't guarantee it is identical to Earth's gravity, but I figure I would have seen more noticeable differences if this world varied much.

With this in mind, I calculate the amount of force I should need based on my estimated mass, and apply an upward force directly beneath myself. This takes a massive amount of mana, far more than simply altering my weight, but I begin to float. As I rise, I also create a light barrier under my dress so any creeps in the family can stare into the void it creates. A good deal of excited chittering quiets as I rise above the crowd. I lessen the force once I reach a suitable height, out of reach of the people below. I then apply light force behind me to push me in the direction of the door to the estate. I also present my middle finger to the woman from before, although I'm not certain the gesture translates.

I successfully reach the front of the crowd and stop the force behind me, slowly easing up on the upward force and descending in front of the door. My display of magic apparently has a greater impact than my smashed grapefruit of a face, as the crowd parts beneath me and allows me through the entrance. As I look back at the gaping crowd, I am pleased to have bypassed the obstacle, and even more pleased that I can, it seems, fly. Or float for a few yards, at least.

Truth be told, with the mana I had to expend for that short distance and the mechanisms it uses, I don't think I'll be truly flying for a good while. Especially at speed; that would be like entering a free fall anytime I had to travel and burning up all my magic as I do it. If I want to hurtle to my probable death at speed, the traditional down direction is as good as any already. Still, it was pretty cool.

My brief satisfaction is cut off as I enter the house, however, and take in the scene inside. My father and Edward are standing in the middle section of our bifurcated staircase, receiving the visiting "family and friends," who I had never met in my life, as if they were Father's loyal subjects. They are both wearing swords they don't know how to use in order to look more like noblemen. Each visitor is addressing Father as "Lord Serf" and offering some kind of tribute, mostly money. I realize the moron is still trying to claim the name Baldwin chose for him, and I nearly face-palm before stopping myself from causing more pain.

He's going to regret that later if he doesn't correct people now. It's too late, he is Lord Endings now; nothing is going to change that. Trying to claim a different name won't impress Baldwin, it'll just piss off the temple. More concerning is that he has been a lord for maybe a few hours and he is already taking bribes and trying to rule over his relatives. This is why I wanted to avoid a noble title; there are now men using my accomplishments to spit on everything I believe.

I do reevaluate the crowd, however. Rather than being a line of vultures, it's possible they are being extorted. Some of them happily, apparently, if the woman outside is to be believed. Some of these people may not have wanted to come here, however. I'll need to investigate this later and ensure my father hasn't used his nobility to harm anyone here.

Even that is not what truly upsets me, however; something else draws my full attention. He has dragged my mother out to receive guests with him. She is clearly upset, overwhelmed, and completely at a loss. He has her on a chair he brought out just for this and his hand rests on her shoulder. Why would he make her do this with him in the state she is in? I march up the stairs, parting the crowd like the Red Sea, rage coloring my face as I go to rescue her.

It's only when her face pales and I see emotion splash across her face that I realize my mistake. She has her eyes locked on my bloody and battered face. Pure horror controls her, and I feel power course through my mana as her heart cries out for her daughter. I often forget that to her, I am still her little innocent girl. Seeing me punished like this causes a shift in her, and I see her mind racing.

Her gaze shifts to my father, who has the audacity to look smug as he evaluates the result of my defiance. Even Edward, my jealous, prideful, asshole of a brother, is looking at me with shock, horror, and even a little bit of guilt. Not my father. And my mother sees it. Decades of living and raising a family with him, years of watching me, and her own intuition seems to put the pieces together. She has no way of knowing if he did this himself or left it to someone else, but I can see in her steely gaze that she knows he is related to it somehow.

Her mouth opens and a wail escapes, the kind of animalistic cry only a grieving mother can make. It morphs into a scream of rage as she slowly rises, and before anyone can respond, she descends on him like a rabid dog. The two fall to the ground and the people around them scatter, one man stumbling down the stairs. Her long-neglected fingernails, jagged from nervous biting, claw at his flesh while she screams in his face.

"SHE IS OUR DAUGHTER, RICHARD! YOU ABANDONED OUR DAUGHTER AGAIN! YOU ARE SMIRKING AT THE BLOODIED FACE OF OUR BABY GIRL!"

She leaves long, shallow gashes on his face as she refuses to relent. After only a second he shoves her off him, first pushing her up and then using a foot to kick her across the stairs. I don't know if his fury completely blinds him. I don't know if his humiliation over his wife attacking him in front of a crowd he wanted to impress takes over. I don't know if he has wanted to do this for years and is only now emboldened by the legal protection of nobility. Whatever it is, as he runs after her crumpled body, he clumsily draws his sword in a fit of rage and tries to swing it down onto her. He doesn't get the chance. A wave of targeted force picks him up off the ground and throws him to the wall. His sword clatters next to him and he falls to the floor, disoriented as he tries to figure out what happened. He rolls so he is sitting with his back to the wall and wipes his bloody nose on his sleeve.

I first look at my mother, who appears to be recovering with Ed's help. Confirming she is okay, I descend on him like a storm, nailing him to the wall with force mana. My cold gaze meets his confused, then terrified, eyes. He begins to struggle as I close the distance and slam my palm into the wall behind his head. I lean in next to his ear and whisper, "You just tried to kill my mother. Do you know why you are still alive?"

He doesn't respond, but I can feel his labored breathing quicken as I continue, "You are alive because if you die, or are crippled, my fiancé will probably become my guardian. Mom's too. So you keep clinging to him. You pray to your precious Collector that he lives a long, long life. Because as soon as it's no longer more dangerous for you to be dead than alive? As soon as Mom isn't technically safer while you have a pulse? You are a dead man."

I go to leave then, but a thought occurs to me. "By the way, the church declared us the house of Endings. They did this at the ceremony Baldwin requested. You are challenging them both by declaring a different name, you fucking idiot."

With that, I leave the terrified rodent who fathered me panting in fear on the ground and call back to the crowd, "Someone take him to a clinic, he probably has a broken rib." If the clinic reports injuries this may raise some eyebrows, but no more than a crowd of witnesses. I should have hidden before my mom saw me, but it's too late to put this genie back in the bottle. Fortunately, my father still relies on me to give his noble title legitimacy and Baldwin still needs me. Nothing will come of it.

I move to my mother, who is panting, tears running down her face, but okay. Edward is not my favorite person, but he is at least my ally as he drapes her arm around his shoulder and helps me walk her to an unused room. We lay her down on the bed and I sit down next to her. "I need to talk to Mom alone," I tell Edward, and he looks at me sharply, his face softening again as he sees my wounds.

"Lillith, I—I . . . You know what, never mind. Let me know when you are done," he agrees, letting out a frustrated scoff before leaving me alone with Mom. I look after him as he leaves. Somewhere, deep down, buried in all that pride and selfishness, is a kernel of empathy. Not a lot, but maybe it can be nursed. I will worry about that later, however.

"Lily, I'm so sorry, I'm so, so sorry," my mom weeps, her arm draped across her eyes. "I haven't been here for you. I still have three kids to take care of and I've let you down. Left you to . . . him. I'm so sorry."

I just run my hand through her hair. "It's all right, Mom. This isn't on you, I promise. I'm all right. I love you," I reassure her. "Actually, Mom, there is something I need to tell you."

She sniffs but nods, signaling me to continue.

Our conversation feels like it lasts forever, and I revel in the joy of my mother's voice. She is heartbroken and scared. She is worried about losing her children. But she is so alive! As our conversation draws to a close, I see the light of hope in her eyes for the first time since Henry was taken.

CHAPTER THIRTY-FOUR

Routine

The next few weeks pass without much fanfare. I rarely work at Godfrey's Bookstore anymore. Instead, I spend most days at the House of Penance and most nights investigating Baldwin. My mother is still plagued by worry, but she is now equally determined to be there for her kids. The entire estate lights up with my mother's presence, and I feel more hope than I have in a long time. Her grief hasn't disappeared. I am uniquely qualified to evaluate this, and she feels it just as deeply and thoroughly as ever. If anything, her depth of feeling has expanded with her husband's betrayals and my injuries.

She is with us though. Completely present and completely invested. My father, on the other hand, has sobered up from his glee at ascending to nobility. When the momentary rage eased—the rage that erased my presence from his mind when he drew a sword on my mother—and the humiliation faded, he grew terrified and paranoid. The feeling of security he got from Baldwin's support held on a while, until Baldwin visited for another interrogation. Relaying my threat to Baldwin like a tattling child only resulted in annoying the man and getting dismissed. Baldwin knows the same thing I do: if my father dies, I just become Baldwin's ward until the wedding.

The only reason Baldwin hasn't killed him himself is, I suspect, caution. He can handle any real consequences of it, but there are already questions surrounding our engagement. Anything that can be perceived as overeagerness might draw the attention of more powerful mages. So my father lives to spare Baldwin the wrong sort of attention and to spare me from Baldwin's attention. My father has realized he isn't safe and has been avoiding me. There have been no further processions of distant relatives and friends. Between my mother and me, the theory that "looks can't kill" has been put to the test enough to confine him to his chambers.

Baldwin has started visiting three times a week instead of one, trying his best to mold me into his ideal designs. Even this may seem like eagerness, and I suspect he is pushing the envelope out of frustration. Now aware of his attempts, I can fend him off fairly easily now. I have even, finally, succeeded in a couple of changes. Most notably, I have finished the poison. I ran into some . . . risk assessment issues with glands for both a toxin and its activator. I realized it would be too easy to cross-contaminate the poison and the activating protein if they were excreted from the same source. So I went with another design. Now my blood contains a toxin similar to the golden poison frog's but is completely harmless unless combined with a protein I can choose to include in my sweat.

I haven't tested it out yet, on account of the need to murder someone to do so, but this is the field I really shine in. I'd love to test it on Baldwin, and I suspect I will, but his divine healing concerns me. If I am going to do it, I want to do it when it will have the maximum effect and I have plans B through Z in place. Currently, Baldwin considers himself so far beyond me that he's sure I wouldn't dare try to kill him. He sees my acts of defiance as temper tantrums at worst. I don't see much benefit in putting him on guard early.

Edward approaches me to talk every few days, but always loses his nerve. At first, he couldn't look me in the face at all, but now that my accelerated healing has, mostly, helped me recover, he can meet my eyes . . . for a moment. I still have a light scar over my left eye; the wound was too severe to heal completely. It's difficult to see if you don't know it's there, but Edward does. He always focuses on it and looks away before saying whatever he wants to say. I want to push him, but his pride has grown no less fragile. I have to wait for now.

Gilbert still visits the House of Penance with me most days, and we talk a lot on our walks back and forth. He struggles to break free from the mindset he was raised with, but he is open and honest enough that my opinion of him is slowly improving.

My etiquette lessons have continued as usual, to my benefit. Sybillia has been extremely helpful in our deal. She always has a hint of guilt in her eyes and a bit of sorrow in her soul when she does it, but she has given me information on Baldwin I can use. She started giving me this information after my last confrontation with Baldwin, and it's mostly information she shouldn't know. Based on all this, I believe she is giving me information that Baldwin, in his arrogance, wants me to have. It's useful anyway.

The stains of Baldwin's filthy soul can be found all over the city. I could almost find each solely from the grief that emanates from them. Every person Sybillia sends me to is another victim of Baldwin's. Someone who insulted or defied Baldwin at some point. I have met mothers of murdered and enslaved children, widowers of women who tried to reject his advances, and widows of servants or workers who failed to meet his standards. I even met a noblewoman whose sister and brother-in-law were murdered in front of her in a restaurant. That one was particularly hard to hear, and she glared at me when I came to meet her. It seems that particular incident was not unrelated to me.

Just a few days ago I met with the children of a tailor who died for failing to remove a stain from a favored tunic. The message Baldwin is trying to send me is crystal clear. Those who defy him suffer and die. The families of those who defy him never recover. Obey, or else. The message he is actually sending is even clearer. Baldwin is an insecure man-child. All his nobility and power can't protect his pride, and it will shatter with a pinprick. The only way he can live with himself is by ruining the lives of the people who make him feel insecure.

This is his response to me declaring myself his ending. Completely unworried about me following through while also unable to live with the challenge. Bless him for it. His arrogance is the sharpest weapon I have. If he were worried about more than his hurt feelings, I wouldn't stand a chance. If he looked under just the right rock, it would all be over. Instead, he is leading me to all his victims. Idiotic little prick.

I have another lead for tonight, one of his former maids and her mother, but first I need to visit the House of Penance. The first batch of mages has now left the circle, and I spend each day teaching them to suppress their mana. I do my best to explain how important this is, but not all of them receive the advice as well as others.

I haven't just been working hard on changing my body. I have added heat, cold, and air mana to my arsenal, and I'm trying to get the hang of them. I had to push hard and sacrifice sleep to aspect them so quickly, but I need them to counter Baldwin's wind mana. As Gilbert and I walk to the house, I practice creating small gusts of air at different temperatures.

"Are you sure this is safe?" Gilbert asks.

"It's just a little hot air, it's not dangerous. Why do you ask?" I inquire.

"Not that—the kids, the people in that house. Are you sure teaching them magic is safe? You aren't worried at all?" he asks, the anxiety clear in his voice. I pause my dribbling for a long moment before responding to him.

"No. It's not safe. I worry about it every day. I see the look in some of those kids' eyes and a chill runs down my spine. At least one of them is going to do something foolish, it's almost certain," I say, only causing the furrow in his brow to grow more pronounced. "The residents of the house worry me too. They can't leave to make bad decisions right now, but they are occasionally collected by the temple. We don't know why they do that and we don't know when they do it. Any one of the residents could be taken and bring the entire temple down on our heads."

He looks horrified, as he often does when I mention my opposition to the temple. I suppose he hadn't considered the risk of making them an enemy.

"Why are you doing it, then? You know it's dangerous; you know it's a massive risk that could come down on you at any moment! I don't understand. You are smarter than that!" he bursts out, scared and upset at the same time.

I examine his face for a moment before responding. "Smarter than that, huh? Well, let me ask you, what is the alternative? What other options do I have?"

He just looks confused at the question.

"Not doing it?" he ventures, and I give him a disbelieving look.

"A house full of people, completely rejected and stepped on by society. A group of kids used to stealing food for the nearest street gang just for the privilege of eating a small portion of it. Brainwashed and manipulated people cut off from their families, unable to so much as walk out of their unlocked prison, and you want me to, what? Put my hands over my ears and close my eyes?" I ask, and Gilbert looks lost for words.

"That's not what I meant, but surely there are less dangerous ways to help them!" he responds.

I nod to him. "Yes, some of them. I only know one way to fight brainwashing though. For those residents, it's teach them this or abandon them to their fate. Yeah, I can feed the kids. I can house them as well, and I will. And what will that do in the long run? Protect one group of kids while cities all over this forsaken country continue to let them starve?" I ask.

I let him contemplate for a moment before I continue. "I'm not going to stop here, Gilbert. This isn't about making the people I've met happier, it's not even about saving Henry. This is about everyone. I want to make knowledge available to everyone, not just the rich. The same knowledge I only barely managed to get lucky enough to read. What happens to the kids then? Do the risks go away?"

I want to explain more. How violent things will have to get before they improve. How many kids will starve or be killed in the meantime. How I need people to have the means to fight back. Full-on treason is a bit too large a secret to entrust to Gilbert, however. I'm not sure he would understand anyway. I have to take huge risks to effect any real change, and I have to give the people I want to help the option to fight for themselves. It doesn't matter that some of them will get greedy. It doesn't matter that I can't trust every single person.

I can either accept the world as it is, replace the current dictator with my own rule, or give the downtrodden the tools to fight for their own lives and decide their own fates. I can't decide they don't deserve to fight for themselves, and I can't tell them it's too unsafe to give them that chance. I can stop the ones who try to hurt someone else with the new power, but that's as much as I can do. Gilbert won't understand that, however.

It's far too easy to interpret a lack of empathy as intelligence. Too easy to rationalize to yourself that without controlling people, it's too risky to give them a choice. This is often the thought process of those who want to remain more powerful than others. If I convince myself it's too risky to give other people the same opportunities I had, I get to remain the most powerful person in the room. As much as Gilbert has improved, it's evident in his view of women that he still believes to an extent that people need to be protected from their own autonomy.

"It still seems like an unnecessary risk," he says as we approach the house. "What will we do when one of them tries to be promoted to nobility?"

"Well, I have done my best to warn them about that, but when it happens, I imagine I will have to commit acts of violence to protect the rest. They did accept the risk when they agreed, and the risk alone is no reason not to give them a chance. Otherwise, we'd be using the same reasoning the nobility uses to keep the knowledge from us," I say, and push open the big wooden door.

We are swarmed with excited kids as we enter. I speak with all the current residents of the house and help the new mages understand their power. I teach lessons on suppressing and aspecting mana while Gilbert passes out food and supplies. With the sale of the hairpin, it's fairly easy to keep them fed and cleanly clothed. I even bring some of my new homemade soap, which only a few of them bother to try. I also have to pull Ozzy aside and have a private conversation with him, one I don't want Diana to hear.

Once I am done speaking to Ozzy, I also talk to Tommy, who has been helping me find other groups of street kids. Eventually, after the city lord and Baldwin have been dealt with, I plan to set up a similar situation in other parts of town, even other cities. I also suspect this isn't the only House of Penance here. Satusmor is too large for the number of people in this house to represent their entire community.

I'm going to get caught, I know that. But if I protect everyone as long as I can, if this circle gets spread to enough people, it will be too late. Especially if the noble leadership in the city has fallen apart. Most nobles won't be able to take advantage of the circle until their children are older, and the common people will have an advantage. It's a massive risk, but it's one I need to take.

Once information has been shared and the people have been fed, I pack up with Gilbert and we head out. I want to meet the maid Sybillia told me about.

CHAPTER THIRTY-FIVE

For Cruelty's Sake

As the sun goes down I arrive alone at a small home in the poorer quarter of the city. I feel the grief emanating from the small wooden building as I approach. This isn't the sharp grief of a fresh loss but the numbing grief of someone who has given up. I take a deep breath and knock on the door.

It takes a few moments, but a middle-aged blonde woman with dark circles decorating her eyes answers. "What do you want?" Her terse greeting assaults me.

"Hello, ma'am. I'm very sorry to bother you. My name is Lillith. I was hoping I could speak to you and your daughter," I respond gently.

"What for?" she asks, keeping her body between me and the inside of the little hovel.

I have been through this song and dance a few times. "Someone close to me is getting involved with Baldwin Tudor. I was told you might have something to say about him?" I ask, flinching as her face is overcome with rage for a moment.

"Tell them to get the fuck away from him if it's a possibility, and if not, may the Collector have mercy on them," she spits out before literally spitting on the ground and starting to close the door.

"Please!" I beg, putting my hand on the door. "This is important, I'm begging you. I don't know what I'll do without your help! He wants me to marry him, I don't know what to do . . ." At this confession and the desperation in my voice, she seems to understand I am asking for myself, and her face softens.

"Oh, sweetheart," she says. "I'm so sorry. Come in." She leads me into the one-room home, where her daughter is sitting on the bed and looking at me nervously out of one eye. Her right eye is completely missing, and that side of her face is marred with severe burns. She doesn't speak as I enter. "What do you want to know?" the older woman asks.

"If it's okay," I say, "can you just tell me your story?"

She is quiet for several moments at this request. She looks at her daughter, who gives her a barely perceptible nod. With that permission, she finally speaks up.

"It's not really my story, but yes, I can tell you," she agrees. "It started about a year and a half ago. Abby, my daughter, was hired as a maid at the Tudor estate. She had been working at our family's flower stall, and Lord Baldwin approached to order an arrangement. He was polite, charming, and seemed to be enamored. She was taken with him immediately," she starts before taking a long contemplative pause. My heart already starts to break.

She continues, "He came to the stall to see her every day for a month. He flirted with her, promised her a better life, and eventually offered her a job. She was ecstatic. I had never before seen her glow like when she accepted that job. She thought he might marry her someday. That he was hiring her as an excuse to spend time with her. She went to work the next day.

"At first, my husband, James, and I didn't notice anything wrong. She seemed okay when I saw her. But I started seeing her less and less. She started forgetting things and losing time. She would refuse to see us when we tried to visit. After a month, it was like she was a different person. We weren't allowed near the estate anymore. We weren't allowed to see our daughter." Her voice quavers as she struggles through the story. I give her the time to compose herself.

After a while she regains control of her voice. "James got desperate. A man contacted him offering to help him get onto the estate. He took him up on the offer and snuck onto the Tudor estate. He crept past the guards and made his way into the home, but his search of the house found no one there. Then, in the servant's quarters, he found a hidden room. A bookcase had been moved, and an opening in the wall was in its place. That's where he found Abby. Chained and barely dressed. She had bruises all over her body, and her eye had been removed.

"The keys to her chains were hanging on the wall and he freed her. He brought her home to me, using the cover of darkness. Lord Baldwin was waiting for him. He knew he had been coming; he'd sent the man to help us, and he let him find her. The guards were instructed not to stop him, and the bookcase was left open on purpose. Baldwin explained all of this to us as my husband stood in our home, trying to wrap a blanket around our daughter.

"He told us he did it for fun. Like a cat and a mouse. He seduced Abby just to torture her. Let James find her just so he could see the hope fading from his eyes. Then he gave him a choice. Return Abby to him, or kill himself. He promised if James took his own life, he would let Abby go. Let her and me live our lives again. James was a good man. He loved us, and he bought our freedom. But not really. That man would never be so kind. No, he took us in as his wards.

He comes to taunt us when he is bored. He'll never really let us go," she finishes, silent tears running down her cheeks as Abby holds her face in her hands.

"I'm so, so sorry," I say, the mana in my body condensing and flooding me with power.

"Don't be sorry," she says bitterly. "Just run. Get as far away from here as you can. If you can't get away from him . . . well, James may have had the right of it," she says, weariness and grief in her voice.

"Thank you," I say with sympathy. "I appreciate you telling me your story." Then I brace myself. It is time to take a risk, the same risk I have had to take dozens of times in the past few weeks. A risk I simply have to accept Baldwin will find out about, and then take anyway. I look at both women in the room and take a deep breath before asking my next question. "Do you want to help me kill him?"

There are a few moments of stunned silence, then the mother speaks up. "No, absolutely not. He'll know. He always knows. He will give us just enough hope, and then he'll use it to hurt us again. Absolutely not. I won't."

"I understand. It's a huge risk, and I know why you are scared to take it. But this is your only chance at ever being free. Please, help me," I plead.

"No. Get out. Get out of my house. I won't go through this again," she demands.

I understand, and I can't push any more than this. She isn't the first victim to refuse, and I can't blame the traumatized for being unable to do what I am asking of them.

"I'm sorry, ma'am. I understand. I'll leave." I turn toward her door. Just as I am about to go, I hear a voice from behind me.

"I'll help," Abby says weakly.

I turn around slowly and the older woman whirls on her daughter.

"No, Abby, it's not worth it! Please, this is a mistake—I can't lose you too," she begs.

Abby is resolute and her voice gains some strength as she speaks again.

"I want to help kill him."

CHAPTER THIRTY-SIX

Hail Mary

For the following two months, my routine is mostly unchanged. The Mages of Penance, my glib nickname for those at the house who have acquired mana, have grown to thirty-two in number. As with the first group, I always start with how to hide their mana. Every time I visit, I try to drive the point home that what we are doing is dangerous. The rumors that you will become a noble if you become a mage are only half-true. The reality is you will either become a noble . . . or you will die.

Nobility doesn't name new noble houses because it's a hobby of theirs nor because they just respect mana so much. It's about control and power. Magic is what keeps the nobility in power, and it is in their best interest to consolidate that power. Promotion to nobility is the easiest way to keep magic a noble-exclusive ability—if and only if a new mage is connected to someone important. If a new mage happens to be someone who is already missing or rejected by society, the easiest solution will be to kill them.

When my magic was discovered—thanks for that, Walter—I was investigated. Baldwin himself came to see where my magic came from. He wanted to know if I was the illegitimate child of someone important. If I hadn't been the "apprentice" of a known mage, I would probably be dead. Actually, if it weren't for how unique my mana gathering is, I might still have been killed. Baldwin and Godfrey seem to have a complex relationship, one in which Godfrey is not in control.

If any of these new mages attempt to ascend to nobility, neither the temple nor the nobility will have any difficulty deciding between the two options. I do warn them of this, even remind them of it so often that the entire house practically groans when I bring it up, but I still worry it isn't getting across. Sometimes, for a better life, people will take great risks. I know that better than anyone; this entire experiment is a massive risk in service of a better world. I hope for all their sakes none of them believe the lie and expose their mana, but I am expecting at least one of them to.

The danger here isn't just death, however, but the investigation before their death. The temple can make them admit where they learned magic. Baldwin can as well. If my experience with Baldwin tells me anything, it's that it will be the latter. Much like with me, he will want to find out if the new mage is useful and monopolize that use for himself if they are. I rely on Baldwin's greed and arrogance more than I'd like, but it is my best chance at beating him. It's easily the biggest weakness he has exposed to me.

Fortunately, there is a sense of community that has prevented any of this from happening . . . so far. Unfortunately, it's more like two communities, and they tend to butt heads. There have been several small problems over the past few weeks. None of these mages have managed to aspect mana yet, much less cast a spell. A few of them already have a sense of superiority, and there have been various unfortunate encounters between mages from either side. For some, living together inside a circle for a few weeks draws them closer together. For others, it fosters hostility.

Overall, however, the sense of reliance on one another has helped develop a sense of trust. This is hardly foolproof, however, and there have been several arguments and physical fights. The most serious fight took place inside the circle while I was gone; one boy was nearly forced out of the circle prematurely. That would have been a huge headache to deal with.

I am not the only one predicting further trouble, especially when they can use spells, and Diana approaches me one day with her concerns.

"What are you going to do when someone violent or dangerous learns magic from you? What if someone refuses to help once they have magic?" she asks, furrowing her brow in concern. "What about when one of these fights breaks out and they have spells that can actually do harm? Do you have some way of restricting their magic?"

I watch the groups, who are spread through the front rooms, interact for a moment while thinking about my response. Eleven of them are meditating, attempting to aspect mana. Seventeen others are trying to suppress the mana they have, while three are discussing endoaspected mana. Something seems wrong that I can't put my finger on, and I rub the back of my neck as I answer. "Well," I say, "that depends. If someone becomes a rapist or something similar, I'll kill them. But that's not the only possibility. Maybe their mind isn't healthy and they can be helped. Maybe they are just assholes and I can recommend denying them the safety of this community. Maybe they can change if you are patient with them. I don't know." I turn to face Diana.

"Ultimately," I continue, "it's not about what I would do, but what all of you would do. I can give my advice, but I can't tell you exactly what the best way to handle it is. Everyone needs to decide how to handle it. I am not your leader; no one is. We are just people helping one another out, and we will all need to figure out how to respond to problems. We can all agree to defend one another from spells and to try and stop someone from casting them to do harm. We can prepare any number of ways to handle it. But I can't give you a rule book to follow with an appendix for punishments. That's not who I am," I explain.

"So you just have no plan to stop someone dangerous?" she asks, shocked.

"Well, not exactly," I respond, rubbing my neck again. Something is tickling the back of my mind, but Diana's question is important. I try to articulate what I mean. "I have a dozen things I can do to stop someone if I need to. If someone does so much harm that I need to end them, I will. If I can provide the ear someone in a panic needs, I'll do that as well. What I'm saying is it can't be up to me. For one, I won't always be here, and for two, that's just a really bad idea."

"Why is that? You are the one teaching us magic, the one giving us this opportunity. No one here would begrudge you calling yourself our leader. Besides, why give us mana at all if you knew that could happen?" she puzzles.

"Have you ever heard the phrase 'everyone is the hero of their own story'?" I ask, and she shakes her head. "I thought not; it's not a saying from around here. It means every person interprets the world through their own desires and their own motivations. Everyone but you is a side character in your story, and you will always respect your own views at least a little more than other people's. To you, you are the main character," I explain.

"So . . . ?" she responds.

"So," I respond, sighing, "I'm the hero of my own story, but I'm not the hero of the world. I want to make the world a better place, Diana. I have my own vision of a better world and my own vision of how I get there. But the odds are stacked against me. I can't get there on my own. But what if my ideas are wrong? What if they don't work? What if some other version of them will, but mine won't?" I ask.

This is a question I have asked myself many times. I was not the only anarchist in my old world. I had a community, and many of them were smarter than I was. Many of them had successfully realized small communities that I hadn't. I was the direct-action girl. I was at the front lines fighting for change, but my ideas weren't the ones that helped people most. I was a spear and a shield, but I had experts in community and mental health to fall back on. Without them, I'm lost.

She looks contemplative, so I continue, "I'm probably not the smartest person in this room. I'm the most educated. I'm the most experienced in some ways. But I'm not the smartest. So you want to know what I'll do if one of these mages becomes a little tyrant? I'll fight them. I'll talk to all of you. But let me ask you, what if I am wrong? What if I die?

"Because I am not the smartest person in the world, I don't have all the answers. What I do know is the current world is wrong, and with help, I can end it. But if the world relies on me to change, to improve, to bring everyone out of the dark and into the light of a new day? If all that weight is on my shoulders alone, there is no hope. I can't lead everyone to a brand-new world. I'm no good at that. But I can help tear down the old one. I can share my ideas about a better world and watch them grow when passed on to other people. And if I die, I can die with the hope that someone is still fighting.

"That's what I want to do. I want to give everyone that option. Maybe I am doing it wrong, I don't know. But right now, I am helping people. Those people will help more people, and eventually, it will have grown so far past me and what I can do that neither I nor the king of this country can take it away from them," I finish, and Diana examines me.

"I knew you wanted us to share what we learn, but I didn't realize you wanted to . . . do so much. You want to challenge the king?" she asks, face turning a sickly green.

Shit, I got a little carried away there, didn't I? I like Diana but she is . . . a bit more loyal than I would be in her situation. I'm about to try some damage control when it hits me. I counted only thirty-one mages. I am missing one. I scan the new mages, trying to figure out which one is missing.

It takes a few scans, but I realize it's Mary, the little girl whose fear inspired me to kill the thug back when I saved the kids from the Manticorps cellar. She's just . . . gone.

"Excuse me a moment," I say, leaving Diana to contemplate our conversation. I really need to talk to her again, but I have a pit in my stomach telling me something is wrong. I search each room, but Mary is nowhere to be found. Running room to room, I ask frantically, "Has anyone seen Mary? Anyone?"

I get a mix of confused and apologetic looks. A few shake their heads or shrug when I focus on them. I'm feeling increasingly desperate when I see a young boy avoiding eye contact with me. I think I may have seen him with Mary a few times? It's hard to know for sure, but I home in on him. "Please, if you know where Mary is, can you tell me? She could be in danger," I plead, and the boy looks around, scared.

He makes eye contact with Tommy, who gives him a slight nod. "Tell 'er if ya know. It ain't safe for 'er out there," he says, answering the boy's unspoken question.

"Um . . . Mary said she was gonna get us outta here. She said she was gonna be a rich lady now, and we'd get to live together in a fancy place," he finally admits.

Fuck. Fuck fuck fuck fuck. I hadn't considered her to be one of the riskiest new mages. She was so slight and gentle. I should have known better. She would have understood my warnings the least and been one of the most desperate for a better life.

I waste no time. I ask the kids without magic, and the ones who can successfully suppress it, for help. I give them a long list of addresses and instructions with a meeting time. Then I whisper a few words to Ozzy before heading out the door. My mind races as I rush to the temple. It's the most likely place she would have gone if she wanted to be promoted to nobility. I use upward force to decrease my weight and practically fly through the roads.

I draw a few stares as I run at breakneck speeds through the streets of the city. When I finally arrive at the temple, I draw a different kind of stare. I didn't have time to change into women's clothing, and my pants and shirt are apparently scandalous in this part of town. I don't care, and I frantically search the courtyard in front of the temple. In a stroke of luck, I spot Emeric walking to the temple and run to him.

"L-lady Lillith? What are you doing? What are you wearing?" he splutters, but I ignore the questions.

"Have any commoners come by claiming to be mages?" I interrogate him, and he looks taken aback.

"My lady, you know I can't—" he starts, but I don't let him finish.

"Please," I beg, "she could be in danger. I really need your help!" I can tell he understands, but he adopts the same serious expression he got last time I spoke with him.

"All right, Lillith, calm down. I'll find out, okay? Come with me," he says, and leads me into the temple. I sweat while I wait for him to speak to another priest in hushed tones, looking back and forth to the interrogating eyes of the other churchgoers.

After an agonizingly long time, he returns. "Okay, Lady Lillith, you are right. A young girl stopped by a few hours ago claiming to be a mage. It was reported to the city lord, and Lord Baldwin came to collect her. She is perfectly safe, all right?" he explains.

I am out the door. I wanted to wait the full year, but this was always a possibility. Things are in motion now and can't be stopped. I failed to stop her in time, and now what plans I have in place will have to do.

As I thought, I have to kill Baldwin. Tonight.

CHAPTER THIRTY-SEVEN

Powerful

My next stop is Baldwin's estate. The first thing I have to do is ensure Baldwin isn't here. If everything goes at least marginally close to plan, I should be able to handle Baldwin alone. If I am fighting him and his father, Reynold, however, it all falls apart. Sneaking around the estate isn't terribly difficult with my mana suppressed. I have sound and light mana, and Baldwin, in his infinite wisdom, has little in the way of security. I suppose he wants to minimize gossip about his hobbies, or he's just arrogant enough to believe he doesn't really need guards. None of them are even mages, except an aid or two. It's my understanding most city lords would employ a corps of knights to protect their estates and assets.

I suppose either Baldwin or Reynold has other priorities, however. From what I gather, even most nobles shy away from the sort of thing Baldwin enjoys, and rumors could harm his standing in court. The only thing that dwarfs his arrogance is his ambition. Using my sound and light mana, it's easy enough to sneak past the mundane guards and into the main manor where I find my way to the maids' quarters. As they are apparently all busy working, it's sparsely populated, and I snag a maid's uniform. This isn't quite the frilly black-and-white getup I've seen on TV. Instead, it is a simple white dress with a green bodice and long skirt.

After donning it I also collect some random papers and, piling them in my arms, I march briskly to Reynold's chambers. I can feel his mana, so it's easy to find him. The pressure of it even helps me imitate the nervousness a maid would likely have when approaching a lord of his power. There is a guard at the door, but he doesn't bother stopping me. Instead, he snickers and simply steps aside for me to enter.

I enter to find Reynold dressed in nightclothes. I open my mouth to tell him about my supposedly urgent business, but he cuts me off. "What do you think you are—oh, just a maid." He gives me the foot-to-face appraisal men like him favor. "I suppose you'll do. I was going to send for one of you anyway. Come here, girl." This is more or less the response I expect and am looking for, so I nod obediently and move over to him.

He grabs my face roughly, moving my head around to examine me. "Are you a new one?" he asks idly. "Hair's a bit short. Not the most attractive quality. You are to grow it out, understood?"

I just smack his hand away.

"Oh no, you don't think I'm pretty?" I snort.

His face contorts from idle lust to rage.

"Who do you think you are?" he snarls at me. "You will show me the respect I am due. Now come here and . . . and . . . let . . ." Drool starts running out of his mouth as he lectures, and a moment later his muscles begin to contract and he starts to spasm. His breathing speeds and he collapses, losing control of his body. Tight knots of anxiety unravel in my shoulders as my blood poison's high-risk field test is successful. But it's not quite fast enough. "H-help!" he manages to scream before losing complete control. His mana flares, but he is unable to cast any spells. The guard runs in, spear in hand, but I throw him through the wall with force mana.

With the dose of poison that just activated in Reynold's system, I actually feel the pressure of his mana evaporate like water in a hot pan, and I know he is dead before I leave the room. I see another guard running as I head to leave the manor. I kill him with a stone bullet, a spell I can cast much more quickly thanks to my growing pool of mana, grief aspect, and practice. His blood splattered on my face and dress, I march out of the estate and fire off light and sound magic to draw as many guards as possible. I beeline across the gardens to a smaller building on the estate.

This building is itself a smaller mansion, supposedly for housing visiting dignitaries. It is, in reality, the most highly guarded building, and the only visitors it ever gets are Baldwin and myself. A few dozen guards respond to the noise I make and run to me, calling for backup along the way. I use powerful force mana to crush one of them, adding light magic to make the spell shine an ominous red. This doesn't make it more dangerous, but it makes it far more frightening.

I hit a few more guards with the same spell, and the rest pause, hesitating to attack me. After a moment of silent appraisal, they flee en masse. I don't bother chasing them. They will be long gone well before anyone else gets here, and that's all I need. I arrive at the smaller mansion and head into the foyer.

Baldwin won't be as easy as Reynold. Divine magic will likely repair any damage my poison can do. This fight is coming earlier than I'd like, and I won't have as much support as I had hoped for. Still, I have been worried about this since the first mages emerged from the circle, and I did have the minimum requirements prepared before that happened. First, I remove the maid's dress and reveal my practical clothing underneath. This is not a battle I want to fight in a dress. I stand in the middle of the opulent foyer.

Now I wait.

I will have to use every trick I have to survive this fight, but hopefully not for too long. I just need him to use enough mana that . . . Sweat trickles down my face as my nerves set in. My heart is as still as ever, but adrenaline still rushes through me, demanding I do something. I have to remain calm. After nearly an hour, my stomach twists as the expected voice breaks the silence.

"Quite the mess you have made of the estate," Baldwin says, striding confidently through the front door and into the foyer. I take note of a messenger bag he has resting on his side. "I'll expect you to be tidier when we marry, my dearest Lillith."

The glare in my eyes conflicts with the smile on my lips. "You think so? I thought I had removed quite a few stains," I retort, eliciting a chuckle from Baldwin. "Although I suppose it was a drop in the bucket compared to the filth that's left."

"Finally come to kill me then, have you?" he laughs. "Finally get all your little chess pieces into place, or are you just here for one of your little pets?" I glare at him without answering. If he wants to talk, I'll let him talk. "You didn't think those were a secret from me, did you? Your plans to team up with all my little toys to kill me? Please," he gloats.

He holds his hands behind his back and begins pacing around me as he lectures. "You can't keep any secrets from me, Lillith. You should know better than to sneak around behind your future husband's back, my darling. Every single one of them betrayed you. Every single one of them told me you asked for help killing me." What he means here is he forced a divine confession on them. I haven't been betrayed, he just exercised his power like he always has and wants me to blame them for it, like the powerful always do.

"Smart of you to not give them any details, but it won't make a difference. Were you going to make an army of little mages? Was that your plan?" He smirks at me. "That's right. Your little pet mage told me everything too. How you have been training little mages in one of the temple's sick houses. Were you going to attack me with a bunch of kids and cripples? I have to say, Lillith, is that really the best you can do?" He has genuine disappointment in his voice, and I sigh inwardly.

He saw me helping children and the injured, the people society threw away, and he assumed I chose them because I wanted a personal army? Sometimes it feels like it's impossible for powerful people to view the world through a lens of anything other than attempts to gain more power. "You know you could have real power. With me, you will become the queen someday. You will rule over this entire country. You don't have to play these silly games. Truly, I am disappointed in you. I hoped you were smarter than this," he says with a mock sigh.

Apparently, it is my fate across all of reality and in any world to disappoint people by not being "smart enough" to do exactly what they want and expect. "The queen has power, yeah, but only the power to do exactly what the king wants. The power to be on your leash isn't power," I finally respond. Even as queen, I wouldn't be able to do much. I could stop nobles under me from some cruelties . . . unless the king said to leave them be. I could use my wealth for charity . . . unless the king decided it was too expensive or made the common people harder to control.

I would have the power to be cruel, I guess, but I couldn't actually change how this country works. Even if I got away with killing Baldwin after becoming queen, I would just be given a new guardian and a new king would take his place.

"Maybe so," Baldwin responds. "But a bunch of broken toys aren't going to help much either, are they? I promise my leash will be more pleasant than watching them all die by my hand." He has a wicked grin on his face as he taunts me.

"You were going to kill them all anyway. Doing it more slowly isn't a kindness, and watching it from your side wouldn't be easier. Besides, you won't live past tonight. So I don't have to choose, do I?" I respond, my glare following him as he paces the white marble floor.

He spins on me, not in anger but with amusement. "Oh, you really think you are going to kill me like you killed Walter, don't you? Do you actually think I'm the same as a disobedient dog like him?" he laughs.

"Of course not," I quip, then look at his throat. "I imagine he tastes like you, only sweeter." He raises an eyebrow at me for two reasons when I say this. He is clearly amused by my confidence, but he also felt the same thing I just did. My mana has begun building in potency and intensity. People have begun to arrive outside. Baldwin's direct victims are showing up, one by one, and circling the house.

He claps his hands, clear joy on his face. "Of course! What a fun plan! You don't have a little mage army to fight me—you actually want to fight me yourself! What aspect are you using to draw power from them? Pity? Helplessness? I could see you easily grasping the concept of helplessness," he bellows. "You made a mistake though, my sweet bride. These are MY toys. I can feel them. Every one of them belongs to me, and they empower me as well. You may have made yourself stronger, but so am I."

"Is that so?" I challenge, maintaining eye contact with him. "But these people came here at my request. All of them willingly, and all with the knowledge of what could happen to them. They have overcome both your dominance and their fear of challenging you. So, who do you think is going to be stronger? You, leaning on them like beasts of burden, or me, acting as their spear?"

This is the moment I see him confused for the first time since the start of the conversation. He doesn't know how I know what his aspects are, and I take advantage of this brief slip to start the battle. I cast my flash-bang spell, trying to blind and deafen him for a few seconds, then charge him with my force-reduced weight. I swing a fist at him, but I am too slow. He saw my mana forming, protected his eyes and ears, and put up a thick wind barrier that tosses my fist aside. I quickly use force to push myself away, my opportunity missed.

The color of my spell was faint, however, and my grief mana is doing its job. He cackles at me, completely unworried as he forms spears and drills of wind in the air. Unlike my jack-of-all-trades approach, Baldwin seems to have mastered a few specific types of mana, wind being his strongest. I run across the foyer, dodging sharp wind, sometimes stopping just before it hits and other times jumping over it. Ditching the dress was definitely the right call.

He is toying with me; I can tell by the speed and force of his weapons. He is happy to injure or badly maim me, but he doesn't want me dead. He isn't being particularly careful of the people outside, but he isn't attacking my allies directly either. He still has a use for all of us, and until he is actually worried, he will want us alive. That is the arrogance I'm counting on.

I try to approach Baldwin again to make contact with him, but a wall of wind separates us. I feel more allies have arrived and my power is growing even more. He traps me between two wind tunnels, one of them blowing a window out behind me, and aims wind blades at all four of my limbs. The force mana I have been using to lighten my body has grown fainter and fainter as more allies arrive to circle the manor. I go to apply upward force to myself before I realize I am boxed in from above as well.

I aspect a massive amount of cold and air mana, creating a huge pocket of freezing air in front of me. As the wind blades hit this mana, they are redirected upward and fly into the wind tunnel above me. I expand the radius of my cold bubble, and the wind tunnels on either side of me also shoot upward, allowing me to escape.

All my allies have arrived now, and I can feel my mana surging. His wind has grown more powerful as well, but I was right. In their current state, they empower me more than him. The gap between us is narrower, though he still outclasses me by a significant amount. I begin rapidly forming earth bullets and firing them with as much force as I can, simulating heavy gunfire. He has been neglecting his wind barrier, opting for offense, and several of my bullets tear through his body and cause a pained look of surprise.

My small victory is short-lived, however, as his wounds immediately close up. I have drawn first blood, however, and Baldwin's amusement is fading. I feel the familiar numbness of his divine magic seizing control of my body and I freeze in place. He brushes dirt and blood off himself and scowls. "Stubborn bitch," he mutters, frustrated he couldn't put me in my place while I was conscious. He dispels all his wind magic and walks slowly over to me. He doesn't attack or restrain me; in fact, over our various sessions I have become convinced he can't do so while I am under his divine power.

Instead, I see him pull familiar chains from the bag at his hip, similar to the ones in Walter's cellar. He plans to bind me as soon as I'm released from his magical control.

I am awake, however, and I break myself free from his control. With the number of grieving allies outside, my mana has become completely invisible. He doesn't seem to realize I am in control of my body since his divine magic still permeates it. As he approaches me, I call on all the extra strength of the mana I have right now and form a massive spike of earth behind him. He unclasps the shackles and orders me to present my hands.

I do as he says. He reaches up, and I feel his divine magic receding before he attempts to make physical contact, lending credence to the theory that he can't touch me while using it. Before he reaches me, I lunge and grab his hand in mine, finally making skin-to-skin contact. As his eyes widen, I launch the earth spike, impaling him. He uses a huge amount of wind mana to throw me away from him, and I collide with a pillar, feeling a rib crack.

When I recover, I see he has forced the spike out with wind and the gaping hole in his chest is healing. Blood is crusting, dark and thick, down his torso.

He's a sturdy fucking bastard.

He looks up and glares at me, the game clearly over. "Fine. If this is how you want to do it, I have other ways to control you. Come here," he commands, wind still blowing around him in force to ward off any attacks. I'm confused until I see him looking toward the front door, where Henry is walking in. Fuck, I was worried about this. Hopefully, I have done enough.

Henry obediently enters the house and begins walking across the wreckage Baldwin has made of it. Before reaching Baldwin, however, he begins to slow down. After another moment, he stops completely. "I said, come here," Baldwin commands again through a pained growl, but Henry stays put. Just as Baldwin is getting ready to give him another command, life floods into Henry's eyes. He stumbles for a second like he just woke up from a deep sleep. Coming to his senses, he takes in the scene in front of him, processes the situation, and runs to a spot up the nearby stairs, close to the back wall. Baldwin reacts by trying further commands, apparently unable to reconcile reality with his expectations.

Henry stomps his foot on the ground when he reaches his destination and immediately everything changes. The powerful wind blowing around Baldwin dissipates. The hole in his abdomen is closed, but scrapes and bruises all over his body aren't healing as quickly. A look of fury descends on his face and he snarls at me, "What the fuck did you do?"

I don't answer. Instead, I begin casting.

CHAPTER THIRTY-EIGHT

Lillith and Henry

Henry

Since Lord Baldwin bought me from the Manticorps, the days have all melted together over time. He only needs me for two things, alchemy and . . . something else. I'm not sure what it is yet, but he visits me most days. He has little to talk about, but when we are done, I always feel exhausted, like I've been working all day. The days are too short, and I've deduced my memories are being erased.

I don't know what the purpose of this is, but it gives me a foreboding feeling. Aside from that, I spend my days concocting green mist for him. The drug itself isn't actually all that dangerous, but Baldwin has me adding ingredients to make it more addictive. I don't know what a man like him needs to sell green mist for, but the one time I had the courage to ask, he just laughed at me. He also has me brew a safer version that he consumes himself.

I tried making it with a poison once, but he knew somehow. He used it anyway, right in front of me. To my horror the mist enveloped us both, and he smiled at me. A second later the mist was gone, and we were both fine. He told me to go ahead and try again, but he would just sell the poisoned mist, and then blood would be on my hands. He seemed to get actual physical enjoyment at my panic.

Today was just like every other day. I lie on the ground in the cell Baldwin keeps me locked in, trying to get some sleep. Tonight, however, things change, as I hear my cell being unlocked. I turn over, wondering why Baldwin is here twice in one day, then freeze. Standing at the entrance to my cell is my sister, Lillith. Tears running down her cheeks as we finally see each other.

Both of us are paralyzed for a single moment, but I scramble to my feet, and she rushes to me. We hold each other in a tight embrace and just sob together for a few moments. We both catch up to our bodies at the same time and speak over each other.

"Henry, I'm so glad you are alive!" she exclaims, eyes watering and voice trembling.

"Lily, what happened? Why are you here?" I worry, my cry wrestling with hers. We regard each other, then silently agree she should speak first.

"It's all right, Henry. He doesn't know I'm here," she assures me.

"Then you need to get out, now," I insist. "He could hear us. He knows everything—I don't know how, but he does!"

She shakes her head at me. "I'm not leaving without you, Henry. Besides, I know how he 'knows everything.' He doesn't know I am here, and we are in a sound bubble," she claims. "I'm here to get you out. We have to leave now!"

Daring to hope again, I start to follow her toward the ladder in the corner of the room. Before we get there I realize something and stop. "Where will we go? We can't go home. Baldwin will find me there and know you came here." I can see she understands the concern but is denying it.

"We'll leave the city," she answers. "Go somewhere far away. We can just run!" I can tell she is lying. I don't know why we matter to Baldwin, but Lillith obviously believes he won't let us go. Any other city would search for us and return us to him. It isn't safe outside the walls. And what about the rest of the family?

"We can't do that, Lily. Besides, I know you better than anyone. You could never run. I believe you would try, for me. But it would kill you," I respond, dismissing the fantasy.

"I could never leave you either, Henry. Not with this man. Not ever. Besides, maybe he won't care. He has power over us anyway, so maybe he'll just see it as one lost game in a war he is winning," she lies again, tears welling back up in her eyes.

"I have been working with him for a while now, Lily. Baldwin doesn't lose games. We both know you can't take me out of here. Not without putting all of us in more danger," I answer, voicing concerns she has clearly already considered.

She slumps her shoulders, abandoning her denial. She hugs me again and we hold each other in silence for a moment. I resign myself to the decision we both have to make, and she speaks again.

"All right, I'll leave you here. For now. But if that's how it has to be, I need you to do something for me," she says, pulling away and putting her fists on her hips. She then catches me up on her recent activities. My emotions range from pride to horror as she relays the different acts of violence and moments of triumph. It is a strange thing, to look up to your little sister.

I embrace the feeling, however. I don't like everything she says she did, and I don't understand how casual she is about the people she has killed. But under all that, I admire her more than ever. I feel relief for Gilbert and sorrow for Dad. When she tells me about Mom, my heart shatters and my resolve to stay here wavers. In the end, however, it only hardens.

"I only just found out Baldwin was the one who had you, and I came to search his estate as soon as I could. He didn't even bother hiding you well. Just shoved you in the basement under his fucking guest house. Arrogant prick," she says, catching me up to the present day. "I have a plan to end all this, and now that I have you I can start putting the pieces together."

"But if what you say is true, won't he just learn your plan through me? In fact, won't he find out you have been here the next time he sees me?" I ask, worry returning. She nods along, confirming my concern.

"Only if he asks about it, but yes, that's a huge risk. Which is why . . ." she starts, and pauses as if nervous, ". . . I want to do a bit of an experiment."

"What kind of experiment?" I inquire apprehensively.

"I want to . . . use my mana to alter your mind a bit," she admits and I gape at her.

"Lily, that's basically a cardinal sin. That's the domain of the Collector. You'll end up on the third plane if you do that!" I exclaim.

"If that's going to happen, it's probably too late; I've already been altering my own body. I won't make you, Henry. I know it's scary. I can do this without you if necessary, or we can risk him finding out. But this is the safest way," she responds.

"Safest? Couldn't this kill me?" I ask, giving her a skeptical stare.

"No, I'm not going to do anything severe. You can trust me, Henry," she assures me.

I study the determined set of her jaw. Well, fuck. Guess I'm going all in.

"All right, what are you going to do?" I ask.

"In my experience," she explains, "Baldwin's magic can be affected by our intent. Even if we aren't aware. The state of mind we are in affects how we answer his questions. My plan is pretty simple, actually. I am going to set a trigger in your brain. If it loses control over your body, a few different, um, things it produces will be released. This will essentially put you to sleep until it regains control. Your body will still do as it's told, but you won't be conscious. Any information you process will be dreamlike and jumbled. My theory is, while he can order your body around, you won't be able to answer questions in a meaningful way."

I nod along while trying to follow her. That doesn't sound possible, but I figure it's still my best option. "And it won't hurt me?" I ask.

"Absolutely not," she promptly responds, "not for an extended period of time. Hopefully. It doesn't last that long though, and I'm certain I can fix any damage if you'll let me."

Well, that doesn't sound encouraging. I have a feeling I'm not the only one taking a risk, however.

"And if it doesn't work?" I ask.

"Well, then we hope he doesn't ask the wrong questions," she responds. "I'm not going to lie to you—this is a huge risk. But anything we do to fight back will be."

I nod, then steel myself.

"Okay, do it," I agree.

She spends the next few hours coursing her mana through my body. At first, nothing happens, but she walks me through opening myself up and allowing her mana to flow through me. Apparently, this would be easier if I were a mage and could help guide the mana, but the willingness to allow my body to be changed by her is what allows it to start working.

After a long while she eventually stops. "Did it work?" I ask as she wipes sweat off her brow.

"I think so, but honestly, we won't know for sure until it's tested," she responds. "All right, so here is the plan."

It takes a while for me to understand, but it seems like a good plan. "And how will we get a sample of . . . what did you call it, tissue?" I ask.

"Well," she answers, "tomorrow I am being christened as a noble. This will be my official introduction as Baldwin's fiancée. If I play my cards right, I think I'll have a chance."

Today, Baldwin was particularly angry when he came to interrogate me. I suppose Lillith must have put her plan into effect. A moment later, I feel like I just woke up from a week of sleep, and Baldwin looks even angrier. I really hope that means her plan for me worked as well. I give him his green mist for the day before he storms off.

Several hours pass before Lillith finally visits me. She looks like she has been stoned in the city marketplace. Her hair is short and ragged, and her face is badly beaten and abused. She is also grinning like she was just gifted an expensive dessert. I don't know whether to worry or feel happy for her.

"Lily, what in the three planes happened to you?" I gasp, rushing over to her and examining her wounds.

"I got what we needed," she exclaims proudly, presenting her hand with two teeth in it. I look between her and the teeth for a moment.

"Are you sure those aren't yours? You look like they might be yours," I say, absolutely dumbfounded.

"And here I was thinking I looked pretty today." She scoffs before sitting down and crossing her legs.

"Why can't you heal those?" I ask in concern. "They look painful, and you managed to alter my brain in a single day? Why not do the same for yourself?"

"An excellent question," she responds distractedly. "I don't know. The question has caused me a great deal of confusion. It seems it's easier to make completely new alterations than to heal a body to its natural state, with regular mana anyway. I would love the time to just sit down and study that alone, but alas, I am busy."

I take this at face value. She would know better than I would, I suppose. "Okay, then . . . So. How exactly are you going to use those teeth to restrict his mana?" I ask.

"Another excellent question. I'm not, not directly anyway. What these give me is knowledge," she explains. "See, when mages gather mana, they store it in their bodies. It's where we draw it from and it's where we aspect it. It's in our blood, our bones, our flesh. With any piece of my body, another mage could discern that I have aspected grief."

"And teeth are bones, so you are using them to find out all the magic he uses?" I ask, trying to catch up.

"No and no," she answers cheerfully. "Teeth aren't bones, but they do have tissue in them and a couple of other things that would have technically been targeted on a surface level. And I won't know every magic he uses, but I will know if he has an endoaspected mana."

"Okay, and if you know that, you can stop him from using them?" I guess.

"Sort of. If I know where he will be, I can draw a magic circle that dissipates the mana he uses. I intend to enlist the help of . . . a few friends to help close the gap. But I don't want to fight fair; I want to be the only one with the advantages of endoaspected mana. Plus, I saw him use wind magic today, so I can dissipate that as well. I can also prevent mana from regenerating inside the circle. This doesn't work on me because of the design of my circle, but it will work on him. He will have a finite amount of mana to use," she explains.

"Why not just dissipate all mana?" I ask. "You are stronger than other people, right? Won't you win in a magicless fight?"

"Maybe." She shrugs. "But Baldwin can alter his body as well. He might be just as strong, or stronger. Plus, he has expanded reach and height. Not a safe gamble. I will restrict his inner aspects and the external ones I know about, then I should have the advantage in a magic fight." Her attention is on the teeth. "What is this, despair? Hopelessness? That doesn't make sense . . ." She trails off.

"What about his divine magic, can you dissipate that?" I ask as she starts to get distracted.

"Hm?" she responds. "Oh, if I can, I don't know how. Maybe a priest will. Remind me to schedule a long talk with Emeric. No, I have another plan for that. Aha! Dominance. That makes sense . . . and fear? Of course this dickhead has two. How did he aspect fear though? Is he more insecure than I thought?"

She doesn't elaborate on her plan for his divine magic as she jumps up and starts drawing a circle in a journal she brought.

Over the next few nights, she works on the circle, and once it's finished, she returns and we begin drawing it. It's a complex design, and I am in awe that she designed it at all. We are drawing it down here. She plans to fight Baldwin in the manor above, and this underground area apparently expands beyond the walls of the building.

One problem occurs to me as we draw together. "Won't he just . . . leave when he feels the difference in mana?" I ask.

"If he was right at the edge, yes. We need him inside before we activate it. I need to draw him in and then activate it somehow. That's where you come in. I will make a loud sound—you should be able to hear it from down here. That's when you draw the final rune in the center. Then I will try to get him to use whatever powerful spells he has left and drain his mana so I have a clear advantage," she answers.

"What if I'm not down here?" I ask. "What if I am somewhere else, or he brings me to the fight?"

She pauses at this.

"Shit, that's a good question . . . One moment," she says, stopping to think. Then she snaps her fingers. "All right. It shouldn't matter what elevation we are at, as long as the rune is in the center of the xy-plane. We will have to carry the rune on us and try to put it in place upstairs if that happens. Either of us can do it. I'll find the center and describe it to you. If the fight goes on too long or you are up there, one of us will place the rune and keep it there. I'll have to use illusions to keep him away from the rune, but at that point, I should have an advantage."

The plan she comes up with feels . . . spotty, but at least it isn't plan A. I suppose it accounts for me being out of the picture entirely—she can activate the circle herself. Let's hope it doesn't come to that. Although it would be a waste since, as I find out soon, "carry the rune on us" means "tattoo it on the bottoms of our feet."

A few weeks later, Lillith is healed. The circle is done, our tattoos are done (a process I hope never to repeat), and she visits me to offer a vial of red liquid.

"Is that . . . ?" I ask.

"Yeah, it's my blood. Don't worry, I manually pulled my mana out of it, it should be fine," she says.

"Okay . . . that begs the question . . . why though?" I probe.

"Put it in the green mist," she answers. "It should manage his divine magic. It's poison."

"He knows when I poison him. He doesn't care, his magic just heals him! Wait, hold on, why is your blood poison?" I protest.

"Yeah, he is an arrogant cock, isn't he? But that's exactly the point. He uses his divine magic for it. This poison is stronger than anything you have ever heard of, but it won't activate until I activate it. It's harmless until I specifically combine another ingredient with it, which I can do in the fight. Poison like this absolutely wrecks the body. Without divine magic he'd be dead in minutes with no cure. With it, however, it will have to work overdrive to protect him. Especially with a huge dose administered over an extended time," she assures me.

I look at my little sister like she is some kind of first-plane spirit. "Where do you get these ideas?" I ask, baffled. I ignore how she dodged my second question.

"I know." She grins. "It's out of this world how cool it is, right? Best part? I have been investigating the estate for weeks. I'm pretty sure Baldwin knows I do it, but he doesn't know what to hide. His father uses your green mist too. Two birds, one stone."

"Two birds, one stone?" I ask, and she punches a fist into her hand.

Sometime later, after many more meetings, I wake up from an interrogation. I've been moved—I'm standing in the middle of a ruined manor. I see Lillith, tired and splattered with blood. Baldwin is cut up as well. He is picking himself up off the ground and snarling at me.

Shit, this is it. No time to waste, then.

I scan the room frantically until I find the spot Lillith described. I march over to it before Baldwin can react, and while he is still trying to order me to do something, I stomp my foot down on a notch Lillith left in the floor for me.

CHAPTER THIRTY-NINE

Powerless

Baldwin

I order the little brat to enter the house. My amusement with these children is not infinite, and if she is going to give me this much trouble . . . well, I have my own backup plans.

"Fine. If this is how you want to do it, I have other ways to control you. Come here," I say, ordering the girl's brother inside. I had a feeling she would come looking for me when I got my hands on that little idiot. It's always best to have a card up your sleeve, even when dealing with a child.

The boy starts slowing down on his way to me. This fucking family and their resistance to divine magic. He hadn't given me trouble at first, but recently the little shit figured out a way to put himself to sleep during my interrogations. Now he is actually stopping in the middle of following my orders? "I said, come here," I demand again. He doesn't do as he's told. Instead, as I get ready to repeat the command, he seems to wake up and start frantically looking around.

Then he begins running, up the staircase to one of the walls. What in the three planes? I order him again and again, but the useless fool fails to comply. That's when I realize the problem. My divine magic is . . . busy? The spike has been removed and the hole in my abdomen is gone, what is it trying to heal? Usually, I can use it on other people even if I'm healing, but now it's not even working on minor cuts I got from Lillith's last attack.

Something in my body is failing so badly that the entirety of my divine magic is struggling to keep up with it. I feel a hot rage boiling up inside me. I don't know what she did, but I am absolutely done with this humiliation. I am going to throw everything I have at her, and I'm going to kill her defiant brother in front of her. I am going to—

He reaches his destination and stomps on the ground for some reason and . . . my thoughts are immediately derailed as my wind mana suddenly dissipates. I try to cast another wind spell and it eddies away as it's forming. This infuriates me further and I summon all the pure mana I can to crush her so she can't cast any of her own spells. As my mana wraps around her, I have a horrifying realization. My dominance mana is gone. So is my fear mana. I am feeling weaker than I have in years. Lillith, however, seems to only be getting stronger, and for the first time inside my own city, I feel another mage's mana overpowering and suppressing mine.

I scream in rage and stand, preparing an earth spell, one of my other two aspects. I'm not an expert with it like I am with wind, but I have been fighting mages for longer than this bitch has been alive. I form massive stone spears to fight by my side. Her fucking tricks won't stop me. I feel disoriented for a moment and the room shifts. Everything looks the same but in the wrong spot. Walls stand in the middle of the room and there are duplicates of each one. This isn't enough to fool me.

I hear the boy panting and send a spear flying in the direction of the noise. It bounces off a plane midair before coming back to me. I can't see any spells being cast. How is this bitch doing it? It doesn't matter, it's just another trick. She must be using some kind of magic circle. Which means all I have to do is get out of this building and I will dominate her. Or kill the boy—he must have been the one to complete it.

I start to run toward the entrance only to collide with another invisible wall. This is going to be irritating. I can handle it, however. I start to cast a water spell. This is my weakest element, but I can use it to find these fucking invisible walls. I am interrupted by small pieces of stone blindsiding me and tearing through one arm. The same fucking spell she used earlier. I use my own stone mana to try to steal control of her projectiles. She must have propelled them with initial mana and isn't controlling them directly now, because it works.

I create stone armor around myself, then finish my water spell. I am satisfied to see the water splashing up against various invisible walls. I can remember where those are easily. I grunt as my divine mana, still busy, fails to heal my arm. Is there something about the stone she uses? No, then I wouldn't have been able to stop them earlier. It doesn't matter—I have to focus. I am going to make this girl scream and beg for mercy after today. Guess the wedding night is coming early. I'll just deal with any nosy fucking priests if they try to raise an eyebrow.

I see some water move through one of the visible walls and smile. Clever little brat, isn't she? I walk through the wall and am met with blackness from all directions. Lillith is standing in front of me, glaring. She is perfectly still as I swing a stone spear through her. Another illusion. Illusions aren't easy, however. Illusion mages can only copy images, not create them convincingly. That means she is nearby. I begin spraying water out and swinging my spears.

A pair of eyes appears in the darkness, but not red ones like the brat's. I swing at them out of instinct, but they are another illusion. Then another pair of eyes and another. All glaring at me. All condemning me with a look of pure hatred. *Like I care about your pathetic condemnations!* Surrounded by dozens of furious eyes in the darkness, a single eye opens to glare at me. That's when I recognize them.

One of the maids I hired, the one whose father killed himself to protect her. The noblewoman from the restaurant. The slave who collapsed and couldn't use his arm right. Servants and slaves I took as property and used to feed my dominance and fear mana. And Lillith. Her eyes bore into me, condemning me with the rest.

Enough of these foolish tricks. I turn around to back out of the darkness, but I can't find the entrance. I try sending water out, but it all just falls to the ground. I can't even see my own body anymore; all I can see is my mana and the mana of my spells. I'm alarmed to see and feel how weak they are getting. I begin swinging my spears wildly, creating huge arcs to cover as much space as possible, but hit nothing but air.

Something hits me in the darkness and I feel my ribs crack. I immediately swing my spear in its direction but fail to make contact. From another direction, out of the silence, my leg is kicked and I feel it break, my body collapsing to the ground. This time I guess the direction of the next attack and swing there instead. Still, my attack meets with nothing.

My anger rises and I scream out in fury, but the sound disappears as it leaves my lips. I scream more, challenging Lillith to stop with the cowardly tactics and fight me honestly, but the all-consuming silence is as unrelenting as the darkness, and I hear none of my own words. Some indescribable force surrounds my arm and I bite back the pain as it is ripped off.

I try to send a spear after it, but nothing happens. I am out of mana, I realize. Fine. My divine mana will catch up soon, and I will make them all kill one another. "Do you think this is enough to kill me? Everything I suffer through you will suffer through a dozen times more. You fucking coward. You pathetic, dishonorable filth!" I scream, but the sound doesn't reach my ears. The same force as before tears my unbroken leg off and my fury only grows. I can't move my other arm, still injured from the stones.

I feel my body rising into the air, then I am gripped like a rat by a snake. I have never felt a rage of this depth before. A fury that flows through my body so deeply. My heart rate is rapidly speeding as anger courses through my veins. I am angry.

I am furious.

I am rage incarnate!

I am . . . I am not afraid. I am incapable of fear.

Lillith's eyes grow larger and approach me, then it is her entire body I see. She places a hand on my cheek and gently rubs her thumb across it. Then her hand moves so her palm is pressed to the front of my face and I can see her glare through the gaps in her fingertips. She has tears welling up in her eyes, but they somehow only make her seem more furious than sad.

My divine mana is still trying to heal me, but it can't catch up. I feel her other hand slide around to the back of my head. She then begins to turn. I try to think of a way to fight back and the world slows to a crawl. Each moment taunts me with the eons it takes to pass. All the eyes in the room are now the full bodies of my property. Circling me. Glaring at me. Condemning me.

All of you can fuck off. I was chosen by the fucking Collector! I am a natural divine mage! I have a fucking Collector-given right to each of you. Do you think I'm afraid of your fucking glares?

She doesn't stop turning. I feel my head reach its natural limit, and she keeps turning. *The Collector will save me.* I hear something pop and she keeps turning. *I am chosen by a god!* I feel my windpipe closing and she keeps turning. *I fucking own all of you!* The skin of my neck tears and she keeps turning. Turning, turning, turning. I feel the break when it happens. My divine mana fights to keep me alive as the bones in my neck shatter. She keeps turning. The flesh separates. She keeps turning. So many glares lock on my eyes as my head is turned past them. Lillith comes into view from the other direction. I am alive only thanks to my divine mana rapidly trying to stitch me back together, one twisted vein of flesh keeping me connected to my body.

Blackness starts to cloud my eyes, and with the pain now gone, I get out one final word.

"Please . . ."

CHAPTER FORTY

Going Home

I toss Baldwin's head aside, panting with exhaustion. I have never maintained so many complex illusions at once before, nor have I ever had such dense mana to work with. The people surrounding me all seem to release a lifetime of tension at once; the abused staff who had been too afraid to flee, the slaves, Baldwin's victims. We all take a moment to appreciate the freedom we just gained. I see shoulders drop and tears of relief from all of them . . . all of us. Not everyone who gathered to help came inside. Ozzy's sweet soul couldn't have watched this.

I survey the battered and broken ruins around us, wipe the serpent's blood from my face, and compose myself. We aren't out of the woods yet. "Everyone, I am looking for a little girl named Mary. She may be on the property somewhere. If you are willing, I could use help finding her. If you aren't, you are free to go. If you are a woman without a guardian, I can give you a safe place to meet me; I'll do what I can to protect you," I announce. I describe Mary and give volunteers directions to the two hidden areas on Baldwin's estate.

Henry runs to me and we embrace like we did the night I first found him. "It's over, Lily, it's really over," he cries into my shoulder as I try not to squeeze him too hard. I don't have the heart to tell him we still have a lot to worry about. He needs to feel the victory for now.

"We got him," I reply instead of agreeing with him. "He's fucking gone." He starts laughing and crying at the same time, and allowing myself to enjoy the moment, I join him.

Most of the group leaves while I talk with Henry, which is for the better. We need to leave as soon as possible; I didn't exactly score a "silent assassin" rating on this mission. Several guards saw my face before fleeing earlier in the night. It was blood-splattered and dark, but I can't guarantee I won't be recognized. There are only so many short-haired women, especially mage women, in the city. Maybe just the one, actually. Of course, guards aren't exactly used to reporting mages for crimes yet, and I did put the fear of God in them.

I can hardly count on that, however. Of course, nobles who demonstrate their power by openly murdering other nobles in public aren't exactly well-loved. The nobility likes feeling safe, and Baldwin made them feel like, well, like commoners. I even had one here, helping me. Baldwin won't be missed. Of course, letting a commoner who killed a noble live won't be acceptable no matter how much they hated the noble. There is a way to cover this up buried in all that, but first, I have to find Mary.

I go to search the basement Henry has been kept in. I get a slight smile as I descend the now-familiar stair treads. All in all, this basement designed to control and torment me and my loved ones is the only room I've been happy in for a long time. Henry really is the only person I trust completely and the only one I really act like myself around. I also have to laugh at Baldwin. He kept Henry in here and forced him to work in the dark, with only a single torch to work by. He visited him every day to taunt him and get his potions.

I use a light spell to illuminate the room, hoping to find Mary. The magic circle we drew is clearly revealed at the edges of the basement in the light Baldwin never allowed Henry to have. I have to remind myself never to grow so arrogant I let my enemies draw a noose around my neck in my own house. Mary isn't here, and I reascend to the ground floor.

I am met by Abby, the one-eyed woman who helped me against her mother's wishes. "We . . . found her, I think," she says, a foreboding melancholy coloring her words.

"Where is she? Is she hurt?" I probe, worry spiking as I pick up Abby's disquiet. Her face only falls further, and I feel her grief answer my second question.

"She's . . . she's dead. She's in the cell he kept me in. I . . . I'm sorry, Lillith," she laments, and I run past her. I find the hidden room in question and see her small body, abandoned on a table. I panic for a moment, realizing I was in the manor before fighting Baldwin; I was so close to this room when I found the maid uniform. Did I abandon her to this? Was she alive when . . . No, she has been dead for hours. I scan her body with mana and realize she was dead long before I came here, and probably even before I left the House of Penance.

I still feel sick. If I hadn't helped her acquire mana . . . I can't help but feel that sinking feeling in my body. I feel that horrible weight on your organs when you feel like nothing will ever be okay again. My skin prickles with the anxiety of failure. I can't hold it back any longer and I let the tears flow down my cheeks, mixing with the blood of the man who did this. I know this isn't because I taught her magic. This is because Baldwin decided she didn't deserve it.

A tool that could keep her alive. That could give her all the chances and opportunities the nobility hoard for themselves, gorge themselves on until they vomit. Because she dared to ask not for power or wealth but just a chance to live her fucking life. So he killed her. Because he thought this world belonged to him and taking any opportunity at all was stealing from him.

My resolve to spread mana to the common people only steels. If the nobles are so afraid of not being the most powerful, most special people in the world that they will kill a child to protect that feeling . . . they must be terrified of what will happen to them if magic is attainable for anyone. They are right to be.

"I'm burning this down," I announce to Abby and a few others who followed me here. No one questions me, and we set to work. The household staff and the estate's slaves have long since fled, at least the ones who didn't join me in killing their master. At a maid's humble vanity, I wipe my face clean of dust and drying blood, slowly and thoroughly. I find another maid's uniform to change into so I won't have to walk through the streets covered in blood. Finally, on the wide, manicured lawns behind the manor, we build a pyre for Mary. She deserves more respect than the other bodies on this estate, but we can't carry her through the streets.

As we leave through the tall metal gates, three houses light up the night with flames. The main manor is the first to burn, followed by the guest mansion, and finally the House of Tudor itself, its most prominent members' bodies burning to ash alongside it.

Henry, Ozzy, Abby, a few other women, and I arrive at the House of Penance. Poor Ozzy has had a rough go of it; his heart is too gentle for the events of the night. He didn't witness the deaths, but he is clearly emotionally spent. It must have been an ordeal just getting out of the house. Tommy and I had planned to blindfold him and push him out while Diana was distracted, and Tommy must have had to do this alone. Even willing to go, Ozzy had been unable to leave the house while under the priest's brainwashing. However he got here, I am glad my final comment to him before leaving had born fruit.

Returning to the House of Penance clearly lifts a weight from his shoulders. As I bring him inside I am greeted by Gilbert and my mother. Both run straight to Henry, already weeping in joy before they reach him. If my mother felt alive when I told her I had found Henry, she is radiant now. She exudes the kind of joy that rises like the sun, and I feel the density and power of my mana actively lessening as she hugs her lost son.

"Henry, oh Collector, you are alive, Henry!" my mother sobs.

"Mom! I missed you so much! I'm so sorry I was gone for so long, I tried to come home so many times, I . . . Lily told me how hard it hit you. I'm so sorry, Mom," Henry responds, his eyes welling up.

"None of that, you did nothing wrong. I never should have given up on you, I'm the one who's sorry!" she argues.

"It doesn't matter," Gilbert cuts in. "What matters is we are all together again."

Gilbert is openly crying as well, and a certain tension he had been holding vanishes from his body as he talks to Henry. Their reunion could have been a bit less comfortable, but I told Henry how Gilbert helped me search for him and how he was changing. As it is, the two brothers are exuberant. We rejoice in one another's company for a while, laughing and joking like nothing has happened.

The moment can't last forever, however. "Is it safe at home?" I finally ask Tommy. I had Gilbert bring Mom here to keep her safe in case I was caught at the Tudor estate. If things went south, Tommy was supposed to run back here and warn them so they could help get everyone out of here. I originally wanted them to hide somewhere that wasn't a likely target for angry nobles, but when Gilbert and my mom heard the plan, they insisted on coming here to help. I gave a somewhat more cryptic warning to Edward, but I don't know where he went.

"'Sall clear, yes'm," Tommy replies, and my heart lightens even more. I need a safe place to bring some of the women, and I'd had Tommy keep an eye on my family's new estate. If the women came with me, it's because they don't have a guardian. This means they were Baldwin's wards and will be handed off to the temple as soon as his body is discovered. Based on what I've learned about the temple, that's not a great idea, especially for Abby.

I don't know how safe it will be, but I have an idea to semipermanently clear my name, at least legally, even if every witness of the murder comes forward. The city lord is dead, in any case, so the government is going to be in a state of chaos until a new, suitably ranked noble can take command. We should be safe while they are in disarray. I thank Tommy, and my family begins to make our way back to our estate, entourage of displaced women in tow.

I don't know how my father will react, but after our last exchange, I suspect he will fall in line. I'm not sure if I want to follow through on my threat or not. I was furious when I made it, but some small part of me still wants to believe he can change. It's a moot worry, however, as when we arrive home, only Edward is there to greet us.

I walk in first, followed by the women I have brought with me. The rest of my family is lagging a bit, catching up. I wanted to join them, but these women are scared. They need someone to help hold them together. "Lillith, I—" Ed starts, then looks at me, confused. "Who are they?"

"Some friends of mine," I answer. "They will be staying here for a while." He looks a bit unsure about this idea and eyes them suspiciously, but I give him a dangerous glare and he stops. "Where is Richard?" I ask, and his face sours.

"No idea," he answers. "As soon as that kid came to get Gilbert and Mom, Dad got spooked. He left right after and hasn't come back." I frown at this. I suppose it was more than out of the ordinary for Mom to leave so urgently, but I didn't think he would have the insight to react to it. I suppose, finally, he took me seriously about something. He'll probably be back tomorrow. I'll worry about him then. "Listen, can we talk in private?" Edward asks, lowering his voice.

I raise an eyebrow at him. I suppose he is finally ready to get off his chest whatever he has been building up courage for. I open my mouth to tell him that's fine but I need to get these women settled in first, when his face pales. He is staring over my shoulder, so I look behind me to see the rest of the family walking in. Edward is staring at Henry like he's the Grim Reaper.

CHAPTER FORTY-ONE

New Beginnings

I feel like I could cut the tension in the room with a knife as Edward and Henry stare at each other.

There is something I'm missing here, something Henry didn't tell me about during our meetings at Baldwin's estate. I need to help our guests settle in, but I also think I might need to be here for . . . whatever this is. I don't think it's a good idea to let a loud confrontation take place with a group of tired and scared abuse victims nearby.

I wish I had known about this before I walked into the house with everyone at once. I am trying to decide what to do when Henry speaks. "Hey, Ed, long time no see," he says. Bless him. I don't know what this is about, but I can make a few guesses. It seems whatever it is, Henry isn't going to press it, at least for now. I have to admire him for that; restraint is not one of my talents, and at times like this, it is incredibly valuable.

"R-right, good to see you, Henry," Edward splutters, confusion warring with relief on his face. Words aside, the two do not embrace like the rest of my family did. Looks like this confrontation is being delayed after all. For now, there is work to do.

"I'll talk to you later, Ed," I say, breaking the tension and gesturing for the women to follow me upstairs. We have several unused bedrooms as well as an empty maid's room. My father tried to requisition a few slaves for the work, as many poorer noble houses do, but his paperwork for the city dungeon's warden always *mysteriously* disappeared. In any case, I have plenty of housing, and everyone but Edward helps our guests find rooms to settle down in.

My mother and I share what clean clothes we can, and although ill-fitting, everyone should have something. The stipend my family receives from the city can finally be put to some use in clothing and feeding them tomorrow. Finally, when I've double-checked each woman is settled and safe, I go looking for my family. Gilbert, Henry, and my mother are all in the kitchen catching up. My heart wants me to join them, but I've been monopolizing Henry for long enough, and I decide to let the three of them have the moment.

Aside from that, it seems I need to talk to Edward. I pad down the long, carpeted hallway to his room and gently knock on the door. There is a moment of silence and I hover, waiting for a response before moving on to look for him elsewhere. Before I leave, however, his voice comes through the door. "Who is it?" he asks.

"It's me," I respond. "I told you we could talk in private, so here I am."

Another moment of quiet. "Come in," he agrees, and I enter my brother's room. His laundry is all over the ground and his bed is a mess. He is sitting on the bed and looking out his window. I take a seat in the chair by his writing desk and wait for him to speak. He was the one to request the conversation, after all. It takes several moments, and he doesn't look at me, but he does break the silence. "Are you okay, Lily? You look like the third plane," he asks.

He's not exactly wrong. He doesn't know what I did tonight, but despite my attempts to clean up, my hair is matted with blood and sinew, my arms are caked with dried sweat and blood, and I can practically feel the dark circles under my eyes. I probably should have bathed before this conversation, but I want to relax in my bath and I didn't want to put this off anymore. "I'm all right, thanks for asking," I reply.

We return to silence for a while, and I can feel Edward's anxiety as he builds up the courage to speak. "Listen, I didn't know, okay? I didn't know Lord Baldwin was going to . . . do that," he says, finally looking at me, or more specifically, at my scar. I tilt my head instead of answering him. It's not hard to tell that the beating I got shook him. The first time I came home injured, he didn't seem to feel any pity at all. Something must have been different about this time. "Well?" he says, an exasperated question in his tone.

"Well what?" I ask. I don't know what response he is expecting me to have to that. I wasn't expecting him to know I was going to get badly beaten like that; even most nobles don't do something like that openly. He looks frustrated as he rubs the back of his neck and looks for the right words.

"Look, I know we don't really get along, I just wanted to say I . . . shit. I don't know. I thought you were being a child about the engagement. I thought you were trying to deny the family some of the luck and opportunities you stumbled into. I thought you were just being self-absorbed and trying to keep everything to yourself again. I thought you were being stupid for wanting to stay in that old common house. I didn't know Lord Baldwin was . . . like that. I didn't want you to actually get hurt, and I should have backed you when you told Dad you didn't want to get married," he vents at me.

My eyebrows reach for my hairline at this. "You truly suck at apologies, you know that?" I retort. He really does. But I suppose it's what I can expect from him. He's not malicious like Baldwin, he's just . . . a prideful asshole. It makes sense my wounds would hit him with a little dose of reality.

"Ugh, you're fucking impossible, you know that?" he snorts. "I am trying here, Lily, okay?"

"Well, I appreciate it, I guess," I reply. "But I never thought you wanted me hurt. I just think you are a general asshole and a bigot. I'd rather an apology for that if you are going to apologize for anything."

"I'm an asshole? You are the asshole! You always look down on everyone and throw a fit over everything! You got lucky a few times and suddenly you thought you were better than everyone!" he shouts at me.

I roll my eyes. "I didn't look down on you, Edward, I just didn't look up to you anymore. Your pride just interpreted that as the same thing," I retort. "You started to hate me the second I stopped being impressed with you. Well, Ed, it's not my job to stroke your ego. If that wasn't a requirement to be your sister, maybe we would feel like a family now."

He looks like I just slapped him in the face. "You know what? Fuck you. I am trying to be the bigger man here! I'm trying to apologize! Why do you have to be like this all the time!" he snaps.

"You literally insulted me during your apology. And yeah, I do appreciate that you were upset when I got hurt; that genuinely means a lot to me. But the resentment over my success has to stop! I don't 'have to be like this.' I have a right to be like this when I am treated poorly. You are just so convinced I should quietly accept the abuse that you see it as a failing of character when I don't." I stand from the chair. "Well, fuck that. You can think I'm a bitch if you want. You won't be alone. It'll just continue to say more about you than me," I fume.

"Go fuck yourself," Edward says, his face twisted into a nasty expression. "I said what I needed to say, you can go. And careful about those women you brought into our home. A couple of them look like actual who—prostitutes," he says, dismissing me.

I find his decision not to say *whore* interesting, and I suspect he meant for this conversation to go more smoothly.

"*Sex worker* is the phrase I would use, and yes. A couple of them are or have been. You shouldn't warn me about them. Just treat them like people. They are just workers. And you are setting yourself above them like they are dirt, like an insult to throw at your little sister," I respond, irritated. This is not a widespread point of view in this world, and it's one of many things that always get under my skin.

He looks at me again with a frustrated look on his face. "Fine, sorry," he says.

That was begrudging, and it wasn't much, but it felt like an actual apology for something. Maybe we both lost our tempers. He definitely deserved it, but I can give it another shot.

"I don't hate you, you know, Edward. I don't like you, but I don't hate you. I'm angry about a lot of things and I wish I could make you see the world through a lens other than pride, and I don't like being around you. I don't blame you for Baldwin's actions though. I don't even entirely blame you for your gambling problem. I understand how it got started and how hard it is to break. I still see my big brother under there somewhere," I say as I'm on my way out of the room.

"Well, yippee," he drawls sardonically, "how fucking benevolent." He turns back to the window, but I do think I see an almost imperceptible release of tension in his shoulders. Just before I close the door, he adds under his breath, "Tell me that again after talking to Henry."

This confirms that something happened between the two of them before Henry was taken, and might explain some of Edward's behavior since then. I just need to find out what. Well, that exchange didn't go amazing. We both have a lot of resentment that needs to be addressed and his pride is still prominent. It was . . . something though. Maybe, and this could be a bit of a stretch, but maybe the aftermath of a violent, if justified, murder was not the best timing to have that conversation.

I will worry about that later, however. Right now, I need a bath more than I need to breathe. I finally arrive at my washroom and draw a bath, tossing the maid's uniform aside. I use heat mana to warm the water faster and slide in, letting my sore muscles soak. A hot cloth soaked in water over my tired eyes helps me finally relax. I let my thoughts drift to future plans. I need to speak to Sybillia and Emeric tomorrow, maybe Godfrey. What I need now is a moderately powerful noble.

Godfrey

I wake up in the middle of the night, more awake than I have been in years. Something has changed. I sit up rapidly and pulse my mana through my body, then create a flame over my hand. It works. The warmth seeps from my hand all the way to my heart. I summon a spear of ice and grip the familiar cold, wet surface, then delight in its shattering against the far wall. I proceed to cycle through dozens of combat spells I've been unable to produce since coming to this shitty little city.

This can only mean one thing. Baldwin is dead. I am finally, finally free. It's strange, the workings of divine mana. I knew I was under his control. I knew I couldn't defy him. It never occurred to me to try. Even when my apprentice came to me and revealed his divine mana was the cause of my confused mind, I didn't do anything. Even when she realized endoaspected mana could free me, I didn't try.

I was dismissed from court for making a fool out of myself, neglecting my duties and my territory, and being unable to contribute either wisdom or combat to the kingdom. When I met Lillith, I thought I could bridge the gap by contributing great knowledge. But the gap was fake. I never would have been allowed to present her circle, that's clear to me now. I was under orders not to do anything to make myself useful or valuable without Baldwin's orders.

When I was in court, I would open my mouth to give advice and nothing would come out. I would try to cast a combat spell and I simply . . . wouldn't. My own mind was used as a shackle on my abilities and took everything from me.

That small, pathetic little mage of middling power commanded me. Because he, apparently, was a natural divine mage, chosen by the Collector. Truly a dangerous thing, unmonitored divine power. He was smart about it too. He could have used my authority to buy more for himself, but he didn't. He would have been discovered if he had. Noticeable changes are monitored by the temple and the king.

If I had tried to do something to elevate him, alarm bells would have gone off. Stopping me from doing anything, however? That wasn't viewed as an attempt to control the country, just as my own laziness. And in return he got a powerful mage as a pet, running a fucking bookshop in his tiny little kingdom to be called on whenever my master needed me. I can think of a dozen things he ordered me to do with the clear intent of paving his way to the throne. It's like a gauze has been lifted from my memories. He didn't want a puppet in the court, he wanted to be king, and he was willing to wait.

I wonder how someone killed him. It's no matter, really. What matters is that someone did.

I am free.

I want to find his corpse and piss on it. But I don't need to. I have Lillith and I have my own mind. I can take back everything. It's time I moved her out of this pointless city and started preparing for the future. She is nearly fourteen—old enough for the academy. Perhaps I should enroll her. I need to travel as well. I doubt Baldwin was working alone, and I need to return home to find out how this happened and why I was targeted.

I am too relieved to return to my rest. I feel as if I have been resting forever. I am ready for action. I am no longer Godfrey, humble bookseller and loyal pet. "Count Godfrey," he always called me. Mocking me. Rubbing my loss of status in my face, daring me to challenge him, knowing I wouldn't be able to. And where did it lead him? He is dead, and I am Godfrey, the Duke of Facinley and third in line for the throne.

CHAPTER FORTY-TWO

Uproar

I wake up a few hours after I finally fell asleep last night. I have a lot to do today, and as much as I wanted to get to it right away, I have learned my lesson about sleep deprivation.

First things first, I need to make sure I am not arrested and executed for murdering the lord of Satusmor. Sybillia should be here soon, although if *my* boss was beheaded and burned, I'd probably take the day off. Town criers are not quite as efficient a method of spreading news as social media, however, and I think there is a decent chance the news of the Tudors' deaths has not made the rounds.

So Sybillia will be plan A. If she is not helpful, I'll speak to Emeric and Godfrey. I need to find and make discreet contact with a noble of some renown, preferably one well-loved by his peers or one who wishes to be so. I'll probably need Gilbert's help if I want to be listened to, as much as the thought makes my skin crawl. Actually, Henry is an option now as well, but . . . I should give him time to rest.

I need to get a disguise or use illusion magic on Gilbert's face. Once I have that handled, I need to seize this moment. The city will be in disarray for months, or as long as it takes to get a suitably ranked noble here to organize things. This will be my best opportunity to spread magic further. The Mages of Penance are able to suppress their magic much faster than I was, since they don't also have to hide ever-gathering mana. Enough of them should master it soon and, if they are willing, I'd like to ask for their help teaching magic to other districts and houses.

I'd also like to gauge the state of some of the farmers and laborers in the area.

It's possible that would be a discreet and helpful community to share the magic with as well. It will also aid in food production and distribution in the long run, which would improve the lives of even the people who elect not to become mages. It will be important that I am not the only one teaching magic. In the not-too-distant future, some of these communities of commoner mages will be discovered.

It is essential magic be spread too far to stop before that happens, which means expanding in full force now while the city government is crippled. It's also best that, should mages be forced to undergo the rite of confession by the temple, they not be able to point to one specific origin for this circle. I'm actually not terribly worried about this; it seems like the temple doesn't use their abilities to help the city guard. Of course, mass insurrection may be an exception to that general rule. I need to learn more about the temple as soon as I am past all this.

I wait in our front parlor for Sybillia to turn up, but she never arrives. I realize, when she is about a quarter-hour late, what I should have realized first thing this morning. She has been receiving instructions from Baldwin this entire time. She probably does know he is dead, or at least missing. Oh well, I haven't wasted too much time. I depart, headed for the bookshop. I'm not sure about Emeric, but I have never failed to find Godfrey at his shop.

When I arrive, however, I am surprised to discover he is, in fact, absent. The front door is locked, the rooms dark. Is news spreading faster than anticipated? The feeling that something is off only increases my sense of urgency, and I make a beeline for the temple. I need to find Emeric.

I find as I walk farther into the noble quarter that the city is in something of an uproar. I suppose I wasn't quiet last night, but this is a big city, and the Tudor estate isn't directly next to anyone else.

But what else could have sent everyone into such a panic?

A lot of nobles appear to be packing carriages with luggage or have mercenaries with them, the type you might hire as bodyguards if you were planning to travel. What's more, when I look closer, the nobles themselves look upset, but not panicked, after all. This is not the reaction I anticipated. The lord is dead, so let's move? I suppose they must be anticipating unrest among the commoners or something, or perhaps there is a financial reason?

I'll ask Emeric when I find him.

I arrive at the temple, which is in a different kind of uproar. There are nobles lined out the door, and each of them looks livid. Well, I'm not getting in their way. I spot Emeric quickly, as he has apparently been enlisted for crowd control. He has a serious look on his face and he is trying to guide nobles in the right direction while others shout complaints at him. Well, I'd rather not stress him out more, but I need to act quickly.

As I approach him and our eyes make contact, he immediately stops what he is doing and marches toward me. Fuck, that's not a good sign. Do they already know about the Mages of Penance? I should have had weeks! Surrounded by mages and priests, I know I cannot run. I shouldn't panic though; I need to know what he knows first.

As he gets to me, he harshly whispers under his breath, "It was Lord BALDWIN who was using divine magic on you?"

Well, that's not quite the question I was expecting.

"How did you—?"

"Lord Baldwin"—he looks around and lowers his voice further—"Lord Baldwin is dead, his father too. All these people were in the same position as you. I put two and two together!"

Oh. Oooooh. Of course that little shit was using his power on other people. He never liked being told no, and by the looks of it, he made sure a third of the nobles in the city couldn't do so. And nobles are exempt from confession, so he was never discovered.

This provides some valuable information for me as well. With divine magic, kill the caster, kill the control. This is good, actually. Well, not the mass number of victims of mind rape, but the information at least. I can help a lot of people by targeting a few priests. I just have to figure out which ones are doing it. Unless my read on Emeric is wrong, which is very possible, I don't think every priest is aware of the cruelties of confession. I can free the people in the House of Penance, however.

This is helpful in other ways as well. The nobles don't just dislike Baldwin—they must hate him. If I can find the right noble, my plan will work even better than I hoped. Even if I can't, I might be able to use the temple itself. Both even, if I play my cards right.

"Listen, I know you must have questions, but there are a lot of other victims," Emeric says. "Can I meet you at the bookshop this evening? I need to speak with you, urgently. I know it must be traumatizing. I will do everything I can to make this right. I have to go back now, but promise you'll meet me," he requests.

I nod and he turns to head back to his duties. "Wait, can you answer just one question?" I plead. The group he was speaking to is already growing rowdy again, and I see urgency in his face as he pauses. "If Baldwin and the city lord are dead, do we have anyone else who will take their place? A particularly prominent noble or anything? I . . . have something to report to them . . ." I trail off lamely. I was hoping to be a bit more subtle, but . . . it seems I need to act quickly.

He raises his eyebrow in suspicion, but more of a parental suspicion than anything else. "You don't know?"

"Know what?" I ask. *Why trail me along, man, I thought you were in a hurry. Spit it out!*

"Sorry, it's just I thought . . . Well, no matter. I suppose he has always allowed people to believe his rank is lower than it is, probably for the same reason he spends his time in this little city instead of the capital . . . and I'm now realizing what that reason is, shit. I just thought, as his apprentice . . . " Emeric ponders, clearly getting distracted.

I, on the other hand, am entirely caught off guard. "Wait, Godfrey? What rank is he? He can't be that important!" I splutter.

"Right, sorry," Emeric says. "Godfrey is the Duke of Facinley. He is probably only here because of Baldwin. I never understood why he was here at all, but that would certainly explain it."

What the fuck. Godfrey is a duke? Shit, that could be trouble. He'll have to do, however.

"Do you know where he is? He wasn't at the shop," I say, surprise lingering in my voice.

Emeric furrows his brow for a moment, then answers, "Well, if my guess is right, he could be anywhere, but I would check the Tudor estate first. It may be hard to enter, but Lord Godfrey may have unfinished business there."

Well, I didn't plan to go there again so soon, but I guess it's true what they say about killers and the scene of the crime.

"Thanks," I say, then begin to turn, but Emeric is the one to stop me this time.

"Wait, Lillith," he says, sadness in his voice. I turn and look at him expectantly. "I'm sorry. I knew he was your fiancé, and I knew you were being confessed outside the church. I should have known. I'm sorry I didn't do anything."

"Don't worry about it," I say dismissively.

Then I turn and run back toward the manor I burned down the night before.

A duke, huh? Short term, that is better than I could have hoped for. Long term . . . well, things could get ugly. I hope they won't, but I will be prepared if they do. I start planning what I will say to Godfrey as I jog down the bustling streets toward Baldwin's estate.

CHAPTER FORTY-THREE

The Duke and the Demon

As I approach the Tudor estate, I find half the city guard surrounding it. I have to slow down as I approach to avoid unwanted attention. The estate is a mockery of its former glory. The two main buildings on the grounds are burnt-out skeletons and the magnificent gardens have been trampled, either last night or this morning. From roughly a hundred yards away, I spot Godfrey speaking with a guard captain.

Emeric was right about Baldwin's control, he must have been. Godfrey looks like a new man. I can't make out his face well, but his demeanor has changed. He stands straight and tall, revealing his stature is literally greater than it appeared before. The most stunning change, however, is his mana. He is no longer suppressing it, but he doesn't allow it to radiate freely from his body either. Instead of suppressing any mages in the area, his mana is dense and surrounds his body like a literal aura of . . . unreality? It's like looking through Baroque glass.

I pause at the open gate for several minutes and ponder how to approach him. I need to speak with him, but getting closer feels like a fantastically stupid idea. If any of the guards who saw me last night are here, which seems likely, there is a good chance they will recognize me. As I examine Godfrey's sharp aura, I get an idea. I can't go to him, but I can bring him to me. I stop suppressing my mana for a moment and flare my power. Godfrey immediately looks in my direction, and I have to slip behind a wall before the guard captain looks as well.

I peek around the corner for a brief moment only to see that Godfrey is gone. As I step back behind the wall and turn my head, I come face-to-face with Godfrey and—

"Gaaah!" I shout, startled. "Jesus, Godfrey, you scared me half to death!" I hold my hand over my heart. I do this out of habit more than anything, as the adrenaline does not actually cause my heart to beat. He simply smiles at me. Up close his aura is truly impressive. His mana is colored yellow for a brief moment before fading back to transparent as whatever aspect he was using dissipates.

The air around him looks . . . unreal. Like looking through intense heat waves but with an even greater effect. It feels like reality itself is bending around him. I can see him and his face clearly, but it's like he doesn't quite belong in this world and you can see where a rough hole has been cut for him to occupy. His hair and long beard are as messy as ever and his old robe is made of no finer material, yet he feels like he is more distinguished and put together. His face looks like it's lost twenty years, although every single wrinkle remains in place.

I don't understand how Baldwin ever controlled this man. I feel like I am confronting a force of nature. To Godfrey, Baldwin's mana must have felt like a fly buzzing around his head. "Thank you, Lillith," Godfrey says, and my face pales.

". . . For what?" I hesitantly inquire, and Godfrey raises a bushy eyebrow at me.

"Shall I announce it, here, so close to your handiwork? I suppose I can do that if you wish . . ." An insincere tone colors his voice. Fuck. I hadn't anticipated a fucking duke organizing an investigation so quickly. I should have had weeks, minimum, before they even started trying to figure out what happened. They should have been kneecapped without someone to direct the investigation. Of course, Godfrey already knows this was me.

He must have already spoken to the guards from last night. Who knows what else he has looked into? Fortunately, I had everyone else wait for the grounds to be clear before helping me and we didn't all leave together, so some secrets should remain safe. This is still far from the ideal scenario, however. Things are getting away from me, quickly. He hasn't acted yet, however, and has only thanked me. Perhaps I can still work with this.

No use in lying at this point. And looking at him, I have no chance of escaping. That leaves negotiations. I'm not bargaining from the position I was hoping to be in, but that doesn't mean I have nothing. "All right," I respond, "you are welcome. So what now?"

Godfrey observes me with that familiar calculating look and tilts his head in thought. "Well, you came to find me, you even drew me away from the guards. Why don't we start with that? What do you want from me?" he asks. This new version of Godfrey is going to be much more difficult to work with.

"That depends," I hedge. "Who else knows?" My plans will need to be adjusted depending on that. I don't think Godfrey would do something right away; I always thought he was too interested in my magical discoveries for that, but it seems I never really knew him at all.

He sniffs dismissively at the question. "I have covered for you, so far," he drawls.

I narrow my eyes at him. "And why is that?" I ask with suspicion.

"Gratitude, perhaps? Why, does a master need a reason to do something kind for his apprentice?" he asks, voice decorated with innocence.

"Yes," I practically snort. "The purely benevolent don't need to be called master."

This actually makes him laugh, and it's a brief moment before he can respond.

"True enough, little Lily. Sometimes I wonder which of us is truly older. All right, I want your help as well. That's all I can tell you right now. Will you tell me what you wanted to speak about?" he inquires. I narrow my eyes again. He's keeping his cards close to the vest. He does have the high ground here, so to speak, so I'll have to budge first.

"You covering for me won't last forever, not if you are just dismissing witnesses and sweeping it under the rug. I want your help with . . . a more permanent solution," I say.

"I suppose you are right; color me intrigued," he responds.

"I want you to confess to killing Baldwin," I announce, leaning back and crossing my arms. Godfrey coughs at this suggestion, then regains his composure and raises an eyebrow at me.

"Why in the world would I do that? You are a good apprentice, Lillith, but you aren't that good," he retorts.

"It's simple," I say. "And it's nothing but upsides. Have you been to the noble quarter today? Closer than your shop, I mean. Baldwin has been playing games with a lot of nobles. A lot of angry nobles. From the looks of it, he forced more than a few of them to move here to increase the influence of this city. He committed heresy, he defied the temple, and he made an enemy out of just about every powerful noble house in the city. He is basically public enemy number one."

Godfrey seems to pick up what I'm implying and he helps complete the thought. "Ah, so whoever killed him, to the nobility and to the temple, is a hero. This isn't a crime, this is an accomplishment, is that what you mean?" he asks.

"That's precisely what I mean. You know as well as I do nobles rarely get charged with crimes. Baldwin killed a couple of nobles in public and no one asked any questions. At your rank, you could kill anyone in this city without consequence. Except in this case, you will actually be praised for contributing to the kingdom," I explain.

Godfrey nods along until the middle, when he raises an eyebrow. "My rank?" he asks.

"Emeric sold you out," I reply.

He sighs but waves it off. "Very well, not a bad plan. So, why don't you just confess?" he asks.

"A commoner who has killed Baldwin may be a hero to the nobility, but they will still kill me for it," I say. That much should be obvious; it's odd he asked at all.

He tilts his head in confusion. "You . . . aren't a commoner, or did you forget, Lillith of Endings?" he asks, somewhat amused.

I flush a little. Actually, I kind of had. I'll never actually be a noble in my mind or heart; I have been planning everything as if everyone saw me that way. I still dismiss the idea.

"It still won't work. I am a recently raised noble, and I am a woman. No matter how much good it does, a woman killing her fiancé is too dangerous to ignore. It would set a terrible precedent. I may be spared the rope but not the chains. No, it has to be you. Besides, this whole issue, for me, started with too many people knowing how capable I am. It'll do me no good if people realize I am capable of . . . that," I answer.

Godfrey nods approvingly. "Hiding your abilities is a good instinct," he says. Of course, I imagine he won't want me to do that forever. "Very well, but I want to do things a little differently."

"And how is that?" I ask.

"We both killed him. You helped me. This will explain your presence to any witnesses who come up and will hide your abilities. It will close any gaps in the story if anyone tries to look too closely. Besides, it makes sense I would take my apprentice with me," he suggests.

I consider this for a moment. I don't think he is being entirely upfront about why he wants me to take some of the credit, and that gives me pause. At the end of the day, however, if that's how he wants to play it, that's kinda what I have to do. It's not ideal but . . . it will work.

"All right," I assent. "If that's what you want to do. I played a small role. A tiny one, okay? Like your murder towel girl, or something."

He chuckles. "Very well. Now, there is something you need to do for me in return," he says, and I groan inwardly. This is why I didn't want the noble I chose to know who I was when I suggested this. "When you are fourteen, you will be able to attend Facinley University in the capital. I want to enroll you."

This catches me off guard. What exactly is he up to? I'm not actually opposed to the idea. Sure, I don't want to go to school with a bunch of noble kids . . . I kinda don't want to go to school at all actually. If dying as Annie had one benefit, it was avoiding my qualifying exams. However, my magical knowledge could grow by leaps and bounds and . . . "Do they have classes on complex item enchantments?" I ask.

Godfrey grins. "The best in the kingdom."

Well, that's it, then. If I am ever going to succeed, there is a certain item I need to create. And I need to get my family out of this city in any case. Even if I did "help" kill Baldwin, I was still his fiancée. When a person who people hate isn't around to receive their vitriol, they will throw it at their closest acquaintance. It doesn't matter if it's logical, this city could grow unsafe for us in the near future. I have several things to wrap up, and I have more work with the House of Penance, but I will need to leave.

"Okay," I agree. "But I need you to get my family out of the city now. Do that, and I'll attend your university." He seems to understand my concern and nods.

"And you?" he asks.

"I can take care of myself," I respond. "I'm only concerned for my family right now."

"Very well, consider it done. I do have one last thing to ask," he adds. I raise an eyebrow. "How did you manage it? You aren't that strong."

I give him a wide grin. "Very carefully," I reply, then turn to leave.

"Oh, and Lillith?" Godfrey calls as I begin to run back toward the main city. "Get me a Danish!"

You know what, fuck it. Godfrey and I are no doubt going to have a rocky future. Eventually, he is going to have to either surrender power or . . .

But for now, he's exactly who I need. I head toward the market, in search of a pastry shop.

About the Author

Dreamer's Riot is the author of the Otherworldly Anarchist series as well as a computer scientist and indie video game developer. Based on his experiences in the US Air Force and later as a student, his stories aim to tackle themes of power and autonomy.

Podium

DISCOVER MORE

STORIES UNBOUND

PodiumEntertainment.com